LAND ON ME

A NOVEL

MATTHEW R. CORR

First Edition: August 2021
Edited by: Alicia Dean
Cover Art by: Dessiree Perez. Illustrations copyright © 2021 by Dessiree Perez
Interior Design by: Matthew R. Corr
Printed in the United States of America
Fiction: New Adult Contemporary
Fiction: LGBT/Gay
Fiction: Coming-of-Age
Content Warnings: Homophobia, Hate-Speech, Underage Drug and Alcohol Use, Strong Language, Sex, Conversion Therapy, School Shooter Drill, Violence, Suicide, Death.
ISBN: 978-1-7351194-6-5 (Paperback)
ISBN 978-1-7351194-7-2 (Hardcover)

ALSO BY MATTHEW R. CORR

For Andrew Norman Coit

You're still here with me, in everything I do.

For anyone who has ever felt like they don't fit into a societal norm. You are still valid, and you are loved.

ONE

My ears rang. I'd heard gunshots in movies, but they were louder than expected in real life. My elbows locked, and my arms shook. I wanted to drop the gun, but my entire body froze. The scent of hot metal emanated from the barrel of the weapon. My mouth was too dry to speak, and I could hardly swallow. I desperately wanted to reach out to make sure he was okay, but there was so much blood. It was so red and coming out so quickly. I didn't want to shoot him, but he wouldn't have stopped otherwise. Tears welled in my eyes. His blood was on my hands now.

My phone's alarm was so loud it jolted me awake every morning, making my heart race. It was like being zapped by the machine that brings you back to life after you've flatlined. All the alarms on my phone failed to wake me up, so I downloaded this app called 'Nuclear', which sounded like one of those old-time nuclear warning sirens. It did the trick every time. I twisted in bed, snatched my phone, and clicked the snooze button. I wasn't a morning person.

Turning on my back, I closed my eyes, ready to let sleep take me again.

"Landon! Get up!" My dad's voice could wake the entire neighborhood.

My face scrunched. "I'm up!" I yelled. Just because I wasn't out of bed didn't mean I wasn't up. My dad was not a fan of that philosophy.

"No, you're not. Hurry up!" He shouted from downstairs.

The same conversation happened most mornings. Dad was a military vet, and he'd been waking up early most of his life. I wished it was as easy for me.

My bedroom faced the street, which meant it got all the sun in the morning. I once tried to convince Dad to let me get blackout curtains, but he said no, saying I'd never get out of bed. Can't say he was wrong. I stood with a big stretch, rubbing my eyes, letting my vision focus on all the commotion outside. Fun fact: I lived across the road from my school, Madison High of Madison, Texas, or "Mad High" as it was better known. Another fun fact; we had the highest use of marijuana in the county.

I shut the curtains in fear that someone would glance up and see me standing there in my underwear, staring at them like a creep. I shuffled to my closet like a zombie, grabbing the first shirt I could reach, then a pair of shorts to slip into.

I trotted down the stairs, which led into the kitchen, and yawned as I sat at the island counter, popping up onto a stool. My dad was leaning against the sink, dressed in a blue suit. He was reading his phone with an intense expression; it was usually the news. The bitter smell of coffee brewing filled the air. It was one of my favorite scents.

"You should start going to bed earlier," Dad said, placing a plate of burned toast in front of me. He wasn't much of a chef.

"That's the benefit of living across the street from the school," I said, taking a bite of the toast. It crunched and crumbled back onto the plate. "I can wake up ten minutes before class starts." I could barely finish my sentence, the toast was terribly dry. "Pass the butter, please?" I reached my hand out like a toddler asking for his bottle. Dad placed the butter dish next to me and handed me a knife before rushing to pour his coffee. I laid the butter on thick while scraping off bits of black flakes.

"How do you think practice went yesterday?" Dad asked, referring to football.

I was the team's running back. It didn't help that my dad was the high school's superintendent and had access to any practice he could get to. Growing up as an only child was great, but it also meant all the pressure to succeed was on me. Not only did he grind me on the field whenever he could, but he always ensured my grades were top-notch. Dad loved football; he played in high school but never had the chance to pursue it after joining military school. Most of the time, it felt like he lived vicariously through me.

"Practice was fine," I said.

Dad sipped his coffee. "You need to work harder if you want a scholarship, Landon."

You need to work harder on your cooking skills. What adult couldn't even make toast? The blame wasn't entirely on him. My mom was the one who had done all the cooking. He'd made nothing for himself for at least fifteen years that didn't take more effort than slapping the meat and cheese between two pieces of bread. I was better off making my food, which I usually did. I took one last bite of toast before giving up. It tasted like buttered ash.

"And it needs to be better than fine if you want scouts to consider you instead of Dan," Dad said.

I rolled my eyes. Dan Wilson was my best friend, quarterback, and captain of the team. That was typical of my dad. All he cared to talk about was football, scholarships, or grades, with a bit of politics sprinkled on top.

I whipped out my phone and scrolled through Instagram, waiting for Dad to mention something else I needed to do. Dan had posted a picture from an hour ago of him holding a fan of $20 bills. I tapped it twice to like it and commented: 'Doooouuucchhheeee.'

Dad's voice took my eyes off of my phone. "Are you hearing what I'm saying?"

"Yes, Dad," I said with a sigh. "I hear you loud and clear. I'll be better." I put my phone on the table and took my plate to the sink. Dad stood next to me, leaning on the counter.

"It's not about being better," he said, facing me. "It's about putting in the work."

I scrubbed the small plate without looking at him.

"What is it you think I'm doing, Dad? Taking a nap on the field every day?" I placed the plate into the drying rack with a little too much force.

My phone vibrated before Dad could say anything.

Lauren Calling.

I clicked the message button and started typing.

ME

Can't talk right now.

LAUREN

I'm outside, I thought we were walking in together?

ME

Sorry, I totally forgot, be out in a sec.

"I gotta go. I'll see you later," I said, slipping my phone into my pocket and rushing for the door.

"You're forgetting something!" Dad called out to me. I spun on my heels, seeing he was holding up my backpack. I grabbed it, but he didn't let it go. "I know I've been hard on you," he said, looking me in the eye. "I'm trying my best. Things have been hard for me too, you know."

"I know," I mumbled, looking at the floor. Dad let go of the bag and I received the full weight of it. "You around later?" I swung the backpack around my shoulders as I walked backward.

"Not sure yet. I have a few meetings later in the day. My campaign manager is putting a lot on our plate," he said, picking up his coffee mug.

My dad was in his first year of campaigning to become Mayor of Madison, which packed on the pressure of being the golden boy. Politics weren't my thing, so we scarcely talked about it. It was weird when I saw signs popping up around town on people's front lawns with my dad's face on them. People looked up to him. People believed in him. I was just along for the ride.

"All right, I'll see ya then," I said, whirling around out the side door.

Lauren Ramirez was waiting for me at the end of the driveway, her backpack slung over one shoulder. She looked great in jean shorts and a flowy white button-up shirt. Lauren was a few inches shorter than me, with long, brown hair kissed by the sun, giving her natural copper highlights. She completed her outfit with a pair of black-framed glasses she used as an accessory. Lauren took me by the hand, and we crossed the street. I caught a whiff of her sweet floral perfume in the breeze. The school's front courtyard was filled with people, clamoring to get inside to feel the first gust of wind from the air conditioning hit their faces.

Lauren and I had been dating for almost a year. She was the president of the school's drama club, and the lead in all the school plays. She was hands down the best actor at our school. She dreamed of going to New York City to become the next big thing. My parents loved her because she was polite and pretty; they assumed we were the perfect match. My mom and dad met in college and got married soon after, I assumed they wanted a similar path for me and Lauren.

We maneuvered through the crowd, my vision filled with blurs of color as kids whizzed by us, heading toward the entrance and their homerooms. Then something strange caught my attention—a shirtless guy. I saw the tanned skin of his back amongst the chaos when my gaze shifted to the right. I squinted to focus, but like a mirage, he disappeared in a blink.

Lauren squeezed my arm. "Are you looking for someone?"

"What?"

"You were just looking around so attentively like you were looking for someone."

"Oh? No, I wasn't. Sorry, I just saw something weird. What were you saying?" I tried playing it cool.

"I was asking if you wanted to go with red for our prom outfits, or if you were feeling another color?"

"Red?" I focused on Lauren, "No. Yeah. I mean, yeah, red is a good choice. I'm ok with that." I said. She smiled in agreement as we walked through the front doors of the school. I didn't care what color we wore to prom. It felt a little early to be thinking of it anyway, as it wasn't for another couple of months. While Lauren was thinking about prom dresses, I was thinking about a guy's back muscles that may or may not have been real.

"Hey, Landon!" A familiar voice rang out. "I need that short story by Thursday, we print on Friday, you know this!" Tasha Morgan yelled as she hurried toward us. Tasha was the editor-in-chief of our school newspaper. Once a month, the *Madison Monthly* was published and handed out to students, chronicling all the important news we all needed to know. But, it also included student works, like poems, essays, pictures, or, in my case, short stories. My brain came up with some pretty wild stuff. I liked to write it and share it with others.

Writing was something I loved doing more than anything. Much more than football, even. I knew it was something I wanted as a career. But I still hadn't told my dad. He'd never read anything I'd written because I'd been too nervous to show him, fearing he'd be disappointed or say that I wasn't focused enough on football.

"Hey girl," Tasha said as she gave Lauren a quick hug. "Sorry for rushing by, I have a meeting about the paper with Mr. Jones." Tasha dashed off just as quickly as she showed up.

"I'll have the story by then, I promise!" I said to Tasha, watching her bouncing curls become lost in the crowd.

Lauren looked at me. "What's this one about?"

"I'm not sure," I said. "I haven't written it yet." I chuckled a bit as Lauren leaned in for a kiss. The bell rang, and everyone pushed through the hallway. Lauren liked to hold the kiss long enough for everyone to notice. She never said it, but I knew she wanted people to think we were a perfect couple. Lauren was the opposite of me—she loved being on stage for a reason. My eyes were closed while I kissed her, as they normally were, but this time I saw the flash of that guy's shirtless back and pulled my lips away. "All right, I need to go, or else we're both gonna be late."

She stepped back, did a cute wave, and trotted off.

I wiped the gloss from my lips and headed for my Advanced Placement Literature class, wondering if anyone had been staring at us kissing. I tried shaking the thought of this shirtless person from my brain before climbing the stairs to the second floor. AP Lit was my favorite class. I enjoyed having in-depth conversations about characters, storytelling, symbolism, and everything else that came with classic literature. Mrs. Donahue was my teacher, a tall, slender woman with tanned skin and short, dark hair. She was one of the few teachers up to date on the latest fashion trends. A lot of the guys from the football team had the hots for her. I mean, she *was* beautiful, in a teacher sort of way.

My seat was in the third row, on the far right side of the class, next to the large windows. I was the last one to arrive as everyone had already filled the room with noise and chatter. I sat at my desk, placing my backpack next to me. I unzipped it and took out a notebook. Just as I sat back up, my eyes caught movement from outside the window. My brows scrunched as my brain processed what I was seeing.

What the...

My eyes hadn't deceived me earlier. I was staring at the same shirtless back for the second time in the courtyard. The way the sun hit him, it was as if he was lighting up the entire street. It was like God had a single light shining down on his most beautiful angel. I felt like a creep, because everything else in my world fell away, and I was locked on him. I couldn't even hear the surrounding chatter anymore. He was doing something to the half wall that separated the courtyard from the sidewalk. Cleaning it, maybe?

I couldn't see his face; only his back. He was slender, with broad shoulders. His jeans sagged a bit, showing off the band of his white underwear; every muscle curve in his back was pure perfection. He had those hard muscles poking out of his lower back, causing indents at either side of his spine that looked like dimples pointing toward his tailbone. His shoulders were perfectly rounded as if high-tech lasers sculpted them. Every time he moved his arm, I caught a glimpse of hair poking out from his armpit. His triceps flexed with every swipe across the stone wall. His hair was wavy, dark brown, and longer on top than the back. I imagined myself being able to zoom in with my eyes like a camera just so I could see every bead of sweat pushing from the pores of his tanned skin. It was as if he was sparkling like a vampire from *Twilight*. The sun was beating down hard. I couldn't help but wonder why anyone would want to stay outside. The boy was a fascinating mystery. Who was he? Why was he there? Why was his shirtless back making me feel some type of way? I watched, desperately waiting for him to turn around so I could see his face, hoping it would stop my wandering thoughts.

"All right, everyone," Mrs. Donahue announced, pulling me out of my trance and settling the hustle and bustle of the roaring class. "Today we are going to discuss obsession, sexuality, and sexual orientation in fiction." She was known for discussing more taboo topics that other teachers were afraid to talk about. "Who are some characters you think of when I say this?" No one raised their hands or even shouted out an answer. "Come on, people, there are some pretty obvious ones."

I hesitantly raised my hand, not wanting to be the first to answer, but I needed to break the ice. I glanced through the window one more time to check on Mystery Boy, but he wasn't there. I was still very unsure if he was real or if I was suffering from heatstroke.

"Yes, Landon?"

My head whipped around to the front of the class when I heard my name. I faced Mrs. Donahue, but my eyes yearned for another peek out the window.

"Jay Gatsby," I said with a burst of energy as if I were holding the answer in my gut for days. He was the first to pop into my head.

"Yes," Mrs. Donahue said with a smile. "Some would say that Gatsby was quite obsessive. Accomplishing everything he could to get the seemingly off-limits girl. Not stopping until he had her. Very good! Anyone else?" She looked around the class.

Steven Mori was the next one to raise his hand. He was the most flamboyant guy in our school, and wore a lot of tight clothes, sometimes even women's clothes, eyeliner, and dyed his hair a different color every two months. Steven had a distinct tone of voice that guys in my school could only describe as girly. Steven had his group of friends that didn't intermingle with mine much, except for Lauren and Tasha. I knew little about him those days other than the constant offerings he got from guys walking by calling him fag or fairy. As much as I wanted to come to his defense, I said nothing to stop the verbal assault. I guess that made me part of the problem. Lauren was better at calling out guys like Dan about it. But guys like Dan seem to feed off the disapproval of others.

"Barbara Covett," Steven said.

"Ah yes!" Mrs. Donahue said. "From Notes on a Scandal, perfect example!" Steven smiled, and Mrs. Donahue continued. "Barbara became obsessed with a female co-worker named Sheba after falling in love with her. She became jealous of Sheba's attention to one of their young students. Barbara began manipulating her way into Sheba's life until she finally felt comfortable enough to make a move on her."

Steven tilted his head. "So, is that how sexuality or sexual orientation comes into this?"

"Sexual orientation has a lot to do with it, which is why I tacked it onto this topic. Sometimes, a person's sexual attraction can lead to obsession, even if it's a same-sex attraction. Some could say that a character with no sort of outlet to express their sexual orientation and seems isolated within it, could cause deviance to brew. It can then of course become dangerous and predatory. Just look at the principal character of Lolita. Of course, not everyone's sexual attractions lead to obsession, but it's something that can make for gripping storytelling in fiction."

I couldn't help but think of Mystery Boy throughout the discussion. Watching him, and even just the thought of him had taken me to a different place that day more than once. I had a girlfriend, yet I couldn't stop fantasizing about what Mystery Boy might look like. I didn't know at the time if I just wanted to know who he was or if I wanted something more from him. I'd be lying if I said it was my first time thinking about a shirtless guy but never like that, or for that long. Normally I'd brush it off and push it from my mind. If people found out, everyone would treat me differently. I'd be the one Dan yelled fag at, and I'd lose my best friend. It could even ruin my dad's chances of getting the votes he needed for mayor. But the tingle I felt down my stomach when I saw Mystery Boy's shiny, sweaty back made me excited and confused. Maybe I was Gatsby, and Mystery Boy was my Daisy, off-limits. But I needed to shake it; enabling those thoughts could ruin everything.

TWO

"Landon Griffin!" Someone hollered my name from the back of the class. I glanced behind me, unable to put a face to the voice.

"Again, excellent example," Mrs. Donahue said with a Cheshire grin. "Landon is the epitome of the word obsessed. It's even caused him to question his own sexual orientation. Mr. Griffin has a classic case of obsessive fascination. He saw a shirtless guy from behind and now he can't stop thinking about him. How can one become infatuated so quickly?"

"Maybe because he's never had a gay crush before?" Someone exclaimed from behind me. I tried to speak up, but my mouth went dry. How did everyone know?

"Maybe he has a back fetish?!" Someone yelled. I didn't recognize their voice either, and began to sweat. The walls were closing in on me and it glued me to my seat. I stared at my desk, hoping no one would notice I was still in the room.

"Does he like men, or does he like women? Because you can't like both!" Mrs. Donahue sneered as she stepped to my desk, glaring down at me. Out of nowhere, the sound of the bell thundered. My eyes came into focus, and I took a deep breath.

"Landon, are you all right? You seemed checked out there."

I looked over my shoulder to find Mrs. Donahue standing over me. Everyone in the class was shuffling out of the room, and I realized I'd fully zoned out from the rest of the class discussion.

"Wow, I'm sorry, Mrs. D. I'm not sure where I went." I lied. I couldn't exactly tell her my dream had transported me to High School Hell. "That won't happen again."

"It's okay." She smiled, walking around to the front of my desk. "Football isn't keeping you up too late, is it?"

"Uh, no, no. That's not it at all." That time I told the truth. I took another breath and collected my things. Steven was the last person to walk out. His bright pink hair was hard to miss. I felt the need to follow him, and started for the door.

"I'm looking forward to your next story in the *Monthly*!" Mrs. Donahue proclaimed at me before I left the room. I wasn't usually that standoffish, but I was still jittery from my nightmare. Mrs. Donahue was one of the biggest supporters of my writing. She was the teacher who gave me honest but constructive feedback. Mrs. D knew what she was talking about. If she liked something, I believed her, unlike my mom, who used to say she loved everything. But if Mrs. D said it was shit, I trusted her. She would tell me if something I wrote was terrible, but in a way that always inspired me to improve it. That's what a brilliant teacher does. She was a published author, so her feedback meant a lot.

I stepped into the hall, looking left and right. The traffic was heavy. Shoulder to shoulder, as teenagers swarmed to their next class, shuffling along like a hoard of zombies. A tuft of pink hair stood out from the crowd, and I hurried toward it. Steven was stuffing books into his locker. I stopped and leaned against the lockers opposite him across the hall to think. I didn't want too many people seeing me talking to Steven, I didn't need the rumors circulating.

The crowd started to thin. Steven grabbed a book and closed the locker heading for his class. I slowly followed behind him, searching for an opportunity to get him alone. Luckily for me, Steven stepped into the bathroom.

Perfect.

I approached the door, glancing left and right before I pushed through. Steven was washing his hands and noticed me in the mirror.

"Hey, Steven," I whispered.

He looked sharply and surveyed me before his eyes returned to the sink. "Um, who are you?"

My brow furrowed. "Wait, are you serious?"

"It was a joke," Steven said with a flat tone. "I know who you are, obviously. What do you want?"

"Oh... right." I let out a small, awkward laugh. "I just wanted to ask you a question, real quick."

He seemed unamused by me. ".... okay."

It was the first time we'd spoken in years.

"How did you know you were gay?" I whispered again.

"Who says I'm gay?" Steven gazed into the mirror, fixing his hair.

"Wait, you're *not* gay?" There was a small crack in my voice.

"Of course I am," Steven said with a giggle as he pantomimed a hair toss.

He was joking... again. With him, it was hard to tell what was a joke and what wasn't. My face relaxed.

"Oh, good. I mean, cool." I almost forgot the point I was trying to get to. "So how did you, like, know though?"

Steven stood there and pondered. "It's hard to explain, I guess. It's just something you feel inside you? Like I've known since I was five. It just seemed normal to me. Why do you care all of a sudden? You sure as hell didn't when I first told you."

An all too familiar bolt of guilt hit my stomach as I searched my brain for an excuse, needing something good enough that my questions wouldn't get back to Lauren. "My next story has a gay character. Just trying to hear a real-life experience," I said. I needed to end the conversation before he got suspicious. "Thanks, man. That was really helpful!" I turned and walked out before he could further the conversation. I glanced back long enough to see him huff with a twisted face.

I walked to my next class, staring at the floor the entire time, holding the straps of my backpack. The bell rang again, and everyone scattered into different rooms like cockroaches. I noticed a familiar back at the end of the hallway, removing a bag from a trash can. This time, he wore a white tank top, but I recognized the bare shoulders and short brown hair. My eyes widened. It was Mystery Boy again!

Before I could step closer to him, Dan tackled me through a door frame. It wasn't a full-on football field tackle but a small one that pushed me into the classroom and out of my Mystery Boy trance.

"What's up, Griffin?" Dan said, slapping me on the shoulder.

Most of the football team called me by my last name. With Dan being the quarterback, he didn't get to do a lot of tackling on the field, so he did it off the field. Dan was a tall, slender guy, standing at 5' 11" who wore a different football jersey every day of the week. He was good-looking with dark hair, shaved on the sides and pushed back and slick on top, and had more girlfriends in the past four years of high school than I could count. The football team used to keep an ongoing tally, but everyone eventually lost count. No one could keep up with him.

"I saw you go into the bathroom after Gay-ven. You goin' over to the pink side?" Dan wrapped his arms around me, making kissing noises.

A pit formed in my stomach. I was worried Dan might be the one to start a rumor, so I shut it down.

"Nope, just needed to take a piss." I scoffed, pushing him off of me.

"All right," Dan said, raising his hands in the air. "Don't get so defensive."

"Well, don't be such a dick." I smiled.

Dan could be rude a lot. Out of all the guys calling Steven a fag in the hallway, Dan did it the most.

"All right, gentlemen," the teacher called out to us, "sit down, please, so we can get started."

As I sat, I wondered what I would've done if Dan hadn't pushed me into class. I remember stepping in Mystery Boy's direction, but what would I do once I got close to him? I was dying to see his face. I could've acted like I had something I needed to throw away before he tied the garbage bag up. That seemed like a normal thing to do. But then what? I just stare at his face? Dan might've saved me from major embarrassment.

Throughout the class, I couldn't stop making up scenarios in my head. I imagined walking by Mystery Boy pretending to talk on my phone or asking if he needed help. Or maybe say, 'Hey, I'm that guy who keeps staring at you from afar; my name's Landon; what's yours? And why are you taking out the trash?'

When my day ended, Lauren met me in the school's front courtyard. I usually had football practice after school, but that day we had off because of a game the next night. Usually, we had football games on Friday nights, but they pushed this particular game up to Wednesday because of impending weather for Friday.

Lauren planted a small kiss. Two guys from the football team had been watching us and hollered in our direction. I rolled my eyes, taking Lauren's hand as I walked toward the street.

My house was bright yellow. Couldn't miss it. I'm not sure whose decision it was to make it the brightest house on the block, but there it was in all its sunny glory. Living across the street from my high school made things very convenient. I didn't have to waste gas going back and forth, not that I even had a car. It sucked having to rely on my dad, or my friends to drive me around places. I couldn't just pick up and go when I wanted when I didn't feel like walking. If my dad wasn't using his car, he'd let me borrow it if I gave him an important enough reason.

"Hey, you want to go to Lucky's for some ice cream?" Lauren asked, pulling on my arm. Lucky's was our local diner. They made the best milkshakes in all of Texas.

"Yeah sure." I smiled. "Just let me put my bag down, I'll be right back."

It took me all of thirty seconds to run across the street and up my driveway. I moved so fast that I practically knocked over my dad, who was coming out the side door.

"Whoa! Slow down, killer," he said, taking me by the shoulders.

"Sorry, Dad." I stepped inside, dropped my bag near the couch, and turned around to head out the door. Dad was getting into his car when I called out for him. He stopped before climbing into the driver's seat and stared at me, waiting to hear what I had to say. I stepped to his car on the opposite side, resting my arms on his blue Ford Taurus roof. "I'm wondering if you'd know about something people have been talking about?"

I didn't want to tell him I was staring at Mystery Boy, so I used gossip as an excuse.

"Make it quick," Dad said.

"Some kids were talking about this guy, like cleaning the wall or something." I pointed across the street at the half-wall. "Do you know anything about that?"

"Yeah, there was some graffiti there," Dad said before sitting in the driver's seat.

I hunched over, resting my arms on the open window, and looked in at him. "Okay, but like, who's the guy?"

"You don't need to concern yourself with that," Dad said, starting the engine.

"Dad, come on." I stared at him with too much desperation. He sighed and tapped his fingers on the steering wheel before looking at me.

"He's here on community service."

"What did he do?"

"That's none of our business." Dad shifted the car into reverse.

"Wait!" I blurted out. "How old is he?"

Dad searched his memory. "Nineteen, I think? Or twenty, I don't know."

"How long is he gonna be here? At the school, I mean?"

"I don't know," Dad said. "A couple of months? I just signed the papers to allow him to be here. Principal Jamison is the one working directly with the kid. Why do you care so much?"

"Just curious."

"Well, don't be," Dad said. "He is not someone I want you hanging around with. He's not like you."

"What's that supposed to mean?"

"He...you aren't... " Dad was hesitating, trying to find the right words to say. "He's a troubled kid, is what I mean. You shouldn't want to be associated with someone who has obviously broken the law. Is that understood?"

"Got it," I mumbled. I looked at the passenger seat, cycling through the other questions my mind came up with.

"Landon, I have a meeting to get to. Is there anything else?"

"Oh!" I said, perking up again. "Can I have a twenty? Lauren wants to go to Lucky's." My dad made a noise, sounding like the Big Bad Wolf before reaching into his pocket for his wallet. He eased off the brake, and the car rolled, forcing me to take a step back.

"Put on some sunblock, would you? You're looking a little red," Dad shouted, backing out of the driveway. "I'll see you later tonight; get your homework done!" I gave him a salute before he sped down the street.

I rushed back inside to grab the sunblock I always kept in my bag. Being a redhead and living in Texas, where the sun was always shining, wasn't the best combination. Like Steven's, my hair was easy to spot in a crowd. The color was just under the tone of flaming hot Cheetos. I couldn't believe I was from Texas. With my pale skin, I was one of the few kids in my school without a tan.

I hopped into Lauren's car, sweating from being outside for eight minutes. She owned a beat-up Volkswagen bug that used to be her mom's. The AC took a while to kick in. Lauren was sitting in the driver's seat, adjusting the rear-view mirror. Her eyes swiveled to me, and she let out an abrupt laugh.

I grinned. "What?"

"You have sunscreen on your face." She smiled back.

My cheeks warmed, and I pulled down the visor to look in its mirror. There was a small white dollop on the side of my nose. I brushed it off and smoothed it into my hands.

A loud thud against my door made Lauren gasp. Dan stood there, peering in, appearing out of nowhere. I rolled the window down, letting more hot air in.

"Where you goin', Carrot Top?" Dan's tone was perky. Like the jerseys he wore, he also had a new ginger-related word to call me every day; most weren't very original.

"Lucky's," I said.

"Cool, I'll grab the guys and meet you there." Dan rubbed my head as if he were a dad ruffling his child's hair. Lauren rolled her eyes. Before she could interject, Dan was halfway to his car, rounding up the troops. I shrugged at Lauren. She huffed and put the car in drive.

Lauren and I got to the diner before everyone else. We took a booth at the back of the restaurant. Every tabletop had a different theme, put together like a scrapbook under the plexiglass casing. One table had a space theme with pictures of astronauts and planets. Another table had a video game theme with images of Mario and Sonic the Hedgehog. The one we sat at was a 50s nostalgia theme, complete with pictures of Elvis Presley, old cars, and even a few cigarette ads. They placed the menus in a rack on the table along with the mustard and ketchup bottles. We never touched the menu because we knew it by heart. The diner smelled like a sugar factory that day.

A tall woman with stylish glasses greeted us. Her hair was cut into a short bob, dyed black and silver, wearing an apron with 'Lucky's' branded across her chest. Her long arms were covered in intricate tattoos. She even had a small rainbow flag button clipped to her apron beside a small Mexican flag pin.

"Hey there, my name's Steph," she said with a toothy smile. She must have been new because I'd been there a hundred times over the years and didn't recognize her face. "Can I start y'all with something to drink?"

Lauren must have noticed the Mexican flag pin because she ordered in Spanish. Steph smiled and jotted down the order. After four years of Spanish classes, I still wasn't confident enough to speak the language, but I understood most of it.

"I'll do a strawberry and chocolate milkshake, too," I said.

Steph nodded and walked off. I heard the bell above the front door chime and in walked Dan with four other boys from the football team. Trailing behind was Chris Wilson, Dan's younger brother, who was shorter and stockier. On the field, Chris's job was to stop the other team from tackling Dan. Not much was different off the field; Chris was always there to back Dan up if need be. The brothers sat in our booth while the other three guys sat at an adjacent table.

Lauren and I had hardly said anything to each other when Dan struck up the conversation about the day. "So what was actually going on between you and the faggot today, Landon?"

Chris, meanwhile, looked over the menu. I glanced at Lauren, who tilted her head at me with squinted eyes.

"Just because we were in the bathroom at the same time doesn't mean anything is going on," I said.

Lauren peered at Dan. "Wish you wouldn't call him that. His name is Steven." Lauren knew Steven from the drama club. He made most of the costumes for the shows.

Dan rolled his eyes. "I know his name. Fag just suits him better."

"Stop being such an asshole, for once," Lauren said.

Chris shook his head, still staring at the menu. Steph walked up before the conversation went any further. The brothers ordered fries and soda.

"Fuck, she's hot," Dan said as Steph walked away. "Too bad she's a dyke."

Chris watched her, too. "How do you know?"

"She just has that look," Dan said. "The tattoos, the hair, and the flag pin she's wearing." Chris nodded in agreement as Dan continued, "I bet I could turn her, she just needs the right dick, you know?"

"Wow," Lauren said in disgust. "Is there anything that comes out of your mouth that isn't offensive?"

Dan pointed a thumb at Steph. "Landon, you wouldn't bang her?"

Lauren's eyes shot to me, ready to cut my head off if I answered. I looked away, rubbing my forehead. The more Dan spoke, the more I questioned whether I wanted to continue to use the word 'friend' to describe him. It was like puberty turned him into an entitled macho man that very much differed from the person he was when we were kids.

"I wonder if she has a hot girlfriend," Chris said.

Dan wiggled his brows, practically drooling over the thought.

"Okay," Lauren said. "So it's okay for Steph to be gay because she's an attractive woman that gets you all tingly? But it's not okay for a guy to be gay because that makes him a fag?"

"It's just gross," Dan said, twisting his face.

Chris put up his hands in defense. "Hey, I don't care if a guy is gay."

Finally, something good to come out of this conversation.

"As long as he isn't hitting on me," Chris finished.

Okay, not the best, still not terrible.

Lauren stood, agitated by the entire conversation, rolling her eyes. "Yeah, because you're every gay guy's type," she said before stomping to the restroom. The guys just laughed her off. I shook my head and told them to shut up again.

Steph arrived with our milkshakes and placed them on the table. "Is she okay?"

"Yeah, she's fine," Dan said, putting on his best attempt at a charming voice. "We were just talking about how I could turn you straight, how bout you and I go out sometime?" The guy had no shame.

"Turn me? Really?" Steph's eyes narrowed and she crossed her arms. "Well, to me it seems like you don't even have a dick big enough to please a woman, never mind 'turn' her. I'd have to decline seeing as I already have someone who can do things that you couldn't even wrap your fragile masculinity ass mind around on your best day." She turned on her heels and walked back to the counter without batting an eye. Chris and I hollered laughing, bouncing in our seats, while Dan sank lower in his.

Through my tears of laughter, I spotted Lauren standing outside the restroom, smiling, having heard the whole conversation. Dan shut up and moved on to other topics. However, he continued his douchebaggery when he refused to tip Steph before we left. I wondered what Dan would say if I told him about my feelings toward Mystery Boy. Perhaps he'd call me a faggot, too, and drop me like trash. I needed to keep better company.

When we left, Lauren thanked me before starting the car.

"For what?" I said, thinking it was for paying for the milkshakes.

"For not being like him," she said.

That made me smile.

THREE

I busted through the front door and threw my helmet to the ground; I was headed for my room with mud trailing the floor behind me. I had almost reached my bedroom door before my dad screamed, chasing after me.

"Where the hell was your head tonight?! There could have been scouts there! If they had seen the way you played, they would've left at halftime and not even considered your ass for a scholarship. Has everything I've taught you this season gone out the window?" I just stood there with clenched fists. "Landon, answer me!"

I couldn't take it; the best I could do was slam the door in his face and lock it. My poor, thin wooden door barely kept his loud voice back. I expected it to crack up the middle and explode until his volume calmed, and I heard him sigh and walk away. The tension left my body as I flicked on my desk lamp, peeled off my greasy jersey and pads, and dropped onto my bed. I laid there, still in my muddy pants and leg gear, staring at the ceiling.

Where was my head tonight?

The obvious answer was Mystery Boy. I spent the entire game looking at the stands to see if Mystery Boy might be sitting there, watching. I'd do double-takes whenever I noticed a guy with brown hair walk through the crowd of spectators. Catching the football was the farthest thing from my mind, and that was my most important job on the field. I couldn't focus for one damn minute. All I thought about was his sweaty back and what his face might look like, and I didn't know why.

Thanks to me, we lost the game. My team would've killed me if they could see inside my mind. My entire life had been football and scholarships, and now some alleged criminal comes into my life that I couldn't stop thinking about and screws everything up? I was usually flawless on the field; I was used to getting praise after every game. Nothing had ever distracted me as much as Mystery Boy. Why was it happening now? I didn't even know him! At that moment, I decided to stop obsessing over Mystery Boy. He was ruining things.

My phone dinged from across the room. I groaned, not wanting to get up yet. I could lie there forever, burying myself in pity and guilt for losing the game for the rest of the guys. When I got up, I searched my backpack for my phone. It was a text from Lauren.

LAUREN

Hey babe, you okay?

ME

Yeah, why, what's up?

LAUREN

Oh, you just didn't say bye after the game.

ME

Sorry, I just wanted to get out of there. My head wasn't in it tonight.

LAUREN

Yeah, I think everyone noticed that. What's going on?

A couple different answers came to mind. Like: Oh nothing, just feeling too much pressure from my dad. Oh nothing, I'm pretty sure I'm failing trig. Oh nothing, I'm obsessing over a GUY I've never met.

ME

Just not feeling well.

LAUREN

Are you sick?

Another text popped in from the top of my screen from Tasha.

TASHA

Landon, the deadline is tomorrow! You haven't emailed me the story yet.

Shit. I'd forgotten to write the new story. *Thanks again, Mystery Boy.*

ME

I'll get it to you by tonight.

LAUREN

What?

ME

Shit, sorry, wrong text.

I did that a lot.

ME

I'll get it to you by tonight.

TASHA

Great, thank you.

LAUREN

Who was that for?

ME

Tasha. I forgot about my deadline. I gotta go. I need to finish this. I'll talk to you later?

LAUREN

All right.

Wait one more thing. Let's go out somewhere on Saturday? Just you and me, give us a chance to talk about what's on your mind.

ME

Sounds good. I'll see you at school tomorrow.

LAUREN

<3

I placed my phone on the desk and flipped open my laptop, clicking through to an empty Word document. I took a deep breath and closed my eyes. Coming up with something would not be as easy as I hoped, not with my mind in so many places. I imagined myself in the world of magic, waving my wand in front of the computer as it typed the most amazing, addictive story. But I opened my eyes to white nothingness on the screen.

My phone chimed again. I picked it up, annoyed by the distraction.

DAN

WTF man, what happened out there tonight?

I tossed my phone back on the desk with more force than intended. I had that quick moment of panic, wondering if I might have cracked the screen. I didn't have the patience for Dan, so I stood and walked to my window. People were still crowded around the school post-game. I noticed Dan walking to his car with an unfamiliar girl on his left and Chris on his right. I closed my curtains before he looked up and saw me standing there shirtless.

With a huff, I plopped down on my bed again, closing my eyes. I wanted to get rid of the thoughts of Mystery Boy, but it was so hard. Flashes of his sparkling back passed through my mind again. The thought was so vivid I felt like I could smell him. It was a combination of freshly cut grass and sweat.

No! Stop.

I took a deep breath in through my nose, yearning to smell even more. I fantasized about waking up next to him on a bright, sunny morning in my bed and turning him around to see what he looked like. I could feel his skin; it was soft and damp. I'd never fantasized about Lauren in my bed or about touching her so intimately.

Different combinations of facial features came and went as if his face were a Rubik's cube and I was trying to match everything just right. I imagined myself looking down, studying Mystery Boy's shirtless body. My hand instinctively slid under my football pants, where I could feel my lust for him growing. The thoughts were so new and exciting, and I let them take over.

Stop thinking about him!

"Landon!" My dad burst through my bedroom door without knocking. My eyes exploded open, and I sat up in my bed faster than any human being should be able to move. My chest heaved, and my heart beat as fast as a hummingbird's.

"Dad! Jesus, I swear I locked that door!" I yelled between fits of breath.

"You know the lock comes loose if you jiggle the handle," he said. "I'm sorry, I should've knocked."

"Yes, you should have." I grabbed the pillow from behind me and covered my bare chest. "I could've been changing!" *or worse.*

"I'm sorry, I'm sorry," he said, raising his hands in defense. He took a breath, walking further into my room. He hadn't seemed to notice anything out of the ordinary. "I just wanted to say that, I shouldn't have yelled at you like that. I was going to bed, but it was bothering me too much. I had to come in and apologize."

"It's fine," I said, calming my breath. My heart slowed down to a normal rhythm again. Any arousal I had going was shut down and would stay that way for a while.

"You just seemed a little off tonight."

"I just have a lot on my mind," I said, pushing my fingers through my buzzed hair. So much for forgetting about Mystery Boy; that lasted all of two minutes.

"Right," Dad said as he crossed his arms. "I know it may not seem like it all the time, but I'm here if you need to talk about anything." His eyes darted around my room, looking for anything to focus on that wasn't me. There was obvious tension that still floated through the air between us. He noticed I was still wearing my dirty football pants. "Landon, you're getting your sheets all dirty. Throw them in the hamper before you go to bed, I'll try to wash them tomorrow."

"It's ok, I can put them in tonight," I said, swinging my legs off the bed. "You probably have a busy day tomorrow, and I might not get to bed for a while anyway. I have a deadline I forgot about."

"All right, I'll let you get to it then." He turned. "Again," he said, stopping in the doorframe and looking back at me. "I'm sorry I got overheated. This has been such a sudden change for me, I'm still trying to find the balance."

I sighed. "I know, Dad. I am too."

He gave me a half-smile, closing my door behind him.

My room filled with light through my window. Cars were leaving the school, their headlights reflecting off my house as they drove by. I pushed myself off the bed, hiked back to my desk, and sat in front of my laptop again. I clicked my phone to check the time and saw Dan's text on the screen. I didn't want to respond yet. Staring at his text message, I thought about how he used to act when we were younger. He was nicer; he cared more about people. I thought about our long history as I typed out some plot points. It became clearer the more my fingers pressed the keys. I was gonna write a story about two best friends that grew apart as they got older.

SEVEN YEARS AGO.

Dan and I met on the first day of 5th grade. I was ten years old. He and his family had just moved to town from North Carolina. I sat with him at lunch one day after noticing him sitting alone, and I remember he had a cool *Ninja Turtles* lunch box that caught my eye. I liked that. Turns out he liked my *Spider-Man* lunch box. That day we traded lunchboxes and promised to sit together the next day to get them back, which we did. Then we sat together the next day and the day after that, and the day after that, until it just became automatic. We talked about everything and anything: our favorite superheroes, cartoons, action figures, bugs, sports, pizza, and video games. I realized everything I liked, he liked, too. We always made each other laugh; we were in our own little bubble, no other kid in the school could penetrate it. We were a club of two.

That year, on picture day, my mom made me wear a purple collared shirt, which, when you were ten years old, was like wearing a giant neon sign that said, "Please make fun of me." I pleaded with her not to send me to school wearing it. I wanted to wear a shirt with skateboards on it, but she said that wasn't appropriate for picture day. I wore my windbreaker for most of the day, trying to hide my embarrassment. When the teacher took my class to the gym to take the pictures, we all had to line up against the wall alphabetically and move one by one until we made it to the cameraman.

I was next, but with my last name being Griffin, there were still a good number of kids behind me in line who I didn't want to see my purple shirt. I decided to keep my windbreaker on and make up some excuse for my mom when she saw the picture, an excuse I'd worry about later.

Confident in my decision, I strolled up to the small stool in front of a dark blue background. I sat and practiced my smile while the cameraman reset the lights. To my surprise, my teacher popped up next to me and kneeled to eye level. "Hun, take this off," she said, pointing to my windbreaker.

"No," I said, shaking my head back and forth.

"Now come on, your mother put you in this nice collared shirt for a reason. Take it off, please."

I unzipped the jacket as slowly as I could, hoping she'd change her mind and tell me to keep it on in a fit of impatience. But she was an elementary school teacher, her patience level was through the roof. She waited politely until I handed it to her. Once in hand, my teacher walked away, leaving me in plain sight of all the other kids in line to feast their eyes upon my Barney-colored polo. To make things worse, another class lined up behind mine. I didn't dare glance over to see if anyone was looking. I didn't have to because I could hear the tiny giggles. It started with one or two kids, and then it spread down the line like wildfire.

"Look! He's wearing a girl color!" a voice shouted out, followed by more laughter. We all considered purple a girl's color, along with pink and yellow. Kids had already been making fun of my ginger hair, but now they had another thing to make fun of me for. I'd forever be seen as the redhead with freckles who wore purple. My jaw clenched as I fought back tears. They couldn't see me cry, too; that would just fuel the fire. More than anything, I wanted to sprout wings and fly away, busting through the gym roof and never coming back.

"I think he looks awesome!" a voice rang out. Those five words from someone in the newly formed line caused the laughter to go silent. I gained the courage to look over to the line of kids and saw Dan leaning out from everyone else with a thumb in the air.

I smiled, suddenly feeling a warm sensation in my stomach for him, until a boy further up in line looked back at Dan and shouted, "You're both losers!" That's when the laughter started up again. My boost in confidence shattered, I felt defeated as I looked back at the cameraman, unwilling to show my face to the crowd of devils any longer. The next second came with a flash and I was told to move on. It should go without saying, I wasn't smiling in my school picture that year.

The next day I didn't see Dan until lunchtime because we were in separate classes. The only time we got to interact was at lunch and recess. I sat down at a table by myself, still feeling the social pain from the day before. I assumed Dan would be too embarrassed to be seen with me now.

"Hey, Landon," Dan said, smiling. I looked up from my lunch box in awe of him standing across the table. He was wearing an oversized, frayed purple shirt. My mouth dropped open. It looked to be an adult shirt, cut to his size with a pair of scissors. He sat across from me and talked about what we would do at recess as if he wasn't making some major fashion statement. My body filled with warmth as I sat there watching him talk. My eyes darted around to see if anyone was staring at him, which they were, but he didn't care!

He didn't wear a purple shirt because he liked it; he wore it for me. Dan wore it to show he was on my side and that no one could infiltrate our bubble. My small brain couldn't register my emotions that day. All I felt was warmth and happiness, that's the only way I could describe it back then. My smile couldn't be shattered after that.

As our friendship grew, so did our desire to hang outside of school. Soon enough, we were having sleepovers almost every weekend. We spent our nights reading comic books and playing video games way past our bedtime. Dan shared a bedroom with Chris, who was eight years old. Chris was constantly wanting to hang out with us or do what we were doing; he was Dan's little shadow.

"You're so lucky you don't have a little brother," Dan said to me before his face lit up. "We should camp outside tonight so we don't have to play with Chris!" Dan was so excited by the idea; before I could even say anything, he ran off to ask his parents if we could set up the tent in his backyard.

Once Dan's dad set everything up for us, we got to work on the signs that said: No Little Brother Allowed. We had our flashlights, sleeping bags, snacks, and action figures; we were ready for the night. It got dark fast, so we flipped on our flashlights and placed them between our sleeping bags, illuminating the Great War between Ninja Turtles and professional wrestlers.

"Hey Dan," I mumbled, not wanting to interrupt our action figure fight, but something was on my mind. Dan looked at me, so I continued. "I never thanked you for what you did." Dan tilted his head as if he'd forgotten about the lunch after picture day. "Coming into school wearing your dad's purple shirt that day. That was really cool."

"No problem. That's what friends do," Dan said. The way he smiled at me made me feel that rush of warmth again.

"Can I kiss you?" The words projected out of my 10-year-old mouth like vomit. My brain didn't have a second to think about what I'd said before I said it. My throat held back any words that could've come next. Time seemed to slow.

What did I just say?

It felt excruciatingly long before Dan spoke.

"Boys aren't supposed to kiss other boys, stupid," he said, laughing it off and going back to his Ninja Turtles. I laughed, too, not giving the topic any more attention. The warmth faded at that moment, but the happiness didn't. Luckily for me, he still wanted to be my best friend after that.

My alarm blared, and I pushed my head up from my desk. It was 7:00 a.m. I panicked, realizing I'd fallen asleep. I clicked the trackpad of my laptop to wake it up, and I couldn't remember if I'd finished writing. Once the screen came back to life, I saw my email dashboard. I had an unread message from Tasha that said, 'Thanks!' I slumped back in my chair; I'd made my Thursday deadline. I stayed up so late that it was hard to remember what I'd written. Pieces of my story were coming back to me, and I panicked again. I knew I had written the story of Dan and I's friendship, but I couldn't remember if I changed the names or if I left out the part about me wanting to kiss him. My heart raced. If Tasha had already read it, she'd know my biggest secret, and even worse, if she'd printed it, it could force me out of my very confused closet to face the entire school.

FOUR

I jolted out of my seat, smashing my fingers on the edge of my desk, trying to reach the trackpad of my laptop. Bolts of pain shot up my forearm, and I let out an agitated growl. I moved the small cursor as fast as I could to click the file. My eyes passed from left to right like a speed reader trying to win a Guinness world record, and I saw I changed the names. My tired eyes slowed down to ensure I didn't miss the part about the kiss. I sighed in relief. The kiss was nowhere to be found. How could I be stupid enough to think I would add that? I closed my laptop, noticing my knuckles had gone red from the collision with the hardwood. I tried to shake the pain away, but it just felt like pins and needles.

I stood and cracked my neck; it kinked from sleeping on the desk. I peered out the window; people had already started parking their cars and filling up the front courtyard. I got closer to look for Mystery Boy, and caught my reflection out of my peripheral in the mirror hanging on my closet door. I was still wearing nothing but my football pants; I looked down at myself, still caked in a few patches of mud and dirt. I needed a shower ASAP.

"It was good," Tasha said as she flipped through a printed copy of my short story. "There was actual heart and emotion there, you know?" A red headband held Tasha's curls back. Her dark skin was flawless, and she wore a black T-shirt with 'QUEEN' across her chest in bold white letters. She was sitting across from me at a table in the library. When it was a free period for us, we liked to get together and talk about the *Monthly*.

"Really? You think so?"

"Yes." She smiled as she checked a text on her phone. "Have you been looking at any colleges for writing? I hear Columbia has a great program."

I scoffed. "Yeah, right."

Tasha placed her phone on the table. Her bright red nails matched her headband. "Maybe NYU, then?"

"My dad would be devastated if I moved halfway across the country." I'd never thought about living in New York City. I'd never even been there, only seeing it in pictures and movies. The people would be more open-minded, for sure. Folks in my town thought the same way Dan did, with ignorance and fear. Tasha and Lauren were two of the few that were different. Tasha was outspoken about social justice and human rights. She and Lauren attended at least three women's marches across the state that year, even Steven tagged along with them. "Plus, my dad wants me to pursue football so—"

Tasha cut me off. "But what do you want?" That was a hard question for me. Tasha sat up straight and interlocked her fingers as if it were an interview.

"I don't know," I said with an awkward smirk. "I mean, I love football, but I love writing, too. I just don't think my dad would let me do it. He's worked so hard with me on the field over the years." I averted making eye contact. The library was a sea of whispers, typing fingers, and turning pages.

"Boy, look at me," Tasha said, with a few finger snaps in my direction. My eyes darted back to her. "Do what makes you happy, not what makes your dad happy. I wouldn't want to see your talent go to waste."

I chuckled. "You sound like Mrs. Donahue. Maybe I can do both," I said, puffing my chest out.

"How scandalous!" Tasha said as she brought her hands to her cheeks, playing along with my charade. We laughed louder, and it was met with an anonymous 'shush' from somewhere in the room. "Continue writing so that when you make it big, I can be the one to say I discovered you."

I rolled my eyes at her and laughed more.

ONE YEAR AGO.

During my junior year English class, the teacher assigned us to write an essay about our most prized possession. I remember sitting in my room, looking around at all my useless things, wracking my brain to think of an item I truly cherished. It was probably my cell phone; what teenager didn't always have their phone glued to their hand? But writing about it would be the dumbest teenage decision I could make. After twenty long minutes of empty thought, I decided to make it up. I would turn this true-life personal essay into pure fiction and play it off as if it were real.

I wrote an entire paper about a picture of me and my grandma dancing at a family reunion and how I had made a copy to bury with her after she passed away. None of which was true at all because, one, I didn't even have a family large enough for a reunion, and two, my grandmother was still alive and well. Was it morally wrong? Yes, absolutely, but it got me an A.

During my free period, I was in the library on my laptop, finishing the essay before I had to turn it in. Unbeknownst to me, Tasha had been walking by and spotted me writing. She stopped and stared at my computer screen from behind. I was in one of my power modes, where the entire world went silent and my fingers typed a mile a minute, I never felt her eyes on me. Tasha dropped her books on the table beside me, releasing me from the spell.

Tasha plopped in a chair. "What is this?"

My brow furrowed. "What is what?"

"This?" She pointed a blue-painted nail at my computer screen. "What is this that you're writing?"

Taken aback by her assertiveness, I said, "It's an essay for my English class. Why?"

"I like what I saw," Tasha said.

I turned my computer away and squinted at her. "Were you reading over my shoulder?"

"Of course. What is it about?"

"Uh," I said, unsure if I should tell her to go away. My school housed about a thousand kids, so I was having trouble placing her name, but I had seen her around before. "It's about my most prized possession, a picture of my grandmother and me."

Tasha bounced in her seat. "Can I read it?"

"Oh God, no."

"Oh, come on! It looked good! Why won't you let me read it?"

"It's personal, all right?" I was hoping that would send her on her way. Tasha didn't blink; she just stared at me, tapping her fingers on the table. "I made it up, okay?"

Tasha raised an eyebrow, "What?"

"This is supposed to be true, about my life, but I made it up because I couldn't think of anything," I confessed as I rubbed my forehead.

"Oh, now I have to read it," Tasha said with a growing smile. She gestured for me to pass the computer as she bounced up and down in her seat. I was confused about why she was so excited by it. I pushed the laptop over to her. She was a fast reader. I watched her eyes scroll from side to side as she enveloped my fictionalized true story. Now and then her eyebrows would scrunch or raise. "So you made this up?" She asked, and I nodded. "Is your grandma even dead?"

"No," I whispered, reclining in my chair and looking away in embarrassment.

"Oh, that's cold!" Tasha laughed her words out. "That. Is. Cold," she said again, this time clapping with each word. I wasn't sure how to respond. I assumed she didn't like it because of how hard she laughed at it until she said, "This is brilliant."

"What?" It surprised me. I was so confused by her.

Tasha pushed my laptop back. "I think it's great. How did you come up with this?"

"I don't know. My brain just does it, and I write it down." The heat in my face disappeared.

"That's perfect! Can you write more?" She pulled her chair closer.

"What? What do you mean write more?"

"I just took over as editor for the *Madison Monthly*." Tasha's face lit up. "I've been looking for someone who can write short stories. We have way too many poems and essays and reports, it's so boring. I need something fun and new!"

"You want me to write for the *Monthly*? Seriously?" I said, flabbergasted. "No one's ever read anything I've written besides my teachers."

"The way you told that story felt so real," Tasha spoke with her hands. "The way your words flowed together was captivating and emotional. I want to see what else you have. I want to know what else your brain can come up with."

I didn't know what to say. A brief scenario played through my head where this was all a practical joke. I would answer yes, and Dan would jump out from behind the bookshelves and start laughing, calling me names. But so far, there were no surprise appearances by Dan Wilson. I hesitated, glancing back and forth a few times between her and my computer screen before saying yes.

"Great!" Tasha stood from her chair. "It's Landon, right?"

"Yeah, how d'you know?"

"We had health class together freshman year."

"Of course, yeah," I said, playing it off as if I remembered her, but she saw right through me.

"I'm Tasha," she said after extending a hand. I completed her gesture, still sitting. "Well, all documents are due next Thursday and we print on Friday!" She dug through her stack of books until she found a notepad. She ripped out a page and scribbled something. "Just send it to me at this email. I'll be looking forward to it!"

"Thanks," I said, smiling as I watched her strut away.

I remember the first short story I submitted to her. It was a post-apocalyptic tale of a flesh-eating disease that took over a small Texas town. Thirty minutes after I sent it to Tasha, I got an email asking me to turn down the dial on the gore in the story. I had no problem doing it. Mad High just wasn't ready for that yet, I understood. To my surprise, the story was a hit. Many people were talking about it after the paper was passed out that morning. Even Dan liked it for someone who barely had the attention span to tolerate a book. He didn't read a single one of my stories that were published after that. One was enough for him. That first story got Mrs. Donahue's attention as well. One afternoon, she pulled me aside in the hallway and praised my storytelling abilities. She asked me if I wouldn't mind if she helped me out. Since then, she's read most of my stories before I've published them, helping me with formatting or editing and sometimes even story development. Football was such a team effort, but with writing, I could do something successful on my own.

"I'll be sure to give you full credit for discovering me." I chuckled.

Tasha pointed a polished red nail at me. "You better."

The bell rang, and we both said our goodbyes. That morning, I had dropped off a copy of my latest story on Mrs. Donahue's desk. I was in her class next and was curious about what she thought of it. It wouldn't be printed until the next day, so I thought I could bounce the edits off her if needed.

"Just the man I wanted to see," Mrs. Donahue said as I entered the classroom. Not everyone had shown up yet, so we had time to talk.

"What'd you think? Be honest."

"It felt... very personal," she said. It wasn't the response I expected. A big part of the story was about my purple shirt incident, so she wasn't wrong.

"There may have been a little non-fiction thrown in there," I said with a smile, sitting at my usual desk. I wondered if anyone who read it would remember that real-life event from elementary school. If Dan took the time to read it, he'd remember. But it was safe from him since he didn't give a crap about the *Monthly*.

"It was sort of heartbreaking at the end. I was sad they couldn't stay friends after everything. It seemed like they had a fondness for each other," she said, standing and walking to me. She placed the story on my desk. "I made a few edits, nothing major. You're getting better at this, Landon," she said with a smile.

"Thank you!" I plucked through the pages. "I'll make sure I get this to Tasha in time for tomorrow's print."

My mind fluttered at the thought of Mystery Boy again as I walked to my next class and sat next to the windows. I hadn't seen him since I glimpsed him cutting grass the morning before. My eyes flicked to the windows; that classroom overlooked the parking lot on the side of the school, but there was no one outside. I'd hoped I would see him as if I had the power to summon him. I wondered if anyone else around the school knew him. I could ask some people. Mystery Boy could be a drug addict. Maybe I'd ask the stoner kids if they knew who he was. He could be their dealer.

After class, I was putting books away in my locker when Dan rolled up behind me and slapped me on the back. "What's up, pumpkin head?"

"It feels like you've just forgotten my name," I said, rolling my eyes.

Lauren also appeared out of the crowd and kissed my cheek. The three of us made small talk and complained about homework before Lauren brought up a much more interesting topic.

"I heard these girls in the bathroom talking about a new janitor or something? Apparently, he works outside shirtless," she said, asking Dan and me if we had heard of him. If girls were talking about Mystery Boy, maybe I wasn't the only one obsessed.

Dan scratched his head. "That's weird, I haven't seen him."

"Yeah, I've seen him," I interjected, closing my locker. "A couple days ago. My dad said he was here for some community service thing."

"Oh shit, wait," Dan said. "Yeah, I've heard of him. Some kids were talking about him the other day. They said he burned down his school or something and got into all this trouble. That's why they made him do community service at a school." Dan seemed confident in his statement, but its logic made little sense.

"The girls were saying something different in the bathroom," Lauren said as she looked back and forth between Dan and me. "They said he was here because he beat someone half to death over some drugs."

"That doesn't seem right," I said, "Wouldn't he get more than community service for doing any of that? It couldn't have been something that bad."

"I don't know, but he freaks me out. I hope I don't see him around," Lauren said, hooking her arm around mine.

"The guy shouldn't even be around kids," Dan said.

"We aren't kids. And he's not that much older than us," I said with more of a defensive tone than intended.

Dan tried to call my bluff. "How do you know?"

"Because my dad told me he was like nineteen or twenty." I realized I'd given away everything I'd learned about Mystery Boy. Two things, his age and his criminal sentencing. I thought I knew more, but everything else was stuff I'd made up in my head. I yearned for more information about him; he was like a drug I wanted another hit of.

Now I knew two rumors, one of which could be true but seemed very unlikely. I knew nothing about the justice system and how they treated certain crimes. I was certain that he'd be in prison for anything violent, so I determined right then he wasn't dangerous. This led me to assume that he was a nice guy and would talk to me if I approached him. I might've been a little too optimistic. As I walked to my next class, I made a mental checklist of things to say if I ever saw him again.

FIVE

Class was over, and I stepped into the hall of never-ending bodies. The last bell had rung, and everyone was trying to escape the educated concrete walls. I doubted people would find my new story interesting once they published it in the *Monthly* the next day. I wondered if it was too dry for a high school reader. The student body that read the *Monthly* was so used to my wild, imaginative stories. I had yet to write something so true to life and personal. I sighed, no longer wanting to ridicule my mind with self-deprecating thoughts.

Pushing through the crowds, I noticed a familiar tank top and broad shoulders, and my eyes focused. I was seeing tunnel vision. It was Mystery Boy again. He was about twenty feet ahead of me, the closest we'd ever been to each other. I wanted to see his face so desperately that it unleashed a frenzy inside of me. It seemed like the faster I moved, the more bodies got in my way, and I accidentally shoulder-bumped a kid, knocking his backpack off of him and spilling its contents onto the floor. I twirled around, walking backward. "Sorry!" I shouted to him, and then spun forward in a snap. My eyes searched the crowd, I zeroed in on the shoulders again. I was gaining on him, pushing through more bodies, but it felt like treading quicksand.

Mystery Boy turned a corner; he was headed for the front doors. I raced now, turning the corner myself, but a crouching girl sipping from the water fountain met me. My hip slammed into the side of her body, causing me to spin out of control. I was in a car making my last lap in the Indy 500 to peel out and crash right before I passed the finish line. My body hit the floor, and I rolled into a pack of denim-covered legs. Before I could propel myself up, I was already hoisted back to my feet.

"What the hell, dude," Chris said, pulling me up from under my arms.

Dan was there, too. "Landon, you okay? What's up with you lately?"

My eyes fixated on the exit. I nudged the guys aside and ran the rest of the way through the front doors. The sun was too bright to ignore as I shielded my eyes, squinting and darting my head from left to right, hoping to spot the one guy in a tank top. But he was gone. I groaned as I bent, holding myself up on my knees, trying to catch my breath.

"Landon, what the hell was that?" Dan was behind me. Chris was close by, waiting for an answer, too.

I shook my head, standing upright. "Nothing. I was just looking for someone."

Chris shrugged. "Who?"

Dan looked at me. "Lauren?"

My eyes widened. "No," I said, realizing I hadn't thought about Lauren in days. I had physically been around her, but even then, my mind was on Mystery Boy. I felt terrible; I wasn't thinking about my girlfriend because he'd taken priority. I wondered for a second if I should tell her.

It's too soon. What would I even say? You can't just tell your girlfriend you've been fantasizing about someone you've never met. It would destroy her. This could all go away tomorrow.

I'd hoped the feelings and desires would've fizzled out by that point. I worried that they never would, at least maybe not until I saw Mystery Boy's face. What the hell was wrong with me? I knew I looked crazy and was worried I'd completely outed myself. I was an idiot for going after Mystery Boy, but I was blinded by obsession.

ONE YEAR AGO.

I met Lauren during our Junior year. I stood outside the auditorium waiting for Dan to meet me before practice. The halls were bustling with movement; waves of kids passed, heading to their after-school activities. My eye caught a tiny boy running past me and outside to catch his bus. His backpack looked as big as he did; he could probably fit inside of it. I wondered why a boy that young was in a high school. Then, another passed me at breakneck speed, and I realized they were freshmen. They seemed to get smaller and smaller every year.

As I watched the munchkins flee, someone bumped into me as they reached for the auditorium door. I scowled as I turned to face the culprit, thinking I'd say something crass, but the person had already run inside. The doors had two slim windows above each handle. I looked inside and saw a skinny guy running toward the stage. The assailant had bright blue, messy hair. Steven was the only kid in school who stood out that much. I rolled my eyes; there was no point in getting into it over a bump.

A girl's voice surprised me from behind. "Are you auditioning?"

I spun around, startled by the voice being so close to me. "Uh, what?" I said, looking her up and down. Her brown hair was pulled back in a messy bun, her backpack over one shoulder. I noticed she was holding a stack of papers in her arms. I recognized her face but didn't know her name.

She spoke slower, with her eyebrows raised. "Are you auditioning?" I had no idea what she was talking about. She pointed over my shoulder after I still hadn't said a word.

My head whipped around. “Oh,” I said. Finally, everything made sense. A sign posted on the auditorium door read: FOOTLOOSE AUDITIONS, 3:00 P.M. I looked back at her. “No, I won’t be auditioning. That’s not really what I do.”

She tilted her head. “Not what you do, huh? What do you do, then?”

“I play football... I guess that’s what I do,” I said, shrugging my shoulders.

She rolled her eyes at me; my guess was she didn’t like football players. “Well, reconsider, auditioning, I mean. We could use more guys like you.”

“Guys like me?”

“Yeah,” she said. “You know, Kevin Bacon types.”

“Who’s that? Does he go to school here?”

She laughed, but I didn’t understand why. “I love all those guys in there, but none of them are really perfect for Ren.”

Everything she said sounded like a different language.

She noticed something through the auditorium window, then grabbed my hand and pulled me toward the door.

“Wait, what are you doing?”

“You’re coming to the audition,” she said without looking back at me, tugging me.

“I can’t,” I scoffed, stopping her. “I’m waiting for someone.”

She turned to look at me. “Oh, do you have a girlfriend?”

That was direct.

“No,” I said, but she quickly pulled me again before I could explain who I was waiting for.

“Good,” she said with a smile. I didn’t stop her that time. Her messy bun bounced up and down as she guided me through the auditorium doors. Steven had been there, holding it open for us. She didn’t let go of my hand until we made it to the ramp. She parked me in front of the stage. Steven trailed behind us.

“Lauren! I’m so excited!” Steven hugged the girl that forced me through the doors. She hugged him back with giggles. I looked around at the mostly empty seats. The front row housed most of the auditioners. I counted the number of girls versus guys. Only six guys and twenty girls showed up.

"What's he doing here?" Steven's high timbre interrupted my mental investigation.

"He's gonna audition," Lauren said with a beaming grin. Steven glared at me.

"Landon," Steven said with a monotone voice.

"Steven," I said, matching his tone and nodding.

Lauren fluttered to the hard plastic table against the front row of seats and dropped her stack of papers, which I then realized were scenes from a script. I stood there with my hands in my pockets while Lauren hugged everyone else in the room. I glanced toward the auditorium doors, wondering if Dan was on the other side waiting for me, and why I was still standing there.

I'm not really gonna audition.

Lauren finished her rounds and was back on me like white on rice. She sat me down in the front row and plopped in the seat to my right. Steven sat to my left. I heard coughing from behind us, and I turned to discover an older man walking toward the stage. He wore a sweater; a button-up shirt and tie peeked out of the top. A pair of khakis occupied his bottom half. His coughing continued the whole way down the ramp, covering his mouth with a handkerchief. The coughs sounded strong and phlegm-soaked. I assumed he was a chain smoker and turned forward in my seat, adjusting my posture. The cream-orange upholstered seats weren't exactly luxurious.

"Welcome, students," the old man said after his coughing subsided. "I have a list of your names here. I'll call all of you up to the stage in pairs to read the scenes. Break legs, everyone!"

I had no idea who this man was; I assumed he was the director of the school shows, but I wasn't sure if he was an actual teacher there. I also didn't understand why he told us to break our legs.

Lauren jumped from her seat, skipped to the table where the old man sat, and wrote on his paper. *Is she adding my name to the list? Locking me into this?* Yes, I could've gotten up and left, but I was too nervous about what Lauren and the drama kids would do to me.

The older man looked at me with squinted eyes. I assumed he was trying to figure out who I was and if he had seen me before. I slouched in my seat, not wanting him to see my face. "Lauren will pass out the scenes, and we'll start with a Ren and Ariel scene first," the old man said.

Lauren placed the scene down on my lap. At the top of the photocopy, someone had written FOOTLOOSE: THE MUSICAL in black Sharpie. I leaned over to Steven. Without looking at him, I whispered, "What's a Footloose?" My words caused him to stop reading and dramatically slap his lap with the papers.

He whipped his head at me and scrunched his eyebrows. "Are you serious?" I suddenly felt small. His words came at me like shards of ice.

I hesitated. "... yes." I imagined him turning into a cobra, and I was his prey. If I said one more word, he would swallow me whole.

He sighed. "Wow, okay, you really don't know." He may have noticed my face turning red, so he eased up. "It's like one of the most iconic 80's movies of all time. The soundtrack alone makes up the entire musical."

"What's a musical?"

"You're kidding..."

"Yes, that one was a joke," I said. The additional information made me even more reluctant. I'd describe my singing voice as a cat trapped in a burlap sack being set on fire. Lauren finished passing out the scenes and returned to her seat next to me. I leaned close to her, trying not to be heard by the others. "I can't sing, are they gonna make me sing?"

"No," she told me with a smile. "That part is tomorrow for the callbacks; maybe you'll make it through!" She looked at the pages and mumbled the lines to herself.

"God, I hope not," I said under my breath, leaning back into my seat. I stared at the pages in my lap, reading over the scene. Ren and Ariel were the two leads of the show. The scene in question was very flirtatious. I kept telling myself to get up and leave. I couldn't go up on stage, not in front of everyone. My leg bounced. I could feel myself shaking the entire row of seats.

I stood, but as soon as I stepped toward the aisle, the old man shouted, “Landon and Lauren, you two can go first.” I looked down at Lauren in shock. Her face beamed up at me as if she’d planned it. I looked out to the small crowd of my peers; they were all staring at me, awaiting my performance. I swear my nervous gulp echoed throughout the auditorium. Lauren was pulling me onto the stage before I could think about running out of the building.

Standing at the edge, I was taken aback by how bright and hot the lights were and immediately started sweating. My eyes shot to my feet; all I focused on was the shiny wooden floor, feeling like I could pass out at any moment.

“Psst.” Lauren caught my attention. “It’s your line first.”

“Oh,” I said, clearing my throat a dozen times. I brought the pages close to my face; my eyes struggled to focus on the words, and my mouth went dry. I took the deepest breath I could. “You are something!” I shouted at her. My body had projected the words out of me like a rocket launching into space. I looked to Lauren, who was standing about six feet from me. She didn’t let my roar affect her at all; a real professional.

“What do you mean?” Lauren asked without even looking at the paper. She already had her lines memorized. I stood there, watching her twirl her hair before realizing I had to say something. I pulled the paper close again.

“I mean, the whole p-p-package,” I stuttered, licking my lips, trying to compose myself. “Minister’s daughter, Ch-ch-chuck Cranston’s girlfriend.”

Lauren chuckled. “Guilty,” she said, throwing up her hands.

“Just a cha-cha-church goin’ gal with some b-b-badass red cowboy boots.” I couldn’t fathom what was happening. I wiped the sweat from my forehead and glanced into the audience as Lauren said her next line.

“My father hates me wearing these things.”

My quick glance at the audience became a long, hard stare. I could hardly see anyone except the old man sitting at his fold-out table. His hand rubbed his forehead; everything I was doing appalled him. I imagined huge, white, feathery wings sprouting from my shoulder blades, flying me straight through the roof of the stage. My breath sharpened, and I must have blacked out.

I remember things returning to focus because Lauren said, "Do you wanna kiss me?" I shook my head to find Lauren much closer to my face.

"Um... what?"

"That's not the line," she whispered.

"Oh... um." I pulled the paper back into my line of sight and realized I'd spaced on most of the scene but somehow made it to the end. "Someday."

"Someday?" Lauren took a step back. "What do you mean someday?"

"Ok, thank you, you two!" The old man barked at us. He had put me out of my misery, and I'd never felt more grateful. I stumbled off the stage and beelined for the doors, dropping my papers on the table as I passed. I couldn't get out of there fast enough as I pushed through the doors, vowing never to step on a stage again.

A voice called out from behind me. "You were right," Lauren had followed me into the hallway. "This really isn't your thing."

"I told you," I said, wiping the last beads of sweat from my face. She just smiled and stared at me. I grinned back. "What?"

"You go do your thing. I'll do mine," she said, pointing a thumb behind her at the auditorium. "But, think we can do something together sometime?"

"Oh." I was a little shocked; she put me through the wringer because she was flirting with me? "Uh, yeah, sure, that'd be cool."

"Great, give me your phone," she said, holding out her hand. I gave in to her request, and she typed in her number. "Text me?"

"Yeah," I said, still feeling jarred by my debut stage appearance. Lauren smiled at me, turned around, and disappeared into the auditorium. Just as fast as Lauren vanished, Dan appeared behind me, shoving me down the hall.

"Dude! We have to get to practice; we're late!"

I shoved him. "Where have you been? I've been waiting for you." I chose to leave out the last twenty minutes of my stage adventures.

"I had shit to do. Don't worry about it, fireball."

It seemed a little odd, the way Dan had shrugged off my question, but at the time, I let it slide.

A week later, Lauren and I hung out, walked around the mall, and went to the movies. Everything seemed to happen so fast. Before I knew it, we were official. Lauren had become my very first girlfriend. I never would've thought to ask her out. She was the one to ask me. At the time, I wasn't sure I should say yes because I didn't know if I liked her as much as she liked me. But I felt the pressure. Saying yes felt like something I *had* to do rather than *wanted* to do. Over time, we got closer, and I started to enjoy her company more. She became a person I liked being around, and I loved her for that. But I never felt the way I was supposed to feel toward her or how I thought people would assume I should feel toward her. The first time we kissed was so awkward and sloppy that she stopped me and had to teach me how to do it well. Lauren was always the one to initiate a kiss.

———

SIX

"Goddammit," I whispered to myself. All I could feel was frustration. I'd been obsessing over Mystery Boy for days, and yet I had no details about who he was. I was so close to seeing him; my hopes were high but instantly smashed. I thought maybe it was all a dream.

How could I go days without seeing this guy's face?

I ran my fingers through my hair, wondering what to do next. Standing in the courtyard, in the center of a human tornado, I watched my peers swerve around me. I didn't care that the sun was baking me.

"Landon..." Dan tried to grab my attention, but I walked away. Not wanting to lie about how I felt, so I started moving. I wanted to find him. I wanted to see him. He couldn't have gone that far; he had to be around somewhere. Dan and Chris didn't follow me. They just let me wander.

My eyes scanned every person who walked by. The sun caused me to squint and move my face away from the shining beams. I was afraid I'd miss a glimpse of him. I could already feel my skin burning, and I'd only been outside for fewer than five minutes. I hadn't applied sunblock that day. I could picture the tube sitting in my backpack that had fallen off my shoulder when I crashed to the ground and left it there in hopes of seeing Mystery Boy's face.

I pressed my hand to my forehead, creating a visor-like shape to shield the sun so I could look around without squinting. Taking giant steps, I walked to the front corner of the school. I was almost to the end of the street where an intersection started, about half a football field away from my house. Being that far from the school's entrance, kids still flooded the space. They moved like schools of fish. I heard bits and pieces of conversations as I passed by each mob. Discussions of homework, TV shows, who was having sex with whom, who broke up, and who got back together. Even conversations of hatred for a certain teacher. Some walked by me talking about volleyball, then another about tennis. The conversations would go in one ear and out the other. I was determined to hunt Mystery Boy down.

Face after face, I searched and scanned until I spotted a pair of tank-topped shoulders. He stood out like a great white shark in a sea of backpacks. For a moment, I thought it was a mirage the sun made me see. But I had memorized the back of his body since the first time I saw it. I studied it in my mind every night before I fell asleep. I daydreamed about it in class, so I knew for sure it was him.

I stood there for a bit, waiting to see which way Mystery Boy would go. He was about to step onto the crosswalk through the intersection. I thought of crossing to the other side of the street and following him. There was no doubt in my mind that I wouldn't be able to see his face. My heart pounded again; it was finally going to happen.

I dodged a few goth kids, about to walk onto the crosswalk, until Lauren appeared, stepping in front of me. "Landon," she said. "Where are you going? People were saying, you, like, freaked out in the hall."

I couldn't believe I'd failed again. My frustration grew to sudden anger; if life were a cartoon, my ears would've shot steam, my face would've turned bright red, and my head would've skyrocketed off my body.

"Is this a dream?" My eyes widened. Steven stood with her,

looking as perplexed as Lauren. My eyes shot to my left, trying to see if Mystery Boy had already crossed the street. Once again, he disappeared. It was as if he had the power to evaporate into thin air. "This has to be a fucking dream, right?"

Lauren crossed her arms. "Landon, what are you talking about?"

Steven stepped toward me. "Are you all right?"

I couldn't answer their questions. I felt like the world was coming down on my head, and I couldn't take it anymore. "I gotta go," I said as I pushed between them, crossing the street. I hadn't noticed the traffic moving as a car came to a screeching halt before almost taking me out. My heart jumped into my throat as the person behind the wheel blasted the car's horn. I flipped them the middle finger and picked up my pace.

I reached the front door of my house and pushed through, hoping no one had followed. The cold air of the AC impaled me. It felt so refreshing. My temper cooled. My movements slowed as I ascended the stairs.

People were talking, Lauren said it herself. I needed to come up with an excuse in case anyone asked me about my freak-out the next day at school. Maybe I could play it off as trying to catch my lab partner for a science project who'd been ignoring my texts. I could only imagine what people might've been thinking or saying.

The rollercoaster ride was over, and my body was drained. Once in my room, I removed the shirt I'd sweat through. Dad knocked on my door frame as I opened a drawer for a fresh one.

"You didn't say hello when you walked in," Dad said.

"Sorry, I didn't know you were home." I hadn't noticed his car in the driveway. I grabbed a plain black shirt and slipped it over my head. The static sent a weird sensation through my hair.

Dad was holding my backpack. "Lauren just dropped this off," he said.

I shuffled over and took it off his hands, wondering if Lauren had spilled the beans about my mini-meltdown. "Did she say anything?"

"No, but she seemed a little off. Are you two okay?"

"Yeah, Dad, we're okay." I sat on my bed, letting the backpack fall to my feet. Dad tilted his head as if to say he didn't believe me. The body language was there, but the words never came out of his mouth.

"Well," he said. "My campaign manager got sick, so they postponed our meeting. I figured I'd try cooking something tonight. Want to come to the store with me?"

"Yes!" I said as I shot to my feet. I don't think he expected that sort of reaction. I needed to do something that wasn't sulking in my room, obsessing over Mystery Boy.

As we pulled out of the driveway, a song by The Chicks came on the radio and it reminded me how much I used to enjoy car rides with my mom. When I was little, I would always sing in the backseat. As soon as we would get in the car, I'd beg her to play whatever song I was obsessed with. Sometimes, it was The Lion King soundtrack; other times, it would be *Alvin and the Chipmunks*. I was even partial to "Achy Breaky Heart" by Billy Ray Cyrus.

My mom enjoyed her country music. The Chicks were one of her favorite bands. She and I would sing their songs at the top of our lungs; even if we didn't sound the best, we didn't care. A special bond develops between a mother and her only son; that's the only word I can fathom to describe it, special.

Dad pulled into the parking lot of our local grocery store, Shop 'n' Go. Parking as close as he could to the entrance.

"I was thinking pork chops," Dad said as he grabbed a basket before entering the automatic doors.

I smiled. "Whoa, that sounds risky. Think you can handle it?"

Dad chuckled. "I used to be a grill master back in my day."

"Oh yeah, sure."

The AC washed over us in a wave. I wondered what it would be like to live somewhere with different seasons, where it got cold. Maybe New York, like Tasha mentioned. I daydreamed about what throwing a snowball or making a snow angel would feel like.

I followed Dad, waiting for him to hand me the basket when he got tired of holding it. He started bopping along to the song playing over the loudspeakers. I grinned, watching him pick through heads of broccoli; It was exactly what I needed to mellow out.

"Hey," Dad said, handing me the basket. "Is that Steven Mori?" I took a glance behind me. It was Steven; he was shopping with his mom. His pink hair caused him to stick out from the cardboard cutouts of Shop 'n' Go customers.

"Yeah, that's him," I said, returning to the produce, grabbing a handful of green beans to shove into a plastic bag. I think Dad sensed my discomfort.

"I haven't seen him much outside the school. Do you two still talk?"

"No," I said. "Not really." I tried to keep my back to Steven so he wouldn't see me.

"That's a shame." He looked over at me as I rearranged the green peppers. "You guys used to be so close."

"Well, people change," I said, staring down at the sea of veggies. "They grow apart."

FIVE YEARS AGO

Steven had come into our school district at the beginning of our eighth-grade year. He had lived a few towns over, but his dad got a new job that forced them to move. I immediately noticed him on the first day of school because he walked differently than the other boys. He wasn't obnoxious like Dan and the rest of our friends; he didn't seem confident in his shoes. He kept to himself the first few weeks, not saying much to anyone. But I kept my eye on him.

The first time we spoke was in gym class, about a month into the school year. I was in the locker room changing into my gym clothes. I'd gotten there a little early because I'd been to the nurse with a headache. She gave me some Tylenol and sent me on my way. I headed to the locker room instead of going back to class, knowing I had gym next. To my surprise, Steven walked in while I was changing.

"You're here early," I said to him, pulling on my shorts. He didn't make eye contact with me. I just watched him sway to his locker.

"My teacher lets me leave class if we aren't doing anything important," Steven said, looking in every direction but mine.

"Why?" I pulled off my shirt and caught him glancing at me out of the corner of his eye.

Steven hesitated. "I, um, I don't really like changing in front of people."

"Oh, okay," I said with a shrug, sensing he was uncomfortable with me there. I assumed he was just as surprised to see me as I was to see him. As someone involved in sports for most of my life, I was used to changing in front of other boys.

I picked up my day clothes and shoved them into my locker, closed it, and spun the number dial. When I looked at Steven, he was already in a different outfit. He'd changed so quickly. I sat on the bench in the middle of the aisle, surveying his choice of clothes. He wore black sweatpants and a long-sleeved shirt.

"You're gonna die outside wearing that," I said, grinning in his direction. I thought his outfit choice was a joke. "You should wear shorts; you're gonna sweat big time."

"I can't," Steven said, looking down at the floor.

"You can't sweat?"

"No," he said, rolling his eyes. "I can't wear shorts."

I tilted my head like a confused dog. "Why?" Steven shrugged and sat on the wooden bench five feet from me. "Dude, you can tell me, no one's around," I said, holding out my arms. A moment passed in silence. I stared at Steven, trying to penetrate his mind to see what he held back. He sighed and lifted his pant leg. My eyes dropped, discovering what he had been keeping a secret. His leg was hairy.

"My dad says I'm an early bloomer," he admitted, letting his pant leg fall. "I'm like the sasquatch of the locker room. That's why I wear sweatpants because I don't want any of the other guys seeing my hairy legs and making fun of me."

I looked down at my legs; they were bare and pale, with a few hairs here and there. Steven's dad was right; he was an early bloomer. He would've won if there were a contest for the hairiest eighth grader. Puberty had hit him like a brick wall. Meanwhile, puberty had hit me like a soft feather to the cheek. I had two little hairs growing in my armpits.

"Hey, it's gonna happen to all of us," I whispered, trying to ease his embarrassment.

Steven pressed the toe of his shoe into the Linoleum floor. "I know, but why did it happen to me first?"

"Hey," I said. "How do you think I feel? All my hair is gonna be orange!" Steven busted into a giant, squeaky laugh; it was the first time I'd seen him smile. His laugh was contagious as I followed suit.

"Yeah, you're right," Steven said through his smile. "That is pretty bad." The bell rang and caught us both off guard; we jumped at the sound of it and started laughing again.

I slid down the bench closer to him and nudged him with my elbow. "Your secret's safe with me," I whispered. He smiled at me again. I could tell he was about to thank me when loud boys clamored into the locker room. They surrounded me; Dan was among them. Steven stood and walked away. The guys had scared him off like a timid baby deer.

The next week I spotted Steven sitting alone at lunch. Dan and I were walking to our usual table when I stopped him. "We should sit with him," I said to Dan.

My best friend looked at me as if I had two heads. "What? No, he's weird."

"He isn't that weird," I said, slapping Dan's arm. "I talked to him last week in gym class; he's pretty cool." Dan wasn't convinced, so I looked him in the eyes. "I think I recall you sitting alone at lunch when you were the new kid. Who knows where you'd be now if I hadn't sat with you?" I winked at him. Dan took a breath and weighed his options. He looked at our usual table with our usual friends, then back at Steven, then back at our table, then back at me.

"Fine," Dan said with a huff. I took the lead, setting my tray down.

"Hey man," I said. "This is Dan. Dan, this is..." My voice trailed off, and my smile faded. I didn't know the new kid's name yet.

"Steven, my name's Steven."

I swung my legs under the table, sitting across from Steven. "I'm

Landon," I said with a smile. Dan looked at me. I could feel his eyes digging into the side of my face. That first lunch was sort of awkward, but as time went on, it got easier. I had to convince Dan to sit with Steven a couple more times before he enjoyed it. The three of us got along well. Our duo that Dan and I had established was opening up to a trio.

Dan and I decided to let him into our bubble when we invited Steven to hang out with us on the weekends. We spent most of our time at my house. Being an only child, my house didn't have the burden of younger siblings. I also had violent video games that Steven and Dan weren't allowed to have. Over time, I noticed Steven liked our indoor activities more than outdoor ones. Anytime Dan and I wanted to throw a football around, Steven would either sit on the sidelines and watch or exclude himself altogether.

We spent almost every weekend together for the entire school year. It was getting close to summer, and we were camping out in my basement. Each of us had a sleeping bag set up parallel to one another. I was in the middle, with Dan on my right and Steven on my left. We stayed up into the early morning talking about what we would do over the break, like ride our bikes through the trails at Howard Hill. Or go to a trampoline park that just opened. Play basketball at Dan's house, or have as many *Mortal Kombat* tournaments as possible.

Things simmered down, but Steven had one last thing on his mind. "Guys, I have to tell you something," Steven said, breaking the room's silence. The three of us were in our sleeping bags, staring into the darkness.

"Okay," I said with a chuckle, not knowing where the conversation would go.

"I think," Steven started, chewing on those words momentarily. "I think I might be gay."

He'd sucked the air out of the room. It was silent, as if we were floating in space with no tether holding us to our ship. My young brain had no idea how to respond. Dan and I didn't speak, and Steven didn't say another word either. I could hear his breathing getting heavier. I expected him to laugh, admitting it was just a joke, but he stayed silent. None of us knew how to react. Until that point, we had never heard the word gay used seriously. We always used it as an insult to our friends as a joke. Dan and I both knew what it actually meant.

The only real experience I'd had at that point with anything gay-related was watching reruns of *Will & Grace* with my mom. Dad had a fit when he came home to us watching it. 'Landon shouldn't be watching this', he said. 'He's too young, I won't allow it. He doesn't need to be seeing that shit.' We never watched it after that. Whenever I came across an episode being played on TV, I'd hurry to change the channel as if I'd committed a crime for even seeing a glimpse of it.

Dan finally broke the quiet. "I need to sleep, guys."

The sleeping bag made swishing noises, and he turned to his side, facing away from us. Then Steven's sleeping bag made the same noise as he also turned away from me. I held my position, staring up at the ceiling until my eyelids got heavy enough to take me into a deep slumber.

The next morning I woke to a beam of light shining through the basement window. I propped myself up on my elbows and looked around. Both Dan and Steven were gone, their sleeping bags all askew. I walked upstairs, expecting them to be at the kitchen counter as my mom served them breakfast, but the table was empty. I checked my room, but no luck.

I called Dan's house to clear up the confusion.

Dan's mom answered the phone. "Hello?"

"Hi, is Dan there?"

"Oh, hi, Landon. He just walked in. Let me get him." I heard a clunk as she put the phone down, then some mumbles before Dan spoke. "Hello?"

"Dan? Where'd you go? I woke up, and you and Steven were gone. I thought we were gonna play Call of Duty all day."

"Sorry," Dan said. "I just felt weird."

"What are you talking about?"

"What Steven said."

I had honestly forgotten the conversation.

"Steven told us he was gay last night," Dan whispered into the receiver.

I let out a nervous laugh. "I'm sure he was joking. He always jokes."

"I don't want to hang out with him anymore."

"Seriously?"

"Yeah. I don't think we should, and if you're really my friend, you won't hang out with him either."

I tried to protest, but Dan had already decided. He gave me an ultimatum: Steven or him. He made me choose, and of course, I picked Dan. I had no other choice; we'd been friends for much longer.

That Monday at school, Dan and I got off the bus together. Steven was waiting for us by the entrance like he usually did. Dan leaned and reminded me not to acknowledge him.

"Hey, guys!" Steven said, waving at us. Dan never looked in his direction; he just kept walking. I wanted to stop, but I was too afraid of what Dan would do. I glanced at Steven; then my eyes shot to the ground. I walked past him without saying a word. Steven didn't follow us. He just let us go; I think he knew something in the air was different. I looked back at him and saw his face turn upside down. My heart dropped into my stomach; I felt so guilty.

Steven tried to sit with Dan and me at lunch the next day. Dan got up and walked away without a word. Steven sat across from me, his eyebrows furrowed, and he shook his head, not understanding what was happening. "I'm sorry," I whispered before standing and following Dan to another table. I left Steven sitting alone like we had found him earlier that school year.

The summer came and went. Both Dan and I didn't speak to Steven at all. We didn't even see him around the neighborhood. We continued doing our own thing, and Steven became a distant memory. Three months of summer vacation could make a kid forget about anything.

That fall, we entered high school. It was great not having to take the bus. Now, all I had to do was cross the street. Strolling down the halls, everyone, including Dan and me, had changed a little. We were a little taller and had a bit more fuzz on our upper lip. Dan greeted me with a fist bump as we gathered around some lockers with our other friends, updating each other on our lives.

"No fucking way," Dan said. His jaw went loose, and his eyes were laser-focused on something behind me. I turned around, curious about his reaction. That's when I saw Steven walking toward us down the hall; he'd changed more than anyone. He'd grown out his hair and dyed it yellow, and wore very tight jeans and black combat boots with rainbow laces keeping them in place. His bellowing T-shirt had the words 'Kiss Me' printed in a sparkly font. The guys in my cluster, including Dan, watched as Steven strode by us and greeted a group of girls near a water fountain. "Look at this fucking queer," Dan said. This was the first time he'd said anything about Steven in months. "Guys, let's go fuck with him."

I rolled my eyes. "Why?"

Dan ignored me, walking toward Steven and motioning for the other guys to follow. I trailed behind the horde, watching. Dan was on Steven without warning and grabbed him by the neck of his shirt, slamming him against the wall. I heard the smack of Steven's head against the brick. I had never seen Dan that aggressive off the football field. The simple sight of Steven set something off in him.

"It's been a while, faggot," Dan sneered in Steven's face. I could see the spit from the F syllable fly onto Steven's shirt. "Do you realize where you are, fairy boy? What's gotten into you? Suddenly, you decide to wear your mom's clothes to school?"

"You honestly pushed me to have more confidence in myself, Dan," Steven said with a devilish smile. "You should be proud." He winked, setting Dan off even more. I remember thinking Steven's words sounded deliberate. Dan threw Steven to the ground and kicked him hard in the stomach as if kicking a football to a goal. I'll never forget the sound of air escaping Steven's body. He clenched his torso, gasping for breath. Dan's aggression sent the surrounding girls screaming as they ran away.

The rest of the guys started in on Steven; like a pack of hungry wolves, they followed Dan's lead. The kicking was relentless. Stephen was crying out for help as I stood there stuck. My eyes locked with Steven's. The desperation in his face crippled me. With just one look, he begged me to make it stop, but I couldn't. I was a coward, frozen in fear, too scared to face repercussions from the alpha and his pack.

One of Dan's kicks met Steven's face, knocking him out cold. A teacher then rushed to Steven's aid, breaking up the pack. I looked down at Steven's helpless, skinny body, holding back my tears. Blood trickled off his face and onto the floor. That was the first time I'd experienced actual violence, and I felt so powerless.

Dan was suspended for the first week of school, while Steven spent time in the hospital. Steven's parents fought to have Dan expelled, but the principal wasn't convinced that the sole purpose of Dan's attack was because Steven was gay. When Steven eventually returned, I continued to ignore him, like nothing happened. I wouldn't have known what to say if he approached me.

"Mom used to do applesauce with her chops. Remember that? Can you go grab some?"

"Sure," I said. I crossed the store, glancing at each sign as I passed an aisle, looking for the canned fruit section. I took a hard left down aisle six and reached the abundance of applesauce selection. I grabbed the cheapest jar and turned back the way I came, just to bump into a tuft of pink hair. "Shit, sorry," I said, composing myself.

Steven chuckled. "It's okay." He realized it was me and huffed. I walked away, but he stopped me, asking, "Why?"

I turned to him. "What?"

"Why did you talk to me the other day in the bathroom? You haven't really said a word to me in almost four years." Steven crossed his arms. "So why now?"

I stared at him, unsure of what to say. It took a moment for the words to form in my mind. "Like I said, research."

Steven scoffed, grabbing a can of mixed fruit off the shelf. "Research, right. And what about your scene at school today? What was that about?"

I scratched my head and straightened my shirt a little, nervous by his questioning. He was referencing my chase of Mystery Boy earlier that day. I must've looked like a freak. "I'm just kind of going through some stuff right now."

"Anything I can help with?" He was being uncharacteristically genuine for the sarcastic high school version of Steven I'd seen develop over the years.

"No, no..." My words trailed off in an awkward chuckle. Then, a light bulb popped on in my brain. "Well, maybe?" I took a deep breath. "If you wanted to find someone to like, find out what they looked like, how would you do it?"

"Easy," Steven said with a hand flick. "Do you know their name?"

"Um," I said. Why the hell hadn't I thought of that already? Finding out someone's name was the simplest thing in the world, I could've asked my dad for it. "No."

"Well, it would be easy to look them up on Facebook if you knew their name. If that doesn't work, I usually use Grindr."

"What's Grindr?"

"Oh," Steven laughed. "Obviously you've never heard of it. It's like this hookup app for gay guys."

"Gotcha," I said. The thought of Steven hooking up with someone was weird. "Well, thanks, man. I appreciate it."

"No problem!" Steven said with a curtsy before walking away.

"Steven," I called out.

He stopped and turned to me with an eyebrow raised.

"I'm sorry... " I said, swallowing the lump in my throat. "...for not stopping Dan when I could have. I'm... I'm just really sorry."

Steven tilted his head, giving me a half-smile. "Wow. You know, never in a million years did I think those words would come out of your mouth after everything. I've had a long time to think about if I could ever forgive you, and I just might be able to, but I'll never forget." he said.

"Right," I said with a nod. Steven had every right not to forgive me. What happened to him was fucked up, and I had a part in it. I turned to walk away but his words caught me.

"I never had the chance to say anything, but I was sorry to hear about... ya know..." Steven's voice softened as he fiddled with the can of fruit in his hands. I knew what he was trying to say. "She was always nice to me. I never felt judgment from her."

My jaw clenched. It sent a chill through my body. "She was never the type," I said. He smiled before walking off. My shoulders relaxed around Steven for the first time in years. Anytime I'd been around him before that, I replayed the violent event in my head, causing me to keep my distance.

At that moment, I broke off from the pack to become an alpha of my own. My first order of business was to rush back to my dad and ask for Mystery Boy's name.

SEVEN

My eyes popped open, then clenched from the painful, bright fluorescent light in the ceiling. I rubbed my eyes, blinking away the fog.

What the hell?

I was in a hospital room, lying on a gurney, wearing a thin, white gown with nothing underneath. I propped myself up, but a sting from my left arm stopped me. An I.V. attached to the bend in my elbow. I ripped off the clear tape, pinched the needle, and held my breath as I dragged it from my skin. It felt like pulling out a shard of glass. I threw the needle to the ground and heard it clink against the floor. I swung my legs off the bed and connected my bare feet to the cold tile. A breeze up my backside told me my hospital gown was open, so I pulled at the strings and tied them while I looked for my clothes.

The room was bare, except for the bed and a single green cushioned chair; it stood out like a sore thumb against the stark whiteness of the area. I crossed to the window and drew the curtains. It was dark outside and foggy. I couldn't see the ground; only gray mist. I turned to study the space again. My body felt so cold.

Why am I here?

I looked at a beige door, and I scrambled to it, turning the handle.

It was the bathroom, just as barren. I glimpsed myself in the mirror. My breath heavied. I trudged closer, admiring my face, and touched my nose. It was bandaged and bloody. Both eyes were shades of black and blue. I had no memory of how I got there or what caused my wounds.

A sound came from behind me. I twirled around with force, having to catch myself on the sink. "Hello?" I called out, but no one answered. I crept back into the room, walking on my tiptoes to the only other door. I slowly opened it, peeking my head out first. The corridor of the hospital was empty and dead silent. I looked right and left, but not a soul lingered, just emptiness. I stepped into the hallway. "Hello?" I said again, hearing my voice echo. I sauntered down the linoleum path, feeling my left arm, discovering a skinny trail of blood moving down my skin from where I'd pulled the needle. Then I heard something in the distance. It was faint, but I could hear it. I moved toward the small noise, turning a corner before the sound became clear; it was a dial tone.

The lights flickered from above, which startled me to a stop. My heart raced. I followed the sound; it was getting louder. A nurse station sat at the end of the hallway. I picked up my pace, and the dial tone got louder and louder as I approached. The dial tone became ear-piercingly loud when I reached the nurse's counter. Then I heard a splat, and a small splash hit my leg. I was standing in a pool of dark red blood. I screamed, stepping away, slipping on its slick layer, and falling against the wall. That's when I saw the body.

A hand covered my mouth; I couldn't believe what I saw. The blood was coming from a woman wearing white scrubs. She was face down in her own mess. Someone had stabbed her torso multiple times. I then realized the dial tone had stopped, and everything went silent again. That's when I heard the footsteps.

They were heavy; the person was wearing boots. The lights went out before I looked in the sound's direction, but I still heard the footsteps. They weren't fast, but at a steady pace. I could tell they were getting closer. I pushed myself to my feet again, but my fear cemented me in my place. The lights flashed again, and I saw a dark, shadowed man walking toward me at the same pace as the footsteps I'd heard. The light reflected off the long hunter's knife in his right hand; the blade stained red. My eyes widened, and my heart dropped into my stomach. I tried to run but slipped and fell to the ground as my feet were still slick from the blood.

A firm hand latched onto my ankle. I screamed and clawed at the floor, trying to get any sort of traction. My heart thudded in my chest, too terrified to look back at the person controlling my fate.

"Landon..." I heard a voice say, then again a little louder.

I jumped awake, struggling to catch my breath. I was in Dad's car. I'd fallen asleep on the ride home from the grocery store. Dad had given me a good shake to wake me. I panted, rubbed my face, and tried to calm my breathing.

"Didn't mean to scare you," Dad said.

I glanced at him still sitting in the driver's seat. "It's okay. Just a weird dream."

I stood from the car in a daze, still shaken from my nightmare, as I sauntered to the trunk to help with the groceries. I was used to having strange, vivid dreams, but never that dark. I knew my mind had been in a weird place, but something mysterious was stalking me.

As I stepped through the side door, I remembered I wanted to talk to Dad about Mystery Boy. After my chat with Steven in the canned fruit aisle, Dad was already paying for the groceries, so I decided to wait until we got home to ask my questions. I placed the grocery bags on the kitchen counter and emptied them. Dad sat at the kitchen island and started a video on his phone. I stepped behind him, curious about what was keeping his attention. He was playing clips of football games from another high school team.

"Look at this," he said. "This team is slaughtering North Valley High."

I watched the screen, but I didn't respond to his comment. Whatever team this was, they were throwing some impressive plays on the field, but I couldn't care less about football at that moment.

"Dad," I said but paused. I wasn't sure how to segue into my question. There was no perfect strategy, and I didn't have time to work it out like the perfect plays on the phone screen. I just had to come out with it. "That guy working at the school, what's his name?" The words sounded glued together.

Dad didn't take his eyes off his phone. "What guy? There are a lot of guys working at the school."

I moved from behind his chair and sat to his left. "The guy doing community service or whatever."

Dad paused the video to look at me. "Why do you care?"

"I don't," I lied. "I just heard some people at school talking about him, and I was wondering what his name was."

So I can look him up on Facebook.

"Oh, I don't know," he huffed, looking back at his screen.

"Come on, Dad."

"He doesn't report to me," he said.

I slumped in my chair. "You've gotta know something."

Dad stared at me with curious eyes, and his mustache moved. "It's something with a C, I think." He looked around the room, searching his brain for a name. "Charlie, maybe? No, Cole?" I perked up from my slouch, itching for any information about Mystery Boy. Dad continued. "It wasn't Chase, was it? Ah, I don't remember Landon; I'm sorry." Breath escaped my lungs like someone had let go of a full balloon. I was instantly deflated; he'd killed my high.

"All right," I said, standing from the stool. "Thanks, I guess."

He played the video, and the smacking football helmets started up again from behind me as I ascended the stairs. I tried to look at the positives. If Dad's information was correct, I at least knew the first letter of Mystery Boy's name was C.

I closed my bedroom door and found my phone on my bed. I had hoped to be scouring Facebook for Mystery Boy, but I wasn't so lucky. I looked at my screen, noticing the missed call from Lauren and three unread texts.

LAUREN

What happened today, are you okay?

You sort of snapped at me, so I'm kinda confused.

You're freaking me out.

She must've sent the texts as I left for the grocery store.

ME

Hey, sorry I didn't respond, I fell asleep after school. Thanks for dropping off my bag.

She was already typing back.

LAUREN

You've been acting so weird this week, what's been going on?

ME

I just have a lot on my mind, it's senior year, things are crazy right now.

LAUREN

I understand that, but you've just seemed a little distant, I don't know. I feel like I've barely talked to you this week.

My fingers didn't move; I stared at the screen, searching for the right words. I didn't want to lie, but I had no other choice.

ME

I'm sorry, but really I'm okay.

LAUREN

All right :/

Are we still on for Saturday?

ME

Yeah :)

I flung myself onto the bed and perched my pillow against the headboard for support and leaned back on it. I thought about what Steven said at the grocery store—that if he couldn't find someone on Facebook, he used...

What was the name of that app?

I felt like my dad. I replayed our conversation like a video in my mind, rewinding and fast-forwarding, scanning the way Steven's mouth formed his words, trying to figure out the answer.

Then it popped into my head.

Grindr!

My thumb moved around the screen of my phone. I searched the app store and found it within seconds. I hovered over the download button for a bit, fearing the unknown. I had no clue what type of door I was about to open. I wasn't sure how it worked or what my chances were of finding Mystery Boy. I didn't even know if he liked guys.

If someone sees this on my phone, I'm screwed. If Dad knew about this app, he'd disown me. I'll delete it when I'm done; it'll be quick.

I pushed the thoughts aside and clicked download. I was in, but I needed to create a username first. It obviously couldn't be my actual name. I pondered for a sec, then typed 'SportyGuy' and clicked next, but the app informed me the name had already been taken. So I added my jersey number to the end, letting me continue.

Next, I had to fill in my stats, age, height, weight, and tribe.

Tribe? What the hell is a tribe?

I clicked the drop-down menu to survey my options. There were about ten different tribes, which included bear, twink, fem, sub, dom, jock, etc.

Overwhelmed and also not understanding what any of it meant, I clicked jock and moved on. Next, I had to add a picture. That part stressed me out; I knew I couldn't use my face. I thought about adding a picture of a celebrity, but that would make it seem like I was trolling people. I went with a picture of a Dallas Cowboys jersey. I skipped the part where I had to fill in my bio because, at that point, I just wanted to search.

The app's main dashboard was just a bunch of square pictures. I had to click on one square to talk to the person and read their stats. I quickly realized I wouldn't have any luck with Grindr either because I had no idea what Mystery Boy's face looked like. If a picture of his face *was* on the app, I'd scroll right by it, not knowing it was him. I hoped I'd see a picture of a guy's back and recognize it as Mystery Boy. Then my phone vibrated, and I had a message. I clicked to a thread with a little blue text bubble on a gray background.

GUYLOOKING, 45

Hey handsome ;)

I had no idea how to respond. It surprised me; I wasn't expecting anyone to message me. And how did he know if I was handsome?

GUYLOOKING, 45

I'm looking to meet up with someone tonight to fool around.

"Wow," I said to myself, staring at my screen. "That was forward." It was making me nervous.

SPORTYGUY83, 18

No.

GUYLOOKING, 45

:(

GuyLooking sent a picture of his face. He had salt-and-pepper hair and serious uncle vibes. It made me feel weird. I clicked out of the chat and continued my search for Mystery Boy on the main dashboard. Scrolling through, I imagined Mystery Boy to have dark eyes to match his brown hair. I imagined him to have a dimpled chin with a little patch of hair growing under it.

Most of the pictures were bare chests, underwear shots, or guys who looked like professional models. I suppose one guy could be him, but I'd never know. My phone vibrated again, and I clicked over to the messages. HornyDaddy, 38, had sent me a photo. I held my breath and clicked the message to open it.

My eyes met a picture of HornyDaddy's erection.

"Jesus Christ!"

"What happened?" Dad yelled from downstairs. "Are you all right?"

I clutched the phone to my chest, acting as if he were standing behind me trying to peek at what I'd seen.

"Yes!" I called back. "Nothing happened. I'm fine!"

I looked at the phone again. My jaw popped open. I didn't think anyone's dick could get that big. I was suddenly feeling very inadequate. I clicked away from the message and doubted what I felt for Mystery Boy because, looking through all the faces on Grindr, I wasn't attracted to any of them.

Another vibration.

. . .

THEATRENERD245, 18

Hey there, I don't think I've seen you on here before.

Finally, a normal thing to say to someone.

SPORTYGUY83, 18

Yeah, I'm kind of new.

THEATRENERD245, 18

That's cool, welcome! :) What're you looking for?

SPORTYGUY83, 18

Not really sure. Just looking around, I guess.

THEATRENERD245, 18

Cool. Wanna trade pics?

SPORTYGUY83, 18

What kind of pics?

I started to sweat a little.

THEATRENERD245, 18

Just face pics, for now.

Another vibration, GuyLooking was back.

. . .

GUYLOOKING, 45

Maybe you can send some nudes then?

SPORTYGUY83, 18

No thanks.

GUYLOOKING, 45

:(

THEATRENERD245, 18

I can send one first.

SPORTYGUY83, 18

Okay, sure.

HORNYDADDY, 38

You like my cook?

Cock*

GUYLOOKING, 45

Am I not hot enough for you?

HORNYDADDY, 38

Are you a top or a bottom?

GUYLOOKING, 45

You're probably some stuck up twink.

You don't deserve me, asshole!

HORNYDADDY, 38

I want to fuck you so badly.

Message after message kept coming, even though I wasn't responding to any of them. The app was scaring me; I didn't blame guys for being so confident and forward behind a screen, but did those messages ever really work for them? Another vibration, Theatrenerd245 had sent a photo. I opened it with caution and choked on my spit. Theatrenerd245 was Steven, in all his pink-haired glory, posing for a selfie in his room! I quickly closed the app and threw my phone face down on my bed as if Steven could see me through my front-facing camera. I ran my fingers through my hair, wiping the sweat from my head. I wasn't going to find Mystery Boy on Grindr; that much was clear.

EIGHT

The next morning I walked into school to find the *Monthly* had been printed and people were already reading it. My mind still raced from the night before, horrified over my first Grindr experience. My eyes flickered from face to face as I shuffled through the mass of bodies, hoping I wouldn't see Steven. It was an irrational thought, but as soon as he sent me his picture, I assumed he knew Sportyguy83 was me. There was no way he knew that. But it's something I felt in my stomach.

"It's a hit so far!" Tasha said, popping up in front of me, taking me by surprise. "I'm so glad I added you to the team. Besides Corey's comic strip, your stories are always the part people like the most." Tasha smiled at me but noticed my face was stuck in a distant gaze. "Are you okay? You've been acting strange all week."

"I keep hearing that from people."

Tasha shrugged. "Well, a lot of people saw your little freak-out yesterday. So I want to make sure you're okay."

"Yes, I'm fine," I said, dodging eye contact. "And it wasn't a freak-out. I'm just tired of people saying I'm acting weird."

"Well," Tasha's expression warmed as she touched my arm. "If you need to talk about anything, don't hesitate. We can do coffee or whatever."

"Thanks, Tasha," I said, grinning and shrugging her off. My mind wasn't in the most conscious state. I headed toward the cafeteria; my stomach growled during my brief conversation with Tasha. I tried to look into each classroom as I passed by, hoping to notice Mystery Boy mopping the floor or removing pieces of gum from desks, but I didn't see him. I wondered if he came in every day, every other day, or once a week. That was a question I should've asked my dad; he might've at least known Mystery Boy's schedule.

Lauren flagged me down from a table ten feet away when I entered the cafeteria. Again, my eyes darted from table to table as I walked to Lauren's spot, searching for a pink-headed mop of hair.

"Are you feeling any better today?" Lauren asked as I slipped into the bench seat across from her. She touched my hand. My eyes locked onto her for the first real-time in days..

"Yeah. I think so." I lied. I was on edge; I was already so anxious to glimpse Mystery Boy, and worried Steven knew my secret.

"Ok, good," she said. She may have been unconvinced. "So, what did you mean yesterday when you asked me if this was a dream?"

I'd forgotten I blurted that out in frustration.

I've been dying to see this guy's face, but every time I get close, something gets in the way. Yesterday, that thing was you.

That would've been too rude and more honest than I was ready to be. That was the first time Lauren had seen me truly frustrated.

"I said that?" I was playing dumb.

"Yeah," Lauren said. "You seemed pretty annoyed."

"The sun, I was out in the sun too long." I lied again. It wouldn't be the last time I lied to her face. "You know it fries my brain sometimes." I gave a weak smile. "I have this group project due in chemistry, and I was trying to find my partner, but he ran out before I could talk to him, so I was pretty annoyed. I'm sorry I took it out on you." I wondered how far I could go with the lie before it wore me down. I squeezed her hand a little, hoping she believed my fairytale.

"Okay," Lauren said with a genuine smile that told me she wasn't holding any grudges. "Oh! I made this new playlist last night! Can I download it to your phone?"

"Yeah, sure," I said without thinking. In one swift motion, I pulled my phone from my pocket and placed it on the table before her.

"I need to grab something to eat," I said, glancing at the long line at the food bar. I wasn't sure I had the patience, so I stayed put.

"It's sort of this blend of 90s R&B and early 2000s pop," Lauren said, flicking through my phone. "Um," suddenly, her face turned upside down. "Why do you have Grindr on your phone?"

My heart jumped into my throat. *Shit, shit, shit! I forgot to delete it!*

After I saw Steven's selfie, Dad called me downstairs to help him with dinner. By the time I got back to my phone after eating and doing homework, I'd forgotten the app was there.

I practically leaped over the table to grab my phone back from her. My face felt red hot as I tried to think of an excuse. "Dan must've downloaded it as a joke or something." I struggled to play it as smoothly as I could. "I'm deleting it now," I said, which was another lie. Waiting in line at the food bar suddenly didn't seem so tiresome. "I'm gonna grab some food real quick. I'll be right back," I said as I stood, leaving Lauren alone and confused by how quickly everything had happened.

While in line, I tried not to look back at the table, afraid Lauren would be staring me down. I hoped she believed what I said. I didn't think it would be beyond Dan's intellectual capacity to download a gay app onto someone's phone as a prank. Right? I pulled my phone out and deleted Grindr.

"Do you want to try the new breakfast burrito?" A woman in a hairnet asked from behind the bar. It took me a second to realize the line had moved, and I was standing there with a blank look. I could smell the fresh eggs and bacon circling the air.

"Sure," I said, grabbing the foil-wrapped cylinder. As I approached the cashier, I looked at Lauren's table. Dan, Chris, and a few others had joined her. I took a relaxed breath, hoping she'd become distracted enough to forget about finding Grindr. Hopefully, she wouldn't bother asking Dan about it. My stomach growled. I was getting excited to scarf down the burrito.

"Sup, Cheeto," Dan said as I reached my spot back at the table. I gave him a quick nod and unwrapped my breakfast. The cafeteria had gotten louder, with random chatter around us as kids piled in before the first bell. I started taking large bites, worrying I wouldn't have enough time to finish. To my very satisfying surprise, the burrito housed eggs with cheddar cheese, sausage, and bacon. It was everything you could want in the morning when your stomach yelled at you. I glanced at Lauren between a massive bite. She was texting, seemingly unfazed by her recent discovery on my phone.

Dan babbled about some girl he hooked up with the previous night, which I tried to tune out. But then he said something that caught my ear. "Have you guys heard the latest about this new janitor?" I focused on Dan's face, ready to receive additional information about Mystery Boy. My mouth chewed, but everything else was still. I focused on his lips just in case I couldn't hear what he said over the roar of the growing breakfast crowd.

Everyone at the table was listening. It made me suspect that Mystery Boy's popularity was increasing. The gossip spread about who he was and what he did to get community service. "Someone told me they saw some sort of, like, anarchy tattoo on his hand. It's like an A marking," Dan said. My mind moved the information to a little box labeled Mystery Boy with a small lock on the front.

A tattoo. Interesting.

I whipped out my phone to google what an anarchy symbol looked like, wondering if it meant what Dan said it did. The questions continued to build.

"The guy burns down his old school AND has an anarchy tattoo? He's probably part of some cult," Dan said.

My thoughts traveled to a ridiculous vision of a man walking into the cafeteria. I couldn't see his face because a large hood attached to a Jedi-like robe covered it. He meandered toward a trash can and turned his back to me, removing his hood and dropping the robe. The familiar back was Mystery Boy. Then he pulled a large hunting knife from the waistband of his pants and raised it in the air, triumphantly displaying his tattoo. He was about to commit a sacrifice, but Chris's words brought me back to reality.

"Do you think this will all end in a murder spree?" Chris smirked.

"If anyone gets killed, he's definitely gonna be suspect number one," Dan said, causing the other meatheads to chuckle along with him. By that point, my burrito was gone, and I could feel the grease coating my stomach. Then it made a sound that didn't mean I was hungry; it was bubbling, rejecting everything I had just guzzled down.

I sat up straight, asking, "Have any of you actually seen him?"

"How could you not?" Lauren said, looking up from her phone. "He's always doing something around here."

A pang of jealousy shot through me like a bolt of lightning. How had she seen him, but I hadn't? I felt like I was searching for him every hour of every school day. I wondered if I should interrogate her for more details, but it might be too soon after she found Grindr on my phone. The first bell rang, and everyone stood, putting an end to my personal debate.

The day flew by faster than usual. It was a half-day because of parent-teacher conferences happening later that evening. My stomach progressively worsened throughout the day, bubbling up like a pot of liquid left on the stove for too long. I headed toward the locker room to change before football practice. As I passed the cafeteria, I got a strong whiff of pizza that made me want to vomit.

Stepping into the boy's locker room made my stomach turn again. The whole place smelled like decaying feet mixed with Axe body spray. I threw my bag on the bench and crossed to a sink. Turning on the cold water, I cupped my hands, using the puddle to soak my face. I leaned on the cold porcelain, staring at my reflection. The fluorescent light made my ginger buzz cut look even brighter than it was. I strolled back to my bag and grabbed my jersey. Pulling it over my head, it met me with a pleasant scent of floral breeze. It was my mom's favorite laundry detergent that Dad continued to use. It didn't last long as I pulled my head back into the stench of the room. My stomach gurgled again, forcing me to the bench, feeling lightheaded. Other guys trickled in to change, and the smelly room filled with energy.

Our football field was behind the school. You had to walk through the gym, out the backside of the school, and across a large parking lot to get to it. I held my helmet by the face mask, letting it swing back and forth as I weaved through parked cars, still scanning for Mystery Boy at every opportunity. I hadn't seen him that day, so I assumed he didn't work every day.

Then my eyes fixed on Dan. He was standing behind his car with the trunk popped open, already in his practice gear. His helmet was resting on the roof. I continued toward the field, but my eyes stayed on him, confused by what he was doing. As I made my way through the cars, another person came into my line of sight, standing next to Dan. He was a tall, skinny guy with a goatee and stringy, long hair. His clothes looked two sizes too big, and he stood with slumped shoulders.

The strange man pulled out some crumpled cash from his pocket and gave it to Dan. Dan quickly looked in each direction before reaching for something in his trunk. He didn't realize I was watching him. Whatever Dan grabbed for, he kept it concealed in his fist before passing it off to the skinny man. The exchange had happened so fast, if I blinked, I would've missed it. The man hurried away, and Dan closed his trunk, grabbing his helmet. I looked forward again and almost walked into a parked car. If I watched them any longer, I'd surely have a bruised knee.

Who the hell was that?

My mind raced with questions. I'd know if my best friend was selling drugs. Dan wouldn't be stupid enough to do it on school grounds. Then I thought it was probably something school-related, like a USB or something.

I stepped through the four-foot-high chain-link fence that surrounded the field area. My shoes first met the brown racing track around the football field. I always liked the way it felt under my feet, it had a slight bounce to it that made it fun to walk on. I heard a whistle blow and saw kids running down the track. A group of guys huddled on the grass ten feet ahead of me. The grass crunched under my feet; it had just been cut, and the smell made my stomach flip again. I closed my eyes and exhaled, letting my cheeks blow up like balloons. The nauseous feeling hadn't disappeared, and I knew any strenuous activity would only worsen it. I wasn't sure which end the greasy breakfast burrito would come out, but I could feel it gearing up for its exit. It was just a matter of when.

"Looking a little sweaty, Griffin," Chris said, bringing all the attention to me. "We haven't even done anything yet."

"Never eat the breakfast burrito from the cafeteria," I said, dropping my helmet and rubbing my stomach. "I'm learning that lesson the hard way." The other guys laughed it off, and it seemed to make my stomach angrier. It was pushing its way out, but I held it back. I wanted to get through practice.

Dad walked onto the field with Coach, which wasn't uncommon. They were good friends, and my dad had to be on school grounds that night for the teacher meetings.

Coach's voice roared. "Take a knee, boys." We all turned around, doing as he commanded. Dan ran up from behind him and joined us. "We've got a lot of work to do," Coach said. His whistle hung around his neck, and he held a clipboard in his right hand. His daily tie was loosened, and he undid the top button of his shirt. "We could've done better when we faced Glendale last Wednesday. What I saw on that field was not what I expected from you guys." He stroked his goatee, and his eyes passed over us individually. "I expect focus and hard work. That's not what I saw on this field. As you know, we have a game against Skowhegan in a few weeks. Those guys are serious business. I saw them kill the North Valley team last night." Coach must've been the one who sent my dad that video. "I'd be scared if I were you because, with the shape we're in right now, they're going to use us to wipe their asses. Y'all need to show me what it takes to win. The work starts now," he said, pointing to the ground. "Fifty crunches, fifty push-ups, let's go."

"Yes, coach!" We all screamed.

Dan positioned himself next to me, giving me a greeting nod. Lying on my back in the grass, I wanted to stay there forever. It made my stomach feel a little better. Everyone else had started, but I didn't. Dad was quick to notice.

"Landon, pick it up!" He hollered in my direction.

I pushed up toward my knees and winced; I could feel the bile in my gut sloshing around. Dan was counting out loud, already ten crunches ahead of me.

"Who..." I said to Dan, speaking my words between each wince of a sit-up. "... Was... that guy you were talking to?"

Dan's head turned. I could see the concerned look on his face out of the corner of my eye. "Don't worry about it," Dan said.

"He just seemed really odd. I haven't seen him around here before."

"Drop it, Landon. Like I said, you don't need to worry about it." He was being standoffish, more than usual. I winced again. "What the hell is wrong with you?"

"Fuck," I whispered, grabbing my stomach as I laid flat against the grass. "That burrito I ate this morning hasn't been sitting well with me all day." I felt a cramp building in my bowels, I knew I needed to find a bathroom. I stood on my feet too quickly, getting a sudden head rush. "Coach," I called out, raising my hand.

He looked at me with scrunched brows. "Why are you on your feet, Griffin?"

"I have to go."

"What do you mean? We haven't even started yet."

"I need to find a bathroom," I said, holding my stomach.

"Landon, you can hold it, now get back down with the rest," Dad said, motioning me back toward the group.

"No, I'm gonna be sick. I think I have, like, food poisoning or something." My stomach flipped again, causing my jaw to clench.

"Food poisoning?" Dad asked as if he had never heard of it. "From what?"

"Dad," I said, frustrated. "If you don't let me go now, I'm gonna shit all over this field." That statement alone turned my dad's confused expression into a disgusted one.

"Go then, go!" He waved me off.

I power-walked through the gate and into the parking lot, afraid that if I ran too fast, the bile in my stomach would push through. I was wearing tight, white, padded pants; I didn't need that happening in front of everyone. I swayed around people entering their vehicles to go home for the day. My eyes were laser-focused on the door to the gym, not caring to scan for Mystery Boy.

"Hey, Landon!" I heard a voice call out from my right. My power walk continued as I inched closer to the building. "Wait up!" The voice called closer than before. I stopped just outside the metal door and turned toward the voice. It was Steven, he was running to me.

"Goddammit," I mumbled under my breath. I avoided him all day, thinking I was scot-free. I clenched my jaw again, trying to keep everything in. Steven jogged to me in his red short-shorts and a white tee. The shirt's sleeves were short and hugged his shoulders at an angle.

"Hey," he said, catching his breath. "Sorry. I know you're busy, I just wanted to ask you something."

My heartbeat quickened, and my hands clammed up.

He's gonna ask me about Grindr. Please don't ask me about Grindr. How does he even know Sportyguy83 is me?

Beads of sweat ran down the back of my neck.

"Are you okay?" Steven tilted his head. "You don't look so good."

I swear to God if someone asks me if I'm okay one more time.

"I don't feel well," I mumbled, reaching an arm out to support myself against the brick wall of the building.

"Oh, well, I'll be quick."

Please be quick.

"The story you wrote for the *Monthly*," Steven said. "It was great, by the way. But I was wondering..." His words trailed off as he hesitated. "Was it about me?"

My breath caught in my throat. It was not the question I expected. The day that Dan and I ignored him flashed through my mind, and I felt guilty again. “Uh,” I couldn’t form words fast enough. “No, it wasn’t. Why would you think that?”

“Oh, I was just curious,” Steven said. “It just seemed very familiar. A story about two young friends drifting apart? It felt like too real, ya know?”

“Yeah,” I said. “I get what you mean.” My jaw clenched again as another cramp hit me, reminding me of what would soon come. “It wasn’t specifically about us, no. But I mean, people always say, ‘Write what you know,’ right? So maybe it just came out subconsciously.”

“Right.” Steven nodded but didn’t seem to understand what I meant.

My stomach bubbled again. “Steven, I really gotta go, I’m sorry,” I said as I ran into the building, not letting him ask any further questions. I took long leaps across the gymnasium, hoping nothing would come out before reaching the locker room. My heavy steps echoed in the empty changing area. I darted to the stalls, pushed through the door, and fumbled with the lock before pulling down my pants and sitting on the porcelain throne. My body knew it was time to open the floodgates as my stomach pushed out everything it had. I’d never felt so much relief, but with it came a smell that could only be described as ungodly.

When it was over, I felt like I could breathe again. I closed my eyes and rubbed my forehead, taking long, unstrained breaths. I reached for toilet paper with my other hand, but my fingers clinked against an empty plastic rod where it should have been.

Are you kidding me?

I heard footsteps. Sneakers squealed across the tiled floor as they got closer to my stall. I watched the open space under the door as the feet passed by. The person wheeled a yellow mop bucket behind them. I cleared my throat to announce my existence so they wouldn’t attempt to open the door. But the smell of what I had just done probably gave me away first.

“Oh, sorry,” a man’s voice said. “I didn’t know anyone was in here.” The voice had a slight rasp to it but still sounded young. At first, I said nothing. I didn’t want to further out myself as the person who stunk up the bathroom. But then I looked at the empty roll and knew the guy was my only hope.

"Could you, um, possibly hand me some toilet paper? I'm all out in here."

"Sure, one sec," he said, sounding happy to do so.

"Thanks," I said. "You're a lifesaver; you have no idea."

"Here you go," the guy said, popping his hand under the stall door. I reached for it. That's when I saw the tattooed A on his hand and stopped breathing.

Holy shit. Holy shitty fucking shit.

It was Mystery Boy! A lump caught in my throat, and my outstretched arm froze. I locked my eyes on the A. The tattoo was placed on the back of his right hand, between his thumb and pointer finger. It was a simple letter A in a circle. But it wasn't the anarchy symbol where the lines of the letter came outside the ring. The letter fit perfectly in the middle of it.

"Are you gonna take it?" His voice brought me back to reality. I wondered how long I'd made him wait.

"Thank you!" I shouted, grabbing the toilet paper from him.

"No problem," he said, rolling his mop bucket out of the bathroom.

I pressed my face into the fresh toilet paper roll, desperately wanting to scream. All that separated him and me was a thin door. His face was on the other side of it. It embarrassed me that our very first interaction, something I'd dreamed about, was through a bathroom stall. I couldn't believe that he'd know it was me who stunk up the entire bathroom.

Wait, he doesn't know it was me. He doesn't even know who I am.

I used what he gave me and pulled my pants up, ready to storm out the door and find him in the locker room. He couldn't have gotten far. Then I stopped before unlocking the door.

If I go out now, he'll know who I am and that I created this horrid smell; that's even worse than him not knowing I exist.

I placed my palms and forehead against the door. "Why?" I whispered. "Why is this happening?"

NINE

I'd waited almost ten minutes to leave the stall after I was done in the bathroom. My body wanted to burst out to get my first look at Mystery Boy, but the fear of embarrassment held me in the small rectangular space. I waited there until it was silent in the locker room. Despite that, I tiptoed my way out of the stall just in case he was still lingering. Once I was out of the locker room, my searching eyes kicked back into gear. It felt like I was released from prison after a fifteen-year stint, free to explore the world for Mystery Boy once again.

I pushed my way through the rest of the practice, doing minimal movement to exert my body, which felt like it had nothing left in it. I tried to chug as much water as I could between running, catching, and tackling. I couldn't wait to get home just to lie in bed and let myself recover from the food poisoning.

On the field, my eyes would drift to the parking lot, searching. But again, no luck. I'd lost my chance. It seemed Mystery Boy had the power of teleportation. Every time I saw him, he would disappear as fast as he came into my line of sight. After two hours of non-stop running and sweating, the practice was finally over.

"Y'all are off tomorrow," Coach said, huddled by the water cooler.

"But I'll see you here again in two days. Rest up, we go hard again at practice on Sunday."

The guys started shedding their gear and walking toward the school; I spotted Steven sitting in the bleachers with two girls. They were chatting and laughing.

"I bet he gets off on watching us," Dan said, popping up next to me, and chugging a cup of water. He watched Steven and his friends, just like I was. "Faggots shouldn't be allowed to just sit there and watch us; it gives me the creeps," Dan said.

I remembered Steven's question in the parking lot before I got sick. "Do you ever feel bad for what we did?" I realize now it was a stupid question to ask someone like Dan.

"Hell no," Dan said. "Do you wanna be associated with queers? I sure as fuck don't."

"I feel bad sometimes; he was our friend."

"Don't tell me you're going soft, Griffin," Dan pushed my shoulder. "He stopped being our friend the second he told us he was gay. Besides, you weren't even part of the worst of it."

His words confused me. "What does that mean? What are you talking about?" I first thought he meant the attack on Steven, but Dan's words made it feel like he was talking about something else.

"Don't worry about it."

"You know," I said. "You've been saying that a lot to me lately. What the hell is going on with you?"

Chris had caught on to our conversation and stopped before exiting the track to watch us.

"What's been going on with me? You're the one who's been acting weird. We've barely seen you out of school," Dan said.

Chris jogged over to us before I could say anything. "Guys, chill. If Coach sees you arguing, he'll make you stay here all night doing drills."

Chris was right. The coach's way of making teammates work out their issues was to drill them on the field until he heard a sincere apology or their feet bled. I didn't have an excuse to prove Dan wrong. He was right. I had been distant from my friends that past week.

"I'm sorry," I said, picking up my gear and shoving it all into a duffle bag. "You guys should come over tomorrow. We can hang out and play video games or something. We haven't chilled in a while."

"Finally," Dan said, crumpling up his water cup and spiking it to the grass. "About time you started making sense. See you tomorrow, then." Dan ran off to the school with the other guys. Chris picked up the cup before we exited the field together. I wondered if he noticed the guy Dan was hanging out with in the parking lot earlier.

"Have you seen Dan hanging out with anyone weird lately?"

"Nah." Chris shook his head. He tossed the crumpled cup into a trash bin before stepping onto the parking lot's asphalt. "Why?"

"I saw him with someone earlier, like someone who doesn't go to school here."

"Was it that weird janitor?" Chris let out a small laugh.

"No," I said with a chuckle. "It definitely wasn't him."

I wished it were Mystery Boy; then I'd finally know what he looked like. The thought of him never left my mind while walking home.

Where did he go? Where does he go when he leaves the school?

Later that night, after dinner, I was washing dishes when Lauren called me. She wanted to talk about our date the following night.

"We should go to La Villa!" Lauren said.

La Villa was a local Italian restaurant, and I suddenly craved chicken parm just hearing the name.

"Sure," I said. "I'll ask my dad for some money. Though I don't think he'll wanna pay for both of us."

"That's fine. I can ask my mom for some money, too."

As I climbed the stairs toward my room. I felt a cool breeze come through my open window. Dad sometimes turned off the central air and opened all the windows in the house. I could hear the next-door neighbor's dog barking at a couple of kids skateboarding down the street. It was a German Shepherd named Sparky; its owners made it sleep outside at night. My mom used to think it was cruel and unnecessary.

"We should see a movie after, maybe?"

"Dang," I said, laughing. "You're an expensive date."

"I thought you knew what you were signing up for."

"Apparently not."

"I'll swing by your place tomorrow, and we'll go. Sound good?"

"Works for me,"

"Okay, babe, I'll text you."

"Sweet."

"Love you," Lauren said. She was saying it more while I hesitated.

"You too." I had yet to say the actual words to her. It just didn't feel right. I hung up and sat on my bed, feeling the pull of social media, seeing as I hadn't checked it in hours. I scrolled through my phone, intending to click on Instagram, but my thoughts gravitated toward Grindr, wondering if Steven had sent anything after his picture. I bit my lip a little, feeling the curiosity strike me again. I hopped up, closed my door, and returned to my bed. Laying on my stomach, I re-downloaded the app, hoping my messages with Steven hadn't been deleted.

Once I opened Grindr, I was met with several vibrations. I'd received more messages while I was offline. I opened the first one from a person with the username Anthonyorgy, 30. He didn't even say hi. All he sent me were naked pictures of himself standing in a mirror at several angles. I groaned and deleted the message thread. Then I noticed Steven had messaged me again.

THEATRENERD245, 18

Gonna send me any pics of you?

SPORTYGUY83, 18

Sorry. But I don't think I'm ready to show my face.

I assumed he wasn't online, so I clicked away and scrolled through Instagram until a notification popped up, telling me Steven had written back.

THEATRENERD245, 18

It's okay, I get it. This app can be pretty intimidating sometimes.

SPORTYGUY83, 18

More like terrifying haha. Why do so many guys send random nudes without even saying anything first?

THEATRENERD245, 18

LOL yeah you kind of get used to that. Some guys are into it, but it's mostly creepy. I like to get to know a guy before showing him the goods, ya know? ;)

Is Steven trying to flirt with me?

THEATRENERD245, 18

So, what're you looking for on here then?

SPORTYGUY83, 18

To be honest, I was looking for someone in particular. It's dumb because I don't even know what he looks like or what his name is.

THEATRENERD245, 18

Hmm, well there are a lot of faceless guys on here, maybe he's already messaged you.

SPORTYGUY83, 18:

Haha, I doubt it. I don't think he's on here. I call him Mystery Boy, how lame is that?

THEATRENERD245, 18

I think that's kinda cute. So you've never even met this guy?

SPORTYGUY83, 18

Nope. Which sounds ridiculous. I've only seen him from afar, but he's completely taken over my thoughts. I've become infatuated with him to the point where I'm dreaming about what he might look like.

THEATRENERD245, 18

Oh, so you're like a stalker?

I didn't know what to say. I felt like a total freak.

THEATRENERD245, 18

I'm kidding lol I've been in that situation before, crushing on someone from a distance. It happens to me a lot.

SPORTYGUY83, 18

Really?

THEATRENERD245, 18

Oh yes, Hunny. I've been at this a long time, lol. When did you come out, if you don't mind me asking?

I paused, thinking over the question. It was great to talk about what I felt, but coming out had yet to pass my mind. My feelings for another guy had hit me all at once. It was the first time they'd stuck. For me, attractions usually came and went faster than I could run a football to the end zone. Seeing all the hate Steven got over the years, I didn't think all that pain was worth coming out and telling anyone about my feelings in real life.

. . .

SPORTYGUY83, 18

I'm not out, actually. No one knows about me, except you.

THEATRENERD245, 18

gay gasp Well clutch my pearls! I'm so honored! I'll just consider myself your fairy gay mother. You can come to me for anything.

Our conversation continued throughout the night. Steven gave me a crash course on all things gay. Which gay movies to watch, his favorite gay books I should read, even his favorite porn website if I was ever feeling extra gay. I felt confident in my anonymity. Like I wasn't being judged or laughed at. I still felt like me, but a different me. An honest me. I was actually enjoying my conversation with Steven. I wondered what he would do if he found out SportyGuy83 was me. Would he shout it to the entire school or keep it to himself?.

For the first time in a while, I felt I could relate to someone. The past week, it felt like I'd been screaming underwater while my friends watched from the shoreline, waiting to see if I would drown or make it back to the sand.

"Dude, wake up!" Dan's voice pulled me out of a deep sleep the next morning, howling through my open window. The sun shined so brightly in my room that it was hard to open my eyes. I blindly reached for my phone to check the time. It was almost noon.

My body felt sticky. I propped myself up, noticing I'd sweat through my sheets. Dad had forgotten to turn the AC back on; the heat poured in all morning. I walked to my window in nothing but underwear and poked my head out.

Dan and Chris stood on my front lawn, looking much more awake than I was. "Let's throw the ball around!" Dan said.

"I'll be down in a sec!" I stumbled to my closet and slipped on a tank top and basketball shorts. I pulled my desk drawer open and grabbed a tube of sunblock, slathering on as much as possible. I hurried down the stairs and grabbed a power bar before heading out the front door. "What's up, guys?" I said, unwrapping the bar. It only lasted three bites before it was gone. "Throw me the ball." I ran out to the street and caught the first toss. Chris and Dan followed. We formed a large triangle and tossed to each other casually.

"Get it in with Lauren yet?" Dan said, catching the ball.

I rolled my eyes. "No, I haven't," I said, stepping back to increase the distance between us. "Sorry to disappoint."

"You guys have been dating for what? Almost a year now?" Dan threw the ball to me, I jumped to catch it with both hands. Dan tended to throw a little high.

"Yeah, that's kinda sad, man," Chris said.

I brought the ball to the side of my face, prepping for a throw. The wind whipped against me, and I could smell the leather before I chucked it toward Chris in a perfect spiral.

"I don't know," I said. "It just hasn't happened yet. It hasn't really been an issue." I could hear some kids laughing behind me and the sound of their scooter wheels racing toward us.

Chris and Dan both had sex before I had. A few months before I started dating Lauren, I attended my cousin's wedding in Houston. When I came back, I told the guys I hooked up with a random girl who was there as her friend's plus one. The guys believed me, even though none of it was true. I felt a lot of pressure from them since Dan lost his virginity sophomore year. Chris lost his a couple of months before the start of his junior year.

"You can't go into college a virgin," Chris said, running backward. He jumped, catching it with one hand. "That's just weak."

Before resuming our game, we let the kids pass through our triangle on their scooters.

"Landon, go long!" Dan shouted.

I turned and ran, sporadically looking over my shoulder. Dan threw the ball with power like the talented quarterback he was, but I undershot it. I tried to jump to reach it, but I was too short. The ball zipped through the air and into the school's front courtyard.

"Weak!" Dan shouted, making Chris laugh.

I hopped the stone wall, landing on the grass. The ball was in my sights, but so was the sun. I approached it, squinting, not letting the rays burn my eyes. I was about to reach for the ball, but another set of hands grabbed it first. I was taken aback, as I hadn't noticed anyone standing in the courtyard. I stood up straight and locked onto the person to whom the hands attached. My entire body immediately turned to ice. It was Mystery Boy.

"Here you go," he said with ease, holding out the ball. I wondered if the sun was playing tricks on me. Had I been baking that long, I was seeing things I only saw in my dreams? I squinted harder. The sun was glowing from behind his silhouette, like he was a muse sent to me by the Greek gods. Words couldn't form properly. I imagined my brain was a mess of nonsensical numbers, like binary code I didn't understand. I tried to speak, but nothing came out. My eyes were the only part of my body I could move. Again, he was shirtless and sparkling. The front of his body was even more pleasing than his back. Mystery Boy's skin was bronze and looked smooth to the touch. His chest looked like someone had sculpted it from marble, and his torso was long, with toned abs. I couldn't see each square, but his stomach was flat.

I wanted nothing more than to see his face since I first saw him. The thought of it kept me from paying attention in class that whole week. And finally, I was staring into his big hazel eyes. They were like quicksand, and I was sinking fast. His eyebrows were thick, and his hair was long enough to cover most of his forehead. But then his smile hit me like a brick wall. His teeth were almost as bright and blinding as the sun. But the dimples that formed at his cheeks practically made my knees buckle.

He looked at me with one eye squinted. "You okay?"

I hadn't moved or said anything in what felt like hours. My mouth was so dry that my tongue was stuck to its roof.

Speak! My brain was shouting. *Say anything!*

"Uh yeah," I said, reaching out to grab the ball. "Sorry. The sun, it um, gets hot."

What the hell did I just say?

I had no idea what was wrong with me. It was like I'd turned into a limp noodle. Feeling completely incompetent, I panicked, swiped the ball from him, and turned away, feeling idiotic.

This may be your only chance, I thought as I flipped to face him again. "Landon," I spat out. "I'm...my name's Landon."

"Caleb," he said, extending a hand. I grasped it, feeling the calluses on his palms formed from hours of manual labor.

"You wanna join us?" I pointed a thumb behind me to the street. It was worth a try.

"Oh, no thanks," Caleb said with a smirk. "I still got a lot of work to do." He sauntered backward. "It was nice to meet you, Landon," he said before turning away.

"You too!" I said, causing him to look over his shoulder at me again with a smile. Then I stood there watching him walk away.

Caleb, holy shit, his name is Caleb.

The ice had melted away, and I could move again. I smiled to myself before jogging back to the street.

"So," Dan said as I came back into earshot. "What's his deal? Is he a psycho?" Chris moved in closer to us.

"Nope," I said with a grin. "Seems pretty normal to me."

"I'm not convinced," Chris said, stealing the football from my hands. "Someone told me he got expelled because he tried to bomb the place. Said he literally brought a homemade bomb into his school."

"You know that's all gossip, right?" I said, looking at Chris with a goofy smirk. "No one knows for sure."

"Got that right," Dan said. "Guy's a total mystery."

Not anymore. He's Caleb now.

Throughout the rest of that afternoon, I'd look at the school, hoping to see him again and that Chris and Dan wouldn't notice.

Later that night I was in my room getting dressed, waiting for Lauren to pick me up for our date, when I heard music play from outside. I glanced out my window and saw Caleb standing under a streetlight; he'd found a shirt since I last saw him.

Is he just finishing up now?

The music came from his phone; it played, and he failed to untangle his earbuds. I checked my phone for the time. Lauren wouldn't arrive for another twenty minutes. I took a breath and decided to go talk to him. I felt like I had to prove I knew how to speak a proper sentence.

I barely touched a single step as I leaped down the stairs, worried he'd be gone before I got outside. When I stepped out the front door, Caleb was halfway down the street. It was dark, and the air felt cool. I jogged and called out his name, but he had untangled his wires and had the earbuds in.

"Caleb!" I said a little louder. That time he heard me and looked back with his eyebrows raised. He pulled an earbud out of his right ear and smirked.

"Oh, hey," Caleb said, stopping in the street. "What's up?"

I caught up to him. "Figured I'd say hi. Are you just finishing...at the school, I mean. It's kinda late."

"Yeah, the asshole guys that run the school thought it'd be best if I stayed until I finished their laundry list," Caleb said with a scrunched face. I walked with him. "They all need to take the stick out of their asses."

"Yeah." I looked at the pavement. "One of em's my dad."

"Oh shit! The principal is your dad?"

"No, no, he's the superintendent."

"Damn, that must suck. I'm sorry, I didn't mean to sound like a dick."

"You're fine. And you're right, he does have a stick up his ass. It's pretty annoying." We chuckled a bit, then fell silent. We walked a few steps, looking forward until I spoke again. "Headed home?"

"Yeah. I live a town over."

"In Skowhegan?" I glanced at him. "That's like a two-mile walk from here."

"It's cool. I just cut through the baseball field. Makes it a little shorter." Caleb spoke with ease, like he'd been doing it every night for years. I wondered why he didn't have a car.

Somehow, we got lost in a simple conversation, and I walked with him to the baseball field. His laugh was so damn charming I could've listened to it on repeat. His voice had a rasp that could soothe anyone who listened. I'd once heard a 1940s radio host who told bedtime stories during one of Dad's History Channel shows, making me picture Caleb's voice booming from an old radio.

The baseball field was creepy at night. It was dark, except for a light over one dugout. I wasn't going any further, so I sat on a metal bench, looking at the chain-link fence surrounding the field.

"You cut through the woods?" I looked up at Caleb, who stood next to me. A dark forest surrounded the entire back of the baseball field.

"Yeah," he said, looking toward the line of trees. "There's a clear path. It's not too bad; I just use the light on my phone."

"Seems a little too creepy for me." I felt a chill up my spine just thinking about walking through the woods alone. I figured Caleb and I would say a quick goodbye, and he'd be on his way, but to my surprise, he sat beside me.

"It's not like *The Blair Witch Project* if that's what you're thinking," Caleb said with a chuckle.

"What's that?"

"What?" His mouth dropped open. "It's a horror movie. You've never seen it?"

"No." I smiled. "I haven't seen a lot of movies. I auditioned for the musical *Footloose* once. I heard that was a movie."

"Go home," Caleb said, looking at me with a deadpan expression.

He wiped his face with his hand. "You've never seen *Footloose*? That's like one of the best 80s movies of all time!" He seemed genuinely shocked. "Blair Witch, I can understand, sure, but *Footloose*? Wow."

"I didn't watch a lot of movies growing up."

Caleb turned his entire body toward me, and our pinkies touched as our hands rested on the bench. It sent a shock wave through my body.

"Okay, uh... " Caleb looked to the sky. "...what about *Jurassic Park*?"

"Nope," I said with a sour face.

"Oh, my god!" He jumped from his seat and shook his head. "I don't know if I should even talk to you right now," he said with a laugh. I would've stopped time to watch a thousand movies if it meant he would continue to talk to me for the rest of the night. "*Jurassic Park* is an all-time classic, one of the greatest! For being made in 1993, it still holds up to this day! The dinosaurs look so real compared to the CGI bullshit they use now." Watching him spaz out made me smile.

"What are you? Some kind of movie buff or something?" I was genuinely amused by his tidbit of information.

"Maybe a little." He sat next to me again. I was taken off guard by how cute his dimples were, they melted my insides. They were pulling me in like a tractor beam from an alien spaceship. Then he switched gears so fast, it nearly knocked me off the bench. "You remind me of someone special to me." He paused. "You both have red hair."

I stared at him, staring at my hair. I didn't know what he meant by it or how to take it. I could've stared at him until the sun came up.

He looked away before standing again. "Thanks for walking me this far." Caleb shoved his hand out for a shake.

"No problem." I stood and returned his gesture, noticing the A tattoo on his hand. "What's this stand for?"

"It's a long story," he said flatly. Caleb brushed by me and headed toward the woods. "Catch ya later."

"Maybe tomorrow? Gonna be around?" I was feeling desperate, wondering when I'd see him again.

He turned on his heels to face me, walking backward. "Probably not. Got a date tomorrow." Caleb turned to the woods again. His words burst my bubble. I crashed hard from the high he had given me like a little kid after he'd downed five Pixie Stix. I wondered who the lucky girl could be. Was she the special one with red hair who I reminded him of? I tried to hide my disappointment.

"Careful of the Blair Witch!" I said, cupping my hands around the sides of my mouth to make sure he'd hear me.

"Watch the movie, kid!"

I smiled and watched him disappear past the dark tree line.

My phone vibrated as I walked back to the street. I pulled it out, and the screen lit up my face, causing my smile to fade when I saw I had three missed calls from Lauren.

Fuck.

TEN

I jogged most of the way home, sweating through my date-night clothes. Though it was a bit cooler, it was still a warm Texas night. I was an idiot for letting myself get swept up with Caleb, forgetting all about my date with Lauren.

How did I not feel my phone vibrate? Three missed calls?

Lauren was going to have questions. I needed to make up an excuse fast.

On my jog home, though, I couldn't stop thinking about Caleb. I scratched out the label on the small box in my mind. Now instead of saying Mystery Boy, it read Caleb. A few more tidbits of information about him were downloaded and stored. He was a movie buff, and he lived in Skowhegan. I imagined the files being dropped into the box, like when you drag a file into a folder on your computer.

Skowhegan was one town over from Madison, but they couldn't be more different. My town was very suburban with lots of cul-de-sacs. Skowhegan was a bit more rundown. A lot of condemned buildings, a few trailer parks, and even a cornfield. I pictured Caleb living in a house that kids thought was haunted because it looked decrepit on the outside. I pictured him having to chase them away as they attempted to throw rocks through the windows.

As I approached my house, I thought about what Caleb said—that he had a date. Jealousy shot through me again. Though I was about to have dinner with my girlfriend, I desperately wanted to be on a date with Caleb.

A car horn lifted me from my thoughts. I returned to my house, about to step through the front door, when Lauren honked her horn at me. I was so distracted by my dreamed-up scenario that I hadn't noticed she parked on the street in front of my house. I stood on my front steps and watched as she exited her car and stomped up the lawn.

"Where've you been?" she asked. "I've been calling you."

"I know, I'm really sorry."

Lauren crossed her arms. "Landon, we had plans. I thought you were ditching me. We missed our reservation."

"I'm sorry, I didn't feel my phone go off, I don't know how."

"You're all sweaty. What've you been doing?"

I searched my brain for an excuse. Knowing I had to lie to her again killed me. "I went for a walk," I spat out. "To think about some stuff. I lost track of time. When I finally realized, I ran back, hoping you wouldn't be here yet."

"To think about stuff?" She asked. "Like what, Landon? What the hell is so important that you blew me off?"

I felt like I was on a witness stand, a pot of boiling water with a lid about to burst. "Wanna come inside?"

"Are you gonna tell me what's going on with you?"

"Yes." The pot I'd become cooled as a lightbulb went off instead. I knew something I could tell her that wasn't necessarily a lie, but it wasn't my biggest secret either. I took her by the hand, leading her through the door.

"Where's your dad?"

"Probably with his campaign team," I said, glancing over my shoulder. I led her to my room and sat her on my unmade bed. She tossed a sock to the floor.

"I haven't been up here in a while," Lauren said.

My dad was pretty traditional about having my girlfriend over. He didn't like us hanging out in my bedroom, knowing what might happen if he left us behind a closed door. 'I was a teenager once,' he loved to say.

"Yeah, sorry it's such a mess," I said, stumbling over my football shoulder pads, trying to scrounge up anything I could from my floor to throw in my closet. I unbuttoned my sweaty shirt and threw it into the hamper as I looked for a new one.

"Landon, come sit."

I did what I was told before I could find a shirt. I sat next to her on my bed and apologized again, feeling terrible for blowing her off.

Lauren popped onto the bed and crossed her legs. Her jeans were skin tight. She grabbed my hand, interlocking her fingers with mine. "So, what's going on?"

"All this college stuff," I said, glancing at the floor. I couldn't bring myself to lie while looking her in the eyes. "It's really stressing me out. My dad is putting all this pressure on me about football scholarships. But I don't think I even want to play football anymore."

"What do you want to do, then?"

"I think I want to major in creative writing, but if I tell my dad, he's gonna go berserk. Unless I make it to the NFL, nothing will be good enough for him."

Lauren pulled my face up, forcing me to look at her. "You're gonna have to tell him soon, babe. Application deadlines are coming up fast."

"I know. I think I'm gonna go see my counselor on Monday."

"Have you thought about where you want to apply?"

"Not sure. Tasha recommended NYU, maybe."

"Oh my god." Lauren perked up. "How amazing would being in New York City together be?!" Lauren hoped to get into Marymount Manhattan's musical theater program,

I smiled and nodded, wondering how many high school couples lasted through college. "When is your audition again?"

"Not this weekend, but the next, so like, two weeks?"

"What are you gonna sing? Are you nervous?

"Oh god, yes," Lauren said, moving her hair from one shoulder to another. "I'm singing 'Astonishing' from Little Women. It's a white girl song, but I feel like I'd be a cliché if I sang something from I*n the Heights* or *West Side Story*, ya know?"

I nodded, having no idea what she was talking about. The only words that made sense were "Little Women." I loved that book. I stood and continued my hunt for a shirt.

"We can still make the movie if you wanna go," Lauren said as she stood. She moved closer, wrapping her arms around my neck.

I needed to redeem myself and get my mind off of Caleb. My thoughts turned into a hailstorm.

Maybe I'm bi. I could easily be bisexual. I just need to make a move.

I turned, grabbing Lauren's hips. I wanted to prove Caleb didn't have control over me. I wanted to finally be able to tell Dan I had sex with my girlfriend.

I leaned, pressing my lips against hers. The small buttons of her shirt scratched against my bare stomach, tickling me. She kissed me back. Our breathing intensified as my tongue found hers.

"I'm still mad at you," Lauren said between breaths.

I smiled against her lips as she furiously unbuttoned my pants, but before she could reach inside, I walked her backward, laying her on my bed. I came down easy on top of her; our lips never detached. Her hands continued their mission. My fly was down next, and she pushed my pants and underwear down at the same time. It was the most naked I'd ever been in front of her, or anyone for that matter. It was the first time another person had touched me where I'd only touched myself.

My heart raced. I wasn't sure what to do next. My hands stayed flat on the bed, holding myself over her. She reached down to discover I was still flaccid. The image of my pinky touching Caleb's on the bench flashed through my mind, sending a shudder down my spine. It felt like an earthquake in my bones, and I stopped kissing Lauren. My eyes clenched, and I shook my head a few times.

"Are you okay?"

"Yeah.... sorry," I said, moving to continue kissing her. One of her hands slithered up to mine and guided it under her shirt to her chest. I tried my best to touch her in a way I thought she would enjoy, but nothing triggered me. I assumed I'd feel a tingle in my stomach, wanting her the way she wanted me. I assumed I was supposed to be erect, but I wasn't, I couldn't. Caleb's face flashed in the darkness behind my eyelids. Again, it felt like my bones shook, forcing me to leap off of her. I just stood there naked at the foot of my bed, rubbing my eyes.

"Landon, what's wrong? You're not even hard."

Thank you for reminding me.

I sighed, pulling my pants up from around my ankles. "I'm sorry... I..." I turned away, desperately searching for a shirt, needing to feel clothed. Not wanting Lauren's eyes to spend any more time on me.

"What's wrong?" She asked again.

I opened a drawer and grabbed the first T-shirt I saw.

Lauren continued her questions. "Is it me? Are you, like, not attracted to me?"

That feeling of boiling water erupted in my stomach again. I didn't have an answer for her, and that scared me. I placed both hands on my dresser, facing away, feeling like I could pass out at any moment from the pressure building inside me.

"Landon?"

"I think you should go," I whispered, still staring at the stained paint of my dresser drawer.

"What?" She stood from the bed, taking a step toward me.

"I want you to leave. I'm sorry."

"Landon, please tell me what's going on." She placed a hand on my arm. I wanted to look at her, but my body wouldn't let me. Lauren sighed and turned to go without saying goodbye. When the front door finally slammed, I felt I could breathe again.

I sat at the edge of my bed. My hands rubbed back and forth against my thighs as I took deep breaths. My face warmed and my eyes filled with tears. Caleb was corrupting my thoughts, corrupting my body. He *did* have control of me. But how was that possible? I'd only interacted with him twice. I was so confused about what I was feeling and why.

I could still feel the boiling pot inside me, and when it was too much to bear, I let out a visceral scream that filled my room until I had no breath left in my lungs. Tears streamed my cheeks, but I wiped them away. My nose was running, I was a complete mess. I pulled the bottom of my T-shirt up, wiped my nose with it, and took a few more deep breaths. I laid back on my bed, staring at the ceiling. If Caleb saw me at that moment, he'd think I was psychotic. He had a date; he confirmed it. Some girl was taking up the attention I dreamed he would give me. She's got him, and I've got...tears.

I guessed it was all but confirmed that Lauren thought I must be insane. I was afraid to check my phone, scared to see the inevitable texts from her. I thought it was something I wanted. Sex is what's supposed to happen with a guy and his girlfriend in high school. It's what's supposed to happen after you've been dating for a year. I'd imagined it so many times, Lauren and me hooking up. Talked about wanting it. And thought I could do it when the time came. I'd imagined it would be this fantastic thing I could brag to Dan and Chris about, but I was wrong. When Lauren touched me, I felt nothing. I seriously wanted to feel something. I tried to connect the dots to make my dick work, but my body already knew something my brain didn't.

I laid back on my bed and closed my eyes, depleted. I was so emotionally exhausted that it only took a minute for sleep to take over.

I saw myself sitting at a white cloth-covered table at La Villa, dressed in a button-up shirt and khakis, waiting for Caleb to arrive. I'd told him to meet me there at eight. The server had asked me if I'd like to sample some wine while I waited, and I accepted. I checked my phone; it was eight-twenty. When Caleb arrived, he sat across from me, looking confused.

"What are you doing here?" He asked,

I tilted my head. "What do you mean?"

"I'm meeting a date here," Caleb said.

My brow furrowed. "I am your..." I couldn't get the words out fast enough before a beautiful red-headed woman wearing a short black dress touched my shoulder.

She looked at Caleb. "Who's this?"

"This is Landon. He and I met during my community service. Not sure how he ended up at our table."

I quickly realized she was his date for the night, not me. Caleb was about to introduce her when my eyes opened. I sat up and checked my phone. I'd only been asleep for ten minutes.

I pulled my shit together and took a shower, washing away the embarrassment. I didn't bother sending Lauren any texts. I needed to get my head straight before I could talk to her.

After my shower, I returned to my room in nothing but a towel and sat at my desk in front of my laptop. I had left my phone charging with the USB plugged into my computer. I opened Grindr and swiped through my chat with Steven, looking for the recommendations he'd given me for good porn sites. I wasn't that horny, especially after what happened with Lauren, but I couldn't get aroused by her. I needed to know if my body responded to gay porn instead.

I opened my computer and clicked the incognito window of my browser.

I should lock the door.

I hobbled over, twisted the lock, then plopped back down at my laptop. I typed in the first site Steven gave me. The page looked like YouTube, but the thumbnails had naked bodies. I clicked on a tab called 'categories' first. I wasn't sure what kind of porn I was into or what type of guy I might like. There were so many options. I knew I was attracted to Caleb, who wasn't super skinny but wasn't too muscular either; he was in-between. The image of shirtless Caleb popped into my mind from meeting him earlier that day. I licked my lips subconsciously. Thinking of Caleb shirtless stirred something inside me.

I surveyed the options on my screen. They labeled one category, 'Gingers.' I chuckled to myself, not realizing we deserved our own category. People had made fun of my red hair most of my life, making me think few people found us attractive.

I clicked on a category called 'College Guys' and scrolled through the countless thumbnails until I came across the title 'Freshman Learns a Lesson.'

"Here we go," I whispered. The video started with a guy in a white polo attempting to unlock a door. 'Hey, Michael,' another guy said out of frame. The guy wearing the white polo, who I gathered was Michael, spun around toward the voice. 'Yeah?' A taller guy stepped into frame, wearing a blue polo.

Should I stock up on polos before college?

Both men had tanned skin and dark hair. Michael wore a white puka shell necklace. It was hard to pinpoint the year they could have filmed it. Blue polo guy continued: 'Heard you were talkin' shit'. Michael was backed against the door, looking nervous. 'What?' Michael asked. I rolled my eyes; the acting was pretty cringe-worthy. 'Let's go to your room,' the taller guy said. 'I need to show you what we do with loud-mouth freshmen.'

Did all gay porn start that way, with lines written for people who didn't have any acting experience? Not that I was an expert on acting ability. Once they walked into the room, they started making out on the bed. Michael was enjoying it, which was a major plot hole. Two seconds ago, he looked scared, like he would get beaten up. But now they were smiling and taking each other's clothes off. I fast-forwarded the video, hoping to get to the action. When I hit play again, loud moans erupted from my speakers, and I quickly hit the mute button. Dad had gotten home while I was in the shower. I listened attentively, ensuring Dad wasn't lurking outside my door. I focused on the video again, biting my lip, and my pulse pounded. The towel around my waist tented. I liked what I was seeing, and my body was responding.

I heard my doorknob jiggle.

Fuck!

My eyes widened, and my heart stopped as I pushed myself out of my chair and stood. Dad barreled into my room, and I faced him in nothing but my towel, crossing my arms in front of me, trying to hide my erection.

"Jesus, Dad!" I shouted.

He didn't even try to shield his eyes or look away; he was used to seeing guys in towels in the locker room. "Sorry, I should've knocked," Dad said.

"Uh, yeah! That's twice this week you've done that!" I needed to check if the lock actually worked.

Beads of sweat dripped down my forehead out of fear that he'd seen my computer screen. But my body was covering the video that continued to play. My half-naked, pale figure was the only thing separating my dad's eyes from two men having sex. It terrified me. Thank God I'd muted the video. I needed something to get him out of my room quickly. Or, I at least needed to get his line of sight away from my computer.

"I think there's a leak," I spat out; it was the first thing that came to mind.

Dad's face scrunched. "What?"

"I think there might be a leak... up there." I pointed up toward the corner of the ceiling behind him. Dad turned his back to me, looking up to study it.

"I don't see anything,"

"It's there; just look a little closer." My voice cracked. I cleared my throat and walked past him. I could move now that all the blood from my crotch had rushed to my face. I stood in front of him so that his back was facing my computer. I stared at him as he squinted at the ceiling, tilting his head back and forth. Out of the corner of my eye, just over Dad's shoulder, I could see my computer screen; they were going at it like a pair of rabbits.

Jesus Christ, why didn't I close the screen?!

I wiped the sweat from my forehead with the back of my hand.

"Landon, I really don't see anything. I mean, I know my eyesight isn't getting any better these days, but maybe you should get yours checked." Dad turned around. I panicked again; he would see my screen if I didn't stop him.

"Wait!" I grabbed his shoulder. He looked at me with a furrowed brow. "My door, um, it's been, like, creaking lately? Can you just check that real quick?"

Dad huffed. "I guess."

He stepped into the hallway to check the door. I took two enormous steps toward my desk. If it were the savanna, I'd have been a gazelle. I closed my laptop before sitting at the edge of my bed, finally able to breathe.

"Landon... " Dad was down on one knee, bent at the waist with his ear close to the bottom hinge. He hung on the doorknob, swinging it back and forth. "I don't hear anything." He grunted, pulling himself back up. "Are you okay? You're seeing and hearing things that aren't there." He stood in front of me with his arms out to his sides.

I answered his question with another. "What did you want, anyway?"

"My computer is dead. I was hoping I could use yours for a second." Before he finished his sentence, he reached for my computer and opened the screen. I shot off my bed, almost losing my towel.

"WAIT!" I screamed, scaring him out of his skin. I felt like I was leaping into the air to catch a pass. I shoved his hands away and slammed the computer screen shut. Luckily, it didn't have enough time to turn on.

"What in the hell is wrong with you, boy?"

"You can't use it," I said, leaning against the desk, trying to be as casual as possible.

"Why the hell not?"

"It's broken."

"What?"

"Yep. It just died and never came back to life. I'm throwing it out, actually."

"What happened to it? I feel like you just got the damn thing."

"I don't know, just stopped working." I shrugged. "Technology, man. I don't get it."

Dad scoffed. "Yeah, me neither." He gave me an awkward stare, then started for the hallway. "I guess I'll just wait for mine to charge."

"What did you need it for?"

Dad stopped before stepping out of my room. "Facebook. My

campaign manager set up a page for me that people could follow, I wanted to check it out before it goes live."

I rolled my eyes and crossed my arms; I was almost outed because my dad wanted to use Facebook.

"You know you can do that on your phone, right?"

"My damn phone screen is too small, I wanted to see it bigger." He waved me off before walking out. "Put some clothes on, will ya?"

I shut the door and locked it before slumping back into my computer chair. I opened my laptop, and there it was. The video continued to play where it left off. I closed out the tab. It proved its point: I liked it. But it didn't need to go any further. I'd had enough gay stress for one night.

ELEVEN

The following Monday, I stopped by the guidance office. I needed to talk to my counselor about college options before it was too late. To be honest, I'd already waited too long. Most students figure out where they want to go to college during their junior year, but I procrastinated. I'd already applied to a few state schools where Dad was sure I could get a football scholarship, like the University of Texas in Austin, Texas A&M, University of Houston, and Rice University. I hadn't looked much into any of them. Dad just handed me the applications and told me to fill them out. Now that I knew the major I wanted, it was best to visit my counselor.

I stepped to the counter in the main office to find eighty-six-year-old Mrs. Darcy about to announce something over the loudspeakers. It was a running joke at Madison High if Mrs. Darcy would still be there on the first day when everyone returned from summer vacation. Some people had running bets about whether she'd retire first or die. Her crypt-keeper-like hand switched on the microphone, and her warble voice boomed from the overhead speakers.

"Reminder to students and staff," she said. "A mandatory assembly will be held in the auditorium after the last lunch period."

Mrs. Darcy clicked off the microphone, noticing me out of the corner of her eye. She reminded me of a sloth as she made her way over. "Can I help you, sweetie?"

"Yeah," I said. "I was wondering if Mr. Reily was available."

"Let me check." She wobbled to her desk, picked up the receiver, and dialed a number. She tapped her nails against the wood, waiting for him to answer. "Yes, hello. A young man here is asking to see you. Great, thank you." She hung up the phone. You can go on back, hun."

"Thanks," I said, hurrying around the counter and walking through a glass door to the back office. I knocked on a thick door, staring at Mr. Reily's nameplate. A muffled 'come in' spoke from the other side before I turned the handle.

"Hey Landon, what can I help you with?" Mr. Reily was an overweight African-American man with a bald head and goatee who wore a lot of argyle sweater vests. He typed something into his computer. I assumed he was pulling up my file.

"Hey, Mr. Reily," I said as I sat in a cushioned chair on the opposite side of his desk. "I was wondering about a few other schools. I wanted to apply to some that have a good creative writing program. I know it's kinda late to apply, but I just wanted to get some options... if there are any."

"Hmm, it is pretty late in the game, but let me see." He typed again, mumbling to himself as his eyes scanned back and forth. "I see you've already applied to a few state schools, which is good; you should hear from them soon. But let me see." My legs bounced in anticipation. Mr. Reily finally looked away from his computer and said, "All right, plenty of schools have great creative writing programs, but I'm only seeing three here that take late applications. Those three are uh..." He looked back to his computer screen. "The University of Southern California, Emerson College in Boston, and New York University."

"Okay." I nodded.

"Looks like you have to turn in some work based on the prompt they provide and a letter of recommendation, of course."

The bell rang as a five-minute warning for the day's first period.

"Thanks, Mr. Reily. I really appreciate it."

He smiled. "Of course. You can fill out the applications online, but I'll print the list of schools for you. Just grab it from the printer on your way out."

I nodded and headed out the door, whizzing by Mrs. Darcy, who was reading a book. I snatched the paper from the printer and shoved it into a folder from my backpack to look it over later.

I was hoping to find Lauren. She and I hadn't spoken for the rest of the weekend after she left my house Saturday night. I needed to apologize for acting cold toward her. I turned a corner just as Lauren closed her locker. There were only a few people left scattered around the hall. She didn't notice me before walking away. I jogged to her, calling out her name.

"Hi," Lauren said flatly.

"Can I talk to you?"

"We don't have a lot of time." Again, her words felt cold, which I deserved.

"I know." I leaned against the wall of gray lockers with one backpack strap around my shoulder. "I just wanted to apologize."

"I just don't get it," she said.

"I don't either, I sort of panicked. I thought I was ready, but I guess I wasn't?"

"You could've been nicer about it. You made me feel like I molested you or something."

"I'm sorry," I said. "I didn't mean for it to be that way."

Lauren leaned into one hip. "I just need to know if it's me."

I took a deep breath and held it, not on purpose but because I was becoming a pressure cooker again.

God, give me something so I don't have to talk about this anymore.

I pictured a tornado ripping through the school and taking out most of the hallway behind Lauren. It would scare her enough to forget about her question. Then I pictured the hallway filling with water, and we needed to find a way out, again avoiding her curiosity.

No natural disasters were going to save me, though. Then the bell rang.

Thank you, God.

"We should go. We're officially late," I said, grabbing her hand. "Can we sit together at the assembly later?"

"Yeah, sure." She walked backward; our connected hands brought our arms in the air. Then she let go and walked away. I stood there, watching, feeling like she was getting suspicious. Unsure how long I could pretend everything was fine. I rubbed a hand through my hair and sighed. I wasn't ready to break her heart because I still wasn't ready to accept everything I felt.

I whipped around, crashing chest-first into someone. My eyes scrunched closed on impact. It all happened lightning-fast; I didn't even hear anyone walking behind me. My shirt dampened with splotches. I opened my eyes. It was Caleb. My bad luck continued. He was carrying a large bucket of gray-colored water. He wore a black T-shirt, so seeing where the water landed was difficult. But it was clear when I slammed into him that the water from the mop bucket soaked his face. I wiped the drops of water from my chin with the back of my hands as Caleb put down the bucket.

"Shit," I blurted out. "I am so, so sorry. I had no idea you were behind me."

At first, he said nothing; he just stood there looking like a grumpy dog dripping wet after a bath he didn't want to take. Then he cracked a smile. "It's all right, Mad Max," Caleb said with ease. "Maybe pump the brakes a little quicker next time."

Mad Max? Did he forget my name?

Caleb lifted the bottom of his shirt to wipe his face. I took in his smooth, toned stomach. He was taunting, tempting me to reach out and touch it. My eyes became a camera; every time I blinked, a picture was saved in the Caleb box in my brain.

Seconds later, his stomach was covered again, and I felt I could focus. "What were you doing?" I asked.

"There was a leak in the utility closet. They've been using this to catch all the water instead of fixing it."

Great, I covered him in dirty pipe water.

I looked at the bucket. "Why are you carrying it down the hall? I thought every utility closet had a sink."

"Oddly enough, this one doesn't. And someone's gotta dump it. That someone is me. The closet by the cafeteria has a slop sink, so I'm just gonna dump it there." Caleb scooped the bucket into his arms again.

I'd never been jealous of plastic until that moment. Ugh, to feel what that bucket was feeling in Caleb's arms. The tightness he held it with made my jeans tight. I needed to think of another question before I exposed myself. I thought of asking about his weekend date. But what if he said it was great? I wasn't prepared to hear about the beautiful red-headed woman and how many kids they wanted together.

"Do you go to school?" The words came out of my mouth like a dragon spraying its fire breath.

Caleb's eyebrows raised, probably feeling the question came out of nowhere. He stared at me for a second. I could picture the gears in his brain working hard to decide what to tell me.

"Maybe, maybe not," Caleb smirked, teasing me with one dimple as he strutted by. Was he playing with me? Was he being mysterious on purpose? Did he know he was killing me? As he passed, I got a whiff of his mix of sweat and cologne that would haunt me in my dreams later that night.

"Are you coming to the assembly later?" I called out to him. He didn't look back at me when he spoke; he let his voice echo the halls as he had at the baseball field, walking into the sea of trees.

"That's gonna be a hard no from me, kid."

I found it interesting that he called me a kid again. He wasn't much older than me, so why the nickname? Caleb disappeared around the corner, and I instantly wondered when I'd see him again.

Mid-afternoon rolled around, and students were instructed to go to the auditorium. They already had the assembly for the underclassmen. It was time for the juniors and seniors to assemble in the as there weren't enough seats to fit the entire student body. I shuffled along with the rest of the hoard, pulled a slip of folded paper from my pocket, and stared at it. It was a detention slip that Ms. Pepper had given me for being late to calculus because of my Caleb distraction earlier in the day. The detention was for the next day, after school.

I scanned the theater's faded seats, searching for Lauren. Spotting her toward the front, sitting next to Dan and Chris. She had her backpack in the chair to her left, hopefully saving it for me.

Chris waved at me from the end of the row. "Hey!"

I squeezed past him; Dan was in the middle, and Lauren was to Dan's left. I moved her backpack and sat. The projector screen was pulled down on the stage, ready to show us whatever slideshow my dad had created.

"Dude," Dan said, leaning forward to see me. "I want to have a huge bash for my birthday! I'm thinking of a costume party."

I chuckled. "A costume party? Halloween was months ago."

"I know," Dan said with a smile. "It's not a Halloween thing; it's a costume thing."

"... okay," I said. "When?"

"Two weeks from now, on the weekend, Dan said.

"It's gonna be sick," Chris said. "Our parents are visiting our uncle in San Antonio, so it'll be perfect."

"I'll be in New York for my audition," Lauren said with a pouty look. "So I won't be able to go."

"Damn, I'm sorry," I said, placing a hand on her thigh, but she didn't respond to my touch.

Tasha turned around; I hadn't noticed her sitting in front of us. "Did you say party?" Tasha said with a smile.

"Yeah," Dan and Chris said at the same time.

"You wanna come?" Dan asked.

"Duh," Tasha said. "Can I make an online event for it? How many people are you thinking?"

Dan shrugged. "I want this party to be lit."

"Done," Tasha said, whipping back around in her seat. I peeked over her shoulder; she was already on her phone, creating the event.

"Oh!" Dan said, tapping Tasha on the shoulder. "Make sure you add that everyone has to wear a costume, or they aren't getting in." Tasha nodded, and Dan sat back, looking proud as if he was the first person to come up with the idea of a costume party.

Dad appeared on stage, and his voice boomed in the auditorium. He spoke into a microphone and told everyone to get to a seat. The roar of the chatter died down as Dad continued. "As you all know, tomorrow is our second annual intruder drill," Dad said. "Today's assembly will be a reminder of how it works and what to expect."

I'd completely forgotten the drill was happening. Last year, the school brought in a non-profit organization that works with local police departments to run school shooting drills. They formed the program to give students and staff the best ways to stay safe in a live shooter scenario and plan out evacuation techniques and strategies. The company started about five years prior and was met with a lot of controversy. They strived to make the drills as realistic as possible. They even recruit the local police department as "shooters." The school goes into lockdown while the police officers walk around with paintball guns that look like automatic rifles, and they simulate gunfire sounds through speakers. Parents thought it could be too triggering, but the company insists that they had done countless studies on the program that proved the more realistic, the higher the success rate was of keeping students safe.

My junior year was the first year we did the drill; they instructed us on how to stay safe, specifically inside the classroom. The school spent a bunch of money installing a specific type of lock on every door. During that first drill, I was in Mrs. Donahue's English class. The school went into lockdown, so all the students huddled together on the floor in the farthest corner of the room, away from the door. Dan was also in that class and kept mocking the drill and how stupid he thought it was. He said the obvious move would be to attack the shooter if they ever came into the room.

Once we were all huddled in the corner, it was Mrs. Donahue's job to lock the door. But since the school had installed the new lock, she had trouble with how it worked. She eventually gave up and huddled with us. Four or five minutes later, we saw a figure dressed in black pass by the door's small square window. Then we saw the handle jiggle. Everyone stopped breathing. The man in black pushed through the door and pointed his gun at us, announcing we'd all been shot and killed. Dan got pretty angry afterward, blaming Mrs. Donahue for causing all of our deaths. She studied how the locks worked after that. She even told me it sometimes kept her up at night, knowing she couldn't have saved us if it had been a real scenario.

My senior year, things were a little different, things had gotten even more realistic. In the second year, we were told that we had the choice to leave the classroom and evacuate using one of the practiced evacuation paths or stay put. Leaving meant you risked being caught by a shooter. If they saw you, the police could shoot paintballs at your legs, which meant they'd killed you.

Coming out of the assembly that day was an odd feeling. The tension was high, and you could tell people felt nervous about the drill the next day. Others were treating it as a game.

"I can't believe they can actually shoot us," Lauren said as we walked down the hall back to our respective classes.

"Yeah, but they're just paintballs," Dan said. "So it'll hurt, but only for like three seconds."

"Plus," Chris said. "They're only allowed to shoot our legs; believe me, it hurts a lot more getting shot with a paintball in the chest."

"Or the neck!" Dan said, grabbing hold of his throat, acting as if he'd been shot.

"Shit, the neck is the worst!" Chris shouted.

"I'm staying in the classroom," Lauren said. She walked close to me and wrapped an arm around my waist. I threw my arm over her shoulder and pulled her close. "I do not want to get shot at, no thanks."

"I'm choosing to get the fuck out," Dan said. "Especially after what happened last year. I'm not getting killed this year; I'm in control of my own life. I'm not letting a teacher fuck us over again."

"Ease up," I said. "Mrs. Donahue made a mistake."

"Mistakes get people killed," Dan said.

Chris looked at me. "What're you gonna do?"

"I'm not sure," I said.

I thought about it the rest of the day. At first, I was nervous about the whole situation, but I kept reminding myself it wasn't real. That nothing would harm me. The whole thing seemed like a scare tactic, which I understood. They wanted us to experience the fear we'd feel during a real-life lockdown. I wondered what I'd do during an actual school shooting. Stay put or run. Of course, there were pros and cons to both. But what was stopping a gunman from shooting through the door or even the windows? Maybe evacuating rather than sitting around like a fish in a barrel would be better. But then, of course, if you leave the classroom, you have a chance of running into the shooter, which might lead to your death, with no locked doors standing in between you and the gun.

I thought about who a shooter could be. Plenty of people in my grade had motivation to bring a gun to school. My first thought was Steven. How many times can one person tolerate getting beat up over four years for being gay? At what point would Steven snap and eliminate the entire football team?

There was also Susan Townsend, who had suffered from bipolar and schizophrenia most of her life. During our sophomore year, they hospitalized her for hearing violent voices in her head. Of course, when she returned to school, kids were calling her Schizo Sue. Her depression got worse after that, which led to a suicide attempt in our junior year. She survived, but she didn't come back to school after that. What's stopping her from returning and taking revenge on everyone who made fun of her?

Then there was Ms. Henderson, who worked with the special needs kids. She spent her days following the mentally challenged around the school and helping them in their classes. I'd seen her get cussed out and even bitten, pinched, and punched by these kids who don't know any better. Every time I saw her, the circles under her eyes seemed darker. She was an exhausted and worn-down woman, which was justified; she had one of the most demanding jobs. One that got very little praise. How far could she go before they pushed her to end it all?

And of course, the last person I thought of was Caleb. I did a mental recap of the facts. He lived in Skowhegan, a run-down town, and had a criminal record. He had a mysterious tattoo and seemed obsessed with movies. That was it. People already thought he was weird. Dan already said that Caleb would be suspect number one if someone turned up dead. What if he got his community service on purpose? What if he was hoping to get assigned to a school so he could scope it out? What if his love for violent movies inspired him to try his hand at some violence of his own? People say video games contribute to real-life violence, so why couldn't movies inspire the same?

I combated my thoughts, but there was no way Caleb could do anything like that. The idea of him pulling his shirt up to dry his face blinded me. He seemed normal, based on the few times I'd spoken to him face-to-face, but I had to be honest with myself; I had no idea who he was. I wanted to change that so badly.

The next day at school, everyone was on edge. No one knew when the lockdown would start, and any sort of loud noise would make people jump. The first period went by, then the second and third, but nothing happened. We were told to go about our day as if everything was normal. I even had lunch with Lauren and Chris that day.

It was the final period. I was in chemistry class with Dan. He and I sat toward the back because we were the only seniors in a room full of juniors. We both failed our biology class freshman year, which caused us to take extra science credits during senior year. Mr. Butler was our teacher. Most kids called him the penguin. He was severely overweight and waddled when he walked. Mr. Butler's pointy nose held up thin-framed glasses. He had hair but only on the sides of his head; the only thing connecting one side to the other was a few long strands he combed over the bald space.

Mr. Butler was explaining the chemical reactions of soap when three industrial alarms blared from the loudspeakers and the emergency lights turned on.

"All right everyone, this is it," Mr. Butler said. "Everyone, please move to the back of the room."

We obeyed, shuffling to the back of the class while Mr. Butler waddled to lock the door. Dan and I sat toward the front of the huddle, watching Mr. Butler struggle to join us on the floor. Then we heard the gunshots, which made a few girls in the class scream.

Dan jumped to his feet. "All right, I'm not sitting here anymore!"

"Mr. Wilson, sit back down now!" Mr. Butler whispered.

"No, they said we could go or we could stay. I'm choosing to go. Who's coming with me?"

Everyone stayed quiet. I looked behind me at all the nervous faces before standing.

"I'll go," I said.

"Damn right, you will!" Dan said as he slapped me on the back. Mr. Butler didn't bother to stop us. We started for the door, but when Dan tried the handle, he remembered Mr. Butler locked it. Dan glanced over to the huddle. "How do you unlock this?"

"You need this key and the passcode. But if you leave, I can't let you back in," Mr. Butler said. Dan stomped to our teacher and took the key from him. He jogged back to the door and inserted it. "Now keep the key turned," Mr. Butler said. "And type in three, six, eight, six, and four."

I stood behind Dan, unable to see what he was doing, but I could hear the beep of the number pad every time he pushed a button. The door unlatched, and Dan threw the key back to Mr. Butler.

"Let's go," Dan said to me over his shoulder.

We slithered out the door and closed it behind us, keeping our backs against the wall.

"Do you remember the evacuation route?" I whispered.

"No," Dan said. "I wasn't paying attention to that shit."

"Damn it, me either. We're gonna have to wing it."

Again, we heard gunshots, making us flinch; they were louder outside the classroom. The halls were deserted; it didn't seem like anyone else had chosen to leave their room.

My phone vibrated. It was a text from Lauren.

LAUREN

Landon I'm scared.

ME

It'll be fine, it's not real.

LAUREN

The gunshots sound real.

ME

I know, but they aren't. It's all fake.

"Who is texting you right now?" Dan asked.

"It's Lauren," I said, looking up from my phone. "She's scared."

"Tell her we'll come get her."

ME

Dan and I left the classroom.

LAUREN

OMG!

ME

He said we can come to get you.

LAUREN

You're insane.

ME

Where are you?

LAUREN

Second floor, room 204.

ME

Okay, we'll try to get there.

LAUREN

Be careful.

"She's on the second floor," I whispered.

"Okay, we need to get to the stairs then." Dan led the way. We moved quickly, trying to stay as light on our feet as possible. We were about to turn a corner, but Dan suddenly backed into me. He put his finger to his lips. I could hear footsteps, so we backed ourselves against the wall again.

Dan peeked around the corner and turned to me. "There's a guy holding a gun; he's walking to each door and checking the handles." Then we heard a classroom's worth of screams. The man with the gun must have found an unlocked door. Dan turned me around, and we ran in the opposite direction.

"Stop!" someone shouted from behind. A red paintball splattered against the ground in front of us right before we slid around the corner. We bolted but slowed close to the cafeteria. A bunch of lunch tables were folded up and stacked close to a wall. Dan and I stayed low and hid behind the tables. The cafeteria had a wall of windows facing a small courtyard before leading into the staff parking lot. Within that wall of windows was an exit door.

"We have to go for it," Dan whispered.

"I don't know," I said. "There could be a shooter anywhere in this cafeteria."

We couldn't see past the stack of folded tables without exposing ourselves.

"This may be our only chance." Dan attempted to run toward the door, but I grabbed his shirt.

"Dan, this could be a mistake. Don't."

"I have to take that risk," he said.

"Mistakes get people killed; those are your words."

Dan stared at me with a furrowed brow and clenched jaw before he shoved me and ran toward the door. I didn't follow him, but I heard his clunky footsteps and then a single shot.

"Goddammit!" Dan shouted.

I peeked one eye in his direction and saw the red splat on his pant leg. A man dressed in black escorted Dan through the exit door. I pressed my back against the tables, looking in the direction we came from. I needed to get to the second floor. Each corner I approached, I peeked out to ensure no one was around.

I turned left and saw the stairs at the other end of the hallway. I was about to run to them, but a man stepped out from underneath the staircase, pointing his gun. I panicked, jumping around the nearest corner behind me, when I felt a hand wrap around my mouth and pull me backward.

"It's me, it's me," the voice said. I was turned around and face to face with Caleb. "What the fuck is going on?" He wore a white tank top and a janitor's jumpsuit, but it was unzipped halfway, and the sleeves were wrapped and tied around his waist.

My brow creased. "What do you mean?"

"There are a bunch of guys walking around with guns," Caleb whispered. "Have you not seen them?"

"It's a drill."

Caleb's face twisted. "What?"

"A drill," I said again. "A school shooting drill. The guns are just paintball guns."

"Jesus Christ, it would've been nice if the principal told me about this."

"Hey, you're the one that skipped the assembly yesterday." I had a dumb smile on my face. "If the guys see us, they'll shoot us."

Caleb tisked. "They don't see me as part of the staff. I'm just a guy completing his sentence; they couldn't give two shits about. Come on," Caleb said, pulling me down the hall. The top of Caleb's hand felt smooth. I would've let him pull me off a cliff. I didn't care at that point as long as he didn't let go. I didn't even look up to see where we were going. I just stared at our hands clasped together. Before I knew it, Caleb swept me into a closet and closed the door. It was pitch black, and both of us were panting. He cracked the door, peeked out, and closed it again. "Someone was following us." My eyes widened. I couldn't see Caleb, but I could feel his breath when he spoke. "This is kinda fucked up."

"I agree," I said. "But it's intended to feel real."

"They sure fooled me," Caleb said.

Our hips brushed together, and my heartbeat jolted. The closet was so small that my chin rested on Caleb's shoulder.

"I came in to clean the bathrooms today and heard the alarm. When I came out, I saw these guys walking around with guns, and I thought something serious was going on," Caleb said.

Beads of sweat trickled down my face; it was getting hot.

Caleb cracked the door again. "We should head for the front exit."

I was about to mention Lauren on the second floor, but the door closed, and Caleb pushed his hand against my stomach.

"Shh, someone's coming." Caleb's hand rested there, and a fire erupted inside me. I closed my eyes tight, trying to push down the flames.

Don't get hard, don't get hard.

I clenched my jaw, hoping it would help, but my body wasn't listening to my brain. Thank God it was dark. Heavy boots stepped past the thin wooden door.

I waited a beat, then whispered, "Think it's safe?"

Caleb slowly opened the door. A wave of cool air pushed against us. The heat of our heavy breaths turned the closet into a mini-sauna. Caleb grabbed my hand again and rushed out, leading me down the hall and around two corners before we reached the front foyer.

"It's clear, as far as I can see," Caleb said.

"Should we make a run for it?" I could see the front entrance and half my house across the street.

"Go!" Caleb yelled, and we dashed forward. I ran as if on the football field, whizzing past the auditorium. Caleb kept up with me. Out of the corner of my eye, I could see him smiling. We jumped down the front steps and through the courtyard. He slowed down, but I kept running until I reached my front yard. I collapsed on the grass and stared at the sky, breathing heavily.

Caleb appeared, standing over me, looking down with a smile. "So, did I just like, rescue you? I felt like I was in *Die Hard* or something."

I laughed, sitting up. "I have no idea what that is."

Caleb sat next to me. "You have so much to learn."

"And you didn't save me," I said, gliding a hand over the short grass. "I was already trying to escape. I was with my friend Dan, but he got shot."

"Jesus, this school is intense." Caleb leaned back on his hands. "So, what happened to him?"

"I'm not sure, I saw a guy escort him out after he shot him."

"How is this okay? I don't get it," Caleb said. "Why were you out in the halls? I assume they locked everyone in the classrooms."

"This year, we had a choice: we could stay in the classrooms and wait, or we could choose to leave the building ourselves."

"And you left, huh?" Caleb bumped his shoulder into mine. "How James Bond of you."

"Hey, I actually know who that is," I said, looking at him for the first time since we took off running, getting trapped in his eyes.

Caleb laughed. "Thank God."

I was suddenly thrust into thinking about Caleb and his red-headed goddess. I imagined myself sitting in the audience at their wedding, watching them exchange their vows. Caleb looked so happy holding her hands. I looked around but was the only one sitting in the space, surrounded by empty white chairs.

"How was your date?" I blurted out.

Caleb stared at me. "What?"

"Your date this past weekend?"

"How'd you know about that?"

I hesitated. "Uh, you told me about it."

"Oh," he said, looking toward the school. "Right."

"Did it go well? Was she everything you hoped?"

"Meh." Caleb shrugged. "It was all right, I guess."

"Think she'll want to see you again?" I was torturing myself, getting in too deep with the truth I didn't want or need to know.

"I hope so," Caleb said. We both went quiet and stared at the school. "But," Caleb said as he stood, wiping the dirt from his pants. "I never said my date was a she."

Holy shit.

TWELVE

My mind was reeling. I had to stop my jaw from hitting the ground. The street remained quiet until the school bell rang, announcing the shooting drill was over.

"See ya, Lan," Caleb said as he strutted across the street.

My brain was so rattled I couldn't even say goodbye. I just watched as Caleb walked away, suspecting he knew how much he was torturing me with every word he spoke and that he enjoyed it. Was he being honest or busting my balls?

My mind switched gears. He gave me a nickname. No one had ever called me Lan before, not even my parents. Thinking about it warmed my chest. Was it strange to think he cared about me enough to give me a nickname, or was I being childish? What made me so special?

My phone buzzed, and I pulled it out. Texts from Lauren filled the lockscreen.

LAUREN

Where are you? I thought you were coming to get me?

ME

It got too risky, I'm sorry. There were guys everywhere. I barely got out of the building.

LAUREN

Is Dan with you?

ME

No, he got shot.

LAUREN

OMG!

ME

Yeah, I don't know where he is.

LAUREN

I'm coming to find you.

ME

Okay, I'm out front. I'll meet you by the tree.

LAUREN

K.

I stood, dusting off my pants. Kids exited the school as I crossed the street, wondering where Caleb was off to. I assumed he had things left to do since the men with paintball guns interrupted him.

A large oak tree sat at the center of the school's front courtyard. It was the usual meeting place for Lauren and me most mornings. I leaned against it, noticing I didn't have my backpack. I'd left it in Mr. Butler's classroom, not thinking to grab it amid the chaos of the drill.

Could use some sunblock right now.

The tree's leaves were in full bloom, so I found a shaded area to stand under, shielding myself from the sun.

"Hey," Lauren said as she approached.

I held out my arms so she could embrace me. She hesitated but gave in.

"That was so scary."

"I know," I said into her neck as I held her. The fruitiness of the shampoo she used clung to her hair. My mind flickered to the scent of sweat and cologne I'd gotten from Caleb, wishing I could be as close to him as I was to Lauren.

"I hope we never have to go through that," Lauren said, pulling away.

"Same, but at least this is giving us some sort of prep if it does." Lauren held my hand as I spoke; I could sense her eased attitude.

"I'm sorry," she said, looking me in the eye. "I went too fast the other night."

"You have nothing to apologize for; I'm the one who started it. I could've been a little nicer about it. I just got nervous, I guess." A wave of guilt pushed through me. How could I say that getting physical with her may never happen at all? The last thing I wanted was to hurt her feelings, especially after all our time together.

More and more kids filed out of the building, and I let go of Lauren's hand. "Shit, what time is it?" I checked my phone, confirming I was late for my detention. "I gotta go," I said.

"What? Where?"

"I almost forgot that I have detention."

"For what?"

Getting detention wasn't a usual thing for me. I'm sure Lauren found the words odd coming out of my mouth.

"Yesterday," I said. "Ms. Pepper gave me one for being late after I talked to you in the hall."

Lauren cocked her head. "Her class was right around the corner. How were you late?"

She caught me. "Caleb." I blurted. My words could no longer keep themselves in as if they had a mind of their own.

Lauren's brow pinched. "Who's Caleb?"

There it was; I had to tell her but was so nervous my feelings for Caleb would show in the words I used to describe him. I somehow thought she'd know I was with him the other night and that I lied.

"He's that new janitor guy," I said, after searching the entire English language for words that wouldn't give me away.

"Okay..." Lauren's hands moved in a way that told me she wanted more information. "What does he have to do with you being late?"

My pulse rose, feeling like I was being interrogated.

Just tell her what happened; it wasn't a big deal!

I felt like Jekyll and Hyde. Going back and forth, deciding what information to give her.

"I bumped into him and made him spill mop water everywhere," I said.

"And now you guys are suddenly friends?" Lauren asked.

I searched my brain as if it were Google, but all I kept seeing was the box labeled 'Caleb' and all the information files shooting out of it like a magician throwing cards around a stage.

"Cool," Lauren said before I could answer her question. "So is he weird? Is he scary?"

"Uh," I said, shocked by the conversation's outcome. "No?" It was all I could muster to answer both of her questions. Then panic set in again. "I need to go, Ms. Pepper is gonna give me another detention for being late to this one."

Lauren nodded and gave me a quick kiss. "Okay, go. We can talk later."

"See ya," I said before jogging into the building.

"Late again?" Ms. Pepper said, looking over her glasses at me. I plopped into a desk in the second row. The woman had an awful fashion sense. She wore a long-sleeve, brown turtleneck and an overall denim dress that met her clogs.

"I'm so sorry," I said, trying to catch my breath. I wiped the sweat from my forehead with my arm. "I had to run to Mr. Butler's room to grab my backpack first." Glancing around the classroom, I was the only one in the seats.

"I'll let this one slide," Ms. Pepper said. "Because of the hectic events today."

"Thank you."

Ms. Pepper stood from her desk and walked to the door."Ah, Mr.

Montes," Ms. Pepper said as I pulled my water bottle from my backpack. The clunk of her steps echoed through the empty room. I almost spit out my water when Caleb walked in. Ms. Pepper and Caleb stood side by side, looking at me. "This is Mr. Montes, he will be watching you during your detention."

Caleb smirked. His face looked devilish and handsome.

Ms. Pepper continued, "I have a teacher's meeting about today's drill, or else it would be me. Mr. Montes was the only one available to take over."

"Okay," I said with a hard gulp. My palms felt clammy, so I rubbed them against my jeans.

"He's not allowed on his cell phone," Ms. Pepper said to Caleb. "That's about it. Sit at my desk, and I'll be back in an hour to release Mr. Griffin."

It was official; we knew each other's last names. I pictured another file going into my Caleb box. The other scattered files from earlier whisked themselves up, returning neatly to the box.

"He's in good hands," Caleb said with a nod. I remembered the way his hand felt against mine. I wanted to feel his skin again. Caleb started for the desk as Ms. Pepper left the room. He sat and kicked his feet up, crossing his ankles, while a smug look grew on his face. Chunks of dirt stuck in the grooves under his tan work boots. Caleb leaned back in the chair, interlocking his fingers behind his head, and asked, "Are you stalking me?"

"Ha! You wish," I said.

Caleb chuckled. "What're you in for?"

"You tell me first."

Caleb raised an eyebrow as if to say 'touché.' "It's complicated."

"Try me," I said, sitting up straight.

"I know people around here have been talking about me, spreading rumors."

"Are any of them true?" I was desperate for any word that came from his lips.

"Like I said, It's complicated."

I sensed he didn't want to talk about it, so I made a joke. "They have you doing everything around here, huh?"

"What can I say? I'm a jack of all trades."

"Is this conflicting with school or anything?" I wanted to become a Caleb Encyclopedia.

"Nope. It's just easier not to be in school right now."

"Because of what?" I couldn't stop myself. I was a freight train bursting through the walls of Caleb's boundaries.

He was quick to change the topic. "You're lookin' a little red, kid."

"I just had to run from..." I stopped myself, I needed answers. "Wait, why do you call me that?"

Caleb sighed and removed his feet from the desk, leaning on it with his forearms instead. "Sorry, it's a habit," Caleb said. The rasp in his voice was endearing. "You're younger than me, so it just comes out."

I laughed. "Oh, come on, how old are you?"

"Just turned twenty-one."

I threw my hands out toward him, smiling like a clown. "You're barely three years older than me!"

"You're right." Caleb smiled, flashing his perfect dimples. "I won't call you kid anymore."

I would've asked for an entire week of detention if it meant I had to spend an hour with Caleb every day after school.

"I'm not saying it's a bad thing, I was just curious." I noticed Caleb get rosy in the cheeks and wondered if he sensed my playfulness. Then he split the air again.

"You can use your phone. I won't narc on you." Caleb whipped out his cell. It was two generations old.

"Thanks," I said through my smile.

I cupped my phone in my lap, and stared at the screen, keeping a low profile in case Ms. Pepper popped her head through the door. I texted Dan, asking what happened after I saw him get led out of the cafeteria, but he didn't answer. Then, in a weird coincidence, I got a text from Chris.

CHRIS

Hey, do you know where Dan is?

ME

That's so weird, I just texted him asking the same thing.

CHRIS

lol.

I'll check around. I wonder if he left during the drill.

ME

I was in class with him.

I looked up and surveyed my surroundings, ensuring no teacher was in sight. I could see Caleb texting out of the corner of my eye, and he'd returned his feet to the top of the desk.

ME

We left the classroom together during the drill.

I looked at Caleb again, wondering if asking for his phone number would be weird.

CHRIS

I just found him and saw the red paint on his pants lol.

ME

He was an idiot and got himself shot haha.

CHRIS

Sounds about right.

When I found him by his car, he was talking to a weird, smelly guy.

ME

The guy I told you about at practice last week?

CHRIS

Yeah, I think so.

Dude, I think he's selling drugs or something because this guy was sketch.

ME

Are you serious?

It suddenly made sense why Dan got defensive when I asked him who that guy was. I wondered what Dan had gotten himself mixed up in, and if he needed help. Who was he selling drugs for, and why? Even though he'd been being more of a dick, I still didn't want Dan getting in trouble.

I sniffed the air, recalling a memory.

Caleb caught me. "What is it?"

"Huh?"

"It looked like you were smelling something," Caleb said.

Was he watching me when I wasn't looking?

"I had a math class here during my sophomore year. I can still smell the vomit."

Caleb put his phone away, smirking at me. "What happened?"

"One day during class, a kid named Jared raised his hand, saying he needed to go to the nurse, which the teacher allowed, but before he could leave the room, he threw up all over the floor in front of the desk you're sitting at."

"Gross," Caleb said with a chuckle.

"Oh, it gets worse." I grinned. "Everyone screamed. Jared curled over and vomited again, splashing some chunks onto the pant legs of other kids. I remember seeing the puddle of orange goo all over the floor. Then, the smell dusted the room like a sandstorm. It was so rotten that it made a girl named Alexis vomit all over her desk, which then caused a boy named Dustin to vomit in his hands. Jared had single-handedly created a chain reaction so disgusting that people started running from the room in fear, as if the vomit was poisonous. I remember laughing so hard, thinking it was something you'd only see in cartoons."

Caleb laughed. "Oh my god, I feel like I can smell it now!"

The smell lingered for weeks after the incident. I looked at my phone in my lap, anticipating a text from Chris, when the sudden screech of Caleb's chair startled me.

"I gotta go," Caleb said as he stood. "Tell Ms. Pepper I'm sorry."

"Wait!" I hollered, trying to stop him. "Where are you going?"

"A date!" Caleb shot through the door and took a hard left.

Another one?

The rest of the hour passed, and Ms. Pepper returned to release me, shocked to see Caleb had ducked out. She commended me for staying the whole time before letting me go. As I walked home, I wondered if Caleb was dating multiple people. I pictured him at a dinner table, sitting across from a man and a woman holding both their hands. Why was Caleb so hard to figure out? I tried to think of something else to occupy my mind, then remembered I hadn't reviewed the college applications Mr. Reily gave me.

When I entered the door, I smelled a Hot Pocket Dad had microwaved. He sat at the kitchen counter with his laptop open in front of him.

"Hey, son," he said without looking up.

I nodded to greet him and walked to the fridge. As usual, I had set the latest edition of the *Madison Monthly* on the counter next to the fridge, but it wasn't there anymore.

"Dad," I said as I twirled around. "I put the *Monthly* here. Did you move it?"

He looked at me. "I might've accidentally scooped it up with my stuff. Check the office on my desk." His eyes returned to the computer while my heart sank to my stomach.

"Can you go get it?" I asked with a lump in my throat. "Please?"

"Landon, I have to finish this email. And I need the office for a Zoom meeting in ten minutes, so be quick."

Dad didn't know I hadn't stepped foot in his office for months. I'd been too scared to even touch the doorknob, afraid I'd get a whiff of her perfume or see a pair of her shoes in the corner and break into pieces. But I knew Dad wouldn't budge. It was time I faced my fear.

THIRTEEN

There were only two rooms down the short hallway off the living room: a bathroom and Dad's office. I hadn't stepped down that hallway in six months. Even a glance in its direction sent a chill down my spine. It was a dark place of pain, anger, and sorrow. I avoided it at all costs. Anytime I needed to use the bathroom, I'd go upstairs.

I reached for the knob of the office and took a deep breath as if I were about to go underwater. I opened the door a crack just to peek in.

It's just a room.

The door creaked as I pushed it open and stepped in. The hallway was carpeted, but the office had a dark hardwood floor. In front of me was a large bay window looking into the backyard behind my dad's oak desk that he'd built himself when I was nine. I made a chip in the wood of one leg with a screwdriver, saying that I was helping with the build. It was the only imperfection on the desk. The walls to the left and right were floor-to-ceiling white shelves that made the room feel brighter. These shelves held everything from books to trophies, miniature flags, and things Dad collected from his military days. The ceiling was the only one in the house with exposed beams. A few potted plants scattered around the space had seen better days.

I took in the room as I'd done before, but it was different that time. I could almost hear her voice telling Dad to come to bed after a long night or saying 'knock, knock' before she entered the room to tell Dad dinner was ready. My chest heaved. I closed my eyes for a second to regroup before I noticed a stack of papers on the desk.

I rounded the large oak fixture and pulled out the leather chair. The sun was setting, reflecting off a frame on the desk that caught my eye. That picture was the only one in Dad's office. I picked it up as I sat in the chair. The chrome frame held a picture of my mom and me sitting on a haystack. I assumed we were at the annual fall county fair. I was only about a year old. We were wearing matching overalls. I was sitting between my mom's legs, looking up at her, smiling back at me. Her red hair was still long and wavy.

God, she looks so young.

It was long before the pain, before she lost her hair, and before the depression hit. She looked so carefree. The longer I stared at it, the easier I could hear her laugh. It was loud and contagious. I missed it so much.

"I wish you were here," I whispered. My chest tightened again as my eyes watered. I wiped them, sniffling a bit, setting the picture back down. I rubbed my forehead, wondering what she might say about my feelings for Caleb.

You probably already knew.

She told me when I was in second grade, I would come home every day gushing about a boy named Aaron. 'Aaron said this today,' I would tell her. 'Aaron wore this today.' 'Aaron and I played catch today! You're never gonna believe what Aaron had for lunch today!' All the signs must've been there, but they weren't important to her. As long as I was happy, she was happy.

I shuffled through the papers until I found the *Monthly* and stood, taking one last look at Mom before starting for the door. The air in that office felt cold, even without the AC running. It was a different cold, an empty cold. I felt like I could breathe again when I closed the door behind me.

I climbed the stairs to my room, slapped the paper on my desk, and plopped into the little wheely chair that always hurt my tailbone the longer I sat in it. I pulled the list of colleges out of my bag, picturing myself walking around each campus while googling them. The prompt of each application was simple: write an original short story no longer than 50 pages and no shorter than 20.

Easy. I can finish this and send it tomorrow!

I opened my laptop and clicked into a new Word document, ready to type anything that came to mind. But I sat there starring at the blank screen for five minutes, watching that little cursor line on the page blip in and out. Nothing was coming to me. I wiggled my fingers over the keyboard as if to conjure up any sort of inspiration. I had several stories saved on my desktop, but most of them were shit and underdeveloped. I wanted something new.

"Landon!" Dad called out from downstairs. I sighed and cupped my hands around my face in frustration that my thinking process had been interrupted.

"Yeah?" I yelled back.

"I need you for something!" The neighbors could probably hear us from down the street. I hopped down the stairs, eager to see what he wanted so I could get back to thinking.

"What is it?" I asked.

He collected his computer off the table and started toward his office. "I need you to deposit that check for me," he said, pointing at the kitchen island. "The card is there, too; it's a donation, so I need it done today."

"Dad, you know you can deposit it from your phone, right?"

"I don't trust that." He headed down the short hallway. "Just do it, please. I have to get to this meeting." The last words were muffled as he'd already closed himself in his office.

I sauntered to the counter and picked up the check. The donation was $2,000 from a woman named Ruth Steinberg. I checked the back for Dad's signature before folding it in half and slipping it into my pocket. I grabbed the ATM card with COLOSSAL BANK in bold letters across the front. Colossal was a local bank unique to Madison County. It was a good ten-minute drive away.

Colossal Bank was in a plaza with a few other businesses. I parked just in front of the ATM attached to the outside wall of the bank. As I stepped out of the car, a little boy exiting Sal's ice cream shop gave a high-pitched laugh.

I walked up to the ATM and inserted Dad's card. Every time I hit a button, an obnoxious beeping sang. I slid the check into a slot, and it sucked in the paper. I imagined a round, furry monster inside the machine that fed on paper and threw up dollar bills. I chuckled, thinking what the beast might sound like, until a familiar voice caught my ear. Youthful and raspy. I knew right away it was Caleb.

I turned to follow his voice. He was sitting at a picnic table outside Sal's ice cream shop, across from the boy I had seen seconds before. They were both laughing. Hours ago, Caleb ran out of my detention flustered, saying he had a date.

BEEP! BEEP! BEEP! The machine yelled at me to take my dad's card, startling me.

Caleb had noticed, too. "Landon?" He called out.

I pulled the card from the machine, slipped it into my pocket, and turned to Caleb, trying to act surprised. Looking everywhere but the ice cream shop, I wanted to play it cool as if I wasn't just watching him and the boy. Then I focused on Caleb, and waved. "Oh, hey!" To my surprise, Caleb motioned for me to join them. I nodded and took a deep breath, trying not to freak out as I approached.

Holy shit. Is that his son?

I searched the ice cream shop through the window for Caleb's potential girlfriend. My hands balled to fists in my pockets. I wasn't ready to know that Caleb had a kid or a woman in his life. As I got closer, I saw that there weren't any customers inside. Caleb and his son were the only ones there. I shuffled to the front of the picnic table, where the scent of sweet sugar danced in the air.

Caleb looked up at me, squinting his eyes from the setting sun. "Wanna sit?"

"Uh, yeah, sure." My body felt stiff as I sat beside Caleb, still unsure what was happening.

"Hi!" the little voice said from across the table.

"Hey," I said. Glancing at Caleb, I think he could tell I was confused.

"This is Parker," Caleb said. "My little brother."

The weight of confusion and worry lifted off my shoulders. *I'm such an idiot.* "Oh," I said with a dopey smile before looking at Parker. "I'm Landon."

"Hi, Landon," Parker said. His words came between each lick to his soft-serve cone with rainbow sprinkles. "I'm nine, how old are you?"

"Sorry," Caleb said. "He's very inquisitive."

I smiled. Parker and I had that in common. "I'm eighteen."

Caleb's ice cream of choice was a banana split. Then he caught me looking.

"You want a bite?"

"Um," I said, lingering on the word. "Sure." I reached for the utensil, but Caleb was already moving to feed me a clump of vanilla and chocolate stuck together. I accepted his offer and closed my teeth over the cold spoon, which sent a chill down my spine. I just nodded as I moved the ice cream around the roof of my mouth to melt it.

Caleb returned his spoon to the frozen dessert. "Good, right?"

"Yeah," I said, letting the ice cream melt before I spoke again. "What happened to your date?"

Caleb flashed his dimples. "He is my date." He was the type of person who chewed his ice cream. My teeth ached just watching him do it. "Once a week, we see a movie, and then we have ice cream," Caleb said.

Everything about him was a surprise. What would he say next? I was a sponge, letting every one of his words seep into my pores. I imagined the small box labeled 'Caleb' in my mind overflowing with files.

"Yeah," Parker said before another lick of his cone. "We like movies."

"Listen to this," Caleb said to Parker, pointing a thumb at me, "he's never seen Jurassic Park."

"What?!" Parker said. He'd gone into a complete sugar rage, standing out of his seat. "That's impossible! It's like the best movie ever made!"

"That's what I said!" Caleb pointed his spoon at Parker, matching the younger boy's excitement. They laughed together, making me laugh too.

"I'll see it soon, I promise," I said, covering my face in shame.

"Caleb has the Blu-ray," Parker said proudly. "Come to our house, you can watch it!"

The words made Caleb go silent. He just sat there, looking down at his ice cream as he cleared his throat.

"Finish your ice cream, kid," Caleb said. Awkwardness hung in the air.

"So," I said to Caleb. "Your date from this past weekend you told me about..."

Caleb nodded. "I was with Parker."

Wow, now I really feel dumb.

All the women I had conjured up in my head, all the restaurants I pictured Caleb sitting in, it was all for nothing. I was so naïve. Nothing about Caleb so far was stereotypical, I had to stop thinking about him that way.

"Our home life isn't the best," Caleb said, looking at me. "So we try to get away every once in a while."

"Yeah, Luke is a real asshole," Parker spouted.

Caleb shot a look at Parker, "Language, kid. I told you, you can't say that till you're ten." Caleb eyed me again. "Luke's a real asshole."

Parker smiled.

"Who's Luke?" I asked

Caleb huffed. "Our mom's boyfriend."

"Oh, okay," I said, unsure how to respond appropriately. "Cool." My eyes widened. "I mean, not cool, as in, like, cool that your home life isn't the best." My cheeks warmed.

"No," Caleb said, chuckling. "I get it."

It was cute that he took his little brother to the movies. My eyes traveled to Parker again, inspecting him. He was a unique-looking kid. He had a similar face shape as Caleb and even had the same bronze skin, but he had red hair and freckles all over his face. Caleb's words replayed in my mind from that night at the baseball field as if they were on a tape recorder being rewound and played repeatedly.

You remind me of someone special to me. You both have red hair.

The realization crashed over me like a tidal wave. Caleb was talking about Parker. Just thinking about it made me smile again, and I noticed something else unique about the boy. His left eye caught some reflection, and his pupil was clouded.

"I have to pee," Parker said. "I'll be right back."

"I'll be here," Caleb said as Parker stood and glided into the shop, already crunching through his cone.

"I didn't know you had a brother," I said, watching Caleb take another bite.

"You don't know a lot of things about me," Caleb said with a mouth full of ice cream and a smirk.

"Okay," I said, slapping the picnic table. "Do you like, get off on being mysterious or something? I don't get it."

Caleb laughed and wiped his mouth with a napkin. "No. I just don't need everyone knowing my business."

"How does anyone ever get to know you then?"

"Fine." Caleb placed his napkin on the empty bowl and swung his leg around to straddle the bench and face me. "Today's your lucky day. What do you wanna know?"

My eyes widened. The lights and circuits in my brain erupted. *Anything?!* I imagined an arrow hitting the bullseye of a target as I found my question. "What's going on at home?"

"Wow." Caleb chuckled. "I was expecting, like, 'What's your favorite color?' Or, 'What's your favorite movie?' But you're starting deep."

"I'm sorry." I waved my hands in front of me. "You don't have to answer that; that's way too personal."

"No, no," Caleb said. "You took the leap; you're in deep now, Lan."

Hearing him call me Lan again warmed my chest. "All right, all right," I said, resting my hands on my lap.

"We don't have much." Caleb glanced into the ice cream shop. Parker had sat at a table inside, flipping through a magazine. "We don't have the nicest clothes or even a car. We walk everywhere. And we don't have the nicest house. We live with our mom and her shitty boyfriend. The house is his. Our mom is only with him because he keeps her doped up. The roof over our heads is just a bonus." Caleb spoke directly and to the point, not adding unnecessary detail. "They fight all the time. We all do. He hits her, so I hit him, and he hits me back." Caleb rubbed the top of his right hand. I glanced at minor bruises on his knuckles. Caleb looked toward Parker again. "He knows I'd kill him if he ever touched Parker."

"Has he tried?"

"Not yet," Caleb said, looking at me. "I hate that Parker has to be around all that."

"So, you and Parker have the same dad?" I was prying, but he answered quickly.

"Yeah." Caleb leaned an arm against the table. "He left when I was eleven. I used to think it was my fault," Caleb laughed.

"Wow," I said with a lump in my throat. "I'm sorry." I was stunned by Caleb's honesty. He wasn't this beast of a criminal that everyone at school thought he was. He was a person with real trauma and feelings.

"Soon after my dad left, my mom found out she was pregnant with Parker. We moved around a lot until she found the only guy who didn't mind a woman with two kids. And we've been with him ever since."

A bell rang from behind me as the shop door swung open. Parker walked out and up to Caleb, placing his small hands on Caleb's broad shoulders. "Can we go home now?"

"Sure, kid," Caleb said with a smile.

I hopped up. "Let me give you a ride."

"Oh, no," Caleb said. "You don't have to."

"It's no problem. I swear."

Caleb shook his head. "You probably have other things you could—"

"Please, Caleb?" Parker said, smushing his face into the side of Caleb's. "I don't feel like walking back."

Caleb hesitated, staring at his brother. "Okay, fine," he said, wrapping his arms around Parker's little body and squeezing him. I could tell Parker held Caleb in the palm of his hand. Watching them together really warmed my heart.

FOURTEEN

"I like this car," Parker said after he'd been sitting in the back seat for all of ten minutes.

Caleb twisted in the passenger seat. "Why this car of all cars?"

"I don't know."

I glanced in the rearview mirror just in time to see Parker's exaggerated shoulder shrug. We laughed as Caleb uncoiled back into his seat.

"Seems legit," I said, glancing at a smiling Caleb. I swear his teeth could reflect the sun.

"Oh," Caleb said. "Take this right coming up."

He pointed to a large wooden sign. In an old western font, it read, 'Skowhegan Trailer Park Housing.'

I turned through the gate onto the dirt road. It was a straight, narrow path that looked forgotten about, and it continued as far as I could see. On each side were trailer houses, all similar in build but different colors.

"It's the sixth one in, on the right," Caleb said, scratching at his jeans.

I pulled up in front of a gray trailer—one of the longer ones. The porch was unpainted wood, as if it had just been built. Two beach chairs rested to the right side, with a small white plastic table in between.

I had barely stopped before Parker unbuckled himself and rushed out the door.

"Parker!" Caleb shouted through his open window. Parker stopped in his tracks before ascending the three small steps of the porch. "What do you say to Landon?"

Parker rushed to the passenger side window with as much excitement as he used to exit the car. He popped his head through the window and looked me in the eye. "Thank you," he said, making two words into a one-syllable sound. And just like that, Parker was off in a flash, returning to his original route.

"Anytime!" I shouted just before he slipped through the screen door. I glanced at Caleb, who smiled as he watched Parker enter the house. "His eyes are—"

"I know," Caleb said, looking at me. "It's one of the first things people notice."

"I've never seen anything like that before. Mind if I ask what happened?"

"My mom caused that one," Caleb said, scratching the back of his head. "Cocaine is her favorite, but meth has always been cheaper." I turned the car off as Caleb spoke. "She started using after my dad left. Even though she knew she was pregnant, she didn't stop. The doctors noticed something was wrong while giving Parker an exam a week after he was born. They figured out his left eye wasn't responding to light at all. The meth my mom was smoking had destroyed Parker's retina. He doesn't have sight in that eye." Caleb glanced out the windshield as a woman walked toward us with her small dog on a leash trailing behind her. "There wasn't anything the doctors could do. As time went on, his eye got cloudy."

"Damn. That must be tough for him."

"Naw, he's never known anything different, so I don't think it bothers him much."

"Everyone has their imperfections, I guess." I shrugged, feeling like that was something my dad would say.

"What're yours?" Caleb chuckled. "Red hair and pale skin?"

"Oh, okay!" I said, acting offended. I pantomimed, opening the driver-side door to storm out. Caleb laughed. "We can't all have perfect tanned skin!"

"I get it from my dad's side of the family," Caleb said with a smile. Every time I saw the dimples in his cheeks, it sent me soaring through the air. "He's Puerto Rican. Luckily, Parker got most of our dad's traits. He's kind and curious... for now."

"And your mom?" I asked.

"She's white." His brow perked. "You're all Irish, I assume?"

"Oh, completely! My mom is..." I paused and then tried to speed up my next set of words as if I had lost no time in between. "... She was a redhead too." Caleb smirked and nodded. I hoped he couldn't tell I was thrown off. As much as I loved Caleb opening up to me, I wasn't ready to do the same.

"Parker gets his red hair from our mom too."

The conversation came to a lull, and the awkward air returned. We stared as the woman with her dog passed the car. Caleb waved at her.

"Do you ever talk to Parker about your dad?" It surprised me I hadn't scared him off yet.

"We've shown him a few pictures," Caleb said, unfazed by my constant questions. "I tell him things I remember. How gentle he used to be. He was the polar opposite of the guy that my mom's with now. I try to remind Parker that not every guy is a bully." Caleb's eyes met mine, and I glanced at my lap as a lightning bolt shot through my stomach.

"My dad used to be more of a hard ass," I said. "He's cooled down a lot over the past couple of months. But he used to talk to me like a drill sergeant."

"At least he had the balls to stick around," Caleb said with a tone I hadn't heard from him. It was colder.

"So," I said, unsure if I should continue my questions.

He's still in the car, I haven't scared him off yet.

"Earlier, you said you felt like it was your fault; why is that?"

Caleb let out a small huff. He didn't answer right away, so I panicked and said, "You totally don't have to answer that. My questions are way too much, I'm sorry."

"You're good," Caleb said, staring out his window. "It was almost ten years ago, but it still feels fresh in my head. The Christmas before he left, he was excited to give me a specific present. I remember him handing me the gift, and I noticed how messy the wrapping job was." I stared at him. His eyes followed a flock of birds flying by. "I ripped through the paper and stared at what was inside. A baseball cap." Caleb looked at me and laughed, "I swear it was the ugliest hat I'd ever seen."

"Oh, no," I said through gritted teeth.

"It was like this weird combination of blues and browns, like someone had stitched two separate ugly hats together into one. I made a face and tossed it aside with a quick thank you. 'Well, try it on.' my dad said. I grabbed it off the floor and put it on. I wasn't a kid that was into wearing hats." Caleb reenacted the scene with his hands, pretending to put on the hat and unwrap a gift. "I pulled it off just as quickly as I put it on. My dad was disappointed, but I was too excited for more gifts to notice. I remember tossing it under my bed that night and forgetting about it." Caleb sighed. "Two days after Christmas, I woke up and could hear my mom crying in her bedroom. I checked on her; the room was a mess. She was sitting alone on the bed, just sobbing. I was so confused. Then I noticed the top of their dresser was empty. All of my dad's deodorants and colognes were gone. The closet door was open, most of his clothes were missing, and hangers were scattered on the floor."

A small pit formed in my stomach. I knew what it felt like to find a parent crying alone.

Caleb continued as he fiddled with the strings hanging from his thin hoodie, "I asked her where Dad was, and all I could hear between her sobs was that he left. I didn't believe her and searched every room, hoping he'd be there, but he wasn't. Then I thought about that ugly hat." The sun was set, and the street lights popped around us. Our eyes caught the porch light turn on from Caleb's trailer. "Every time I left the house, I'd put on the hat he got me. I wore it everywhere, I guess. I hoped he would somehow see me wearing it and want to come home with us. But we never saw him again."

I pictured a smaller version of Caleb with the same face but shaggier hair, walking around the mall with his ugly hat on, holding his mom's hand with hope in his eyes that would never be fulfilled.

"It was probably my mom that drove him away with her budding drug habits," Caleb said. "Of course, we've never talked about it. Her relationship with drugs got stronger. I was always the one taking care of Parker. Made me feel like an adult real quick."

"I'm sorry. That's a lot to go through as a kid," I said.

"You'd be surprised."

Suddenly, the screen door was thrown open, and a tall, bald man stepped onto the porch.

"Speak of the devil," Caleb mumbled, looking through the window at the man wearing a dark blue jumpsuit covered in grease stains. His beer belly seemed to be pushing the buttons to their limits. He stood there barefoot, staring at us.

"Yer ma needs ya fer somethin'," the bald man in our direction.

"Coming," Caleb said before turning to me. "So, think you've got enough information for the book I assume you're writing about me?" He smiled.

"Damn, I forgot to take notes. Can you say all that again?"

It felt good to make Caleb laugh.

"Thanks again for the ride," Caleb said, opening the car door. "I'll see you around."

"Yeah, see ya," I said, watching him walk up the steps, his work boots clunked against the wood. He pushed past the tall man without a word of acknowledgment. My eyes locked on the porch; I didn't want Caleb to leave. The tall man stood there, giving my car the once over before disappearing inside. I turned the key in the ignition, rolled up the passenger window, did a U-turn, and drove back toward the main road.

The car was so quiet after they left. I couldn't stop thinking about

Caleb and the story he told. Still surprised he opened up to me. I wondered if he had that kind of relationship with anyone else or if I was a fluke. Maybe my questions were enough to nag him into submission. Or he was telling me so I would shut up. I couldn't stop thinking about how he acted with Parker, either. For a guy so mysterious and brooding, he was so warm and patient with his little brother. Seeing them eating ice cream, I would never imagine them having a tough time at home. I imagined Caleb arguing loudly with the bald man, whom I assumed was his mom's boyfriend. I pictured Caleb playing with army men in Parker's bedroom to distract him from the voices growing louder as their mom and the bald man got drunk. I honestly couldn't imagine Caleb breaking the law. But as he said, there's a lot I didn't know about him.

As soon as I walked back into my house, I remembered my college applications. Inspiration hit, and I was ready to write my short story.

"You were gone a while," Dad said from the couch, scaring me half to death. The entire living room was dark except for the small lamp that was lit next to the recliner he was sitting in. His phone screen illuminated his lap.

"Yeah, sorry, I ran into a friend who needed a ride," I said, moving toward the stairs.

"Hang on, son," Dad said before I could touch the first carpeted step. I was eager to get to my computer before the inspiration faded. I stopped and turned toward him. "This article says I'm a few points ahead in the race."

"That's great, Dad." I pretended to care and started for the steps, but his voice stopped me.

"Landon, can you wait just a second?"

"I'm sorry, but I have this assignment."

"Well, my team recommended I speak at a church tomorrow, and they think it would look good if my son were there with me."

"Dad, I have school tomorrow, it's a Wednesday."

"It's after school."

"I have practice; I can't," I said, thankful I could use it as an excuse. I didn't want to go to church.

"Coach told me he pushed practice to Thursday. He's gonna announce it tomorrow morning." He pocketed his phone as my excuse burned up.

I rolled my eyes. *Of all the days to reschedule practice.* "Who goes to church on a Wednesday?"

Dad stood. "A lot of people." He crossed the living room to the kitchen counter. "And we'll be two of them tomorrow, so come home right after school and put on something nice. You don't have a say in this one."

"Fine," I said as I started up the stairs, leaping over every other step. I sat at my desk and revived my sleeping laptop. The familiar blank page popped on my screen, and my fingers danced across the keyboard. For the next two hours, I was transported into my little world, where characters came to life, and all I could hear was the clicking of the keys.

FIFTEEN

"I can't believe you got yourself shot," I said to Dan as we stepped out of the school and into the front courtyard.

Dan puffed his chest. "I told you that if it came down to it, I was gonna control my fate."

"You're such an idiot." I laughed, shoving him. "Did it hurt?"

"Have you ever been shot with a paintball, Griffin?"

"No, I can't say I have."

"Well, it hurts like a bitch," Dan said.

My brow raised. "You got shot in the leg, princess," I said. "I'm sure you'll survive."

Dan returned the shove. "Fuck off."

I tried to catch my footing but backed into someone. I turned to say sorry, meeting eyes with Steven. Thanks to my bump, Steven spilled his green juice all over himself. His white shirt was splattered with what looked like an infant's vomit. Dan laughed, whereas I clamored to apologize. "Steven, I'm so sorry. Dan pushed—"

"Did we ruin your blouse, faggot?" Dan said, mimicking a crying baby, and bringing his fists to his eyes to wipe the fake tears.

"You're such an asshole!" Steven said, storming off toward the school's entrance.

His words triggered Dan into rage mode. "What did you call me?!" I had to block Dan from going after Steven. "Come say that to my face, pussy!"

"Dan, stop!" I said, trying to pull his focus. Dan's eyes remained on Steven, but his body language calmed. "Why does he set you off so easily?" My hand dropped off his chest.

"Because he's a fuckin' freak, bro. Every time I see his fairy face, I want to slap the shit out of him." Dan bent down, picking up his backpack that fell off his shoulder. "His parents should send him to one of those conversion camps or some shit and set him straight."

"You don't seriously think that works, do you?" Tasha asked as she and Lauren approached us on the sidewalk. Dan was speaking loud enough for everyone to hear.

"I remember my pastor talking about it when we would go to church," Dan said. His breathing had gone back to normal. "One time, he brought this guy to the altar as an example. He said the guy went through this program that turned him straight after being gay his whole life."

"That's impossible," Lauren said. "You can't just switch it off."

"Yeah, it sounds like a bunch of bullshit to me," Tasha said, eyeing Dan. "Not all Christians and Catholics support conversation therapy."

Dan clasped his hands together with a slap. "The guy had a wife and kids! They were sitting right there in the front row! It fuckin' works, trust me."

I pictured older versions of Lauren and me. We were living in my parent's house. Everything was the same except for the baby playpen in the living room. And no more carpet up the steps; everything was glistening hardwood. I had a few gray hairs poking through on the sides of my head, and I could hear Lauren in the upstairs bathroom laughing. A smaller giggle echoed down the stairway, accompanied by water splashing about. *Could this be my future?* I saw myself standing at the kitchen counter, watching the side door as the knob turned, and Caleb walked through, startling me back to reality when I saw his face in the vision.

"You can't argue science!" Lauren said with a scoff as she reached for my arm.

"Someone needs to check that guy's browser history," Tasha said with a chuckle. "Then we'd know for sure." We all laughed.

I wondered if my dad would send me away if he found out I had feelings for Caleb. He might see conversion camp as a sort of boot camp. From the way Dad reacted to *Will & Grace*, it wouldn't surprise me if he knew about conversion therapy. I imagined running away from pastors trying to force me onto a bus.

Dan's voice broke my thought, "Me and Chris have our costumes for the party. You guys are still in, right?"

"Duh!" Tasha said. "That reminds me, I need to update the event. I should do that tonight."

I still had to pull a costume together for the ridiculous party.

Lauren sighed. "I'm gonna have serious FOMO, you guys! Why'd you have to have a party when I'm in New York?"

"My birthday gets rescheduled for no one!" Dan said dramatically. "I gotta go. Since practice got moved to tomorrow, I'm gonna go see this chick." Dan held out his fist, and I bumped it.

"Wear protection!" I shouted as he walked away. Dan turned and walked backward, flashing a peace sign that he flicked his tongue between.

"He's disgusting," Tasha said. "All right, girlie, I got shit to do. I'll text you later!" Tasha hugged Lauren goodbye, and I got a wave. "Bye, Landon."

"See ya," I said.

Tasha walked away as Lauren placed herself in front of me. Things still felt awkward between us since the night we tried to hook up.

Lauren's hair flowed in the slight breeze that smelled like gas from all the cars leaving the parking lot. She wasn't wearing her fake glasses that day. "What're you gonna wear to the party?" She asked, tucking her hair behind her ear.

"I haven't thought about it yet," I said. "I just want something simple, ya know?"

"I can get you some tights from the costume closet; maybe you can be Peter Pan."

"You think Dan would ever let me live that one down?"

"Absolutely not."

We got quiet, and I wondered if she told Tasha or Steven about how I couldn't get hard that night.

"Let's go to Lucky's," Lauren said, breaking the silence.

"I can't today. I'm sorry," I said with a frown, even though I'd been craving a chocolate milkshake.

"How come?" She asked.

"My dad is making me go to church with him. His team wants him to speak there, hoping to draw in some more voters or something. He's making me go with him. Said it would be good if people saw him with his family. Lucky me..." I raised my fists in jest of celebration, "... I'm the only one left."

Lauren slapped my arm. She didn't like my dark humor. "That sounds nice. Maybe we can go to Lucky's on Sunday, then?"

I shrugged. "Yeah, that works for me."

Lauren grabbed me by the hands, pulling me closer to her. "I feel like we need to have some 'us' time and reconnect."

"I agree," I said, pushing away the thoughts of the night I rejected her.

Lauren smiled widely. "It's a date then!"

I nodded, and she stood on her tiptoes for a kiss. I was surprised when she slipped her tongue between my lips, kissing me deeper. My hands let go of hers, but I continued to kiss her back.

"Landon!" Dad shouted from across the street. I unlocked it from Lauren, seeing Dad beside his car. "We gotta go! Get upstairs and change."

"Coming!" I looked at Lauren. "I'll text you later?"

"Okay," she said. "Have fun."

"Yeah, I'll try." I pulled away from her but could feel she wanted another kiss, so I planted a quick one on her lips before running across the street.

"Love you!"

"You too!" I hollered without looking back.

I opened my closet door and spotted a black blazer I hadn't worn since my junior homecoming dance. I grabbed it off the hanger and tossed it on my bed. My jeans that day were dark and a tighter fit, so I left them on. I glided to the bottom drawer of my dresser, popped it open, and pulled out a red button-up I'd gotten from my grandma for Christmas two years prior. I pulled my T-shirt over my head and slipped into the red one. As I buttoned, it got tighter and tighter around my shoulders. It was almost impossible to button the top without choking myself, so I left it undone. Checking myself in the mirror made me wince; I could see every rib and muscle. "I can't wear this to a church," I said, twisting to see what it looked like from the back.

Dad's car horn blared, so I quickly unbuttoned the shirt and let it fall to the floor. I jogged back to my bottom drawer, pulling out a blue button-up shirt instead. It was much more comfortable than the red one.

"Things seem to be going well with Lauren," Dad said as he turned the steering wheel, pulling off our street.

"Yeah." I shrugged, embarrassed that he'd seen us making out.

"How'd the assignment turn out last night?"

"Fine, actually," I said, staring out the window. "I got it submitted."

The car ahead of us didn't move when the light turned green, so Dad knocked on his horn, "C'mon man."

I hadn't told Dad about the college applications, about them being out of state, or that I was submitting for writing programs.

"You should hear from the state schools any day now," Dad said as if he could read my mind. "I know you'll get a scholarship. I can feel it."

A pit formed in my stomach again. I wanted to make him happy and proud, but how did I tell him I didn't want to pursue football? Thinking of his face shrinking into disappointment filled me with dread. Everything outside my car window was so cookie-cutter. Every house looked the same. Every other front yard had kids playing in it. People walked their perfect little dogs. I thought about the vision I had, hearing Lauren laughing with a baby in the upstairs bathroom. Could I feel fulfilled in that kind of life? I'd never visited a big city. Who knows if I would even like it? I'd be a fish out of water, and everyone would be able to tell how phony I was.

As we pulled into the church parking lot, I read the marquee sign facing the street. It was red at the top, with bold white letters that said, 'Madison Catholic Bible Church.' Underneath the header was a digital screen that read, 'Guest Speaker: Republican Mayoral Candidate Curtis Griffin.'

We exited the car after parking in a spot reserved for someone named Pastor Williams.

I glanced at Dad. "Where should I go?"

"You can go through the front," a voice said behind me. Her heels clicked against the pavement. My dad's campaign manager, Grace, was close to his age and wore a burgundy blazer and a matching knee-length skirt. She held a clipboard in one hand as if about to take roll call. "I'm gonna take your dad around back with me," Grace said.

I nodded. "Okay."

"You look very handsome, Landon," she said, joining Dad behind the car.

"Oh, thanks." I smoothed out my blazer. Compliments made me feel awkward. "Good luck, Dad."

"I'll see you in there, buddy," he said, walking away with Grace. I lingered on them momentarily as she passed Dad some note cards. I shoved my hands in my pockets and followed the crowd of mostly older white people into the church. There were a few empty pews in the back where I sat, hoping no one would join me. Most of the men were dressed in suits. Each seemed to have a woman attached to his arm, wearing some pastel dress that reminded me of a carton of Easter eggs.

The pews filled up; I never expected so many people to want to listen to Dad speak; I always thought his speeches were a snooze. The scent of old wood and upholstered fabric hung as if the seating hadn't changed in a hundred years. The acoustics were strong. The echoes of everyone's voice floated up through the high ceilings, bounced off the rafters, and returned to my ears as one collective sound of chatter. A white-haired man approached the podium at the altar. I wondered if he was Pastor Williams.

"Welcome everyone!" The Pastor said into the microphone, shutting down all forms of conversation from the crowd. "We are so blessed to have Mr. Griffin here to speak to our congregation today; thank you all so much for being here." The pastor pulled a notecard from his pocket and placed it on the podium. "Before we bring out our guest, I just wanted to remind ya'll of all the upcoming fundraising events."

That's when I tuned out.

My family was never the church-going type. My mom would ask us to go to Sunday mass at Easter and Christmas, but we were never in church every week. I assumed it was a ploy by my dad's campaign team to string in the votes of the conservative church folk. I squirmed in my seat. Religion always felt cult-like to me. I never understood the draw to it. I was a co-captain of a football team, so I could appreciate the camaraderie and sense of community, but fearing God while telling other religious people that their beliefs weren't valid just seemed off to me. But those were the people Dad hoped to represent. He'd been lucky enough to stay clear of hot-button political issues so far, like abortion or gun control. He got by on being a blue-collar, military family man. That was enough for most people in Madison.

"Good afternoon, everyone!" Dad said from the podium. By then, he had been superintendent of Madison High School for three years, so he had no trouble speaking to an audience; he was pretty good at it. "It's an honor to speak in front of you today..."

Dad was going into his plan to boost the jobs and wages for working families in Madison when my phone vibrated. I inched it out of my pocket as if Dad had eagle eyes, afraid he'd catch me not paying attention and call me out in front of everyone.

I glanced at my phone. It was a Grindr notification. Every night before bed, I would see the app on my screen, but my fun conversations with Steven kept me from deleting it. I triggered the app, seeing a message from Steven.

THEATRENERD245, 18

Hey!

SPORTYGUY83, 18

Hey, how are you?

THEATRENERD245, 18

I'm okay. Kind of having a shitty afternoon.

SPORTYGUY83, 18

Oh, I'm sorry. You wanna talk about it?

Steven and I had more than a few lengthy conversations on Grindr by then. I was getting to know him, and he was getting to know the real me, not the fake me I portrayed when I was at school. I was weightless and free when I messaged him. Able to talk about Caleb without using his name, of course. Talking about Caleb's dimples, how sexy they were, and how I could stare into his eyes for days felt great. Now and then, Steven would try to slip in questions to figure out who I was, but I always caught on and changed the subject.

THEATRENERD245, 18

There's just this guy at school who continuously makes my life hell.

SPORTYGUY83, 18

Oh?

THEATRENERD245, 18

He seems like he goes out of his way to embarrass me in front of people or threaten me.

SPORTYGUY83, 18

I'm sorry, man.

THEATRENERD245, 18

I've been dealing with this for four years, I'm so tired of it, you know? I can't wait to get out of this white bread town and finally start living.

That sounded nice to me, too.

THEATRENERD245, 18

We used to be friends. The things I know about him could ruin his life. But I'm a nice person!

Steven piqued my curiosity. What did he know about Dan that I didn't?

SPORTYGUY83, 18

What do you mean? Like what?

THEATRENERD245, 18

Ugh, it doesn't matter. I need to get out of this negative headspace! >_< What're you up to?

SPORTYGUY83, 18:

Believe it or not, I'm in a church right now, haha.

THEATRENERD245, 18

OMG no way! How are you not burned to a crisp by now? Lol, I never pictured you as a closeted bible boy!

SPORTYGUY83, 18

Yeah, I'm not exactly.

THEATRENERD245, 18

Well, you better get out of there before they make you straight!

Nothing sounds worse right now than being straight. lol

I heard my name from Dad's booming voice and shoved my phone into my pocket. He was gesturing to me, introducing me as his son. Everyone sitting in the pews turned around and smiled at me. I slid down in my seat a bit. Seeing all of their smiling faces gave me the creeps. Luckily, Dad moved on quickly and brought the attention back to him. I sighed, laying my head against the back of the pew. *This speech is gonna take forever.*

SIXTEEN

I opened my eyes to the rafters of the church. A beam of light shone through a stained-glass window that led to a huge wooden cross at the altar. I sprung up in the pew, realizing the crowd had whittled down to a select few. I saw Dad helping arrange folding chairs into a circle in front of the altar stage. The remaining people congregated around the circle.

"Landon," Dad said. "Come join us, please."

I stood and brushed my hands down my blazer, confused about where everyone had gone without me noticing.

I walked down the aisle as the others took their seats in the circle. "What's going on?" I asked.

"Take a seat," Dad said, motioning to an empty chair.

"Um... okay." I glanced at the others who were seated: men of varying ages. A guy with a thick beard and bandaged wrists sat across from me. Next to him was a skinny teenager, no older than fourteen. The more I looked at everyone's faces, the more I realized how miserable they looked. Then I noticed something even more strange. Everyone wore white slacks and a white shirt—some long sleeves, some short, but all the same shade. Dad stood behind me, and I looked at him over my shoulder. "Dad, what is this?"

"They're here to help, son," he said, staring forward.

"Help with what?" I asked, following his gaze. The white-haired pastor stepped into the chair circle, taking the last empty seat. "Dad..." I said, wondering why he hadn't answered me.

"Don't be nervous, Landon," the pastor said. "My name is Pastor Williams. We are all here today for you."

"What do you mean for me?" I asked. A man with a freshly shaved head to my right fiddling his thumbs stared at his lap.

"Your father came to me with concerns," Pastor Williams said. "I recommended that you join our program here at the church so we could help set you on the right path."

I tilted my head, still in the dark. "What? What path?" I looked at Dad again. "What is he talking about?"

Dad shushed me and placed his hands on my shoulders.

"These men," Pastor Williams said. "Have all been set free under my guidance." He pointed at the man sitting to my right, "Long feminine hair afflicted Lyle. People would often mistake him for a woman. We started him on his path by shaving it off."

Lyle remained silent.

"And Carson." Pastor Williams said, pointing at the bearded man. "He was so distraught over his addiction to pornography that he tried to take his own life." Carson pulled down his sleeves to hide his bandages. "And this poor boy, Kevin," Pastor Williams said as he kneeled, placing his hand on the teenage boy's thigh. Kevin jerked his leg away, and the Pastor continued, "They caught him fornicating with the son of the family next door, so his parents sent him to me."

"This has nothing to do with me," I said, attempting to stand from my chair, but Dad pushed me back down from my shoulders and held them.

"Oh, but it does, Landon," the Pastor said, walking behind Kevin. He stroked the boy's hair as if petting a puppy. Just watching it sent a chill down my spine. "Every man in this circle is plagued by homosexual perversion."

"I'm not!" I squirmed in my seat. "Dad, tell him!"

"We know, Landon," Pastor Williams said, penetrating the circle again and strolling toward me. "We know about the videos you've watched." He inched closer. "We know about the app on your phone. We know..." He kneeled in front of me. "... about the feelings you have for Caleb."

My eyes widened. I wanted to refute the claims but couldn't speak. Pastor Williams placed both hands on my thighs and crawled them toward my crotch. "Do you admit to these sins?" His face moved closer to mine as his hands inched up my legs. I wanted to scream, but my voice was trapped in my throat. "Can you repent for your sins?!" The pastor screamed in my face. Flicks of saliva hit my cheeks. My jaw clenched, and my teeth ground together. The pastor let go of my thighs and stood. "We must start you on your path to righteousness," the Pastor said as he walked around the circle again, his hands clasped behind his back.

Dad pulled me up and guided me onto the altar stage. "Dad, stop!" I shouted, my voice finally breaking through. "What're you doing?!" I glimpsed his face. His eyes were glazed over. A shell of the man I knew. He was a holy bodyguard, hauling me toward my fate. Dad pushed me face-first against the wooden cross behind the podium where he'd given his speech. My right cheek burned from the hard slap against the mahogany, and it smelled like a campfire. "Dad, please!"

Two men dressed in white tied my hands around the other side of the thick cross. The rope squeezed tighter around my wrists, digging into my skin. It all happened so fast, it was difficult for my brain to catch up. Pastor Williams slid a pair of scissors up the middle of my blazer and again to my blue button-up shirt. The frayed fabric tickled my sides as they fell, revealing my bare skin. My knees shook.

"What the fuck!" My voice echoed through the church. "Dad, make them stop!"

"This is for the best, son," Dad whispered.

A searing sting hit my back. I scrunched my eyes and let out a yelp.

"This is where we all must begin on our path!" Pastor Williams' voice boomed through my ears. I looked behind me, struggling to break free from my restraints. Every man dressed in white lined themselves in a single file, ready to take the whip from the person in front. The second man stepped toward me. It was Carson with glazed eyes. He raised his arm and shot down the whip against my skin with no remorse. The pain splintered into my skull, and I let out a loud cry.

It was the fourth lash that sent me crumbling to my knees. The teenage boy held the whip, raised it without hesitation, and connected it to my body with an overwhelming force. My skin ripped open, sending spits of blood into the air. I went numb after the sixth time they hit me. All I could feel was the blood trickling down my back and tears covering my cheeks. I pressed my forehead against the wood as blood pooled around my knees.

"Dad, please make them stop," I said through a shortened breath, sobbing as another strike of the whip hit. "I don't want to be gay, I promise!" I screamed, unable to withstand the torture anymore. I hoped my words would make them subside, but the whip cracked again before feeling the burn.

"Tell God what you're thankful for!" The Pastor yelled. "If you continue to deny this disease that put you here, you will never become clean!"

I was dying. I had no more blood left to lose and no more tears left to cry. I looked to my father for forgiveness, but he was no longer there. Instead, my mother stood where the shell of Dad was moments before.

"Landon," she said. I missed hearing her gentle, warm voice. I smiled weakly at her, finally feeling at peace.

"Landon!" Dad shouted, shaking me awake. I sat up straight in the pew, rubbing a hand down my face as people filed out of the church. "Were you asleep for my entire speech?"

"No," I said with a crack in my voice. "Of course not." I wiped the drool from the corner of my mouth.

"Go to the car," Dad said. I don't think he believed me. "We're going home."

I did what I was told. Walking into the parking lot, I felt terrible. I *was* asleep for most of the speech and couldn't remember when I dozed off. I sat in the passenger seat of my dad's car, still thinking about the terrifying nightmare. I had no desire to step foot in a church again. I knew my dream was extreme, but I'm sure that's how a conversion camp felt to some people. It wouldn't have been in my head if Dan hadn't brought it up earlier. I made a mental note to be more aware of my surroundings while on Grindr. Dad could've seen my phone if it was open while I was asleep.

I looked out the window as people passed, getting back to their cars, and noticed Dad and Grace having a conversation, standing three parking spaces away. My eyes zeroed in on their lips, trying to read them. Grace reached to fix Dad's tie. How she smiled and looked up at him made my stomach turn. Her hands swiftly moved from his tie to his chest, placing them flat against him. A fire lit in my chest as I squinted at them.

I opened the car door. "Dad, let's go!"

He stared at me with a furrowed brow. My tone may have taken him aback. His attention returned to Grace, and they said their goodbyes.

"Bye, Landon," Grace called to me, but I slammed the car door with no response.

"You were incredibly rude," Dad said as we entered the house. I'd been silent the whole ride home. I was about to ascend the stairs, but Dad stopped me with his voice. "What the hell has gotten into you?"

I whipped around and glared at him, taking off my blazer. "It's been six months!" I shouted. "Mom has been gone for six months, and Grace is all over you as if mom died six YEARS ago!" I threw my blazer on the stools at the kitchen island.

"Oh, come on, Landon," Dad scoffed.

"Come on, what?!"

"You don't know what you're talking about," he said.

"I saw it. She couldn't keep her hands off you!" My face heated. "Are you guys like... a thing?"

"No, son," Dad said, sounding deflated. "It's professional, I promise."

"Is that why you have so many late nights? Are you spending them with her?"

Dad pointed at me. "You watch your mouth when you talk to me."

I stood my ground as he sat on one of the island stools. "Do you even think about Mom anymore?"

"Landon, do not go there with me," he said as he raised his hand to stop my questioning.

"Well, do you?!"

"Goddammit!" Dad smacked his fist on the counter. "Of course I do! I can't *stop* thinking about her! I see her everywhere in this house!" He stood from the stool, taking a step toward me. I could see the red around his eyes. "I thank God every damn day that you aren't the one who found her. You're lucky you don't have to live with that. You think it's easy for me to step foot in that office every day?!" He pointed his gorilla-sized arm toward the small hallway that housed his office. "It kills me, but I do it because I HAVE to, Landon, to give us a fuckin' life worth livin'!"

A pain shot into my stomach, and my eyes welled. "Dad, I'm sor—"

"Go to your room," he said, cutting me off. "I'm done with your attitude today."

He sank back onto the stool, rubbing his forehead with one hand. I sighed, grabbed my blazer, and climbed the stairs.

I felt awful for what I said, not realizing what Dad was going through. I got so heated when I saw Grace touching him; it wasn't like she didn't know about my mom. I'm sure Dad liked the attention, or maybe he was oblivious to it all. I knew he eventually had to move on and find someone new, but not that soon. Everything was still fresh and sore. I thought it tortured me, but my dad was right, I'm lucky I wasn't the one who found her in the office. I can't imagine the nightmares I would've had.

I pulled out my phone. My conversation with Steven was still open. I swiped the app closed and opened my photo album. I wasn't the type to take many pictures; that was Lauren's thing. She would take selfies of us all the time and text them to me.

I scrolled past pics of Lauren and covers of books I'd seen at Barnes & Noble, finally reaching the pictures of me and my mom. I took them when she was in the chemo phase of her treatment. She encouraged me to take them in case things got worse, and I'm glad I did.

I clicked on a photo to make it full-screen, staring at it. My mom was sitting in a recliner under the room's fluorescent lights, tubes running from her arm. I was seated in a folding chair next to her. She wore a pink and purple silk scarf with flower patterns around her bald head. A gossip magazine rested on the lap of her hospital gown; it splayed large yellow letters across its cover that said, 'WILL THE BACHELOR CHOOSE TRACY OR SONYA?' My mom loved reading those things, especially when she was in the hospital. She said reading about the lavish lives of celebrities made her forget about her situation.

Our faces were pressed together, looking into the camera lens with big smiles. I cherished that picture so much. Weeks after she died, I'd look at it every night before going to sleep. Sometimes, I'd cry; other times, I'd laugh, thinking about the stupid celebrity gossip she would relay to me. I always kept my phone open on that picture next to my pillow to feel like she was still there. As I stared, thinking she was just as beautiful bald as she was with hair, I realized it wasn't fair that I'd accused Dad of not thinking about her. I wondered if he also looked through pictures at night when he was alone. I couldn't imagine the pain that came with losing your spouse.

I wiped the moisture from my eyes and placed my phone on my desk, with the picture still on the screen. I opened my laptop to check my email, hoping I'd have something from the schools I'd submitted to.

It's only been a day, idiot.

It was too soon. All I had from the schools were confirmation emails that I'd submitted my applications, with NYU's at the top. I closed my laptop with a sigh and thought about Caleb, wondering what he might be doing. Maybe watching a movie with Parker. I imagined them sitting in front of a giant TV with a huge bowl of popcorn. Then I imagined Caleb tossing a piece at Parker, which caused an all-out popcorn war. That made me smile.

SEVENTEEN

I hadn't seen Caleb in two days until I noticed him raking leaves around the perimeter of the football field during our rescheduled practice. Dan and I were discussing a play with the guys when Caleb, wearing a pair of khaki shorts and running shoes, caught my eye. I felt like he knew he was teasing me with the number of tank tops he wore, and on that Thursday afternoon, it was a black one. I could see the definition of his triceps every time he pulled the rake.

"Do you think it'll work?" Dan said to me, but I was a million miles away. He looked up and caught me staring. "Landon," he said, waving a hand before my face.

I woke from my trance and nodded, not truly understanding what he said. Not that I needed to. We had done the plays on the field a hundred times.

"All right, break!" Dan yelled.

Everyone got into formation. I dazedly walked to my spot on the twenty-yard line.

Coach split the team into sub-teams, with one side wearing yellow mesh over their jerseys and the other wearing blue mesh. Dan and I were on the yellow team. Waiting for everyone to get to their places, I heard a tick of rain hit my helmet as it started to sprinkle.

"Red thirty-three!" Dan shouted as he stood behind the guy playing center.

Dan had the ball snapped into his palms, and everyone took off. I needed to get out half a yard before Dan could throw the ball my way. I watched for anyone around me in case I needed to weave through them, but I caught another glimpse of Caleb between the slit of my helmet. I'd never been jealous of the rain until I saw how it slid down Caleb's shoulders. I wanted to touch him like the water, without hesitation or doubt.

SMACK!

Someone laid me out against the soft grass of the field. The crack of our helmets sent an echo through the empty bleachers. As I lay there, I groaned for a second, the rain trickling through my helmet onto my face. He pushed his weight off of me; it was Chris.

"Sorry, not sorry," he said, looking down at me with an evil grin. He reached his arm to help me, but I waved him off.

"I think I'm just gonna lay here for a sec," I said through a quick breath.

"Take a five-minute break, guys!" Coach shouted, sending Chris running toward the bench. I sat up, trying to find my bearings after the tackle. Looking ahead of me, Caleb leaned his forearms on the chain-link fence that separated the football field from the rest of the open greenery. Caleb smiled and waved. I glanced behind me, thinking it might be one of those situations where he was waving at someone else, but no one was there. He was waving at me. I swallowed with a gulp, pushed myself off the ground, and jogged to Caleb, noticing my chest was sore from the impact. My cleats clicked against the hard turf that made up the running track surrounding the football field.

"You okay?" Caleb asked. "Looked like you got hit pretty hard."

"Yeah." I took off my helmet. "I'm all right. Chris forgets this is practice, not an actual game," I said with a groan, rolling my shoulder.

"It sounded like a car crash."

"Yeah, it's even louder when you're getting hit."

"I'm actually glad I saw you," Caleb said with a smirk.

"Really?" I tried to keep the excitement from bursting through my stomach.

"Yeah. I wanted to thank you again for the ride the other night."

"It was no problem." I squeezed my helmet's facemask so hard that my fingers stung.

"Parker won't stop talking about you, believe it or not." Caleb was completely wet from the rain, and his tank top vacuum-formed to his chest. I tried my hardest not to stare. "He's been asking if we're gonna see you again."

"I'd like to see him again, too. He's a cool kid," I said.

"I'm taking him to see a special screening of Jurassic Park at the old theater in Millbrook tomorrow for the movie's anniversary."

"Oh, awesome."

"Since you've never seen it, I hoped you'd come with us?"

"Oh." I tried to play it cool, but on the inside, I was jumping and squealing in an imaginary room, bouncing off the walls like a Looney Toons character. "I don't want to interfere with your sibling time."

Caleb laughed, gripping the top of the chain-link fence. "Parker insists."

"Well, how could I say no to Parker?" I said with a smile.

Caleb chuckled and asked, "What time are you done tomorrow?"

"2:30ish, since I won't have practice."

"Perfect, the movie starts at three-thirty."

I wanted to stay at the fence until my legs gave out, but Coach blew his whistle. I looked behind me to see the guys running onto the field. "Sorry, I gotta get back."

"Yeah, me too."

"You're doing great!" I said, slipping my helmet back on. I ran backward, staring at Caleb as he returned to pick up the rake. "Hey! I'll pick you guys up!"

"Perfect!" Caleb gave me a salute. "Later!"

I turned and jogged back, hanging on Caleb's last word, 'later'. Not a 'see you later' but just a simple 'later. ' I liked that.

I pushed through some guys, and Chris waved me over, still

standing by the benches. "I think Dan is high on something," Chris whispered.

My brow creased. "What? What makes you say that?"

"His eyes are out of control. His pupils are huge."

I glanced at Dan doing push-ups in the grass. "I thought he was selling them, not taking them."

"Guys, c'mon, let's go!" Coach shouted to us.

"Let's keep an eye on him," I said as we returned to the huddle. Chris gave me a nod.

As practice continued, we noticed Dan getting more angry and aggressive. If he threw the ball and someone didn't catch it, he followed it with immediate harassment. I kept reminding him it was only practice, and he would tell me to go fuck myself and move on to the next play. We eventually switched up the sub-teams. The rain pelted harder, making the grass extra slippery. Starting the next play, I looked for Caleb, but he was gone. He wasn't dressed for the eventual downpour, so I assumed he retreated inside.

"Blue sixteen! Hike!" Dan shouted.

And just like that, we were off. Chris and Dan were on the same yellow team that round. Chris ran off in a different direction than the other players, oblivious to the play Dan called out. Chris accidentally ran into another yellow player who was supposed to catch Dan's throw. They both smacked the wet grass, splashing into a puddle.

"Damn it, Chris!" Dan screamed as he charged his brother, pushing him back into the puddle. Chris jumped up and shoved Dan. Some other guys got between them before they could throw punches. "I said blue sixTEEN!" Dan yelled, being held back by his arms as Coach ran over.

"I thought you said sixty," Chris said. "I'm sorry."

"You're a fucking idiot!" Dan screamed at his brother.

"Wilson!" Coach stepped in front of Dan. "Off the field, you need a break."

Dan broke free of the restraining grip. "Are you kidding me? It's not my fault that everyone on this fucking team is too stupid to catch a ball!"

"Go now," Coach said, pointing to the school. "Before I bench you for next week's game."

"Fuck you, this team needs me! Bench me and we'll lose!" Dan said as he pulled off his helmet, spiking it to the ground. We all watched as he walked through the parking lot, ripping off his jersey and shoulder pads, dropping them one by one as if leaving a trail of breadcrumbs to find his way back. Seeing Dan like that on the field disappointed me. I've seen him be a major douche in school, but he was never like that when we were in our jerseys. The disrespect Dan showed would've gotten any other player benched for a month, but Coach knew Dan was right—we needed his arm.

"Griffin," Coach said, turning his attention to me. "You're calling the shots now."

I was still flying high from Caleb asking me to the movie by the time practice ended. The rain had passed, but my uniform was still soaked. As we filed into the locker room, we expected to see Dan, but I should've assumed he wouldn't wait around. I opened my locker and took off my shoes. My socks were sticking to my feet. I reached into my backpack, grabbing my phone to check the time when I saw the text from Lauren.

LAUREN

Hey, babe, meet me in the parking lot.

ME

Sorry, practice just ended. You still there?

I peeled off my jersey, pulled the shoulder pads over my head, and hung them in the locker to dry.

LAUREN

Yeah!

ME

Okay, be there in a sec.

"Dan's been getting worse, it feels like," Chris whispered as he approached me. "He has to be on something, right?"

I pulled on a pair of jeans and dry socks. "Yeah, something seems off."

"I'll try to talk to him about it tonight."

"Good luck." I scoffed, grateful the duty wasn't on my shoulders.

Chris held out a fist, and I gave it a light bump. "Thanks, I'll see ya," he said.

I'd seen Dan and Chris argue a few times over the many years I'd known them, but what happened on the field felt different; I'd never seen Dan show *that* much aggression toward his brother.

I exited the building into the parking lot, hiking my duffle bag over my shoulder, when I saw Lauren standing outside her beat-up car. She held her arms up when she saw me.

"I'm really sweaty," I warned her with a smile.

"I don't care," she said, mocking my tone with her voice. I walked into her as she wrapped her arms around me, and we stumbled against the car. "Okay, you smell," she said, giving me a light shove.

"I told you!"

Lauren wiped my sweat off her cheek with the sleeve of her sweater. "What're you doing tonight?"

"Homework, unfortunately, I have a pile of it," I said.

"Same; I'm going to Tasha's now so we can finish our history project."

"Whoa, so fun!" I raised my fists in a fake celebration.

"We're still on for Sunday, right?" Lauren asked.

"I wouldn't miss it. I can taste the chocolate milkshake already!"

Lauren laughed, pushing to her tiptoes to kiss me. "Good," she said as her lips left mine. "I'll text you." Lauren glided around the car, opening the driver-side door as I said goodbye.

My phone rang as I stepped into my room. I flung the duffle bag on my bed, reached into my pocket, and clicked the green button on the screen.

“Hey, Dad,” I said. “What’s up?”

“Wanted to give you a heads up that we’re pulling a late one tonight,” he said with heavy chatter in the background.

“All right,”

“I left you some money on the counter for when you get hungry.”

My stomach growled on cue. “Got it, thanks.”

“Gotta go,” Dad said.

“Oh wait, can I use the car tomorrow after school? I’m gonna see a movie with a friend.”

“Uh.” Dad lingered on the word for a while. “Yeah, sure, I think we’re doing tomorrow night’s meeting at the house, anyway.”

“Awesome, thanks.”

“All right, stay out of trouble,” Dad said before I heard him start talking to someone else and then hang up, all before I could say goodbye.

Friday rolled around, and I couldn’t sit still in my classes. My excitement for seeing Caleb kept me fueled better than six espresso shots. I watched the clock in every class, counting each excruciating minute. I’d never felt a day go by so slowly. When the last bell finally rang, I sprinted home, not bothering to say goodbye to anyone. I burst through my bedroom door, and the smell of my rotting football gear slapped me. The stench filled the room, forcing me to open a window. The clothes needed an obvious wash, so I moved fast, hoping not to make us late for the movie.

I tripped down the stairs, almost face-planting onto the kitchen floor. I grabbed the wooden railing attached to the wall to save myself, causing my clothes to spill down the stairs. I regained my footing and collected them before rounding the corner to the basement when I heard Dad shout, “Where’s the fire?”

“I don’t want to be late!” I said, hoping my voice would find Dad’s ears. I shoved the clothes into the washer and poured some liquid soap. With a push of a few buttons, I was back leaping up the stairs. I'd already wasted ten minutes.

I ripped open a dresser drawer and pushed through my clothes before landing on a black V-neck T-shirt. I pulled it over my head, doused myself in cologne, and leaped down the stairs and out the door. I pictured the wind from my speed blowing Dad over as I ran by.

My excitement manifested into a lead foot. I remembered the route to Caleb's house perfectly. I'd driven past their trailer community a hundred times, but I'd never been inside until I dropped them off that night after ice cream.

The sixth one in, on the right, I thought, but it was Caleb's voice saying it in my head.

I pulled the car in front of their trailer and honked the horn. Dust crept through my open window that the car's tires spit up.

Parker ran out first, bursting through the screen door, wearing a *Jurassic Park* T-shirt and a pair of khaki shorts. He rushed to the passenger side door and opened it. His small freckled face beamed a smile at me. "Hi, Landon!"

"Hey man," I said, trying to match his enthusiasm.

"Hey!" Caleb's raspy voice caught me as he descended the porch steps. "Backseat, kid."

"Dang," Parker said, removing himself from the passenger seat to open the back door.

Caleb wore a gray tank top with a matching *Jurassic Park* logo on the front under an open white button-up.

"I didn't get the memo for the matching shirts," I said with a smile as Caleb sat beside me.

"It was Parker's idea."

"Landon," Parker said from the backseat. I put the car in drive and started the U-turn. "I can't believe you've never seen this movie! It's gonna blow your mind!"

"Seatbelt," Caleb said, looking over his shoulder.

Parker fumbled with the belt before clicking it in.

"It smells like a Macy's in here," Caleb said with a laugh. I apologized, frantically rolling the windows down. "No, it's fine, I kinda like it."

I smiled at him, catching Caleb's perfect, dimpled cheek.

Millbrook was a twenty-minute drive from Caleb's house. I pulled into the theater's parking lot with ten minutes to spare before the movie started. The theater was a small building with a big neon sign that read MILLBROOK CINEMA. I hadn't been there since I was a kid. My mom took me to see my first movie ever at Millbrook Cinema. They were having a special screening of Snow White. I was only four years old, and I remember my mom telling me I fell asleep to the tune of 'Heigh-Ho.'

Millbrook Cinema looked ancient. It only housed four screens and was known for playing two new movies and two old movies. That day, they had been showing *Jurassic Park*, *Dirty Dancing*, and two new movies called *Hashtag Love* and *Millennium Now*. The building had four spots on the front wall outside displaying the posters of their current movies.

"Aw, I wanna see that!" Parker said, pointing to the poster for *Millennium Now*. I had no idea what the film could be about. My only clue came from the spaceship on the poster.

We were hit with the overwhelming smell of popcorn as we walked through the swinging front door. A wide gray desk was in front of us, with one woman standing behind it selling tickets. To the right was a large concession booth surrounded by different colored neon lights. Three people stood in line waiting for popcorn. The entire floor was a dark blue carpet, with varying shapes of neon sprawling in different directions. The entire place was stuck in the 1980s, but that was part of its charm.

"God, I love this place," Caleb said, leaning into my shoulder and smiling. Parker was beside him, holding his hand, eyeing the concession booth.

"I haven't been here since I was, like, four years old," I said. "I almost forgot about it."

"Welcome back," Caleb said, looking at me. His aura was like an infectious disease taking over my body, inflicting me with a smile I couldn't get rid of. We approached the counter, and Caleb pulled out his wallet. "Three for *Jurassic Park*, please." The woman tapped a few things on her screen before the printer shot out the tickets.

"Caleb," I said. "You don't have to—"

"I got it. The old movies are only five bucks each, it's fine." He handed a twenty-dollar bill to the woman, who took it with haste. "You can get the next one." Caleb said, sending me into a frenzy thinking about the possibility of a "next one." Did that mean he already planned on seeing me again, that he already wanted to? I tried not to hyperventilate over the thought and followed the boys toward screen number three.

"Welcome to *Jurassic Park*!" Parker said in the deepest voice he could muster.

"Hold onto your butts!" Caleb said as we stepped into the theater. They laughed at each other's imitations, but I had no idea what they meant.

EIGHTEEN

"I can't believe how real they looked!" I said as we busted through the doors of Millbrook Cinema.

"I told you!" Parker said. "And what about that part when the T-Rex was like, ROOAARRRR!" Parker jumped in front of us with his hands tucked under his armpits. He stomped around as if forty feet tall and roared as loud as he could, making Caleb and me laugh.

"The scene with the raptors in the kitchen is iconic," Caleb said.

"You guys were right," I said. "I can't believe it took me until now to see that movie; it was so good!"

"Now you gotta see the second one!" Parker said, rushing to me and grabbing my hand.

"Wait, there's more?" I was genuinely curious.

"A lot more," Caleb said. "None of them are as good as the original, but yes, there are a few more."

Parker let go of my hand as we approached the car and rushed to Caleb's side. "Can we go to the playground?!" Parker jumped up and down.

"I don't know, kid," Caleb said. "It's gonna be dark soon, and Landon has to drive us back; we can't take up more of his time."

Parker's excitement turned to disappointment at the snap of a finger.

"What playground?" I asked.

"I'm sorry," Caleb said, looking at me. "It's tradition that when we come here, we go to the playground across the street after. But—"

"Why break tradition?" I said. "We should go."

"Really!?" Parker's high voice jumped over the car.

"Yeah, why not?" I said with a shrug and smirked at Caleb.

"YES!" Parker shouted.

"Get in, we can drive over," I said, catching Caleb's smile as we all jumped into our seats.

The playground was across the main road; we cut through two lanes of traffic to the next lot. The area was desolate, with several parked cars scattered in different spots. The playground was off the parking lot, with an open field behind it before hitting a line of fenced-in backyards. Caleb and I were a little slower to get out than Parker, who raced like a greyhound toward the metal, green-painted play structure. Complete with three slides, a firefighter's pole, and a small rock-climbing wall leading to the top tower, it was a kid's dream. A pair of swings also hung just to the right of everything. Wood chips surrounded the entire area.

Caleb and I sat on a bench facing the playground to monitor Parker. A lot of Texas never saw the change of seasons, but that day it smelled like fall, even though spring was upon us; maybe it was all the woodchips. We watched Parker play with the only two other kids there. No parents lingered, so I wondered if the kids lived in the houses that occupied the edge of the field. Parker laughed as he jumped onto the slide at the top of the tallest tower, zipping down it in a blink. The other two weren't far behind. His laugh was one of the most innocent things I'd ever heard. It reminded me of a chipmunk Snapchat filter.

I turned to Caleb. "Wanna hear something ridiculous?"

"Always," Caleb said.

"When I saw you guys eating ice cream at Sal's, I thought Parker was your son."

Caleb laughed, throwing his head back.

"I told you it was ridiculous," I said.

"No, it's not ridiculous," Caleb said. "You're not the only one who's thought that. We get mistaken for father and son all the time."

I huffed, giving him a light shove for laughing at me. Caleb went with it, pretending to fall off the bench.

"It's funny, 'cause when Parker was little he would call me Dad sometimes. And I'd say 'no, kid. I'm your brother.' He'd get confused a lot 'cause I was the only one taking care of him most of the time." Caleb's gaze followed Parker, playing tag with the other kids. "He would see Dads on TV or at school and just assumed that I was his. Do I look old enough to have a nine-year-old?"

"I don't know," I said with a shrug. "I'd say you're old enough."

"What?!" Caleb spat out. "That means I would've been a very sexually active twelve-year-old."

"Stranger things have happened."

"Naw, I was a late bloomer," Caleb scoffed. "I wasn't getting anyone pregnant at twelve."

Both our hands rested on the seat of the bench. My jaw tightened as my pinky touched Caleb's. I tried not to bring attention to it, even though it felt like a magnet pulling my hand closer to his. Caleb seemed oblivious, while I couldn't stop thinking about it.

"I even looked around for your wife," I said to get my mind off our small connection.

Caleb pulled his hand away, severing the spell over me. "Seriously? I had no idea I gave off this married dad vibe."

"It's all Parker's fault," I said, smiling.

"I gotta get rid of the little twerp."

Caleb's phone rang. He swiftly pulled it from his pocket and checked the screen.

"Sorry," Caleb said. "It's my probation officer. I'll be right back."

"Yeah, of course."

I walked to the swings to see what Parker was up to, but he'd already run off for more tag. I sat on the chained seat, swaying back and forth. I hadn't been on a swing in years; I'd forgotten how fun it was. I pumped my legs to get some air flowing, getting higher and remembering how it made my stomach flutter.

Caleb appeared. "Having fun?"

I put my feet down to stop myself, knocking wood chips into the air.

"That was a quick call," I said, embarrassed that he'd caught me swinging at peak height.

"Yeah." Caleb sat in the swing next to me. He spun in a circle, twisting up the chain. "He just reminded me I have to check in with him tomorrow at the courthouse. It's annoying." He stopped twisting and pulled his legs up, allowing the chain to unwind, sending Caleb into a spinning frenzy. I used to do that a lot as a kid. I imagined I was the Tasmanian Devil, twisting into a little tornado of dust and woodchips, wreaking havoc across the playground.

"Sounds like it sucks. I'm sorry," I said.

We untwisted and faced the parking lot, staring straight ahead.

Caleb leaned his head against the swing's chain. "Yeah, he really has a way of snapping me back to reality,"

"How long do you have left?"

"The rest of the year." He eyed his lap. "I'm sure rumors are running wild around your school about me."

"A few, but I haven't—"

"Like what?"

"Uh. They're all really dumb," I admitted.

"I wanna know."

I looked at him. "Okay. Um, I heard one about how you, like, burned down a school or something."

Caleb scoffed. "Yeah. It wasn't a school."

"Oh," I said. "Caleb..." I tried to get him to look at me, but his focus stayed in his lap. "I'm not gonna judge you."

"It happened while Parker was at school," Caleb said with a sigh as he swayed back and forth in his swing. "Luke was beating on my mom pretty badly, over something dumb, like forgetting to buy him cigarettes. I was in my room when I heard it happening, so I came running out and threw a punch at him. Then all hell broke loose, and we started pushing each other all over the house, connecting punches anywhere we could. I remember hearing my mom screaming for us to stop." Caleb eyed Parker, who was drawing in the woodchips with a stick. "I finally pushed him off me. I was so done with his bullshit that I just wanted out, so when I saw his car keys hanging by the door, I swiped 'em and ran. I didn't even care about leaving my mom. I'd begged her for years to leave him, but he keeps her so doped up that she wouldn't have the energy to move out even if she wanted to."

I imagined what it felt like to have parents who never cared about me. Thinking of everything Caleb had been through and what Parker might've witnessed over the years burned a hole in my heart.

Caleb continued, "I had no idea where I was driving to. I just wanted to get as far away as I could. I found a bottle of whiskey in the glove box and downed it. You know that stretch of road by the train tracks over in Oxford County?"

I nodded. "Yeah."

"That's where I was when I thought about Parker. I turned the car around so fast that I lost control. Next thing I knew I was waking up, realizing I'd wrapped the car around a telephone pole."

"Holy shit," I said, thinking he was lucky to be alive.

Caleb nodded as if he could hear my thoughts. "I pulled myself out through the window before the engine caught fire. By the time the cops found me, most of the car had burned up, and I was sitting nearby with nothing but a nosebleed."

"And they arrested you?"

"Charged me with a DUI and Grand Theft Auto, and took away my license." Caleb paused and glanced at me. "The judge took pity on me since I'd never been in trouble before. I was looking at jail time for at least three years. But I got a year of probation and three hundred hours of community service. I got so fuckin' lucky. I could barely look Parker in the eye after everything was settled. I was selfish."

I turned my swing to face him. "You were fed up; it's understandable."

"I hate thinking about Parker having to live with them while I could've been in prison. I would've gone crazy."

"You're an amazing brother," I said.

Caleb stopped swaying and stared at me like he'd never heard those words. That was the first time I felt Caleb wasn't just passively seeing me but studying me, taking me in. "Sometimes I feel like he's all I have," Caleb said.

I fought the urge to hug him. I wanted to jump off my swing and wrap him in my arms.

"God damn!" Caleb jumped from his swing. He pointed at me, and chuckled. "Is that your superpower or somethin'? Because I open up to you without even realizing it, so spill it!"

"You caught me," I said, standing, raising my hands in defeat. "You figured out my superpower."

Caleb smiled. "Your secret's safe with me."

If only he knew my real secret. I wondered how he'd react if I told him how beautiful he was. Everyone at school thought he was an anarchist who burned schools to the ground, but he was the complete opposite. Caleb was funny, kind, and a big nerd who could talk about movies for hours. Being wrapped up in the world of Caleb, I hadn't noticed how dark it was until he called out to Parker, saying it was time to go.

Caleb pointed as I pulled the car into the trailer park.

"Sixth one in, on the right," I said. "I remember."

"I'm impressed," Caleb said.

I parked in front of their gray trailer and turned off the engine. Parker slumped over in the backseat.

"He's passed out," I whispered.

"I'll grab him," Caleb said, stepping out of the car and lightly closing the passenger door. He leaned with his forearms resting on the open window, looking in at me. "I should get your number. You know, just in case we ever need a ride anywhere." Caleb said. I could tell he was joking by the size of his smile. How could I say no when his dimples were staring me in the face?

"Oh, but of course, sir," I said in a terrible British accent, tipping my invisible hat. Caleb pulled out his phone and typed the numbers as I told them. He gently opened the back door, unbuckled Parker, and scooped him up in his arms, pulling him out like a firefighter carrying a person from a burning building. Caleb bumped the door closed with his hip and stopped at the open window again.

"Later," Caleb said as he crouched to see me again. "Thanks for today. We had fun."

"Me too." I said. It was the first time I'd genuinely smiled in weeks.

NINETEEN

I woke Saturday morning to the sound of my phone vibrating. They were three quick vibrations that meant I was getting multiple texts. I had been checking my phone all night, hoping Caleb would text me, but it never came. I sat up, feeling groggy, and wiped the crust from my eyes. Sunlight filled my room, and I smelled clean laundry. A small wicker basket with my washed football clothes hanging over the edge sat beside my desk. Dad must've dropped the basket in my room while I was asleep.

I reached for my phone, realizing it could be Caleb texting me, and unplugged it from the charger. To my dismay, none of the texts were from Caleb.

LAUREN

Heading to my Grandma's house soon. I'm not looking forward to the two-hour drive. I can't wait to see your face tomorrow!

CHRIS

I tried talking to Dan.

He got pretty defensive.

TASHA

Mr. Reily told me you were applying to NYU. Are you actually going through with it?

I responded to Chris first.

ME

What did he say?

CHRIS

He said to stay out of his business. Typical Dan.

ME

Did you tell him what you saw, though?

I swiped to the text with Lauren.

ME

Same! Have fun with grandma, tell her I said hi! Haha

Last was Tasha.

ME

That seems like a serious breach of counselor/student trust.

TASHA

Boy, you know I have the magic skills to get info out of anyone.

ME

Haha yeah, sure.

TASHA

Is it true?

ME

Yes, I applied. But I haven't told anyone, so don't spread it.

TASHA

OMG, yes! I'm so excited for you. It is pretty late in the game, though.

ME

I know, I only applied because Mr. Reily said they take late applications. I feel like I'm constantly refreshing my email.

TASHA

Be patient! They'd be foolish not to take you! What did your dad say?

ME

I haven't told anyone, remember? My dad included. I'm terrified. I don't think I'll tell him unless I get in. I still haven't heard from any state schools.

TASHA

Me either, but I know a few people have, so they're coming! Slowly but surely!

LAUREN

I will! She always asks about you, she loves you. Lol.

What're you doing today?

Waiting for Caleb to text me is what I wanted to say. It tore me apart, knowing I was gonna hurt Lauren. My feelings had become too strong for Caleb to ignore. The more I saw him, the longer I wanted to be around him. I didn't even know if Caleb was gay, bi, or straight. It felt like I was living in limbo. Either I'd be let down when Caleb told me he was straight or happy when he told me he wasn't. Regardless, I'd still be breaking Lauren's heart.

ME

Not sure what I'm doing yet.

Chris texted me back.

CHRIS

Yeah, but he told me I was wrong. That I didn't see him do anything.

ME

Damn. We need more evidence because he's not gonna admit it.

CHRIS

What's the point of lying? He knows he can tell us anything.

I wished that were true. If I told Dan my biggest secret, he'd probably beat the shit out of me. My phone vibrated. A notification popped up from an unknown number. My heart skipped a beat as I shot upright off of my bed.

UNKNOWN

Hey, it's Caleb.

Holy shit, holy shit. I saved the contact in my phone before sending a text back. *Don't look desperate.*

ME

Hey. What's up?

CALEB

Was wondering if you had any plans tonight?

ME

Tonight? No, I don't think so. Why?

CALEB

I was thinking about meeting up with some friends at this club. Since it's 18+ night, I was gonna ask if you wanted to come?

Holy fuck, holy FUCK!

ME

Sounds awesome.

CALEB

Great. Mind if I meet you at your place at like 9?

9 P.M.?! That seemed so late to start the night, but I'd never been to a club, so what did I know?

. . .

ME

Yeah, sure.

CALEB

Perfect! See you tonight.

ME

Can't wait!

I stared at my phone. *Can't wait?* I hoped he wouldn't think I sounded too needy.

My stomach growled; I needed to eat something. I pulled on some basketball shorts but stayed shirtless. I ran pretty warm most of the time, so I took any opportunity not to wear a shirt.

"Hey, Dad," I said cheerfully as I came down the stairs. He was sitting at the counter with a cup of coffee, staring at his laptop screen. He was fully dressed; he just needed to tighten his tie and throw on a jacket, and he'd be ready to give another speech. Dad looked at me as I poured cornflakes into a bowl, and removed his glasses. "What's wrong with you?"

"What?" I closed the door to the fridge, milk in hand. "Nothing. Why?"

"That goofy grin on your face, for starters."

He closed his laptop and placed it into his satchel. I hadn't even realized I was smiling to myself.

"I don't know what you're talking about," I said, shoving a spoonful of cereal in my mouth, and sitting at the counter.

"It's gonna be another late one tonight," Dad said.

I nodded as milk trickled my chin. "Can I use the car again tonight?"

"For what?"

"Just hanging out with a friend again."

"Who is this friend? Do I know 'em?" He wrapped his satchel

around his shoulder and stood as I flashed back to Dad telling me not to involve myself with a delinquent like Caleb.

I shrugged. "Just a guy from my school." Technically, I wasn't lying.

Dad squinted for a moment. "Sure," he said. "I'll leave you the keys. Grace is picking me up today, anyway." He started for the side door.

I nodded and crossed to the kitchen sink, scarfing down the rest of my cereal.

Dad turned back before walking out. "Wash that bowl," he said, and I reached for the soap.

Grace pulled up to the front of the house, and I watched Dad get into her car from the window above the sink, still unsure of Grace's motives. But I had a lot more to worry about.

I spent the entire day cleaning the house, something I'd never done. I vacuumed the living room rug, wiped down every kitchen surface, and even made my bed! My mom would've fainted in shock if she'd seen it. I didn't expect Caleb to come inside the house, but I couldn't risk him thinking I was a slob.

I thought about Caleb every second. I wondered what he would wear, what he would smell like, and if he would do anything different with his hair.

My phone vibrated. I pulled it from my pocket and read the text.

DAN

Dude, come over tonight! We're gonna get drunk and jump off the roof into the pool. It's gonna be sick.

ME

Exhilarating as that sounds, I can't. I have plans tonight.

DAN

With who? We're your only friends!

. . .

He wasn't wrong.

ME

I'm just busy, man. Sorry.

DAN

gaaaaayyyyy

Rolling my eyes, I placed the phone on my desk and moved to my dresser. *Should I go with shorts or jeans?* I slipped on a pair of khaki shorts and a white T-shirt and stared at myself in the mirror. *No,* I thought, about to remove the shirt when the doorbell rang. My stomach sank and filled with butterflies. I ran down the stairs, around to the front door, and pulled it open a little too forcefully.

"Hey," Caleb said with a nod. My mouth dried as I took him in. He looked so good. I couldn't believe he was standing on my front steps. He wore black skinny jeans with rips in the knees, black boots that made him look taller, and a red flannel over a black T-shirt. His hair was pushed back under a black, flat-brimmed hat he wore backward. Silver studs poked out from each earlobe.

"Hi," I said, trying not to smile as hard as I wanted to.

Caleb looked me up and down. "Is that what you're wearing?"

"Uh..." His forwardness took me by surprise. "I don't know, I was just trying stuff on."

"Mind if I help?"

"Oh, yeah, sure," I said, pointing a thumb behind me. "My room is upstairs."

Caleb walked in while I closed the door behind him. I turned to find him looking at our framed pictures on the wall.

Caleb pointed to a picture with a golden frame. "Is that your mom?"

"Yeah," I said.

"She's really pretty."

I just smiled and headed up the stairs; Caleb stayed close behind. For the first time in my life, my room was spotless. I would've felt comfortable eating off of the floor that night.

"This is where the magic happens," I said as I presented my room, instantly regretting the words.

"Cool," Caleb said, looking around with his hands in his pockets. The first thing he studied was the collection of dusty sports trophies on the top of my dresser. Of course, that was the one thing I forgot to clean. Caleb turned, giving me another once-over. "We're going to a club, Lan. You gotta wear some jeans." Caleb pulled off his flannel and tossed it on my bed.

"Jeans." I pointed at him with a finger gun. "Got it." I stepped to my dresser and pulled out a pair of blue jeans.

Caleb seemed satisfied with my choice. "Put 'em on, I'll find you a shirt."

I nodded as he opened my closet door. He moved through the shirts on hangers as if he were swiping through a dating app, making little disapproving noises as he passed each one. Then, he crouched, picking up a red shirt from the closet's floor.

"Is this one clean?" Caleb asked.

I'd forgotten to hang the shirt after I tried it on before Dad's speech at the church. "Yeah, but it's too tight."

"Perfect," Caleb said with a Cheshire-like grin. "Put it on, let's see."

Caleb tossed the shirt, which hit me in the neck before I caught it. I placed it on the back of my desk chair while I pulled off my white T-shirt. I stood there with my bare chest exposed, wondering if Caleb liked what he saw or if I was just another shirtless guy he paid no mind to in the locker room. My face warmed as embarrassment crept in. I was confident my body was in better shape than most, maybe a bit on the skinnier side, but my thoughts raced, wondering what Caleb thought of it. I tried to watch him for any clue that leaned in my favor, but as usual, he was stoic. I slipped into the red shirt. The silky fabric cooled my warm skin. I buttoned it up to my neck and walked to my closet, closing the door to reveal the full-length mirror.

"See, it's way too tight," I said.

"It's actually perfect for where we're going," Caleb said from behind me, looking in the mirror. "One more thing." He stepped closer, pressing his chest against my back as he wrapped his arms around my shoulders, fiddling with the top button of my shirt. The warm breath from Caleb's nostrils tickled the back of my neck, giving me chills. He unbuttoned the top two of my shirt, exposing my chest. I stared at him through the mirror, enjoying his arms around me.

The last time someone was in my room, it didn't go so well. I couldn't help but wonder what Caleb would do if I pushed him over to my bed like I had with Lauren. I wondered how differently my body would respond. The way Caleb's breath teased my neck sent a fire through me. I wanted to feel his breath move down my torso. I imagined myself leaning over him on my bed, in the same position I had Lauren in.

Breaking my fantasy, Caleb stepped away to observe his work, saying, "There, now you're ready."

"Take a left at Perkins," Caleb said, pointing to the street. I was happy to go wherever he asked me to, imagining us as Lewis and Clark. Caleb glanced at me with a half-smile."So what do you do when you're not driving me around?"

"I write a lot," I said as I pulled onto Perkins Street. "Read books. When I have time, homework and football keep me pretty busy."

"I never would have pegged you as a writer. What do you write, poetry?"

"Fiction, I've never actually tried writing poetry," I said nervously, hoping he wasn't a poetry buff too.

Caleb looked forward again. "Cool. What do you want to do, like write books and stuff?"

"Yeah, that's the dream," I said, braking at a red light. "I have, like, this weirdly active imagination. I'm constantly picturing myself in absurd situations or coming up with stories. My dreams can get pretty wild, too."

"Okay," Caleb said, twisting himself to me in his seat. "What's in your head right now? Come up with something."

"All right," I said with pretend confidence, feeling pressured to impress him. "I look at these traffic lights and see a love story." I pointed to the light. "This one is in love with that traffic light across the street." I pointed to the light opposite of us. "They used to be on the same wire for years and years. Until one of their lights went out. Someone removed the traffic light from the wire altogether to get it fixed. For weeks this one here was left on the wire alone, never thinking it would see its soulmate again. But the day the traffic light returned, they reinstalled it across the street on that wire." Caleb followed along as I pointed, nodding. "They used to change lights in sync when they were on the same wire, but now the only way they can communicate is by displaying the opposite lights to keep the traffic moving." I paused as the light turned green and pulled off the brake, and shrugged. "It's a work in progress."

"I like it." Caleb chuckled. "It's cheesy, but I liked it."

"It wasn't good," I said, shaking my head in shame. We both busted out laughing.

"No, it wasn't good," Caleb said between breaths.

"I'm better than this, I swear!"

Caleb dried his eyes. "I hope I can read your stuff sometime."

"Me too," I said as my laugh calmed. "I write short stories for my school newspaper every month. Maybe I'll let you read one of those."

"All right," Caleb said and rolled down his window. The fast wind felt amazing against my flushed cheeks. A whiff of hot dogs floated in as we passed a vendor standing at his cart. "What's your favorite book?" Caleb asked. "Oh, take a left up here."

I took a wide turn onto the street Caleb pointed out. "That's a hard question. It changes every week." I had so many favorite books it was hard to pick just one; I'd imagine Caleb felt the same about movies.

"All right then, what's your favorite you've read recently?"

"Um…" It had been weeks since I read a book. I racked my brain trying to remember, then it hit me. "Oh! *Ready Player One* by Ernest Cline. It was so good! It's about this guy who lives in a dystopian future where everyone thrives in a virtual world, like a video game. But you can, pretty much do anything you want. It's entertaining, and there's all these references to movies and pop culture, which I didn't always understand, but I bet you would love it!" The nerd in me jumped out, but it made Caleb smile.

"I will now," Caleb said, looking at me with his beautiful hazel eyes. My attention flickered back to the road, afraid I'd crash us, if I got stuck in Caleb's gaze. "I'm not much of a reader, but I'd love to check it out," he said. Caleb turned his attention back to the street. "It's up here on the right."

A tall sign with bold white letters painted on it that read 'PARADISE' came into focus. A neon palm tree lit up from the top right corner. I pulled into the lot, which was packed with cars, but I found an empty spot facing the small brick building.

An eccentric array of people strutted the parking lot. A tall person wearing a skintight dress that stopped at their thighs and high-heeled boots turned the corner. They wore a big afro wig pulled into two poofy buns. Then, two men walked by our car. Both buff with hairy chests. Instead of shirts, they wore leather harnesses around their bulging shoulders. I would've thought they were twins if I hadn't seen them holding hands. A gaggle of girls rushed by, all greeting a skinny, younger-looking boy with a hug.

"I should've given you the heads up," Caleb said as he unbuckled his seatbelt. I think he could tell I was putting the pieces together.

"So, this is a gay club?" I asked. I was barely treading water with my sexuality, and being in that parking lot felt like jumping into the deep end, head first.

"Yeah," Caleb said. "If that makes you uncomfortable, we can leave. We can go somewhere else."

"No, no. I'm fine." I lied. Sweat formed at my hairline.

"She isn't much," Caleb said, looking at the brick building. "But she's felt like home for the last few years."

I eyed the building, too. "I didn't know there was one so close."

"Closest in two counties," Caleb said, smiling at three people standing by a red Jeep missing its doors and roof.

"I didn't realize you were..." I couldn't even say the word. I was such a coward.

Caleb looked at me. "I didn't realize I had to tell you I was."

He was right. He didn't owe me anything. I looked at him with nothing to say but feeling relief, finally knowing Caleb's sexual orientation. Maybe I'd have a chance if I grew the balls to tell him how I felt.

"Those are my friends," Caleb said, jutting his chin at the folks standing by the Jeep. "Are you sure you're all right with this?"

"Yeah," I said, fighting against the pit forming in my stomach.

If anyone sees me here, I'm fucked. Maybe I should say I don't feel good and go home.

My hand hovered over the door handle, not yet ready to open it. Caleb had already gotten out of the car. I closed my eyes and took a few deep breaths. When I opened them, I saw a bus pass with my dad's face on its side, smiling at me.

"Jesus Christ, he's watching me," I whispered.

This is a sign: leave now. Go!

Caleb knocked on the window, startling me. "You comin'?"

Goddammit.

"Yeah," I said with a fake smile, finally opening the door.

TWENTY

"Oh, my, who is this fresh meat you've brought us, Mr. Montes?!" One of Caleb's friends shouted as we approached the group. The short man wearing a mesh tank top, exposing his dark skin, stepped from the huddle and tiptoed to Caleb with his arms outstretched. The man had a thin goatee, and his hair buzzed short. One long earring hung from his right earlobe.

"Don't scare the boy off, Miguel!" A husky person in small heels said between puffs of a cigarette. They wore a feminine pantsuit as if they'd come from a law office and a long black shawl-like scarf wrapped around their neck and shoulders. Despite their clothes, the thick beard told a different story. And yet their hair was long and straight, just passing over the shoulders. A complete blend of masculine and feminine.

Caleb glanced over his shoulder at me. "Landon, this is Miguel. Pronouns are he/him," Caleb said, gesturing to the short man in the mesh tank top. Miguel sashayed toward me with a big embrace. My hands stayed in my pockets, and my chin rested on Miguel's shoulder as he squeezed me. I was taken aback by how touchy-feely he was with someone he didn't know.

"It's so nice to meet you!" Miguel said, easing his hold on me. "What are your preferred pronouns, honey?"

"Um..." I'd never been asked that question before, thinking the answer was obvious. "He/Him."

"Girl, let him breathe," the bearded person said. "Sorry, Miguel can't resist a fresh twink."

I had no idea what a twink was, but I assumed he was referring to me.

"Oh, bitch," Miguel said, pointing a painted fingernail. "Do not try me tonight." He spat out something in Spanish. It made all of them laugh, but I'd missed the joke.

"This is Dennis," Caleb said, gesturing to the bearded person wearing the black shawl. "Pronouns are they/them."

Dennis held out their dainty hand, waiting for me to shake it. I could've been shaking hands with the Queen of England if I'd closed my eyes. It took a second for my brain to wrap around calling someone by they/them. I'd never met anyone who used those pronouns.

"And finally," Caleb said as he gestured to the only person who had yet to speak. "The woman of the hour, Mallory!" Caleb hugged her, and she wrapped her arms around his neck, smiling. Mallory wore a purple cocktail dress cut off at the knees and white pumps on her feet. Her long, strawberry-blonde curly hair reminded me of a sunset. Her eyes matched her dress with a glittery purple shadow. Caleb kept an arm wrapped around her shoulders and faced me. "We're celebrating her approval for gender confirmation surgery!"

"I'm finally becoming the woman on the outside that I've always been on the inside, baby!" Mallory said, making the others cheer.

I was naive. Steven was the only person who lived outside the norm in my day-to-day life. If I had opened my eyes a little sooner, I might've been able to see all of the rainbow colors instead of the black-and-white I was used to.

"Oh, cool. Congrats," I said to Mallory.

Caleb cleared his throat, stood beside me, facing his friends, and said, "This is Landon."

“So, how’d you two meet?” Mallory asked with a thick Puerto Rican accent.

“Caleb rarely brings guys around unless it’s serious,” Dennis said, taking another drag off their cigarette. I hated the smokey smell; of course, the wind blew it all in my direction.

“Oh, I’m not—” I stuttered, and raised my hand in defense. “I have a—”

“We’re just friends,” Caleb said, cutting me off.

“And you wanted to bring him to this dump?” Miguel asked.

“He needed a change of scenery,” Caleb said, glancing at me with a slight smile. “Get out of his bubble, ya know?”

“We can all relate,” Dennis said as he leaned back against the red Jeep.

I wondered how Caleb knew them, as they all looked older. But Caleb was right, I needed something new. Standing in that parking lot felt very out of my element. But I’d never seen so many queer people in one place. It was both scary and exciting.

“How do you all know Caleb?” I asked the group.

Miguel threw his hands up first. “Oooo girl, he was just a sweet lil’ gayby when he walked into Paradise for the first time,” Miguel said. “You and Andy, remember?”

“Yes,” Caleb said, shaking his head at the ground.

“They looked like two lost puppies,” Dennis said with a chuckle.

“And we kind of just took them under our wings,” Mallory said.

“I think that’s the night Miguel went home with that foot fetish guy,” Dennis said, causing a burst of laughter from everyone.

“Bitch, why you gotta do that?” Miguel said to Dennis, puffing his chest. “You always gotta air my dirty laundry in front of somebody new.”

It was funny to see Miguel standing in front of Dennis, acting tough despite the height difference between them. I thought Miguel’s anger was real, but his demeanor flipped on a dime.

“Best damn foot massage I ever had in my life, though, I’ll tell you that.” Miguel spat out as Dennis nudged him away. Everyone laughed again. The whole dynamic of the group shook the foundation of my small world.

"So if it wasn't Grindr," Mallory said. "Then how'd you guys start hangin' out?" She looked to Caleb for the answer. I thought about how I practically stalked him until he noticed me.

"We met at his school," Caleb said, shoving his hands in his pockets. "I'm doing my community service at Madison High. He's a senior there."

My cheeks warmed. I didn't feel old enough or cool enough to be there.

"How's that going, by the way?" Miguel asked.

Caleb shrugged. "It's not too bad. Though my probation officer is a dick most of the time."

"Fuckin' cops," Mallory said under her breath.

"He has this power complex going on," Caleb said. "He treats me like I'm lower than him."

I felt sorry for Caleb; he didn't deserve to be treated that way.

"There have been so many times where I'd love to just put him in his place, but I can't risk getting in more trouble," Caleb said. "I gotta think about Parker."

"Oh, how is that little nugget?" Mallory asked with a baby voice.

Caleb's face lit up. "Good! He's saying more outrageous things every day."

Miguel eagerly interjected. "This one time, I was at the grocery store, right? And this little boy pointed at me and asked his mother if I was pregnant." This sent all of them into a laughing fit. "I swear I was ready to go to jail that day; I said, Lord, you betta stop me from slappin' the shit outta this boy. Best believe I was on the treadmill that night!"

"I don't think it's working," Dennis said through their smile, trying to catch their breath from laughing. Miguel screamed and laughed along with everyone else. It was like they'd known each other for decades. It was so easy for them to bounce words off one another in a lighthearted way. Like I was watching a sitcom, it eased my anxiety. I finally cracked a smile, and it felt amazing.

Loud music spilled into the parking lot whenever someone entered the building. Mallory perked up at the current song playing.

"Oh shit, that's my jam!" She cheered. "Let's go, girlies!" She turned, rushing toward the entrance. We followed suit and formed a line before the entrance as the bouncer checked everyone's ID.

The closer I got to the door, the more anxiety filled my stomach. It reminded me of when I was ten, when my parents took me to a haunted maze around Halloween. The anticipation and screams wrecked my stomach.

I stepped to the closed door and handed my license to the large man dressed in black. His T-shirt had the word 'SECURITY' written in bold white letters across the chest. He shined a small flashlight on my license and asked for my hand, drawing a big X over my skin with a black marker. He opened the door, and I followed Caleb inside.

A wave of booming music slammed us, bass knocking on my chest. The building wasn't very spacious. We were plunged into a crowd waiting to get to the bar. The pungent smell of alcohol clung to the foggy air that shot from the ceiling. Bodies pressed together all over the dance floor. Strobe lights of reds and purples plastered everyone, then switched to blues and greens. Mallory had left us all behind, and I caught her squeezing herself between two shirtless men under a disco ball. I never considered myself a good dancer. Always too afraid I'd look like a fool, so I never fully let loose. I wondered what Caleb expected of me. The thought of getting sweaty next to him, though, was one I liked.

"What's this for?" I yelled to Caleb, grabbing his shoulder to get his attention and showing him the black X on my hand.

"It means you're under twenty-one," Caleb called back. "So the bartenders know not to serve you alcohol."

"Oh, gotcha."

Caleb turned to face me. "Don't worry, I won't be drinking tonight either. Not allowed!" It was so dark I had trouble seeing his face. I'd glimpse him every time a spinning light flashed by. The growing crowd pushed Caleb into me. He grabbed my arms to steady himself.

"Sorry," Caleb said, his face three inches from mine. "It's so crowded on Saturday nights."

The spinning light came around like a lighthouse beacon, illuminating Caleb's dimples. I fought the urge to kiss him as he held onto me. No one would've batted an eye. I could kiss a beautiful man, and no one would judge me. Then I recognized a familiar head of pink hair bouncing toward us, and my heart sank to my toes.

"Fuck!" I shouted, turning my back to Caleb.

"What's wrong?" Caleb strained his voice over the music, trying to turn me back around.

I peeked over my shoulder; Steven weaved between dancing bodies, looking in my direction. My gaze shot to the front door, and I bolted through the crowd until the silence of the parking lot struck me. A slight ring hung in my ears.

"Landon!" Caleb shouted from the entrance, but I rushed around the side of the building to my car. The ringing faded as Caleb's footsteps galloped behind me.

"I have to go," I said. "I can't be here."

Caleb caught up before I reached the driver's side door. His brow creased when he looked at me. "Why? What's going on?"

"I saw this guy Steven from my school."

"Okay, so," Caleb said, not realizing the gravity of the situation.

"Everyone at school knows he's..." Again, I couldn't say the word. "I just don't need him telling people that he saw me here, then everyone is gonna say that I'm..." I pulled my keys from my pocket, feeling disoriented.

"Gay?" Caleb said flatly. The word stopped me as if it had all the power in the world.

"Yes."

"Is that so bad?" Caleb asked.

"It is when you have a dad like mine," I said, opening the car door. "It is when you go to a school like mine. You don't know what it's like."

"You're right. I'm sorry," Caleb said, leaning against the hood.

I sighed and pinched the bridge of my nose. "It's not your fault. I wasn't thinking. If I'm seen here, it could ruin my dad's campaign."

"His campaign? What're you talking about? I thought your dad was a superintendent."

"He is," I said as I stood in the open door. "He's also running for Mayor of Madison. His picture is all over town."

Caleb looked as if he was sifting through memories. "I think Miguel has the hots for your dad," Caleb said.

I was so flustered from seeing Steven that I couldn't even crack a smile. "Look," I said. "I enjoyed hanging out with you, and it was fun, but I can't be here." I tried to get in the car, but Caleb touched my shoulder.

"Let's go somewhere else then," he said.

I shook my head. "No. You're here to celebrate your friend, you should be with them."

"They're very understanding people," Caleb said before gliding around the car. He opened the passenger door and sat in one swift movement. "I have the perfect place. Get in!"

I plopped into the driver's seat, feeling like an idiot for not thinking I'd see someone I knew. Steven was the only person at my school who was out of the closet; of course, he would be at a gay club on 18+ night. I shook away the thought as I turned the key in the ignition and shifted the car into reverse.

I pulled onto the main road. "Where are we going?"

Caleb glanced at me and smiled. "You'll see."

TWENTY-ONE

We parked in front of a chain-link fence, covered in overgrown vines and foliage. The car's beams lit up a sign that read, 'NO TRESPASSING.'

The trees on the other side of the fence had grown over the top, making it difficult to tell how far up it went. I wondered what was beyond the gate and if it was Caleb's plan all along to take me to an abandoned factory to murder me. I turned off the car, and the headlights faded, leaving us in total darkness.

"You sure this is the place?" I asked.

"Yup," Caleb said, stepping out of the car. I followed suit and opened my door, stepping onto the gravel.

"It looks like it might've closed down since the last time you were here," I whispered. Aside from a few chirping crickets, the area was silent.

Caleb switched on his phone's flashlight. "This place was closed long before I got here," Caleb said, touching the fence. My phone's beam followed Caleb as he ran his hands against the chain link.

"What're you doing?"

"Trying to find the spot," he said with a huff. "I haven't been here in a while." He crouched and pushed against the fence. "Got it."

Caleb yanked the chain link apart. The metal fence had been cut, allowing him to bend a chunk outward.

"Wait," I said, grabbing his shoulder. "We're going in there?"

"Yeah," Caleb said, looking up at me, still crouched, holding the fence open. "Andy and I used to come here a lot. It was our favorite spot."

That was the second time that night I'd heard the name Andy. The thought tossed me into a guessing game as Caleb scooted through the opening, getting his T-shirt caught in one of the cut links.

I crouched behind him and released the fabric, still feeling uneasy about the location. "It says no trespassing. Aren't you supposed to be staying out of trouble?" I shined my light through the hole in the fence at Caleb.

He squinted at me. "I promise you, no one is ever here," Caleb whispered, shielding his eyes from my light. "C'mon, scaredy-cat."

I checked to see if anyone was around, but all I saw was darkness. I huffed and pushed through the small hole, letting the fence bounce back into place behind me. Caleb walked, and I followed close behind. The overgrowth was thick, but there was a small path of broken branches and leaves. I flashed my light to the right of us, a few empty beer cans were scattered in the bushes. As we continued, the air got mustier, like we were close to a body of water.

Our path ended at a single white door in a small wooden structure covered in moss and vines. Caleb twisted its doorknob.

This is it. This is where he kills me.

The door opened toward us, pushing a breeze through the small booth.

"Whoa," I said as we stepped inside. The structure was one of those squirt gun game booths where people shot a stream of water at a target to make their stuffed animal race to the top. Everything looked decayed. A few stuffed animals were left on the ground, torn apart by wildlife, and the water guns were covered in rust.

Caleb jumped over the booth's half wall into the dark open area. I shined my light at him as he threw his arms out to the side.

"Welcome to Rocky Lake Amusement Park," Caleb said with a smile.

I hopped the wall, landing in the overgrown grass. I'd heard stories of the place but had never seen it. My parents used to tell me stories of them going to Rocky Lake. It was apparently a popular date spot when they were teenagers. Dad said he'd try to win my mom's affection by collecting game-winning prizes.

The entire park took up the north side of Rocky Lake, a two-mile round body of water. The park was complete with a carousel, a swing ride that brought you up into the air, a bumper car terminal, a small rollercoaster where you rode on the back of a giant fish, and a huge Ferris wheel at the water's edge. An unbroken stretch of game booths and food huts lined up with the one we walked through. I followed Caleb, spotting a booth that read 'Ned's Burgers & Dogs.' Seeing it all in the dark, I couldn't imagine it lit up and functioning without the overflowing bushes and trees.

Due to health and safety regulations, Rocky Lake Amusement Park closed down in September 1990. The rides had gotten old, and the owner was too cheap to fix them. I remember reading about the swing ride breaking down while people were on it. The swings were flying high as usual until smoke started pouring out of the top, then it suddenly dropped everyone back to the ground, snapping ten people's legs on impact. Attendance faltered after the incident until the place went under, and the owner filed for bankruptcy. Oddly enough, the state never removed any of the buildings or rides. The park slowly turned into a place of legend as it sat there rotting.

Caleb pointed things out to look at. My amazement slipped into realizing just how creepy the place was. We walked past the bumper car terminal, most of it had been spray-painted with graffiti, and every bumper car was left flipped over or taken apart.

Caleb's voice split the silence in the air. "This place is awesome, isn't it?"

"Yeah." I nodded, looking in every direction to spot something new. "It's crazy that it was just left here."

"I know, right? Like it's frozen in time." Caleb was like a kid in a candy store, smiling ear to ear with every step.

As we walked, my flashlight faced the ground, so I wouldn't trip over anything. We made it to the enormous white Ferris wheel, equipped with matching carriages with blue roofs. The wheel was so rusty you could get tetanus just looking at it.

"You can probably see the entire lake from the top," Caleb said.

"We're not going up there, are we?"

"Hell no," Caleb said with a laugh. "Do you see that thing? It looks like it could shatter with the next gust of wind."

I chuckled, relieved that climbing wasn't on the agenda. "So," I said, lingering on the word. "Where are we going then?"

"The best spot in the park," Caleb said. "Right behind the Ferris wheel, looking out onto the lake."

I nodded, keeping pace, and the rustle of a nearby bush caught my attention. I snapped my head to a squirrel skittering from the leaves.

I imagined a hoard of zombies pushing through the tree line. Their mangled faces glistened under the moonlight as they reached toward us, hungry for our brains. Then I imagined Caleb whipping out a pistol from his waistband, shooting each one in the head, dropping them like flies.

"Climb through," Caleb said, pulling me from my apocalyptic thoughts. We reached the metal barrier that surrounded the perimeter of the cement slab at the base of the Ferris wheel. I ducked under the fence onto the cement. It was cracked with nature pushing its way through. Looking up at the Ferris wheel, it seemed as tall as a New York City skyscraper. "This was our spot," Caleb said. "We thought we were so cool at seventeen." He walked past the big wheel to the back fence that faced the water. "We had our fake IDs that got us into Paradise every weekend, then we'd come here and just look at the water and talk."

Caleb leaned against the horizontal pole. It wasn't much of a fence. He sat on the cement, hanging his legs over the edge that dropped off into the lake. I did the same, plopping beside him.

The area was the brightest spot in the park. The moon reflected off the water's surface, spreading light streams in each direction. We stared across the lake, taking in a few houses with windows lit up on the other side. Caleb pointed at two turtles sleeping on a stump. The moon was bright enough to light the circled A tattoo on his hand.

"A for Andy?" I asked.

Caleb's hand dropped in his lap, and he rubbed the A with his other thumb. He leaned a shoulder against the pole jutting from the concrete.

"Who was he? If you don't mind me asking."

"He was... a lot," Caleb said. "It's a long story."

I stared at him. "I got all the time in the world."

Caleb glanced at me, gave a weak smile, and looked back at the water. A cool breeze brushed my skin, setting off a blanket of goosebumps. Water splashed on the shoreline under our dangling feet.

"We dated when we were in high school," Caleb said. "But it was always a secret. We were in the same film class, and talking about movies led to hanging out after school. Hanging out turned into other stuff, and I fell pretty hard for him. We were each other's first everything." Caleb's voice trailed off, and I wondered if he was flipping through the memories in his head. "I was already out to a few friends at school, but coming out never interested Andy. His family was conservative, so his parents thought we were best friends and inseparable. When things got serious, we invented our own signal for when we couldn't say I love you out loud." Caleb reached for my wrist and turned my hand so my palm faced up. "If we were at dinner with his parents or something, he would reach for my hand under the table and draw a circle on my palm." Caleb traced a circle in my hand. His light touch sent a chill up to my shoulder. "And that meant he was saying I love you to me without saying the words." Caleb let go of my wrist, and I could tell he relived the memory as his smile was as bright as the moon.

I made a fist, still able to feel his circle. "So what happened with you guys then?"

"I didn't wanna be a secret anymore," Caleb said, peering back to the water. "We got into this big fight over the phone one night. I was so frustrated. I wanted to love him outside the walls of Paradise, ya know? I wanted to hold his hand at school, kiss him in the parking lot, and say I love you at the dinner table. But he was too scared. Andy didn't want any of it." Caleb took a breath, then exhaled slowly. "After we hung up, I texted him to meet me here at the park. I was gonna tell him to his face that things had to change or else I'd break it off."

It felt like I was reading a cliffhanger at the end of a chapter. "And did you?"

"He never showed up," Caleb whispered. "I waited a long time, so I hopped on my bike and rode home." Caleb stared at the water. "When I got to the main road, I saw the flashing lights of the cop cars. I sped up and saw Andy's mangled bike in the middle of the road. A cop stopped me as I tried to run to it, looking for him, but all I saw were drops of blood smeared across the cement. I just collapsed in the cop's arms, screaming, 'What happened?' The cop sat me down and asked if I knew the kid who owned the bike. I remember nodding because I couldn't keep my eyes off the stained street. The cop told me a car had hit a teenager, they could tell it was a drunk driver by the tire marks on the road."

My heart sank, hearing the pain in Caleb's voice. I wanted to hold him close and tell him it would be okay.

"They'd already gotten him into an ambulance by the time I got there," Caleb said. "The cop was nice enough to drive me to the hospital. Andy's parents were already there. I came to them in a waiting room crying, and they told me Andy was gone. I swear it felt like a thousand knives stabbed me."

"My God, Caleb," I whispered. "I'm so sorry."

"The worst part was that his parents didn't let me go to the funeral," Caleb said. "They went through his phone, found our texts, and figured out we were seeing each other. Then they blamed me for his death." Caleb rubbed the tattoo again. "For a long time, I agreed with them. If it weren't for me, he wouldn't have been riding his bike so late."

I shook my head. "Caleb, you couldn't have known."

"They never found who hit him. I came to this spot almost every night for a month to cry," Caleb said, scoffing at his own words. "When I was here alone, I could feel him. It was the only way I could get some resolution."

"My dad likes to say grief is just love with nowhere to go," I said. "So, I understand feeling stuck. I've felt stuck for the last six months." I admitted, leaning back on my hands.

"How come?" Caleb sounded genuinely concerned. He pulled his right leg onto the ledge and sat facing me with his other leg still hanging.

"My mom, she... " My throat tightened, trapping the words. I wanted to tell him everything, but my body wouldn't let me. It knew if I started talking about her, I wouldn't be able to stop crying. "I'm sorry. I haven't talked about this with anyone, so."

"It's okay," Caleb said.

"No, you weren't done talking. I shouldn't have brought it up." I looked at the water again. Every ounce of my being told me to get up and run back to the car.

"Landon," Caleb said with a gentle tone. "I'm a great listener if you give me the chance."

I looked him in the eyes. Caleb had given me so much about his life and his trauma, and I'd given next to nothing in return. I cleared my throat, and my jaw loosened. He deserved to know.

"My mom...died a little over six months ago." My voice trembled.

"Shit," Caleb whispered. "I had no idea."

"It all happened so fast," I said. "She went to a dermatologist on a Sunday and was diagnosed with melanoma by the next Friday. They said it was stage three by the time they started her on chemo. We spent weeks in the hospital, but nothing seemed to work. The cancer was spreading too quickly to too many vital organs." The words came out as if I'd rehearsed them for months, knowing they'd have to come out eventually. Reliving everything out loud for the first time felt awful. My chest filled with the same dread as the day we were told the treatment wasn't working. "She had gotten so depressed and so skinny because she refused to eat most days. It felt like my dad was getting weaker every day, too. The cancer was draining the life out of our entire family."

Caleb touched my knee. "I can only imagine."

"They let us bring her home one weekend," I said, still staring at the moonlit water. "We were told she only had a few weeks left. She looked so different by that point. She was so—frail, I hated seeing her that way." I took a breath as I sat up, filling my lungs with the cool, moist air, and held it for a second, remembering her last day. "That Monday at school, the principal told me to go home. I walked into the house to find Dad sitting at the kitchen counter with a piece of paper in front of him and his face in his hands." My eyes welled as I hesitated to say the words. "He told me she was gone, that he found her hanging from the rafters in his office. I couldn't believe what he was saying until I read the letter she left on his desk." The tears overflowed my lids and dripped down my cheeks. I didn't want to cry in front of Caleb, but I was picking at a scab that had yet to heal. "She wrote about how she wanted to end her pain and that she wasn't suffering anymore. She wrote how proud she was of me and that she'd always be watching me." A lump formed in my throat, trying to hold everything back. "She ended the note with 'I love you more than anything.'"

Caleb gently placed his hand on the back of my neck. I looked at him with a wet face, trying not to sob. He wiped the moisture from my cheek with his thumb.

I sniffled and wiped my nose on my sleeve. "Sorry."

"You never have to apologize for showing emotion."

"I feel like I've cried myself to death," I said. "And yet my dad hasn't shed a single tear, at least that I've seen. Even when we were at her funeral, he was like a statue."

"Do you resent him for that?" Caleb asked.

"Kind of," I said, wiping the remaining tears from my face. "I feel like I'm suffering alone, ya know? It'd be nice if he showed any emotion. It's not fair that he gets to feel numb."

"I'm sure he's suffering in his own way, Lan. You should talk to him about it."

"I don't know. You haven't met him. He isn't the easiest person to talk to." I looked out at the water and shook my head, feeling the embarrassment creep through now that the tears had passed. "I'm sorry; I didn't mean to make this about me after everything you told me."

Caleb stroked the hair at the back of my head. "Thank you for telling me," he said. "It means a lot." Caleb stared at me with a soft smile, looking like an angel. I probably looked like a troll with snot running down my face.

"I have an idea," Caleb said, pulling out his phone.

My brow creased. "Yeah?"

"We never got the chance to dance tonight, so..." Caleb smiled. "Come on, stand up."

"I don't know," I groaned. "I don't really dance."

Caleb jumped to his feet. A song played with a single tap on his phone's screen. He slipped it back into his pocket halfway so the speaker end stuck out.

I pulled myself up using the fence pole, already embarrassed enough, and didn't want to inch deeper into that rut by dancing.

The song echoed through the tall trees. It had a funky 80s beat and a synth melody.

"What is this?" I asked. "It's got a cool sound."

Caleb bopped his head. "It's one of my favorite songs by this band, Walk The Moon. It's called 'Aquaman,'" Caleb said, increasing the volume. "It always puts me in a better mood. It's so easy to dance to." Caleb's smile beamed at me. His body swayed. He looked so nerdy, but I'd never seen a cuter human.

"Come on," Caleb said, pointing a dancing finger at me as the chorus hit.

I had no choice. *He's not gonna let up*, I thought. I followed his lead and swayed my body at his tempo.

"There we go!" Caleb said. I laughed and moved a little smoother, feeling my limbs loosen. Caleb wasn't afraid of looking ridiculous, so why should I?

He performed a swift spin and raised his arms. I was drawn into Caleb's self-confidence and hypnotized by the movements of his hips. He stepped closer to me, swaying back and forth like a snake charmed by its flute player.

I attempted a spin of my own to move closer to him and rocked back and forth. It was very apparent Caleb had more experience than I did. I tripped over my foot a little, making him chuckle. He grabbed my hand and spun himself under my arm. We laughed at each other, moving closer as the music boomed through us. Caleb reached for my other hand as we swayed smoothly. I couldn't take my eyes off his perfect face. His smile was all the light I needed for the rest of my life. Caleb inched closer with his dancing feet, and my heart thudded against my chest.

I moved closer, unable to control my body like years of instinct kicked in. The music was building. We continued to sway our hips in unison, and Caleb let go of my hands. I thought he would pull away, but he rested his arms on my shoulders, and his thumbs stroked the back of my neck. I wrapped my hands around his lower back and pulled him in until our stomachs touched. Dancing that close to him under the night sky felt so freeing. My heart raced faster.

Caleb's hand slid from my neck, caressed my cheek, and he looked me in the eyes as we danced. The song continued to build, and the keychange sang through the trees.

I closed my eyes before Caleb's lips pressed against mine.

Our bodies moved with the music as we continued to kiss. A thousand fireworks erupted in my stomach. A euphoria I'd never felt filled my insides as I cupped Caleb's smooth face. Our tongues mimicked the dance of our bodies, and I didn't want it to end. My heart pounded a mile a minute, excited and nervous. Nothing had ever felt as right as kissing that boy in front of that decaying Ferris wheel.

The song faded, and so did the kiss. Caleb pressed his forehead against mine, still holding onto my face. I opened my eyes to his perfect smile. Everything I'd felt since the first day I saw him came to fruition. I could've stayed in that moment, staring into his hazel eyes for all of eternity.

TWENTY-TWO

We broke our hold of each other when fits of laughter erupted from a distance. Caleb turned off the music as we dashed to the nearest Ferris wheel carriage and hid behind it. We stared at each other and smiled with heavy breaths.

"I thought you said no one ever came here," I whispered.

"That's what I thought. I've never seen anyone else here."

As I listened to the distant chatter, I recognized one voice. "I think that's Dan," I whispered.

"Who?"

"He's a friend. It's all right." I pulled Caleb up from his shirt. "C'mon."

I stepped from the carriage toward the small gate where previous patrons would have entered the ride. Caleb followed behind me.

Dan and a few others appeared from the shadows and into the moonlight, laughing and pushing each other playfully. Each one held a beer bottle.

I reached for my phone and switched on my flashlight so they would notice us. My heart still raced from my dance with Caleb. I wondered if he was thinking the same thing I was. *Did Dan see us kissing?*

"Griffin?" Dan called in my direction. "What the hell are you doing here?"

"I could ask you the same thing," I said, grinning. Four guys flanked Dan. I knew three from the football team, but the fourth guy was new. I gave a quick 'hey' to the others as they approached.

Dan wiped his nose with the back of his finger. With a jittery hand, he gestured to Caleb, standing behind me. "Who's this?" Dan asked, sniffling.

I glanced over my shoulder. "That's Caleb. Caleb, this is my friend Dan and some guys from the football team."

Caleb stepped toward us with his hands in his pockets, offering a nod to the group.

"Wait," Dan said, pointing a beer bottle at us. "You're that guy who's been working at the high school."

"That's me," Caleb said.

"Guys," Dan said over his shoulder to the others. "This is the fucker I told you about. The psycho who burned down a school."

"Don't believe everything you hear," I said.

"Most of the rumors are true," Caleb said sarcastically. I knew Dan wouldn't understand the tone.

"I knew it," Dan slurred as he looked at Caleb. It was apparent he and the guys had been drinking for a while. "Kinda weird finding you two here."

I rolled my eyes. The last thing I wanted to deal with was an intoxicated Dan. I'd been having a good time with Caleb, but he was ruining it.

"I come here to think," Caleb said. "It's one of my favorite spots."

"You must bring all the boys here," Dan said, pulling a laugh from the others.

"It's not like that," I said. The words sprung out of my mouth like a jack in the box. Dan approached Caleb, meeting him at eye level. He sniffled as he looked Caleb up and down, analyzing him. "Dan cut the shit," I said as he stalked around Caleb as if he were a predator hunting his prey. Caleb seemed unfazed by Dan's idiotic display of dominance.

"Only fags wear earrings like that," Dan said.

"You seem to know a lot about fags," Caleb said, face-to-face with Dan. "Wonder why."

Dan's goons busted out laughing, and he grabbed Caleb by his collar, squeezing the fabric in his fists.

"Dan!" I stepped to him. "What the fuck is wrong with you?" I grabbed his shoulder. Caleb was stonefaced.

Dan eased his grip and let go, raising his hands in defense. "I'm just fuckin' with him!" Dan said. His voice echoed through the trees. The other guys laughed like hyenas again, pushing my patience even further. "You seem cool, you seem cool," Dan trailed off.

"What a compliment," Caleb said under his breath.

"What're you doing here, Dan? What happened to jumping off the roof?" I tried to sound as calm as possible, fearing that any raised tone would set him off like a firecracker.

"We got bored," Dan said, wiping his nose again. "We wanted to tear some shit up. Gary said this was the perfect place."

I shined my flashlight to better see the crew and realized Gary was the tired-looking guy I'd seen with Dan in the school's parking lot, giving him crumpled-up dollar bills. Gary's bloodshot eyes reminded me of one of the zombies I'd imagined walking out from the tree line earlier.

"Have fun," I said. "We were just leaving."

"Oh, c'mon!" Dan yelled, spiking his bottle to the ground. The glass shattered in a thousand different directions. "Stay with us; the nights just getting started!"

"Sorry," Caleb said. "I gotta get up early for work tomorrow."

I was unsure if Caleb was telling the truth or using an excuse to escape the awkward situation.

"C'mon," Caleb whispered as he walked by me. I gave the guys a nod and followed.

"Hey, Caleb," Dan called out to us. We both stopped and turned around. "I'm having a birthday party next weekend, you should come." Caleb gave a quick salute to confirm. "Bring a costume." Dan pulled a skinny can of spray paint out of his back pocket and shook it before we continued on our way.

We jumped through the game booth and passed the white door into the woods. “I’m sorry about him, he was really drunk,” I said, pushing branches away from my face.

“He was a lot more than drunk,” Caleb said, leading the way through the path.

“What do you mean?”

“I’ve seen a lot of people on drugs in my life.”

“You think he was high?” I asked, holding the fence open.

“Very.” Caleb ducked the gate with a grunt. “He was sniffling a lot and couldn’t stop touching his nose. I’ve seen it enough to know.”

I crouched, pushing through the fence. I believed Caleb knew what he was talking about, and I couldn’t believe Chris’s suspicion was right.

I turned the car off the dirt path onto a paved road, still thinking about our kiss. I’d never felt that same electricity when I kissed Lauren. Then, the guilt flooded over me when I realized that I’d just cheated on her.

Caleb glanced at me. “You okay?”

“Yeah,” I said after a pause, shooting him a smile for insurance.

“What did Dan mean when he said to bring a costume?”

“Oh,” I chuckled. “His birthday is also a costume party.”

“Halloween was months ago.”

“That’s what I said! You don’t actually have to come. It’s just gonna be a bunch of drunk high schoolers. That doesn’t seem like your kinda thing.”

“Hey,” Caleb said, putting a hand on my thigh. “If you’re gonna be there, it’s my kinda thing.”

Feeling his grip on my leg made my chest warm. “Do you have a costume?” I asked, not allowing the giddiness to escape my stomach.

“I have a decent Michael Myers mask,” Caleb said as he watched the trees speed by out his window. "I can steal a jumpsuit from my mom's boyfriend, Luke."

"Who's Michael Myers?" I winced, knowing Caleb would tease me.

He threw his head against the seat. "Oh, come on! The killer from the Halloween movies?"

"I haven't—"

"Seen them, I should've known." Caleb shook his head with a chuckle. "There's so much to show you."

"Teach me," I said with an exaggerated southern drawl. "I'm just a poor, sheltered boy!"

Caleb laughed. "You have to know the mask. Everyone knows the mask." Caleb looked at me for an answer, but I shrugged. "It's a white face with messy brown hair?"

"Oh yeah. I've seen that one before." I racked my brain, trying to see it, but came up empty. Caleb pulled out his phone and started typing.

"This one," he said, shoving his phone into my field of vision.

"Yep, that's the one I was thinking of." It wasn't, but I said it anyway.

Caleb pulled the phone away and scrolled through more pictures. "Did you know the first movie was so low budget that they just painted a William Shatner mask white?"

Caleb was naïve to think I knew who William Shatner was, but I was so fascinated by his random nuggets of movie trivia.

I shifted the car into park in front of Caleb's trailer. He placed his phone in his lap before looking at me. "Thanks for tonight."

"I didn't do anything," I said with a shrug. I should've thanked him for opening my eyes to something I didn't know I was missing.

"It's not easy opening up to someone," he said. "Especially about losing someone close to you." Caleb rested his hand on my thigh again. I hadn't realized how badly I craved his touch.

I placed my hand on his. "Thanks for listening."

"I should go. I need to check on Parker."

I nodded, already wondering when I would see him again. He smiled at me, and his dimples glowed under the street light. He touched my face and planted a kiss. I closed my eyes, gladly accepting his soft lips, feeling like I could fly.

As I walked into my house, I only thought about Caleb's lips. I could still feel the prickly sensation from his small amount of stubble. That was a big difference between kissing Lauren and kissing Caleb, I'd never kissed someone who shaved their face.

I tore up the stairs and heard Dad rustling around his room. I tried to tiptoe, but the floor creaked.

Dad popped his head into the hallway with wet hair. "It's a little late, Landon."

"I know, I'm sorry," I said, touching my room's doorknob.

"Text me next time you're gonna be out late, or else I won't be lending you the car again."

I stepped into my room. "I will."

"That shirt's too tight, it might be time to retire it, no?" Dad called out as my door shut.

I rolled my eyes, surprised he didn't mention my dumb smile again. My face probably resembled a cracked glow stick.

I unbuttoned my shirt, peeled it off, feeling like my skin could breathe again, and tossed it into the hamper. My eyes widened when I turned to my bed. Caleb had left his flannel there. I sat beside it, pulled it into my lap, pressed its softness between my fingers, and lifted it to my face. Closing my eyes, I inhaled his scent. Imagining it was how Caleb's bedroom smelled. Fresh linen with a hint of cologne. Not the fancy kind you get at a department store, but more like a spray from a can.

I lay down, stared at the ceiling, and blanketed Caleb's flannel over my naked torso. I wanted to feel his warmth and that explosive high again.

A rush of guilt hit me when I remembered my breakfast date with Lauren was the next day. I needed to tell her how I felt before things got in deep with Caleb. Lauren didn't deserve to be strung along.

Lauren and I agreed to drive separately to Lucky's the following day for our 'reconnection date', as she called it. The anxiety bubbled in my stomach the entire drive. I played out a few scenarios in my head. I pictured us sitting at the table eating pancakes, and suddenly, I blurt it out, jumbling the words together so frantically that she doesn't understand what I said; I'm forced to say it a second time, only slower. I imagined myself saying, 'I kissed Caleb' in slow motion, followed by her throwing her coffee all over me. Or another scenario where she shrugs it off and guilts me into staying with her for the rest of our lives.

She wouldn't do that, right? She has gay friends. She knows what it's like. She wouldn't hold me back from being happy, would she?

I spotted Lauren's bug-like car as I parked in the lot. I looked through the passenger side window and waved. Lauren smiled and reciprocated. We met behind our cars. She wore light blue jeans and a gray T-shirt. She pulled her hair into a ponytail before hugging me and planting a peck on the lips. My mind immediately flashed to kissing Caleb.

"You okay?" Lauren asked.

My face must have gone blank for a second. "Yeah, of course," I lied. "How was your grandma's?"

"Boring," she huffed as we started toward the diner. "I was on my phone, like, the whole time. But we did talk about my audition next weekend."

"How's your prep going?" I opened the glass door, and sleigh bells rang through the air.

"I feel ready. Confident," Lauren said.

Stephanie was behind the bar, tattoos on full display. She eyed us and said, "Sit anywhere you'd like."

The diner was bustling every Sunday morning. Lauren and I surveyed the tables. Only two were empty. We sat at a booth next to a large glass window that faced the parking lot. The theme of the table was puppies and kittens.

Lauren chose her side, and I sat next to her. I always hated couples who did that. It was harder to eat or have a conversation. But I felt it might make Lauren feel like I cared. I wrapped my arm around her and smiled.

Tell her. Tell her now!

She looked at me as if she were waiting.

Oh god, what if she cries? And it makes a scene? Maybe I shouldn't do this in such a public place.

I decided to tell Lauren somewhere private instead so she could feel everything she wanted and even scream at me if she needed to.

So much anxiety pushed up my chest that I just kissed her. I moved in quickly, putting passion into it so she wouldn't suspect anything was wrong. Then, a familiar voice approached our table.

"Hey guys, welcome to Luck—"

The voice cut out as I unlocked from Lauren's lips and turned to our server. The sight of Caleb wearing a Lucky's T-shirt, holding a pen and paper, stopped my breath. Our eyes met, and we stayed silent, locked onto each other.

Caleb stiffly turned, crossed the diner, and approached Stephanie behind the bar, whispering something. It was impossible to hear over the chaotic chatter of the other customers. Stephanie glanced at our table, then took his pen and pad.

"That was weird," Lauren said. "Wait, wasn't that the guy that works at our school?"

My throat felt so dry, I couldn't respond. Too distracted by Stephanie walking toward us.

She's gonna ask us to leave.

My mind fired in a hundred different directions. If Stephanie asked us to leave, I'd have to explain why. As Stephanie arrived at our table, a bead of sweat formed on my forehead.

"Sorry about that. I'll be taking your table from Caleb," Steph said. "What can I get you?"

"Can I do the avocado toast with poached eggs, please?" Lauren asked.

I became a block of ice stuck to my seat, paralyzed from the neck down.

Steph looked at me. "And for you, sweetie?"

Caleb caught my eye and then bolted to the restroom.

"Landon?" Lauren nudged me.

The ice holding me in place shattered, and I looked at Steph. "Um, the French toast," I said as if I'd just woken from hibernation. "I'll be right back." I pushed myself from the booth and started for the restroom, wondering how to explain everything to Caleb. If I'd known he worked at Lucky's, I would've suggested we go elsewhere. I weaved through the tables, barely able to catch my breath.

The restrooms at the back of the restaurant were close to the kitchen. As I pushed the door open, all I could smell was bacon. The bathroom was small and stark white with fluorescent lighting, and the smell changed to an overwhelming scent of bleach and urinal cakes. Two stalls lived beside two urinals and two sinks on the opposite wall.

Caleb leaned against a sink and crossed his arms. "So you have a girlfriend?"

"Yes," I said, standing three feet from him, worried about how much he hated me.

"You couldn't have told me that last night before I kissed you?"

"I'm sorry."

"Sorry?" Caleb let his arms fall. "Are you even gay?"

"No," I blurted. "Yes," I said even quicker. "I don't know... It's complicated."

"After everything I told you last night," Caleb said as he rubbed his forehead. "I've already done complicated. I can't go through that again."

Everything Caleb said was valid. I was scratching at an old wound. "I know, but nothing about this has been easy for me. Everything is so new! I've never felt like this."

Caleb frowned. "I can't be someone's secret again, Landon."

He passed, and his cologne hit me in the breeze. It made my heart sink.

"I loved kissing you," I said before turning around. Caleb's hand was on the doorknob, but he hadn't opened it. He stood there with his back to me. "I've never felt happier kissing anyone in my life. I don't know what it's supposed to feel like, but I know when I'm with you, I finally feel free."

Caleb turned to me. His hand lingered on the doorknob. I'll never forget the disappointment on his face.

"Figure your shit out, Lan," Caleb whispered before walking out, leaving me alone under the stark light.

I leaned against the sink, stared into the drain, and exhaled. "Goddammit." I imagined myself falling through the dark hole. Never reaching the bottom. Stuck falling forever.

I shuffled back to our table, afraid to see Caleb if I glanced around the diner. Lauren was swiping through her phone when I approached. I didn't sit back down. "I gotta go," I said.

Lauren looked at me. Her brow clenched. "What? We haven't even gotten our food yet."

"I know, I'm sorry," I said, pulling out my wallet. I placed a folded twenty-dollar bill on the table. "I don't feel good. I just have to go home." I couldn't look at Lauren. Panicked, I fled from the diner and got into my car. I just wanted to be alone. I smacked the steering wheel and leaned my head against the window. *How am I gonna fix this*?

TWENTY-THREE

I lived on autopilot for the next four days, moving through the motions. School, practice, shower, homework, sleep. I'd texted Caleb I was sorry the night after our bathroom conversation, but I never got a text back. I'd completely ruined any chance I had with him.

I felt drained anytime I saw Lauren; all I was doing was lying to her, lying to my dad, lying to myself, and it took a toll on my emotional well-being. I was good at faking it in front of Dad; he had no idea what I was going through. I doubt he would have understood it. All he asked about was football practice, and he moved on with his business. I sat at my bedroom desk, going over a practice quiz for my calculus class. My mind wandered as I scribbled little circles around the page. Suddenly, my phone buzzed. I'd never moved so quickly to grab it in my life. A text from Lauren popped on the screen.

LAUREN

Mind if I stop by tomorrow before school to say goodbye?

ME

Goodbye?

LAUREN

We're leaving for New York tomorrow…

I'd forgotten Lauren was leaving for her audition during my week of numbness.

ME

Right, I'm sorry.

I'll meet you out front.

I tossed the phone on my bed; I didn't want to continue to check it. I'd lost hope that Caleb would text me. The phone buzzed again. Assuming it was Lauren responding, I let it be.

I was back at the amusement park, and everything was operational and new. Kids ran around with giant puffs of cotton candy on a stick. The scent of fresh popcorn filled the air, and people screamed as the roller coaster sped down the track. I stood at the entrance of the Ferris wheel alone, watching crowds of people pass. Then everyone stopped, parting like the Red Sea, revealing Caleb. He walked to me, smiling widely, looking dashing in a black tux. He reached for my hand and pulled me in close to kiss me. The familiar prickle of his upper lip poked mine, and we began to float. I stopped kissing him, looking around as our feet left the gravel, and panicked.

Caleb tightened his arm around my waist, holding me close. "Everything will be okay," he whispered.

I looked him in the eyes, feeling safe in his embrace. The crowd below us clapped as we floated higher and higher.

Caleb moved in for another kiss before my eyes popped open, and I was back in my room. I'd drooled all over my practice quiz.

The digital clock on my desk glowed red; it was close to midnight. I huffed and pushed myself from the desk, groaning as my neck stiffened. I rubbed it with a strong thumb as I approached my bed. I removed my shorts, pulled my shirt over my head, and let them fall to the floor before I plopped down. I shuffled through my blanket to find my phone. Grabbing it, I checked the screen, and my stomach dropped. The buzzing earlier wasn't Lauren responding; it was Caleb, and I'd left it unread for hours. I swiped, going directly to his message.

CALEB

Hey, sorry, I haven't texted you back. I just needed time to think about everything.

I frantically typed, hoping he was still awake.

ME

Sorry I didn't see this earlier, I knocked out early.

I stared at my screen, waiting for the three little dots to pop up, but nothing came. I sighed, plugged my phone into the charger, and placed it on my bedside table before clicking off my lamp. Not wanting to close my eyes, I just stared at the dark ceiling, wondering what Caleb might say next.

He'll probably ask me to delete his number.

My phone vibrated against the wood, sending my heart through my chest. I reached over so quickly that I accidentally punched the phone off the table. "Shit," I whispered, leaning over the edge to search in the dark. I snatched it and pushed myself back up.

CALEB

Sorry if I woke you up.

ME

You didn't, it's okay.

How are you?

CALEB

I think I'm all right.

I just needed time to think about everything, so I'm sorry I didn't text you back.

ME

That's understandable.

CALEB

To be honest, it hurt me after I saw you with your girlfriend. Sorry, what's her name?

ME

Lauren.

CALEB

I assume she doesn't know that we kissed?

ME

No, she doesn't. I swear I wanted to tell her that day, but I just couldn't find the courage.

CALEB

Coming out is tough, and everyone's journey is different. I realized that I have to respect that. But damn it hurt seeing that because I really liked you.

ME

Are you saying you don't anymore?

CALEB

I go back and forth. I wasn't lying when I said I've already done complicated. What you did was shady.

ME

I promise I'll tell her. I like you a lot. It's just not gonna be easy to break up with Lauren.

CALEB

Believe me, I know that. And I don't want you to do this just for me. If this is how you really feel, then it isn't fair to her.

ME

I know. That's why I feel awful.

CALEB

Once you come out, it never really stops for the rest of your life. But every time it gets a little easier, you chip away at the insecurity and gain confidence in its place.

ME:

That's good to know.

I'm sorry I hurt you, I want you to know that it wasn't my intention.

CALEB

I keep thinking about what you said, that when you're with me, you feel free. I want to feel that way too. I just don't want to be your secret.

ME

I know, I don't want you to be either.

Staring at the bright screen in the dark hurt my eyes, so I lowered the brightness before I went blind.

CALEB

So what do we do?

I sat there frozen for a minute, thinking about how to answer his question. I didn't want to call it off just yet. There was still so much I wanted to explore with him.

ME

I just know that I don't want this to end.

CALEB

Don't let it.

ME

I think you should come to my game tomorrow night.

CALEB

I don't know, won't Lauren be there?

ME

She's actually gonna be in New York for a college audition the whole weekend.

CALEB

I don't know. Won't it be weird?

ME

Not unless we make it weird.

CALEB

Okay. I'm fine with seeing you, but nothing beyond that until you're a single man, all right?

ME

Works for me.

CALEB

I don't know much about football...

Maybe I'll bring Parker. He might have fun.

ME

Yeah! :)

CALEB

Maybe I'll watch Friday Night Lights, or Varsity Blues to get in the zone.

ME

Haha, whatever you need to do. The game starts at 7:30. Don't be late!

CALEB

I'm never late ;)

ME

Good. :) I'll see you tomorrow night then!

CALEB

Sleep tight.

ME

Night!

I placed my phone on the bedside table and returned to staring at the dark ceiling, smiling. Now that I knew Caleb would be watching, tomorrow I had a reason to play.

Friday night games always generated a particular electricity. Even in the locker room, we could hear the chants of everyone in the stands explode. The marching band played, and the cheerleaders screamed their playful taunts to pump up the crowd. That night, we played against the Skowhegan Saints, a team known for its aggression. They intentionally tried to hurt guys with their tackles, knocking players out one by one to get an easier win.

"We know how these guys play," Coach said to us in the locker room. I sat on the wooden bench in front of my locker, arms resting on my padded thighs, and wedged my helmet between my feet.

"I want you guys to keep a cool head out there and watch out for each other," Coach said.

Everyone nodded. Big fight night energy powered the room. Dad stood at the exit door, leaning against the frame. He nodded at me before Coach ended his pep talk the way he always did, "Let's go give 'em hell!"

The guys bounced to their feet and hollered, myself included.

I picked up my helmet and turned to close my locker, first reaching into my duffel bag to check my phone. I had texts from Lauren and Caleb.

LAUREN

Good luck tonight! I love you!

ME

Thanks! <3

I swiped to Caleb's text. He'd sent me a selfie of him and Parker sitting in the stands, holding a bag of popcorn and beaming enormous smiles. Parker even had two thick painted lines under his eyes, one black and one red, representing my school's colors.

CALEB:

Turns out you're playing my old high school team. Feel free to kick their asses! ;)

ME

I'll do my best!

I returned my phone to the bag with a smile. Seeing Caleb and Parker, knowing they were in the stands, was all the fuel I needed. I felt strong, like I could pick up a bus over my head. After slamming my locker, I squeezed on my helmet and glimpsed Chris from across the room; he looked at me with concern. He gestured to Dan with his eyes before slipping on his helmet.

I searched the locker room for Dan until I caught his Jersey number, 14. He'd just turned away from his locker, wiping his nose with his fingers, then wiped his fingers on his pants. Whatever he took, he wasn't hiding it very well. Dan pushed his head into his helmet and filed out with the other guys.

The crowd roared as we ran onto the field. The cheerleaders tossed girls into the air, and the band never sounded louder. The announcer called out our team's name over the loudspeakers, and the stomps on the bleachers boomed across the field. I searched the sea of people in the stands to glimpse Caleb and Parker. Even with limited vision through my helmet, I spotted them. They sat toward the bottom, close to the running track that surrounded the grassy turf. Parker jumped and waved, catching my attention. I smiled and waved back, then spotted Tasha and Steven sitting close by, sipping from styrofoam cups.

The other team stared us down. Their blue and gold uniforms had two medieval-looking S letters stretched across the sides of their helmets. It was our second time facing the Skowhegan Saints that season. We looked forward to revenge because they had beaten us in the first game.

Dan popped up in front of me and grabbed the face mask of my helmet. "Let's kill these motherfuckers!" He shouted before running onto the field.

I wanted to beat the team just as badly as he did, but I wasn't about to intentionally hurt anyone. We lined up in the middle of the field, and I looked across to jersey number 29, and he flipped me off.

A part of me wanted to tackle him right there, but that wasn't my job. My job was to get the ball from Dan and run it as far as I could.

"Blue sixteen!" Dan shouted, taking his spot behind the center.

Knowing Caleb was watching from the stands made me feel invincible. I pushed the ball of my foot into the grass, ready to run.

"Hike!" Dan shouted.

I rocketed down the field. Jersey 29 barreled forward. I needed to fake him out. He was a bull that only had eyes for me. As soon as he jumped, I twisted with a spin, avoiding jersey 29's tackle and sending him to the grass.

I glanced over my shoulder, open for the pass. Dan always threw a little high. I saw the ball spiraling toward me and caught it with a jump. When my feet met the grass, I was struck from the side. We crashed to the ground as a whistle echoed through the small holes in my helmet.

"Fuck you, pretty boy," the other guy said as he pushed himself off of me.

I stood, still feeling the pain in my ribs. I glanced at Caleb, whose hands covered his mouth. The tackle must've looked brutal. Parker raised both fists, mouthing my name. I shook off the pain and smiled, jogging back to the scrimmage line. Caleb seeing me get tackled during the first play bruised my ego but fueled my fire.

I pushed into the huddle of guys.

Dan pointed at me. "Landon, watch your fucking nine and three. Don't fuck this up for us."

"Dan, chill out," I said. "We have a hundred plays left."

"We can't play like pussies. Not against these guys," Dan responded.

I rolled my eyes at him. "Just call the next play, and let's go."

The Skowhegan Saints got more aggressive during the second quarter. With three minutes left until halftime, we were on defense. I stood on the back line. My job was to force the player with the ball to run out of bounds. Chris stood in the line in front of me. His job was to prevent the player with the ball from getting too far.

The Saints hiked the ball, and we were off. I followed behind Chris as he pushed through two players, rushing for the ball. If Chris failed, I would run the guy holding the ball off the field. A husky player with the number 43 on his chest barreled toward Chris like a Mack truck. Chris tried to evade him, but 43 wrapped an arm around his waist. Chris wiggled free before another player, number 30, grabbed Chris's face mask and yanked him to the grass.

The whistle blew, but the ref never called out player 30 for the face-mask offense.

I jogged to the old man dressed in black and white, shouting, "You need to flag 30 for the face mask."

"I didn't see it," the ref said calmly.

"I'm telling you it happened," I said, pulling off my helmet.

Dan ran up to us, looking heated, and said, "Don't tell me you're that fucking blind!"

I looked at Dan and pointed at the ref. "He said he didn't see it."

Dan's brows pinched. "The fuck he didn't! Call the penalty!"

Chris jogged over, removing his helmet, too.

"No," the ref said, shaking his head and walking off the field. The three of us stood dumbfounded while the other team strutted by us. Player 30 pulled off his helmet and kissed the air in Dan's direction.

"Pull that shit again, asshole!" Dan shouted at 30. "Come try it on me!"

30 had no hesitation stepping to Dan. The two screamed nonsense in each other's faces. Chris and I held Dan back to his detriment because 30 took a swing, connecting with Dan's jaw. Dan overpowered us, breaking free of our grip, and tackled 30, punching him in the face until the refs and coaches rushed in to separate them. The animosity between our teams cranked to eleven after that.

The Saints had a six-point lead on us during the third quarter when they finally took out a member of our team. Dan had thrown the ball down the center of the field. Two Saints flanked me.

My teammate Ray Bloom ran parallel to me. We locked eyes, and

I tossed him the ball. I was tackled but able to keep my sights on him. Ray ran the ball another two-and-a-half yards before two linebackers came out of nowhere from opposite sides. They lunged, one connected with Ray's torso and the other with Ray's legs, practically ripping him in half. The linebacker's weight landed on Ray's leg, twisting it backward. Ray let out a howling scream, quieting the rowdy crowd.

The ref called the coaches over to inspect Ray's leg. All of us took a knee and watched in horror as Ray sobbed, clutching his leg.

"Those fuckers did this on purpose!" Dan shouted.

The Saints had no respect. They stood on the sidelines laughing, making fake crying faces, mocking us. My blood boiled, and the crowd cheered as they wheeled Ray off the field on a stretcher, holding his fist in the air.

We were four points away from overturning the game with fifteen seconds left in the last quarter. The energy on the field was electric. The crowd boomed. I glanced at the stands. Parker was on Caleb's back, and they both cheered.

We all locked arms, and Dan took the lead. "It's now or never, y'all. We can pull this off. We need to be perfect." With everyone drenched in sweat, we knew the pressure was on. Dan continued, "I want to use Purple Twenty Three. Landon, do you think you can do it?"

"That's twenty yards," Chris said. "It's too risky."

"If Landon says he can do it, then we're doing it," Dan said. "We need risky if we're gonna win this."

All eyes fell on me.

"I can do it," I said, nodding.

"Let's fucking go!" Dan yelled at us. He put his fist out in the middle of the circle, and we all slapped our hands on top of it before we broke.

I stepped to the Scrimmage Line with my heart pounding. My

eyes laser-focused on the end zone. I slowed my breath, and the crowd's noise faded, leaving Dan's voice yelling, "Purple Twenty Three! Purple Twenty Three! Hike!"

I shot from my cannon, with the kind of speed that could split molecules. I dodged three players before looking over my shoulder for the ball. I felt telepathically connected to Dan; he knew exactly when to throw the ball as I turned, running backward. It was the first time in a long time that he didn't throw high. The ball spiraled into my arms like an arrow to its target.

I gripped the leather between my gloved hands and spun toward the end zone. My legs kicked into fourth gear. I soared. Five yards, then ten. I checked my left; one Saint's player trailed me. It was player 30. The path to the endzone was clear, but player 30 gained on me.

I bolted across the field like one of those lizards running on water. I glanced to my left again; 30 was even closer. If he lunged, he could nab me.

Suddenly, Chris ran into view, charging player 30 like a bull seeing red. Chris jumped, wrapping his arms around 30's waist, and slammed him down hard.

The end zone was mine and mine alone. I leaped and rolled onto my padded shoulder across the line, scoring the touchdown, pushing my team six points ahead, and winning the game.

I ripped off my helmet and slammed it to the ground, screaming my best war cry. My head chilled as the wind swept the condensation away. The team stampeded until they smashed into me with open arms, cheering and hollering. It was hard to keep my balance as each body crashed into the pile. It was a massive win for us. The crowd's cheers were deafening even while "We are the Champions" blasted from the loudspeakers. I'd never played better in my entire high school career. No one could catch me.

I chatted with Dan and Chris in the parking lot after the game as Tasha and Steven approached us. Tasha hugged the three of us, gushing about how great the game was. Steven stood by with his hands in his pockets, staring me down; it looked like he wanted to say something, but kept his distance from Dan.

"Landon Griffin?" A voice asked from behind me. I turned to a broad-shouldered man with salt and pepper hair who wore a sweater over a collared shirt and held some folded papers in his hand.

"Yeah, that's me," I said, still in my muddy gear.

"Hi, my name is Chester Redfield." He reached out to shake my hand, and I obliged. "I'm from the University of Texas," Chester said.

My arm went rigid. "Oh, nice to meet you, sir."

"You played a fantastic game tonight," Chester said as he pushed the folded papers into his back pocket. "We've had our eye on you for a while now and like what we see."

I gulped. "Thank you, sir."

"We would love to offer you a full scholarship to come play for us in the fall," Chester said with a half-smile.

Tasha gasped from behind me.

In complete shock, I wondered if I misheard him.

Chester continued, "I know this is very informal telling you in a parking lot full of people, but we like approaching our guys before going over the official stuff."

Chris grabbed my shoulder pads, and shook me, bringing me out of the shock. "Wow," I said. "I'm honored, thank you. Thank you so much." A smile filled my face, and I wished Dad had been there to hear the news with me.

"We'll be in touch," Chester said, reaching for another handshake.

"Thank you, sir. I look forward to it," I said. We all watched Chester walk away. I waited until he was out of earshot to turn around. "Holy shit!" I said through my teeth. Tasha screamed and jumped up and down, whereas Chris picked me up off my feet in a big bear hug. Even Steven clapped along with Tasha, smiling. Everyone seemed happy for me except for Dan, who leaned against a car, looking defeated.

"That should've been me," Dan mumbled.

Tasha shot daggers in Dan's direction. "What?"

Dan straightened. "I said that fucking should've been me!"

Chris tilted his head. "Seriously, bro?"

Dan pointed at me but looked at Chris. "I played just as good as he did!"

"No one is saying you didn't," Steven said.

"No one fucking asked you, faggot! What the fuck do you know?" Dan yelled, stepping toward Steven.

Chris held his brother back with a hand against Dan's chest. "Landon's your best friend," Chris said. "You can't be happy for him?"

Dan shoved Chris's arm away. "For what? Because he's some fucking hot shot now? Fuck all of you." Dan grabbed his helmet off the car, stomped through the parking lot, and yanked the gym door open.

My chest deflated.

Chris turned to us. "He's an asshole, guys. I'm sorry."

"You shouldn't be the one apologizing," I said.

Chris pulled his helmet off the hood of a blue car. "I'm gonna make sure he cools down." He backed away, still looking at me, Tasha, and Steven. "You guys are still coming to the party tomorrow night, right?"

"Of course!" Tasha said.

Steven crossed his arms. "I won't be coming for obvious reasons."

"I know it's Dan's birthday, but I invite everyone no matter if Dan likes them," Chris said, half smiling. "It's my house too."

"Maybe I'll make an appearance then," Steven said, tossing his invisible hair and making Tasha chuckle.

"Cool," Chris said before jogging away. "See you guys tomorrow! Congrats again, Landon!"

Tasha tackled me with a hug. I laughed, hugging her back. A line of cars had formed, leaving the lot. "I'm so freaking proud of you!" Tasha squealed.

"Yeah, you should be really proud, Landon," Steven said, watching us. "Eighty-three must be your lucky number."

I glanced down at my jersey and could smell sweat seeping

through. "Since day one." I pointed a thumb over my shoulder. "I should go tell my dad."

"Yes, yes, go," Tasha said, slapping me on my shoulder pads. "We have face masks to get to." She trotted to Steven and wrapped her arm around him.

"I'll see you guys at the party," I said with a nod.

"Can't wait!" Tasha said as they waved goodbye.

I'd almost forgotten about Caleb and Parker in all the excitement. I started toward the field, cradling my helmet.

Caleb and Parker sat alone in the front row of the stands. Caleb tossed pieces of popcorn into the air as Parker tried to catch them in his mouth. I smiled and jogged the empty field to reach them. My legs begged me to stop.

"Landon!" Parker shouted as he saw me. A piece of popcorn accidentally hit him in the face. I approached with heavy breaths. Parker threw himself at me with a big hug.

"Hey, bud," I said, wrapping my arms around his head. "Did you enjoy the game?"

"It was so cool!" Parker said. He jumped onto the first step of the bleachers with excitement. "When you made that last touchdown and you were like, Aaahhhhhh!" Parker mimicked throwing down a helmet and even added a strongman pose. I laughed, watching him try to flex his scrawny arms.

Caleb faced me, his smile crooked. "I think you have a new fan."

"And what about you?" I asked, stepping toward Caleb.

"Oh, I'll be first in line for your autograph," he teased.

"Shut up," I said with a chuckle, waking the butterflies in my stomach. "Something kind of insane just happened."

Parker jumped off the step and settled next to his big brother.

"I just got offered a scholarship to play at the University of Texas."

"Holy shit!" Caleb shouted before scooping me in a hug. His force knocked me back a bit, causing me to drop my helmet. I wrapped my arms around him, thinking how lucky I was to touch him again. "That's incredible! Congrats, Landon!"

Everything had gone over Parker's head. "What's a scholarship?"

Caleb pulled away and looked at his brother. "That means Landon gets to go to college for free and play football there."

"Sounds cool," Parker said. "But wait, people have to pay to go to college?"

Caleb and I nodded.

"That's dumb," Parker said.

Caleb glanced at me. "He's not wrong."

We busted into laughter.

Caleb and Parker walked me back to the school, where we stopped in front of the big metal door that led into the gym. The parking lot was empty. Everyone was probably at Lucky's or Joe's Pizza Place by then.

I leaned against the door and glanced around the parking lot before reaching for Caleb's hand. I pulled him close, hoping I didn't smell too badly. I wanted to kiss him more than anything.

Caleb eased backward. "Hey, remember what I said? Are you a single man yet?"

I sighed. "You're right, I know, I know."

Caleb squeezed my hand and smiled before letting go. Not being able to touch him more killed me.

"You still wanna go to the party with me tomorrow?" I asked.

"Yeah, I think so. Just text me the address."

"Will do." I smiled as Caleb and Parker walked by me, headed toward the street. "Hey," I called out, causing Caleb to look over his shoulder at me. "You look really cute tonight."

Caleb smiled, and his cheeks flushed. "So do you, football boy." Caleb winked at me, and my chest warmed.

Parker grabbed Caleb's hand as they continued on their way. He looked up at Caleb. "Are you and Landon boyfriends?"

"No," I heard Caleb say with a laugh.

"You must really like him then," Parker said.

"Yeah," Caleb said, looking down at Parker. "I like him a lot."

Just hearing him say that sent me to the moon. I walked into the building, unable to hide my beaming smile.

TWENTY-FOUR

I crossed the street and headed home, looking both ways before I checked my phone. Lauren texted me.

LAUREN:

TASHA JUST TOLD ME THE NEWS!
CONGRATS BABE!

ME:

Haha, thank you! I couldn't believe it.

I walked through the side door. To my surprise, Dad was already there in the kitchen. He popped the cork from a bottle of champagne, scaring me out of my skin.

"Congratulations, son!" Dad yelled as the bottle overflowed. "Oh, shit, shit." He held it over the sink as the fizz poured out. I laughed and tossed my duffel bag on the floor. "I've been saving this for when we got the news. You're not twenty-one, but one glass won't hurt."

"Okay." I shrugged with a smile as I sat at the kitchen island. "How'd you find out?"

"Mr. Redfield talked to me and coach after he approached you," Dad said as he filled two glasses with the bubbly liquid. "I'm proud of you, son. I knew this would happen!" He handed me a glass.

We clinked our drinks. "Thanks!" The bubbles tickled my nose when I took a sip. I hadn't expected it to be so sweet. I couldn't help but wonder if Dad would've shown the same excitement if I'd gotten into the writing program at NYU. I gulped another sip and said, "Dan seemed pretty upset."

Dad wiped his mustache with a paper towel. "About what?"

"I don't know, he just seemed jealous I got a scholarship, and he didn't."

"That's ridiculous. There's still time. Another school could approach him."

"Yeah, you're right." I took another sip. The bubbles crackled down my throat, and I thought about how much Dan had changed throughout high school. A lot of stuff had changed. I placed the glass on the counter. "I wish we could tell Mom," I whispered.

Dad's smile faded as if I'd reminded him she was gone. "She'd be just as proud, and she'd already be planning a party to celebrate," Dad said before gulping the rest of his drink.

I stared at him across the kitchen island. "I miss her."

"I'm gonna head to bed. I'm beat," Dad said, pouring himself another glass, ignoring me. He ascended the stairs, gripping the bottle of champagne in one hand and his full cup in the other.

I stayed in the kitchen alone and took my time sipping the champagne. All the things my mom would miss hit me all at once. She wouldn't be there to take pictures of us before prom, see me graduate, or drop me off at college with tears in her eyes. I thought of an entire lifetime of events where moms celebrate their sons and how I'd never get that.

I downed the rest of my drink and grabbed my duffel bag before climbing the stairs. My bed's mattress bounced when I finally sat. I imagined myself playing college football, going to parties, and skipping class to sleep in. Then I pictured how different it would look if I were in New York, not playing football but writing on my laptop at the library.

My phone vibrated from another text.

LAUREN

If anyone deserves it, it's you!

ME

Dan didn't seem to think so.

LAUREN

Ugh, Tasha told me. :(I wish he would think of someone other than himself for once. I'm sorry, babe.

ME

It's whatever. How's NYC?

LAUREN

OMG it's amazing!

Our hotel is so nice! We're staying at this place on 50th Street like right next to Times Square. It feels so alive here. Everyone is always moving. I love it!

I wanted to visit New York and taste the fast-paced life. I wanted to feel the wind of a subway train as it rushed by, and walk through a crowded Times Square, bumping shoulders with tourists.

ME

I'm jealous, haha.

LAUREN

Well, if I get in, you'll have to come to visit me all the time!

. . .

I wondered what a long-distance relationship would be like if she moved to New York. Maybe she would know about Caleb by then, and I wouldn't have to break up with her over the phone. Anxiety balled in my chest just thinking about it.

ME

You're gonna get in, you're too good not to!

LAUREN

Awww, you're so sweet! <3

Oh!

My dad just told me that my prom dress is ready! And he'll be picking up your tux this week.

ME

Holy crap, I can't believe prom is a little over a month away.

LAUREN

I know, right?! I'm so excited!

I have to sleep cutie, we're getting up early to head to the audition. I miss you so much!

ME

All right, break a leg! Sleep tight. :)

LAUREN

Goodnight! <3

I missed being around Lauren, of course, but the way I missed her and the way I missed Caleb were two very different things. Guilt pierced my stomach.

I can make this all go away if I just had the balls.

My head hit my pillow. I wanted to text Caleb goodnight, but I couldn't keep my eyes open. Not even having the energy to get up to turn my light off or get undressed.

I spent most of the next afternoon figuring out my costume for Dan's party that night. I wanted something that showed a lot of skin, so Caleb couldn't take his eyes off me. Browsing Pinterest boards, I eventually chose an ancient Greek look.

It was simple but hopefully effective. I had to remind myself it was a birthday party, not a Halloween costume contest.

I wondered if Dan would still hold a grudge when I showed up, not wanting to deal with the awkwardness. I just wanted a calm night playing beer pong with Caleb.

Wait, maybe someone on probation shouldn't be around underage drinking.

I grabbed my phone and texted Caleb, airing all my anxious energy.

CALEB

lol, I'm not worried about it. Let's just have fun.

He was annoyingly easygoing about everything.

I'd pulled a vine off the drainpipe in our backyard and tied it together. Then I glued a bunch of green leaves to it and made a very poor-looking crown that rested on my head. I pulled a white sheet from the upstairs closet and brought it to my room. Opening my laptop, I'd already queued up a YouTube video on how to make a toga.

My phone vibrated on my desk. I hopped over to it.

. . .

LAUREN

Okay, I think it went well.

ME

How do you feel?

LAUREN

I was so nervous, but I think I did the best I could.

ME

Don't worry then! I'm sure they loved you!

LAUREN

I hope so! Getting ready for the party?

ME

Yeah, figuring out my costume now!

LAUREN

Aw yay! Send me pics when you're done. We're gonna find a place to eat. I'll text you later!

I returned my phone to the desk, stripped down to my white boxer briefs, held the sheet in one hand, and then pressed play on the video. A buff frat bro appeared on-screen, showing off the toga he wore. "Hey guys, welcome back to my channel," his deep voice boomed from my speakers. "No college experience is complete without a toga party. Today I'm gonna give you ten easy steps to turn your basic bed sheet into a kick-ass toga!"

I had to stop the video and rewind as he went through the steps quickly. The guy was a pro. He seemed to be in the living room of a big house, I could see a coffee table made of beer cans behind him. It felt like it took hours to get the toga configuration correct. I wrapped it over my shoulder and tied a knot, and then through my legs and tied another knot, and then around my waist, tying one more. I already knew unwrapping it would feel like one of those brain puzzles where you have to unlink the two metal pieces.

After tying the last knot, I looked in the mirror, placed the leaf crown on my head, and smiled. I just needed a pair of flip-flops to complete the look. The sheet was mainly wrapped around my waist and under my crotch. My hips looked wider than they were, thanks to the fluffiness of the fabric. The sheet rose across my torso and wrapped around my right shoulder. It exposed the whole left side of my upper body. My hips poked out from the sheet. I tugged the waistband of my underwear down just enough to make it look like I wasn't wearing anything underneath. I was proud of what I'd accomplished and hoped Caleb would find me irresistible.

I glanced at the clock on my desk, I was already late. "Shit!" Hopping to my closet door, I yanked it open. It was dark, so I had to find my one pair of flip-flops, feeling around the floor aimlessly with one foot. Once I'd slipped them on, I ran down the stairs, out the door, and around the backyard to collect my bike. Dad had taken the car, but Dan's house was only five blocks away. I planned to take my bike anyway in case I drank too much.

I regretted wearing flip-flops as I pedaled, not realizing the difficulty. It was already dark, and my exposed nipple hardened as I flew through the breeze. The street lights popped on, and two women, drinking on their porch, whistled at me as I rode by.

By the time I got to Dan's block, I was panting. I jumped off my bike to walk the rest of the way. Butterflies fluttered around my insides as I thought about seeing Caleb. I couldn't wait to introduce him to everyone and prove he wasn't the criminal they thought he was. Eager to show them Caleb's charming side.

Music blasted from Dan's house as I approached. It was a split-level style, four-bedroom home with red siding and white shutters on every window. People congregated around the large front porch, sipping out of red solo cups. I ditched my bike in the front yard and started up the cement path that shot down the middle of the front lawn. I flip-flopped to the porch, taking in all the costumes.

Katie Bear dressed as a nun, which seemed appropriate. Zach Richards dressed as a military person, wearing camouflage shorts and a T-shirt. Dog tags hung from his neck. Chuck Dempsy dressed as a cop, wearing a jacket with the word 'POLICE' across the back and a pair of aviator sunglasses.

I opened the front door and was hit with a sound wave of chatter and loud music. Someone had blown up a bunch of colored balloons that littered the entire first floor. I surveyed the space; there were more people there than I expected. Every room in the house looked shoulder-to-shoulder crowded. The strong scent of marijuana seeped through the ceiling from upstairs. It overwhelmed me. I hated showing up to social events by myself.

I wonder if Caleb's here yet.

"Landon! What's up!" Chris called out to me, leading a girl upstairs. I almost didn't recognize him. He wore a long wig with a tie-dye bandana around his forehead and a tie-dye shirt and shorts.

Is he supposed to be a hippie? "Hey!" I shouted and waved before he disappeared.

"Landon! Here!" Tasha found me and pushed a plastic cup to my chest. "Catch up!"

"Oh," I said, taking the cup from her, putting it to my mouth, and inhaling the drink's hairspray aroma. The liquid burned my insides when I gulped it down. I was never much of a drinker, but when Tasha tells you to do something, you do it. "Jesus." I winced. "What is this?"

"Dan's special!" Tasha yelled over the music as she bopped around. Her flailing dance moves told me she may have already had a few. Tasha dressed as Catwoman in fake leather pants and a whip wrapped around her torso. Cat ears connected to a black mask over her eyes. She looked amazing.

"Hey, girl!" Steven yelled as he approached us. Tasha screamed and hopped around with him as if they hadn't seen each other in years.

Steven was practically naked. He wore very, very short white shorts and nothing else but angel wings, attached to a sparkly halo that hovered over his head. His eyes shimmered with gold eyeshadow, and his lips blossomed from the pink lip gloss. His entire body sparkled with glitter.

I stared at him, thinking, *Am I attracted to Steven? No, it's just the outfit. Right?*

"You look amazing, Landon," Steven said after he and Tasha finished bouncing.

"Thanks, so do you," I said, tipping my cup to his. "I'm kind of hungry. Is there any food around?"

"Yeah, I just saw some in the kitchen. C'mon." Steven gestured that Tasha and I follow. We pushed through the crowds of dancing teens, and I spotted Betty Grass making out with Darren Deckler. People stood around them, cheering them on. It was strange; I'd never seen them talk to each other during our four years at Madison High.

I took another gulp of my mystery drink, and it's fire ripped through my throat. We reached the kitchen, and the counters were filled with bowls of assorted snacks. Beer cans littered the space between them. I reached for some pretzels and baked potato chips, swallowing them with more liquid fire. Jordan Palicki placed a plate of brownies in front of us, knocked some beer cans to the floor, and walked away.

"Oh my god, those look so good," Tasha said.

Steven and I nodded in agreement, but only I reached for one and gobbled it down. The brownie was so fudgy, it stuck to my teeth. Chewing it made me crave a glass of milk, but all I had was the kerosene in my little red cup. I downed it and shoved another brownie in my mouth. A strange taste lingered on my tongue, so I hurried for another handful of pretzels.

"I'm empty," I said, shaking my cup.

"On it." Tasha disappeared into the crowd, leaving Steven and me alone. We bopped our heads to the music. I don't think either of us knew what to say.

Steven broke the ice. "Can you believe Lauren's living it up in New York right now?"

"I know, I'm so jelly," I said with immediate regret. I'd never abbreviated the word jealous before.

"Samesies," Steven shot back. "She said she slayed the audition."

Steven must've gotten a different play-by-play than I had. Lauren seemed unsure when she texted me earlier. Maybe she was catching on to my dismissiveness. The anxiety poured into my stomach like the Dan Special, quick and fiery. I wondered if Lauren had brought up anything about me to Steven.

"Yeah, she told me. I'm excited for her," I strained over the music.

Steven leaned against the kitchen counter and faced me. "So are you guys gonna do long distance if she moves to New York and you're here?"

Am I being interrogated? Will he report my answers back to Lauren?

"Uh, I mean, I guess?" I shoved more pretzels into my mouth. "We haven't talked about it yet." I wanted to get off the subject of Lauren. "You should try a brownie. They're so good!"

"I can't. I'm trying to stay away from sweet stuff," Steven said, rubbing his fingers down his smooth, rippled stomach.

"Steven, I can see each ab of your six-pack. I don't think one brownie is gonna change that."

"Better safe than sorry," Steven said with a shrug.

Tasha bound into the kitchen like she had just run through a tornado. She held a half-empty bottle of vodka under her arm and three shot-sized cups in one hand.

Steven took the bottle from her, and read the label. "Where did you get this?"

"Corey Bashoff," Tasha said with ease. "He just handed it to me before going to the backyard."

"Are you trying to kill me?" I asked. My drinking habits were very few and far between. Other than the cup of champagne I had with my dad, I hadn't touched a drop of alcohol since the night of junior prom.

"Just one shot!" Tasha said with a smile.

"I don't know," I said.

Tasha groaned. "It's senior year! Who knows what'll happen

when we all go to separate schools? This might be one of the last parties we have."

"Well, there's still prom, and graduation," I said.

"He's got a point," Steven said before Tasha gave him a light slap on the arm. She eyed me, and her lips pursed.

She might slap me in the face if I don't take it. "Fine, I'll do it! But just one. My first drink is already fucking me up," I said, raising my plastic cup.

Tasha yelped excitedly and poured the vodka to the rim of each shot cup. We all grabbed one and raised it. Some of mine spilled across my hand before I threw it back. My jaw clenched as the alcohol slid down my throat. Straight vodka was the worst. Tasha and Steven seemed to take the shot like pros.

Steven glanced around the kitchen. "Do you think anyone here is gay?"

"Good luck with that," Tasha scoffed.

"Hey, a girl can dream, okay!" Steven yipped.

I almost spat my drink out, laughing. "Where's Dan?" I asked after another gulp.

"I saw Dan when I first showed up," Tasha said, reaching for a handful of chips from a blue bowl. "But that was like an hour ago."

Steven swayed with the music. "Can we go dance or something?"

"Yaaaassss!" Tasha yelled, grabbing our hands and pulling us to the living room.

We pushed through the sweaty bodies and found a spot in the middle of everyone. The music was even louder in the living room. Everyone danced to a techno beat.

"Does this feel familiar?" Tasha yelled.

My heart skipped. I thought she was asking me, but Steven responded quickly.

"Yes, except there usually aren't this many girls!" Steven shouted back.

My mind flashed to spotting Steven's pink hair at Club Paradise. *Steven would've said something by now if he'd seen me, right?*

"Dude!" I heard a guy yell as he approached Jordan Palicki, who was dancing next to us, dressed in all white. "Where did you put the weed brownies?"

"They're on the kitchen counter!" Jared yelled back.

My world stood still when I realized what I'd done.

"Oh my god," I yelled to the others. "Fuck!"

"What?" Tasha yelled, still dancing.

"I ate two brownies!" I said.

"Yes, we watched you do it," Steven hollered. "So what?"

"I just heard someone ask where the weed brownies were!" I'd never smoked or taken edibles before. Tasha and Steven busted out laughing. I tried to put on a serious face. "Guys! This isn't funny. I've never been high before!"

"Boy, you are about to have a great night!" Tasha said between fits of laughter.

My tongue dried, so I took a mouthful of my drink. We continued to dance and laugh, and I tried to remember if I'd put on deodorant. I raised my arms into a dance move to give myself a whiff. No one seemed to notice or care. I was relieved by the familiar scent of Old Spice.

I scanned the party as we danced, hunting for Caleb. I told him when the party started but had yet to see Michael Myers appear.

I finally spotted Dan through the sliding glass doors that led into the backyard. "Dan's outside, we should say hi," I said with a slight slur of my S syllables. Steven rolled his eyes but followed behind Tasha and I. Sliding the door open, I stepped onto the backyard's grass. The fresh air dipped cooler, and different music played much quieter. A large rectangular, in-ground pool took up the middle of the yard and was lit up from under the water. A dozen balloons floated on the surface. The whole yard was lit by lantern string lights that lined the wooden fence surrounding the yard.

"Dan!" I called out. He was huddled in a small group and looked up when he heard his name. He wore khaki shorts and an oversized Hawaiian shirt. A flower lei hung around his neck, and sunscreen covered his nose. A pair of sunglasses were tucked into the top of

Dan's shirt. He staggered to me and bumped my fist with his. "Happy Birthday," I said, smiling.

"Thanks, man!" Dan said as he sipped his beer. He looked at Tasha and Steven behind me and said, "Guys, we're about to play a game, but I wanna talk to Landon for a sec." Dan wrapped his arm around my neck and dragged me away from my two comrades. He brought me to a quieter corner of his yard. "Hey," he whispered. His sniffles started again, and he wiped his nose with his fingers. "Are you drinking the Dan Special?"

I glanced inside my cup. "Yeah, what the hell is in it?"

"Uh," Dan said, searcing the ground. "Tequila, Rum, Vodka, some orange juice," he paused. "And Sprite!"

"Jesus, it's awful," I said before downing the rest in my cup.

Dan reached into his pocket. "You should try some of this." He looked around the yard, then opened his hand, revealing a small plastic baggie filled with white powder.

I blocked the view of his hand with my body. "Dude, what the fuck."

Dan poked his finger through the top of the bag, scooped a bit onto the tip, brought it to his nose, and snorted it like a pro. "This'll give you energy for hours, bro," Dan said. "It makes me fuck like Superman."

"Dan, where did you get this?"

"I know a guy in Skowhegan. I can hook you up."

"I don't want the hookup. Where do you get the money for this?"

Dan shrugged. "I sell a little too."

"A little what?"

"Whatever he wants me to. Coke, meth, weed, rocks, whatever."

"Jesus, Dan! Do you know how badly this could fuck you up? If Coach finds out, you'd be kicked off the team! You could say goodbye to getting a scholarship."

Dan closed the bag and pushed it back into his pocket. His face twisted. "Fuck, Landon, it's not that serious," Dan said with a deep sniff.

"Are you insane? Of course, it is!" I said through gritted teeth. "And if the cops caught you—"

"Guys!" Tasha yelled from across the yard. "Come on, let's play!"

Dan pushed by me, and I flanked him, heading back across the yard. "Don't show anyone else," I whispered as we passed the pool. Dan just wiped his nose.

Ten people surrounded a circular plastic table on which someone had placed an empty beer bottle. My legs tingled as I stood next to Tasha.

"Okay," Jordan Palicki said. "We're gonna play Spin the Bottle Truth or Dare."

Tasha leaned to me and whispered, "What is this? Middle school?"

I covered my mouth, trying not to laugh as Jordan explained the rules.

"It starts with someone spinning the bottle. Whoever it lands on, the spinner gets to ask that person a truth or dare. If the person refuses that truth or dare, they have to kiss the spinner. No matter what you decide to do, you always gotta take a drink." Jordan finished by placing a full bottle of vodka on the table. Everyone cheered.

I rubbed my left eye, feeling lightheaded. My fingers tingled, too. The alcohol and weed brownies hit me all at once, like two bandits hijacking my body. I blinked and felt my head fill with sand.

Jessica Walters spun the bottle. My eyes locked on it, hypnotized. My head wobbled back and forth, the sand getting heavier. The spinning bottle slowed and landed on Max Gibbons, dressed as a magician. I wanted to see him do a magic trick so badly.

"Truth or dare?" Jessica said as she played with her teased hair. She was dressed as an 80s chick and obnoxiously chewed a piece of gum.

"Dare," Max said.

Please dare him to do a magic trick. I hope he pulls a bunny out of his hat.

"I dare you to take this gum from me," Jessica said with a wink.

Max didn't hesitate, jumping over the table to get to her. He pushed his face against hers, and their tongues fought to the death for the piece of gum.

My breath heavied as my head filled with more sand about to overflow. *Focus, focus. You might miss the magic trick. Bunnies are so cute. I hope it's a white one.*

My head swayed, feeling heavier. I could no longer resist the weight and let my head swing backward. Looking at the night sky as the sand poured down my neck and spine felt so good. The sand rushed down my back as if it were a water slide. It pushed past my tailbone and under my crotch, out my groin. The tickling sensation pushed out an uncontrollable laugh. I hadn't noticed the bottle spinning again or that it stopped on me until Tasha nudged my shoulder.

I'm so fucked.

TWENTY-FIVE

"Landon, hello?" Tasha waved her hand in front of my face.

"Yeah, hi. What's up?" I said with squinted eyes, trying to focus.

"She asked you a question," Tasha said with a grin.

I looked across the table. Maddy Houser dressed as a construction worker. I'd never seen a pink hard hat before. "How many tools can you fit in your tool belt?!" I blurted, pointing at her waist.

"No," Tasha said, pushing my pointed arm down. "She asked *you* a question."

Everyone's laugh pulsed through my skull.

I stared at Maddy, my brows raised high. "Oh. What's the question then?"

"Truth or dare?" Maddy said flatly.

"Truth!" I shouted, straightening like one of those Christmas Nutcracker statues.

"Would you kiss a guy for a hundred dollars?" Maddy asked.

All eyes turned to me, and I glanced at Steven. The way he looked at me set my inner paranoia free. *He knows. He knows I kissed a boy and that I did it for free. Where would the hundred dollars even come from? Who has a hundred dollars they would give away?* I sat on the question for way too long. "No," I said. "Not enough money." Everyone laughed at me. Even Steven chuckled.

I want to kiss Caleb. Where is he?

My eyes whipped around the yard, looking for Caleb. The bottle of vodka had made its way to me, and Dan pushed it to my chest. I'd forgotten the rule: take a shot after answering the question. Leaning back, I let the liquid fill my mouth, tasting a hint of blueberry. I thought the pleasant fruit might help with the burn on the way down, but I was very wrong. I passed the bottle to Tasha, and she gestured to the table. It was my turn to spin the empty bottle.

My whole body felt covered in pixie dust. Convinced if I jumped off the ground, I could fly around the yard like Peter Pan. I gave the empty bottle a delicate spin, terrified I'd somehow break it. My head spun with the bottle. When it stopped, I looked up, following the neck of the bottle. It landed on Jordan Palicki.

"TRUTH?" I shouted, then whispered, "Or dare?" I closed my left eye and scrunched my face, acting like a pirate.

Jordan crossed his arms. "Dare."

"Wait," I said. "Who are you dressed as?"

"John Lennon," Jordan said, sounding offended.

"Okaaayyyyy. John," I spat back like a second-grader. "I dare you..." I stalled with zero ideas. More and more people filed out of the sweaty living room dance party. I completed a 360 and placed my groggy gaze back on Jordan. "I dare you to jump in the pool... naked."

Everyone around us gasped.

Jordan thought about it for a beat, then casually walked to Tasha, took the vodka bottle from her, and chugged it for a few seconds. Jordan oozed confidence as he strutted to the pool. Everyone cheered him on. Jordan was a lanky kid who looked older than eighteen. He stripped off his white shirt and pants and stood at the pool's edge in his tighty whities. People chanted his name.

I joined in screaming, "Jordan! Jordan!" at the top of my lungs.

Within a blink, Jordan pulled down his underwear, exposing his flat ass that had never seen an ounce of sun. Most of the girls shielded their eyes. Everyone else watched as Jordan catapulted himself into a cannonball, headed for the water. Unfortunately for him, his balls hung between his legs after he pulled his knees to his chest, so his nut sack slapped the water first. Every guy watching groaned with a collective wince.

Jordan seemed unfazed as he pulled himself up out of the water. I couldn't help but stare at his wet, naked body as it emerged. That was the first penis I'd seen in real life that wasn't my own. The alcohol rushed through me, sending all the blood to my crotch. I forced myself into a lawn chair to hide my erection. Jordan pulled his dry clothes over his wet body and rejoined the circle. It was his turn, next. Jordan's spin landed on a glistening Steven.

"Truth," Steven replied to the age-old question.

As if he'd waited years, Jordan asked, "How many dicks have you had?"

I sat upright in the lawn chair.

Steven's eyes shot to a jaw-clenched Dan. Tension hung heavy in the crisp air.

"Okay, that's enough," Tasha said.

"It's all right," Steven said. "I don't have to answer."

"If you don't answer, that means you and Jordan have to kiss," Maddy said.

"Exactly," Steven said with an evil grin. I imagined devil horns popping through his forehead, knocking his halo to the ground.

"Rules are rules," Jordan said with a shrug.

Steven placed his hands behind his back and puckered up. Jordan met him and bent, swiftly pecking Steven on his glossy lips. Everyone cheered except for Dan.

"This is fucking disgusting," Dan said, turning away. "Fuck this game!" He stomped to the sliding door and stepped inside.

Steven's face could hardly contain his smile as Jordan walked away. The circle of people playing dispersed in different directions after Dan stormed off. Honestly, I was jealous of the kiss. Except, I didn't want to kiss Steven, or Jordan. I wanted to kiss my perfect boy. I wanted to touch his smooth face and feel his dimples while he smiled. After a long day of working outside, I wanted to smell the musk erupting from Caleb's pores and run my fingers through his thick hair. I wanted the confidence to kiss him when everyone looked and realized why I was jealous of Steven. He got to be himself with no apologies while I was too afraid to twist the knob of the closet door.

"Snacks?" Tasha said, looking down at me in the lawn chair. She and Steven held hands.

"Oh my god, yes!" I said as they helped me up. I glanced around the yard for Caleb again before stepping into the house. "Holy shit, I smell pizza." I imagined myself becoming a bloodhound, frantically sniffing at the floor until I found the baked, cheesy bread. Three boxes were laid on the coffee table, and hungry teenagers clamored for every piece. I swooped in like a seagull in a Burger King parking lot, swiped a slice, and shoved the cheesy triangle into my mouth. Not realizing how hot it was. I chewed while blowing air out to cool it down. I turned to Tasha and Steven. "This is soooo good!"

Tasha grabbed a piece, but Steven held off.

My shoulders bounced to the beat of the blaring music. "Who bought this?" I asked. "I want to shake their hand right now." I'd never been that wasted, but kind of loved every second of it.

Someone knocked into me, and I dropped what was left of my slice. I tried to catch the pizza but only squished it against myself, smearing the red sauce on my white costume and bare chest.

"Jesus," Steven said, clamoring for napkins from the table. "This is why we can't have nice things," he chuckled as he wiped the sauce from my chest. For the first time, I was grateful I couldn't grow chest hair; it would've made for a much harder clean-up job.

I shoved the last bit of crust in my mouth as Steven wiped me down. I looked him in the eyes for the first time since eighth grade. *They're so blue.* Without thinking, but with a mouth full of crust, I said. "Thanks, TheatreNerd."

Steven shot me a look with a face paler than usual and stopped wiping. His eyes widened. "What did you just say?"

I glanced at the sliding door and saw Caleb wearing his full Michael Myers costume. He stood in the yard, leaning against the shed in the back corner. I turned and rushed through the open door, keeping my tunnel vision on the white mask.

Wiping the pizza sauce from my mouth, I pushed through a circle of girls dressed like slutty farm animals and passed the pool. Jordan and a few others splashed at each other. A cold mist hit my bare legs as I approached Caleb, who held a drink in one hand. A girl dressed as a nun chatted with him.

Why didn't he come to look for me?

Caleb wore exactly what he said he would: a dark blue jumpsuit and a white mask with messy brown hair.

"Hey!" I said louder than expected. The nun peeked over her shoulder and walked away as I approached. The white mask nodded at me.

"I've been looking everywhere for you," I said as I grabbed him by the wrist, pulling him to the small space between the back of the shed and the tall wooden fence. It was a tight fit, but I wanted to ensure we weren't visible to anyone. "I can't believe you're here. I mean, I'm so glad you are. I haven't been able to stop thinking about you." I touched his shoulder before sliding my finger to the top button of his jumpsuit. "I haven't stopped thinking about our kiss at the Ferris wheel and how perfect it was. I want to taste you on my lips again." It was complete word vomit, and it showed no signs of stopping. "You drive me crazy. Caleb. Since the first time I saw you, I was so enamor-, what's that word? En something. I know it starts with an E. Whatever, I already thought you were perfect, but then we started hanging out, and I saw how amazing you are with your brother, and I fell even harder for you." Caleb didn't speak as I spewed everything I had at him without taking a breath. I pushed closer until our stomachs touched. "I know I have a girlfriend, and I'm gonna deal with that, I promise, but being around you has made me feel so many things I've never felt, and I want more. I want to kiss you again." I placed his hand against my bare chest and continued to guide it down my stomach, making him caress my skin. His fingers were heaven. "I want to feel you against me," I whispered as I moved his hand lower, past my hip. His fingers made it to the waistband of my underwear when he flinched, jerking his hand away. Caleb shook his head and backed out of the small space. "I'm sorry," I said as I squeezed my way out, but he didn't hear me; he was already halfway across the yard. I wanted to chase after him, but my head spun wildly as if in the center of a tornado. Everything around me twisted into blurred colors, so I found my way into a lawn chair and closed my eyes. *What did I do wrong?*

I woke up face down in my bed. The warm rays of the morning sun baked my bare back. My head lifted an inch off the drool-soaked pillow, and a bass drum pounded against my temples. I rolled onto my back with a groan and shielded my eyes from the sun. It took all the strength I had to prop onto my elbows. A head of familiar curls sat at my desk, staring at my open laptop. "Hello?" I mumbled. "What's going on?"

Tasha whipped around in the desk chair. "Oh, you're up!"

I leaned against the headboard. "Am I dead?"

Tasha rolled the desk chair to my bed. "You probably feel like it."

I glanced at my stomach, realizing I was only in my underwear, and covered my bulge with both hands. "Um. Why am I damp? Please tell me I didn't piss myself."

Tasha rolled her eyes. "You thought jumping off the roof into the pool would be a good idea. You were soaked when I finally got you into bed. I took your costume off, but there was no way in hell I was changing your underwear too."

My eyes widened. "Holy shit. I jumped off the roof?"

"You don't remember that?"

"I don't remember much of last night, no," I said, shaking my head.

Tasha reached for the steaming mug on my bedside table. "Here, I made you some coffee."

I took the cup and whispered, "Oh my god, my dad."

"It's fine. He was already asleep when I brought you home last night. He must be sleeping in because I didn't see him this morning either."

"Thank god." I brought the cup to my lips, blowing on the liquid. "Were you on my computer?"

"Yeah, I was checking my email. Which reminds me." Tasha said, rolling back to my desk. She clicked through my laptop. "I'm releasing a special edition of the *Monthly,* and I noticed you had some stories already written on your desktop. Can I take one?"

"Let me guess," I said with a groan. "You already read them?"

She squinted one eye over her shoulder. "...maybe."

"Sure, take whatever," I said, taking my first sip. It was a warm, sweet, and creamy welcome compared to the poison I drank the night before.

"So," Tasha said as she stood from the desk. "Who's Caleb?"

My heart leaped from my chest, and I choked on my drink. I placed the cup on my nightstand, looking at Tasha dumbfounded. "What?"

"Boy, don't play stupid," Tasha said. "You couldn't stop talking about him during our walk home. You said he wouldn't kiss you at the party or something?"

"Fuck," I said through gritted teeth, pressing my hands to my forehead. *I'm so stupid!* I remembered nothing after Caleb rejected me behind the shed. And my idiot drunken mouth blabbed about it. "Did I tell anyone else?" I asked, panicked.

Tasha calmly picked up clothes around my room and tossed them into the hamper. "No, I don't think so. It was just you and me when I brought you home."

I couldn't even look at her, I was so embarrassed. "I was drunk, and saying stupid shit," I said, trying to backpedal out of it.

"Landon," Tasha said as she sat next to me. "What is going on? Who is Caleb? Was he someone at the party?"

"Just forget it," I pushed back before standing up too quickly. My vision hazed for a second as I stepped to my dresser and pulled on a pair of basketball shorts. I began to pace back and forth. "You should go, I need to shower anyway, and—"

"Landon, relax, it's just me." Tasha stepped in my path and grabbed me by the shoulders. "Whatever happened, I won't judge you."

The drunk cat was out of the bag. I stared at her and my nostrils flared, breathing heavy. *If I tell her, it's all over.* My jaw clenched as the gears in my brain turned hard and fast.

Tasha let go of me. "Landon… I want to make sure you're okay. You can tell me anything."

I sighed. She was right. "Caleb is that guy who has been working at our school."

"Okay…" Tasha said.

"We've kind of been like seeing each other?" I leaned back and sat on my windowsill. "It's complicated."

"Oh, um, okay." Tasha sat on the corner of my bed, facing me. "Are you gay?"

"I don't know."

"All right, that's okay," Tasha reassured me. "So what happened?"

I took a deep breath and swallowed it, still unable to look at her. "We started hanging out. One thing led to another, and we ended up kissing." I felt Tasha's eyes on me.

"And you liked it?" she asked.

"I loved it," I said. "And now he's all I think about. I can't get him out of my head."

"Been there."

The guilt pushed its way up my chest. I knew Tasha would ask about Lauren. They were friends. My face dropped into my hands, and a pressure formed behind my eyes. "I fucked up, Tasha."

She kneeled in front of me and placed her hands on my knees. "I assume you haven't told Lauren?"

I looked at her with damp cheeks. "No. I've been too much of a fucking coward. I've never felt like this. I thought it would all just go away after a day. And now I'm scared because I know it's gonna shatter her."

"I'm not gonna lie to you," Tasha said. "It will. She's crazy for you,

Landon. But it's not fair to her. You need to tell her if you're unhappy with her."

"I know. Please don't tell her. I want to be the one to do it."

Tasha sat back on her heels. "Your secret's safe with me, but I can't let it go unsaid that what you did was wrong and I don't support it. As Lauren's friend, I want to smack you upside the head. But as *your* friend, I want you to know I'm here for you to help you figure this out. Was it just a kiss?"

I nodded. "Yeah."

"Don't lie to me."

My hands flew up. "I swear, it was just one kiss."

"Okay." Tasha said. "Does he know about Lauren?"

"He saw me kissing her, actually, at Lucky's. Where I didn't know he worked."

"Damn, this is some *Gossip Girl* shit."

"He said he wouldn't kiss me or anything again until I was single."

Tasha took a deep breath and stood. "That's somewhat redeemable. So, Caleb was at the party last night?"

"That's the last thing I remember." I moved to my dresser again and sifted through my T-shirts. "It was so strange. I was, like, trying to get him to touch me but got rejected. Maybe he doesn't want me after all."

As I pulled on a white T-shirt, my phone vibrated against my desk. I scooped it up and saw one text from Caleb on the home screen that said, '*Hope you enjoyed the party! :) Text me when you're up.*'

"What?" I mumbled, opening the text thread. A previous message from Caleb was marked as read. He'd texted me back over an hour after I left my house.

CALEB

Hey, I'm really sorry!

Parker has been throwing up for the past hour.

I'm not gonna be able to make it to the party.

I can't trust my mom to take care of him all night. I can make it up to you. Sorry again. :(

CALEB

Hope you enjoyed the party! :) Text me when you're up.

I collapsed into my desk chair, and my jaw hit my lap. My stomach lurched, and I tried to steady my breathing.

Tasha stood and touched my shoulder. "Landon?" She sounded a million miles away.

"Shit," I whispered. "Fucking shit. No, no, no."

"What?"

I tossed my phone onto the desk. "Caleb wasn't at the fucking party last night."

"What're you talking about? You said he was behind the shed with you."

"It wasn't him!" I stood and paced, trying to remember everything from the night before. "Caleb told me he was gonna dress up like Michael Myers. The guy I brought behind the shed was definitely wearing a Michael Myers costume. But it wasn't Caleb because he texted me saying he was with his sick brother all night. But I didn't get the texts because I forgot my phone here before I left."

Tasha's nail-painted hand covered her mouth. "Oh my god."

My skin itched from the inside. "That means someone else knows about me."

TWENTY-SIX

"It's okay, we can figure this out," Tasha said, trying to calm me.

Dad popped his head into my room. "Figure what out?"

I couldn't find an excuse, too freaked out that he might've heard the conversation.

If anyone was quick on their feet, it was Tasha. "This physics project is due next week," she said.

Dad looked satisfied enough, and sniffed the air. "Did someone make coffee?"

"Yeah, it's downstairs," I said.

Dad nodded and continued on his way. We waited to hear the clink of the mugs from downstairs before talking again,

"I'm such an idiot," I said. "Why did I get so fucked up last night?" I crossed to the bedside table, grabbed my mug, and sat next to Tasha on the mattress. My hands trembled. "What if that person goes straight to Lauren or Coach? Then Coach tells my dad, I'd be so fucked. What if I lose my scholarship?"

"Whoa, Landon, relax," Tasha said, placing a hand on my forearm. "Being gay isn't the end of the world. This isn't nineteen-forty. Gay people can play sports, too."

I stared into my cup, knowing she was right, but my mind still raced. "My dad is a Republican running for mayor. He'll never win if people find out about me."

Tasha nudged my shoulder with hers. "He loves you. He'll understand."

"You don't know him like I do."

"Let's just take this one step at a time." She stood. "I have to get home. But I'll review everyone's posted pictures from the party and see if I can hunt down Michael Myers for you. Maybe someone tagged him."

"Thank you," I said.

Tasha collected her things. I noticed she wasn't in her Catwoman costume anymore. Instead, she wore yoga pants and a flannel. "Did you stay here last night?"

Her face scrunched. "Hell no. My mom would've killed me. I dropped you off, and you gave me your keys to check on you this morning."

I smiled, grateful for her friendship. "You're the best."

"Never forget it!" Tasha called over her shoulder, leaving my bedroom. She popped her head back in and said, "Oh, and I suggest you tell Lauren sooner than later."

"I know. I will."

I lay back on my bed, clutching my coffee mug between my hands. I hoped deep breathing would relieve my anxiety, but it didn't work.

Shit, I left Caleb on read.

Pushing myself up with a groan, I placed my mug down. My head still ached. I snatched my phone off the desk. A new text from Lauren popped up.

LAUREN

Just got on the plane, can't wait to see you!

I ignored it, instead swiping to Caleb's contact and tapping the green button.

"Hello?" Caleb's voice sang in my ear. It felt good to hear his raspy tone.

"Hey," I said. "How are you?"

"I'm really sorry about last night."

"It's totally fine," I said, laying back on my bed. "I actually forgot my phone at home, so I didn't even see the texts till this morning."

A TV blared in the background, and Caleb said, "I was wondering why you never responded, I thought you were mad at me."

"Of course not. How's the little guy feelin'?"

"He seems a lot better now. We're watching cartoons on the couch."

"Good, that's good." My voice trailed off.

"Are you okay?" Caleb asked.

"Something kind of happened last night."

"Hold on, let me go outside," Caleb said. I heard Parker mumble, and the phone sounded like it slipped it into a pocket. Then the screen door squeaked and slammed before Caleb spoke again. "Okay. What happened?"

"I got super drunk, accidentally ate two weed brownies, and it really fucked me up."

Caleb laughed. "That's hysterical. You had me worried for a second."

"Oh, there's more."

"Okay… "

"Someone dressed as Michael Myers was there, and I thought it was you. I was so messed up that I pulled him behind a shed and started touching him, and he freaked out and stormed off."

"Oh, shit," Caleb said.

"And now I'm going crazy because someone knows about me." I rolled onto my side, holding the phone between the pillow and my face.

"I don't think it's the end of the world, Lan."

"Yeah, I keep hearing that. It's easy for you to say. You're out, you're proud, I get it. But I'm not. Your reputation isn't on the line here!"

"You're right," Caleb whispered. "I'm sorry."

"All of this is screwing with my head. On top of everything, I have to tell Lauren. Just thinking about it makes my skin crawl. And now some mystery person out there could blab about it. Oh, and while I was drunk last night, I told my friend Tasha about you."

"Oh?" Caleb's voice perked up. "How'd she take it?"

"She was cool about it." My stomach gurgled, but I wasn't sure if it was hunger or the stale alcohol wanting out.

"That's great then! If someone is truly your friend, they won't care," Caleb said.

It all sounded too cliché for me. In Texas, at my school, with my dad, it wasn't as simple as Caleb made it sound. "Any advice on how I should tell Lauren?"

"Coming out is a really personal thing. It's never the same for anyone," Caleb said. "You like books, so maybe there's a book about it?"

"About coming out?"

"Yeah, maybe you should look into it."

The more we talked, the calmer I became. Caleb's voice soothed my anxiety. His advice was perfect. I turned to books for almost everything else, so why not try?

That Monday at school felt like everyone knew what was going on in my head. With every stare I got in the hallway, it felt like they were reading my dirty thoughts about Caleb. I wore my hood all day, trying to blend into the crowd. I barely said anything at lunch. I just listened to Lauren tell the others about her audition and how amazing New York was. She went on about shopping in SoHo, eating in Chinatown, and seeing a Broadway show.

Dan bragged about how awesome the party was and how he hooked up with a college girl who was visiting a friend. He hadn't touched his nose once, so I wondered if he'd gotten rid of the cocaine like I suggested.

My fork poked through the pasta pesto I'd gotten from the cafeteria. It tasted fine, but I didn't have much of an appetite as the anxiety flooded my stomach.

I imagined someone dressed in a Michael Myers costume standing up on one of the lunch tables in the middle of the cafeteria and shouting, 'Landon Griffin is a faggot!'

The bell rang, signaling the end of lunch, and I shuffled out, not saying bye to anyone.

The rest of my day was slow. When the last bell finally rang, I bolted. I'd planned on getting straight into Dad's car and driving to Barnes & Noble to find a book about coming out. With the car in my sight, I began to cross the street, but Lauren stepped in front of me before I could look both ways.

"Hey, you," she said. Her smile faded. "Are you okay?"

"Yeah, I'm fine," I lied, wondering when she'd stop believing me.

"Tasha told me you got pretty messed up at the party. I would've loved to see that."

My pulse quickened. "Did she say anything else?"

"Like what?" Lauren asked.

"Never mind, I gotta go."

"Wait." Lauren followed behind me as I crossed. "Where are you going?"

"I need to go to Barnes and Noble for something," I said, avoiding eye contact. I reached the car and tossed my bag into the back seat.

Lauren met me at the driver's side door. "Want some company?"

"I'm sorry," I said. "I need time alone for a bit, okay?" I hated being standoffish to her. It wasn't fair, she had no idea what was happening in my head.

She frowned. "Oh, all right. Text me after, then?"

"Yeah," I said, kissing her and entering the car.

I scoured the fiction section of the big-box bookstore for any title that jumped out at me. I picked up a book, read the synopsis, and then put it back down. I repeated this about ten times, realizing the procrastination had set in. I knew the LGBTQ section was on the store's back wall, but I avoided it like the plague.

A strong whiff of coffee floated from the small cafe nestled in the store's corner. I passed the blue-carpeted kids' section, littered with unfinished puzzles. A mom read to her little boy as they both sipped their drinks, sitting in oversized bean bag chairs.

My mom used to take me there when I was young. Once a month, the store hired someone to read for the local kids. We used to sit cross-legged on that blue carpet and listen to someone read chapters from *The Chronicles of Narnia.* It was something I always looked forward to.

I reached the LGBTQ section and gave it a once over. There wasn't much—only four shelves out of the stack. A title caught my eye and I reached for it. *Rainbow Boys* by Alex Sanchez. I did the same as I had with others. Just read the synopsis, and put it back. It sounded interesting, but I didn't need fiction.

A book titled *It Gets Better* by Dan Savage and Terry Miller poked from the shelf, and I read the back cover. It was exactly what I needed.

I turned, and headed for the checkout when I spotted Steven walking toward me. "Fuck," I said under my breath as I tossed the book back on the shelf and turned the corner to another aisle, hoping Steven hadn't seen me.

I wanted out. I couldn't focus on finding a book, knowing he was in the store. I slithered from the historical fiction section, bumping shoulders with a random woman. I apologized and took off power-walking through the store. The parking lot called my name as I darted around the new arrivals table and passed the checkout counter, pushing open the heavy glass door. It was the last stretch. I'd just made it to the back of my car, home free, until—

"Landon, stop!"

My stomach sank. Steven caught me. I leaned my arm against the trunk and rested my head on my wrist. *Just play it cool.* I popped up, facing him with a fake smile."Hey, Steven."

He combat boots stomped toward me. "I knew I saw you at Paradise."

I acted as if I'd never heard of the place. "What?"

"Don't play dumb, Landon," Steven said, stopping a few feet in front of me. "I knew that was you! Then you called me TheatreNerd, and that's when I knew I wasn't crazy. Your jersey number is eighty-three. I can't believe I didn't put it together sooner!" I'd never seen Steven that angry, not even with Dan.

I had no memory of calling Steven by his Grindr username. Drunk me really wanted to push sober me out of the closet.

"We've been talking on Grindr for weeks!" Steven shouted. "Why are you doing this? Is this some elaborate plan you and Dan cooked up?"

My brow furrowed. "What? No."

"Oh, fuck you!" People around the parking lot stared at us, but Steven continued. "You made my life fucking hell for being gay. You stood by while I got the shit kicked out of me by *your* best friend, and yet you were just like me this whole time!"

I stood there and let him yell at me because he was right.

"How could you make that Instagram page about me and continue to sleep well at night? You fucking outed me to everyone!"

"Wait, Steven, what're you talking about?" I was genuinely confused.

He shook his head, and his eyes welled. "Why do you think I didn't come back to school after Dan attacked me that first day, freshman year? I found your fake insta page, and saw all the comments, and I thought, fuck it. Everyone wants me to kill myself, so why not give it a try?"

"Oh my god," I whispered, stepping toward him. "Steven, I swear, I don't know anything about a fake insta," I told the truth, something new for me. My stomach twisted into knots.

"Yeah, right."

I poked a thumb at my car. "Can we just sit and talk?" I looked him in the eyes, hoping he'd catch my sincerity. "Please."

Steven sighed and nodded before stepping to the passenger door.

I unlocked everything, and we both sat, letting the silence linger. My eyes couldn't leave the steering wheel. "I had no idea what you were going through." I looked at Steven. "We were friends. Dan was the only person who changed, and I'm sorry I took his side. I never stood up for you, because I'd been too scared of what people would think of me. Too afraid of what Dan would do. But I should've stopped him every time he harassed you. I'm sorry I didn't."

Steven stared at his lap. "You really didn't know about the insta?"

I shook my head, and he leaned back in the seat.

"I knew it was Dan," Steven said. "I just assumed you had something to do with it, too, because you guys were inseparable."

"What even was it?" I asked, unsure if Steven wanted to dive back into the memories.

He stared out the windshield. "Freshman year, when I got back home from the hospital after Dan's attack, I saw a notification on my phone. I'd been tagged in a pic from an account named 'StevenMoriIsAFlamingFaggot.' The account already had fifty people following it. I had no idea it was gonna be as bad as it was," Steven said.

"I'm almost afraid to ask what you saw."

"Pictures of me were posted with drawings over the top. Most of them were knives to my head or dicks. Someone posted a comment that if I killed myself, no one would feel bad. That Madison High would be better off. The comment had 28 likes."

"Jesus Christ," I whispered. "I'm so sorry, Steven."

"I kinda went numb. I didn't wanna deal with anything anymore. So, I went into the bathroom and swallowed every pill I could find in the medicine cabinet, and sat on the floor to wait. I was done with the snarky comments as a defense mechanism. Done feeling alone and unwanted. I thought, it's not gonna get better, so why wait around while it gets worse?" Steven paused and wiped his eye with his sleeve. "The dumbest part of it all was that I tried to justify it in my head while I laid there."

"What do you mean?"

Steven sniffled. "When I was little, my grandma moved to the States from Japan. She used to tell me stories about samurai who took their own lives as an act of bravery. So I kept thinking, well, maybe this is a good thing. I was meant to do this because those stories lived in my head my whole life."

"But think of how much she would've missed you," I said. "Your whole family would've been devastated."

Steven nodded to his lap. "It just didn't feel like it at the time."

"Losing someone to suicide is one of the worst things a person can go through, believe me."

Steven's eyes shot to me. "Landon, I'm sorry I wasn't thinking. I didn't mean to—"

"No, it's okay," I said, cutting him off. "That's a kind of pain I'd never wish on anyone. So I'm glad your parents didn't have to go through it."

"Yeah, luckily, my mom found me passed out on the bathroom floor and called an ambulance."

"If I would've known, I would've come to see you in the hospital."

"No, you wouldn't have," Steven said with a half smile. "You said it yourself, you were too scared, and honestly, I don't blame you. Being gay can be scary as fuck sometimes. Especially when you look like me."

My brow scrunched, and I leaned a shoulder against the steering wheel to face him. "What do you mean?"

Steven chuckled. "Look at you. We're very different, Landon. You're a jock; you blend in with the crowd. I'm a fem boy who practically sweats glitter. It's obvious. No one suspects you because of your deep voice, and your clothes are normal."

"It all feels like a facade most of the time," I said. "The person you were texting with? That's the real me. When I talked to you on Grindr, I felt like my authentic self, not the coward I am in real life."

"I liked that person. He's in there. You just gotta let him out," Steven said, twisting toward me in his seat.

"I don't know how. I was literally in there looking for books on how to come out."

"You don't need a book, just say it."

"What?"

"Say the words," Steven said. "It's just us in the car. No one else will know."

I scoffed, sitting back against my seat. "I can't. That feels dumb."

"Girl, how the hell are you ever gonna come out if you can't even say the words?"

"What do you want me to say?"

"You tell me," he replied.

I closed my eyes to think, but all I could see was Caleb's face. I felt a collection of butterflies fill my stomach and took a deep breath. "I'm..." I hesitated. "...gay," I whispered.

Steven leaned closer. "I'm sorry, what was that?"

"... I'm gay," I said a little louder. My eyes still closed.

"I couldn't hear you. Speak up, please,"

"I'm gay," I said a bit louder, feeling the butterflies push their way to my chest.

"One more time for the people in the back!"

The butterflies forced their way to my throat, and I squeezed my eyes, letting them escape. "I'M GAY!" I screamed toward the car's roof, releasing the butterflies into the air with my words of affirmation. An anvil-sized weight lifted from my shoulders.

Steven's hand clutched mine, and I opened my eyes to look at him. He smiled. "Welcome to the party."

TWENTY-SEVEN

Steven and I stayed in my car talking for hours. We laughed a lot. He told me stories of his nights at Paradise. He knew one of Caleb's friends, telling me he went home with Miguel the first night he stepped foot in the gay club on 18+ night. According to Steven, Miguel worshipped Barbra Streisand; he filled his entire apartment with memorabilia, from records to coffee mugs to framed posters, and even a few blankets with her face on them. Steven said it felt like being in a museum.

I told him everything about Caleb, how I accidentally came out to Tasha while I wasted, and about the Michael Myers mystery. We also talked about Lauren and how I should address the situation. There was no way around it; it would break her heart no matter how or when I told her.

"As much as I love your revelation, Lauren is my friend, too," Steven said. "If this were any other situation, I'd immediately tell her what's going on, but I'd never out someone."

"I appreciate it. I really want her to hear it from me. But every time I'm around her, all I can think about is how upset she'll be. And then I start thinking about all the fun we've had over the last year, making me feel even worse. So, I chicken out."

"Girl, the longer you wait, the harder it's gonna get," Steven said. "I wish I could help more, but you gotta figure this out for yourself."

I stared at the steering wheel "She's gonna hate me."

"She'll be hurt, but I don't think she'll hate you. Dan, on the other hand..."

I scoffed. "That's another thing I'm dreading."

"Maybe he doesn't have to know."

"He wasn't always like this," I said. "We hit freshman year, and he was a different person. I don't know what happened."

"I might know," Steven whispered.

The sun had set, and the parking lot was almost empty. The tall light posts illuminated the remaining employees heading home after their shifts.

I perked up in my seat. "What do you mean?"

Steven took a deep breath. "He made me swear I wouldn't tell anyone, but it's been over four years. With all the shit he's put me through, there's no point in hiding it anymore."

"Wait, did you guys..." Steven glanced at me, then covered his face and laughed into his hands, nodding. "No fucking way!" I shouted.

Steven held up his right hand as if under oath. "I swear to Ariana Grande."

"I can't believe this," I said as I swiveled in my seat, leaning against the car door. "What happened?"

"The summer before high school started, long after you guys stopped talking to me, Dan asked if he could come to my house," Steven said. "I was shocked but excited because I thought he wanted to be friends again. When he came over, I could tell he was nervous. It just felt awkward, you know?"

"Okay," I said, giddy with anticipation.

"I can't believe I'm telling you this." Steven chuckled. "So we ended up sitting on my bed and talking, then he just kissed me out of nowhere."

My eyes widened. "You're lying!"

Steven laughed. "I swear!"

"Okay, so, then what?"

"I let it happen! I'd been fantasizing about kissing boys since I was eight years old, so of course, I didn't want to stop him."

When I was eight years old, I had a poster of Tom Brady next to my bed that I would stare at every night before I fell asleep, but I never fantasized about kissing him.

"Then things went further," Steven said. "We were making out. And oh my god, it was so sloppy. We had no idea what we were doing. Then clothes start coming off."

All I could do was listen, with my hand under my chin to stop my jaw from hitting my lap.

Steven continued, "Hands were exploring uncharted territory if you know what I mean, and it was awkward but exhilarating. When we finished, I could tell he felt different about it than I did."

My forehead tensed. "How so?"

"It felt like he was ashamed? Like he'd just committed the worst crime in history," Steven frowned. "It felt like the room went cold, and all he said was, 'I'll kill you if you tell anyone.' Then he left, and it all felt like a dream. I think that's when everything changed. His internalized homophobia hated what we did so much that he's been taking it out on me ever since."

"It probably doesn't help that his parents are super religious too," I said. Knowing Dan, everything Steven said sounded impossible. "Also, he's slept with so many girls..." I said.

"I'm not saying he's gay. Maybe he's bi, I don't know. Only he knows for sure." Steven side-eyed me. "Did you guys ever..."

"Oh God, no." I'd never thought about Dan that way and never wanted to.

Steven laughed. "But you have, like, done it, right?"

Insecurity poked its head into my side. I could've lied, but what was the point? I'd owned up to everything else that day, so why not my virginity, too? I squinted at him, shaking my head no.

"Oh, honey," Steven said. "So, no one has ever touched your 'between me down there'? Not even Lauren?"

"I mean, she's tried. But nothing... happens."

"Ah, I gotcha."

"Yeah, that was one of the most embarrassing nights of my life. I figured she would've told you and Tasha about it."

"She's never complained about you, at least not to us."

My stomach filled with rocks. Lauren was the perfect girlfriend. I didn't deserve her.

Our conversation didn't go on much longer. We got out of the car and said our goodbyes with our first hug. Steven squeezed me tight before returning to his car. It felt great to reconnect. Things felt normal again. It reminded me of all the weekends we spent at sleep-overs, getting hyper off of Mountain Dew, and playing video games all night. After years of avoiding it, it felt like completing a puzzle that was only collecting dust on the shelf.

The next few days flew by, but my anxiety never flatlined. It was still in the back of my mind that a mystery person knew about me and Caleb, but they hadn't told anyone yet. I was sure it would've spread through the school like wildfire if they had. It helped that I got to steal looks at Caleb when I passed him in the hallways or watch him from a classroom window as he mowed the grass in the front courtyard. It was easy to forget about everything when I looked at him.

It was the Wednesday after Steven and I had our conversation in the Barnes & Noble parking lot. I stood in the lunch line holding my tray, and noticed Jordan Palicki's tall presence standing two people ahead of me, causing a flash image of his naked body emerging from Dan's pool. I'd never been able to look at him the same.

I tried to focus my attention on the food. The line moved quickly for once. I stepped up to the sneeze guard and surveyed my options. I grabbed a paper plate from the stack next to the salad bowl and loaded up, accidentally dropping some lettuce on the floor. Moving farther down the counter to a bunch of foil-wrapped goodies, I grabbed one labeled 'cheeseburger'. As I turned toward the tables, someone's gasp caught my ear. People sprung from their seats, avoiding the action, but a few stepped toward it. I bobbed my head to see what was happening. A group of girls blocked my view until Jordan moved them out of the way. That's when I saw Steven's bright head of hair whiz by. Dan had pushed him to the ground. My heart raced as Dan approached Steven.

The quarterback predator hovered over his flamboyant prey. "Say it again!" Dan yelled down at Steven. The whole cafeteria watched, yet no one tried to stop Dan from pouncing. I gripped my lunch tray, wondering what might've gotten Dan so worked up. He could've overheard Steven talking about a guy he had a crush on. Or maybe Steven made a snarky comment about Dan's outfit? Even from across the cafeteria, I could see the rage in Dan's eyes.

After reconnecting with Steven, I couldn't let Dan harass him anymore. I had to be the one to put Dan in his place to end the attacks. My heart pumped as I tossed my tray onto a nearby table and pushed through the crowd, seeing red.

I threw a folding chair to the side, and it crashed to the floor. It was the last object standing between me and them. Steven braced for the inevitable on the cold tiles as Dan loomed over him. But before Dan could unleash his fury, I lunged forward, grabbing a fistful of his jersey and yanking him back. My fist clenched. Then, as if shot from a cannon, I swung.

The crack of knuckle-on bone echoed through the cafeteria as my punch slammed into Dan's nose. Blood sprayed like a burst pipe, spattering across my shirt. The crowd gasped, but I wasn't done. My fist cocked again, this time striking Dan's left eye with brutal precision. He crumpled to the floor like a rag doll with a heavy thud.

My chest heaved, heart pounding in my ears. I'd never hit anyone before, yet there I was, fists trembling. The entire cafeteria stood frozen.

I looked at Dan on the floor. "Touch him again, and I'll fucking end you."

Dan covered his nose as blood dripped off his chin. A few guys from the football team rushed to his side, helping him off the ground. Dan spat blood on the floor in front of me and stared with fire in his eyes, panting. I knew Dan would've lunged for me if the guys had let him go.

Dan wiped his blood on his pant leg. "If you're gonna choose this faggot over me, then fuck you, Griffin!" The other guys pulled Dan back and escorted him from the cafeteria, swearing down the empty hallway.

I turned and helped Steven to his feet.

"Thank you," Steven whispered. The chatter started again as people returned to their business.

"I should've done that a long time ago," I said. "I'm sorry it took so long."

Steven smiled.

"What the hell set him off, anyway?" I asked

Steven rolled his eyes. "I called him a Neanderthal. I'm surprised he even knew the word." He pointed at my bloodied fist. "You better go wash that off. That's pretty gross."

I decided to spend the rest of the day at home. Dad's car wasn't in the driveway as I crossed the street, thankful I didn't have to explain why I'd left school early. I opened the door and went straight for the kitchen sink. As soon as my knuckles hit the stream of warm water, I winced. So much adrenaline was pumping that I hadn't noticed how much my fist throbbed. I watched the red water spiral down the drain, then patted dry with a paper towel. My knuckles already started bruising. I knew nothing was broken as I could still move my fingers, but it still hurt like hell.

I sat on the couch, finally breathing normally, and snatched the TV remote. I couldn't remember the last time I mindlessly watched TV alone.

My phone vibrated. It was a text from Lauren. I should've known word would travel fast.

LAUREN

OMG Steven just told me what happened, are you okay?

ME

Yeah, I'm fine, just a little sore.

LAUREN

Where are you?

ME

I went home after everything. I didn't feel like getting stared at for the rest of the day.

LAUREN

I'm proud of you.

My phone buzzed, and I swiped to the new message.

CALEB

I think something just went down in the cafeteria. I heard some people talking about it.

ME

Yeah, I don't think Dan and I are friends anymore.

CALEB

Wait, what? Why?

ME

Because I punched him in the face. Twice.

CALEB

Seriously?

ME

Yeah. For years Dan has harassed this gay kid Steven that we used to be friends with. I just kind of snapped. I couldn't stand by and watch it happen anymore.

CALEB

You're a fucking legend! A hero to gays everywhere!

ME

Yeah right haha

CALEB

It's kinda hot ;)

Caleb's text made me smile. The drone of the TV and my depleted adrenaline made my eyelids heavy. After-school naps were something my mom never allowed me to do, so it felt good to let it take me away from everything that had happened.

I found myself on a stage in front of hundreds of people sitting in the audience with a spotlight on me. I was shirtless but wore tights and ballet shoes. Then the violins started.

It was so strange when my body moved. I'd never taken a dance class, yet my moves were effortless. I leaped into the air with ease. I'd never felt so flexible, and I started to enjoy the ride. I reached out a hand, and Lauren ran toward me onstage. She, too, wore ballet gear. I lifted her, and she slithered around my body like a snake.

We continued our perfectly choreographed dance together until Caleb swept me away dressed in a leotard. The audience gasped as Caleb picked me up into a spin. As he and I danced intimately with leaps, spins, and dips, Lauren danced around us, looking distraught.

Caleb let go of me to dance with Lauren, but the choreography wasn't sweet and sensual. Instead, it was dark and menacing. They pulled me into their tornado, yanking me in all directions around the stage until everything went dark and the music halted.

A spotlight showed me alone, breathing heavily, and crying at center stage. The whole audience clapped, and one by one, they all stood, cheering.

The sound of Dad rushing through the door jolted me awake. I tapped my phone on the couch next to me. It was almost 4:00 p.m.

Dad walked into the living room with his hands on his hips and a stern look on his face. "Coach called me," he said. "Told me you and Dan got into a fight at school today?"

I sat up straight, sliding to the edge of the couch. "It wasn't exactly a fight," I said, rubbing my neck.

Dad crossed his arms. "What does that mean?"

"Well, I punched him. He didn't punch me, so it wasn't a fight."

"Jesus, Landon. I want you to go to his house and apologize. Now."

I shot up from the couch. "What? No!"

"He's your best friend, Landon. I get that friends don't always see eye to eye, but we didn't raise you to work it out with your fists. You guys need to talk it out."

"You're not even gonna ask me why I punched him? He was bullying Steven!"

"Oh."

"Oh? That's all you're gonna say? How about nice job, son, for sticking up for someone?"

"I'm not saying Dan didn't deserve it, but I won't let you ruin your friendship over it. We still need you guys working together on the field."

"Jesus Christ, Dad. Is that all you care about?" I pushed past him and headed for the side door that led to the driveway. "There's more to life than fucking football!"

The door slammed behind me, and I heard him yell my name from the other side, but he didn't follow me. I needed to take a walk before I said something I'd regret. I dreaded seeing Dan at the next football practice. He'd definitely take his anger out on me on the field. My punch had changed everything.

TWENTY-EIGHT

I wanted to bike around the neighborhood to clear my head. I glanced around the driveway but my bike was nowhere to be found. I sighed, remembering I'd left it in Dan's front yard when I rode it to the party.

Damn it, now I don't have a choice.

The setting sun was locked behind a sheet of ominous gray clouds, and the air felt damp. I was already two blocks from my house and didn't feel like going back for an umbrella. During the walk, I debated whether to grab my bike or ring the doorbell to talk to Dan. *What would I say?*

I didn't regret punching him. It needed to happen. I was over all of his bullshit, his bullying, his homophobia. We didn't have to be friends, but I wanted to be civil, so it felt less awkward when forced to be around each other.

I shoved my hands in my pockets as the breeze gave me goosebumps. I thought about Chris and whether our friendship would change after what happened. He and I were never as close, but we'd been in each other's lives for so long. Chris often followed Dan's lead, but I could tell he wanted to forge his own path, especially after Dan became more of a selfish bigot.

I reached Dan's house, nestled on the corner of Packard Street and Willow Drive. I surveyed the yard for my bike, deciding to grab it and go. I remembered leaving it in the grass near the sidewalk, but it wasn't there. I'd have to ask someone in the house if they'd seen it. A raindrop hit my forehead when I walked the cement path to the porch. I hoped to get my bike and race back home before it downpoured.

My shoes knocked against the wooden floorboards. I rang the bell as my mind raced, trying to find the right words for Dan. My shoulders tensed as the door opened, but I relaxed when Chris answered.

"Hey," I said.

Chris' brows raised. "Hey, man. What're you doing here?"

My thumb pointed to the empty yard behind me. "I left my bike here the other night. I hoped to grab it, but it's not where I left it."

"I think my dad moved it," Chris said as he stepped through the doorway, closing it behind him. "C'mon, I'm pretty sure it's in the back."

I nodded, let him pass, followed around the side of the house, and through the gate into the backyard.

"Everyone's talking about what happened," Chris said.

"Is Dan around?" I asked as the gate swung closed behind me.

"No, he split." Chris leaned against the edge of the tabletop we'd used for spin the bottle. "He seemed pretty angry over everything."

"Figured he would be," I said. Another drop of rain hit my head and another on my shoulder.

Chris glanced at the sliding glass door. His parents cuddled on the couch. "I think they're starting to worry about Dan. He's touching his nose all the time, and his temper's getting worse."

"He was snorting coke at the party and wasn't afraid to show it off," I whispered.

Chris rubbed the side of his face and kept his gaze low. "I found a gun in his car."

Living in Texas, it was common to see people walking around with holstered guns, so I wasn't taken aback by the idea of Dan having one. "Okay," I said, wanting to give Dan the benefit of the doubt. "Doesn't your dad have a gun?"

Chris shrugged. "Most people from our church do. But this was different, though. The serial number was scratched off. Dan knows how much our mom hates guns. She'd flip if she found out. "

I wiped a hand down my face. "Jesus Christ. He's fucked if he's found with drugs and an unlicensed gun."

Chris straightened and shushed me. "No shit." He glanced at the sliding door again, then stepped closer to me. "He's been hanging out with these sleazy-looking guys lately."

"You have to tell your parents. This is getting scary now."

"Dan will kill me, I can't. Plus, my parents are dealing with a lot of shit right now."

"Okay," I scoffed. "Then let's get rid of it."

Chris sighed. "I was going to. But when I went back to his car, it was gone."

"Fuck." I paced toward the pool, thinking about how to help. The smell of chlorine penetrated my nostrils. I turned to Chris. "Maybe I'll text him when I get home and see if I can talk to him about everything."

"Don't mention the gun," Chris whispered. "He's gonna know it's me that told you."

"I won't, I won't."

What the fuck has Dan gotten himself into?

Chris's face shifted before he shuffled to the shed at the corner of the yard. My bike leaned against the barn-like door of the small structure. Chris grabbed the handlebars and steered the bike toward me, calmly running the tires over a Michael Myers mask lying in the grass. My heart dropped, and I rushed to snatch it.

I looked at Chris with wide eyes. "What is this doing here?"

His brows scrunched as if I had three heads. "What do you mean?"

"Whose mask is this?"

"Mine, you psycho." Chris chuckled. "I probably left it out here when I was drunk."

A wave of panic washed over me. "Holy shit, it was you?"

"Yeah. Who else would it be?"

"No, no. I saw you going upstairs. You were dressed like a hippie."

"Yeah," Chris scoffed. "That was before that girl threw up all over me in my room. It was nasty, bro."

I closed my eyes. My stomach dropped thinking about my confession behind the shed.

Chris continued. "The Michael Myers costume was my backup anyway, so I changed it after cleaning up the mess."

I tossed the mask back to the ground. "Do you not remember?" I flashed back to pushing Chris's hand toward my underwear.

Chris tilted his head and laughed. "Remember what? I was so fucked up that night."

"Never mind. I gotta go." I said, taking my bike from him. The rain dropped faster.

"All right." Chris watched me leave through the gate. "See ya."

The rain dropped faster. I hopped on my bike so fast that I smashed my tailbone against the seat and grunted in a quick burst of discomfort. Once on the slick pavement, I pumped the pedals, pushing through the sharp droplets. The streets were calm, and all I could hear was the rain pounding the pavement and thunder in the distance.

Am I that lucky?

Chris not remembering a single second of my drunken rant, felt too good to be true. I needed to text Tasha. By the time I pedaled into my driveway, I was soaked. I set my bike against my house and rushed inside, stumbling to remove my shoes. My slimy socks squelched between my toes as I peeled them off. Every inch of my shirt stuck to my body.

I hurried up the stairs and into my room. With the AC on full blast, I shivered as I pulled off my pants and shirt, like shedding a layer of skin. Then, I grabbed a towel from the hamper and patted myself dry.

I pulled my phone from the pocket of my damp jeans and wiped the screen across the side of my underwear before opening it. Caleb had texted.

CALEB

Doing anything tomorrow after school?

ME

I don't think so. Why?

I swiped to text Tasha.

ME

It was Chris.

Next, I found Dan's text thread and typed.

ME

Hey, can we talk?

My phone buzzed.

CALEB

It's just gonna be me and Parker at the house tomorrow. I was hoping maybe you could come over and keep us company?

ME

Too scared to be on your own? Haha.

CALEB

Lol, we need a strong football player to protect us.

ME

When you find one, let me know. ;p

CALEB

Maybe I can wine and dine you.

ME

In that case, I'm in!

Another buzz.

TASHA

Wait, what?!

ME

Chris was Michael Myers.

TASHA

How did you find out?

ME

I was at his house and saw the mask in his backyard. He said it was his.

TASHA

OMG! What did he say?

ME

I didn't tell him what happened. He told me he was blacked out and doesn't remember much. He didn't say anything about what I did, so I just left.

TASHA

Do you think he's telling the truth?

ME

I hope so.

Dan texted me back.

DAN

Why? As far as I'm concerned, we aren't friends anymore.

ME

I'm sorry I hit you, but I'm just tired of seeing you torture Steven.

DAN

He deserves it!

ME

Why?

DAN

Because he makes me sick.

ME

Are you gonna be a bully in college too? You need to grow up and stop choosing to hate people who are different than you.

DAN

Fuck off, Landon.

ME

I'm worried about you. If you're going through some shit, I'm here to help you figure it out.

DAN

I don't need your help. FUCK OFF!

. . .

I wanted to tell him I knew about the gun, to grab his attention, but didn't want to cause any trouble for Chris. I had so many questions for Dan. I wondered if he had the gun for protection or intimidation.

Caleb texted again.

CALEB

Want to come over around 7?

ME

Sure.

CALEB

Or whenever, doesn't matter.

ME

No, 7 is fine. Sorry, I'm just dealing with Dan stuff.

CALEB

Is everything okay?

ME

I don't know. Dan just seems like he's in over his head with some stuff, and I tried to apologize for the fight, but it didn't go well.

CALEB

You can't do much for someone who doesn't want to be helped.

I saw Dan in the hallway the next day at school, sporting a shiner under his left eye, and the bridge of his nose was purple. He stared me down and puffed his chest as he walked by. I was on his shit list and half expected him to jump me in the bathroom or trip me in the cafeteria. But, he showed his disdain with silence and sharp looks.

Lauren met me by my locker after the last period. I tossed my math book onto the top shelf when she walked up behind me and squeezed my ass. My entire body flinched. Lauren laughed. "Jeez, what's got you all tense?"

"I just wasn't expecting it," I said with a smile. I pulled my backpack off a hook and closed the locker door. "I tried texting Dan last night to apologize, but he wanted nothing to do with me."

Lauren slid her hand into mine as we walked toward the front exit. "I'm sorry, babe. I'm sure he'll come around."

"That's the thing, I don't think I'd be upset if he didn't." I shrugged as the loudspeakers announced an AV club meeting in the auditorium. "Dan and I have been growing apart, so maybe it's for the best." We stepped outside, and I shielded my eyes from the blazing sun.

"I have to start this chemistry project with Dan tomorrow, I hope it's not awkward," Lauren said.

"I'm sure he won't even talk about me, he told me to fuck off last night. so."

At the sidewalk, I let go of Lauren's hand as Steven approached us.

"Hey guys," he said with a cheerful wave. "We're seeing a movie later; you want to come?" Steven asked me.

I shook my head. "Can't. I'm meeting up with a friend tonight."

Lauren raised an eyebrow. "Oh, who?"

I hesitated. "We're doing this writing project for Mrs. Donahue's class. We really need to get it done."

I avoided answering her question like a scared dog avoids a mean cat. I glanced at Steven, who tilted his head at me with wide eyes. Every lie I told felt like a brick of guilt being added to the wall I built between Lauren and me. Soon enough, I wouldn't be able to see her on the other side.

"Okay," Lauren said, looking from me to Steven. "I guess I'll text you later and tell you how the movie was."

"All right." I pecked Lauren on the cheek. "Have fun," I said, waving as I crossed the street. Thinking about kissing Caleb again made me giddy, but I wouldn't be able to do that until I ended it with Lauren.

Walking up the driveway, I noticed Dad's car wasn't there. I unlocked the side door and sent him a text.

ME

Hey Dad, Are you gonna be home later? I kinda need the car to get to my friend's house.

Opening the fridge, I grabbed the package of sliced cheese. I trapped two pieces between some bread and popped it into the toaster oven. My pocket buzzed with a text from Steven.

STEVEN

That was so awkward. Do you realize what kind of position this puts me in?

ME

What do you mean?

STEVEN

I know you're going to see Caleb. Now you're making us both liars. How long are you going to drag this on before you tell her?

ME

I feel just as shitty, believe me.

STEVEN

Doesn't seem that way.

ME

I can tell her tomorrow then, okay? Just give me the night to think about how I'm gonna do it.

STEVEN

Try not to do anything tonight that you'll regret, all right SportyGuy?

ME

Who are you, my dad?

STEVEN

Only if you call me Daddy!

ME

Omg, shut up haha

DAD

Sorry, bud, I need the car for the night. Won't be home till late.

Damn. Now I have to ride my bike to Caleb's place.

I leaned against the counter and checked my email. No rejections yet. I opened Instagram, typed NYU into the search bar, and scrolled through their photos. So many students wore purple hoodies or T-shirts with the purple NYU logo. I wanted to be one of them so badly. I clicked on a pic of a guy standing next to a purple tree, with purple buildings behind him. They quoted him in the caption, saying, "You belong here," and it filled me with hope. I pictured myself walking the streets, admiring the architecture of the surrounding buildings, and writing in their massive library that reminded me of a beehive. My thoughts of NYU made me so much happier than picturing myself at the University of Texas. I'm sure I could find a writing program at UT, but I'd have to play football for all four years. Thinking about it exhausted me. I wanted to focus on writing the next influential novel that everyone became obsessed with, not getting tackled by guys twice my size.

The toaster oven chimed, and I opened it. A puff of smoke escaped as cheese had burned against the rack. Using a paper towel wrapped around my fingers, I pulled the crunchy sandwich out, licking my lips in anticipation, and brought it to my room to do some homework before heading to Caleb's house.

Riding my bike took double the time it would've taken to get to Caleb's with the car. Sweat covered my back when I turned into the trailer park, and my shirt stuck to me like glue. My handlebars vibrated under my grip as I cycled over the rocks and potholes, wondering if I smelled bad.

I squeezed the brakes as I approached the trailer and hopped off my bike. I pinched my shirt's fabric and pulled it back and forth away from my body, trying to fan my damp skin.

Why did I wear a gray shirt? I'm a mess.

I'd tied Caleb's flannel around my waist during the ride but slung it over my shoulder as I made my way up the narrow wooden steps and knocked on the door. With my sweaty brow, I must've looked like an ogre who'd run a marathon. I lifted my arm to sniff, and that's when Caleb opened the door, catching me in the act.

TWENTY-NINE

My arm dropped with the weight of a sack of footballs.

"Hey," Caleb said, leaning to hug me.

"Sorry, I'm sweaty," I said as I hugged him back. My arms fit perfectly around his broad shoulders. The scent of garlic whipped past me in the air.

Caleb pulled away, but his hand lingered on the side of my ribs. "What happened?"

I wiped my forehead with the back of my hand. "My dad has the car, so I had to bike here."

"Damn, I'm sorry."

I handed Caleb his flannel shirt. "You left this in my room, I kept forgetting to give it to you at school." The truth was, I didn't want to give it up.

He smiled and took it. "Thanks."

Caleb stepped back and gestured for me to come inside. I stepped in, and a chilly breeze hit me from an old AC unit in the living room window. It was loud as if it had been on for ten years straight, working its hardest to stay alive. The inside of the trailer was wider than I imagined. The floor was worn down wood, and a long, fluffy brown couch sat before a beat-up TV stand. A matching coffee table nestled in between. A forty-two-inch TV rested atop the stand, held up by two skinny legs, looking like they could give out at any second. To the left of the TV was a vast, five-foot shelf filled top to bottom with DVDs.

I pointed to the shelf. "I assume those are all yours?"

"Yup," Caleb said, looking proud with his hands at his hips. "My pride and joy."

I laughed. "How many are there?"

"Close to four hundred?"

"Holy shit! I've never even watched a hundred movies in my life."

"Well, hopefully, that'll change," Caleb said. He winked at me when I looked at him, making my knees weak. A small dining table took up the rest of the living room. Caleb pointed a thumb behind him and said, "We're in the kitchen."

"Mind if I used your bathroom first?"

"Sure."

Caleb stepped the few feet it took to arrive at the alley kitchen's tiled floor and gestured to a door to his left.

The bathroom made me claustrophobic with its small sink, toilet, and one of those rectangle standing showers that reminded me of a casket propped up on its side. I could see the hint of a little square window through the foggy glass door. I approached the mirror and raised my arms, revealing wet stains underneath. "Shit," I whispered, frantically reaching for a wad of toilet paper. I crumpled the thin stack, reaching under my shirt to dab the moisture, and tossed the paper into a small trash bin under the sink.

He won't see the sweat stains if I don't raise my arms.

I slowly opened the mirror, trying not to make a sound that would alert Caleb's attention. Inside were four toothbrushes in a cup, mouthwash, toothpaste, a few pill bottles, and a deodorant stick. I reached for it, hoping it was Caleb's, before pressing it into my sweaty pits and returning it to the shelf. I washed my hands, splashing some water on my face, hoping to eliminate any redness in my cheeks.

Parker rushed me as I walked out of the bathroom, wrapping his arms around my waist. "Landon!"

"Hey!"

Parker grabbed me by the hand. "You *have* to see our room!" I didn't have a choice as he pulled me through the kitchen. A pot of water boiled, and a pan of red sauce simmered atop a stove half the size of my house's oven. The smell of fresh herbs made my stomach growl. We pushed past Caleb, and I smiled as Parker pulled me to the end of the trailer with two doors across from one another. He pushed open the door on the right and brought me inside. The room's baby blue walls reminded me of a clear sky. The square room was big enough for two twin-sized beds and a nightstand between them.

Parker hopped on the left-side bed and sat cross-legged. "This is mine." He pointed to the opposite bed with gray sheets and a single pillow without a case. "And that's Caleb's."

Even without Parker's help, it was clear which side of the room was Caleb's, as he'd covered the walls with movie posters. At the head of the bed, there was a poster of *E.T.* with the image of the little boy on his bike and his little alien friend in the front basket. The other posters were films I hadn't seen. *The Departed,* and *Pulp Fiction*. The last was a silhouette of four boys walking on train tracks, titled *Stand By Me.*

Caleb poked his head in as I noticed a book on his pillow. I sat on his mattress and picked it up; surprised to see it was *Ready Player One*.

I looked at Caleb, who leaned against the door frame, and a smile pulled at my lips. "You're reading it?"

"Yeah," Caleb said. "It's great so far."

I placed the book on the nightstand. "Which part are you on?"

Caleb looked around the room as if searching his brain. "Um, they just blew up his house."

"It gets even better after that."

Parker slumped over on his bed as if he'd passed out. "I'm starving."

Caleb chuckled, "All right, the pasta is almost ready. Go set the table."

"Okay!" Parker rose from the dead and shuffled into the hallway. I stood to follow him, but Caleb didn't let me pass. His shoulders almost filled the skinny door frame. He pinched my shirt and pulled me close to him.

"I'm glad you're reading the book," I said. "No one ever takes my recommendations."

"How could I not?" Caleb cupped my hand in his. My face scrunched as he grazed the knuckles of my right hand. "Sorry, sorry. I forgot, let me see." Caleb said, examining the bruises. "I'd hate to see the other guy," Caleb whispered. He looked at me with his hazel eyes, I was swimming in them. Accompanied by his long eyelashes and thick brows, they were the most stunning eyes I'd ever seen; they were more beautiful than any sunset or rainbow, or solar eclipse. Caleb's eyes were a maze I could get lost in for hours.

"Caleb, I think it's burning," Parker called out.

"Oh, shit!" Caleb winced before rushing back to the oven. I followed to the edge of the kitchen. Caleb slipped on a pair of mitts, opened the oven door, and waved some smoke away. He pulled out a sheet pan and placed it on the counter behind him. Garlic danced in the rising steam of the sliced baguette. "She's a little toasty," Caleb said of the bread's dark edges.

Parker popped into frame out of the corner of my eye. "That'll do, donkey, that'll do," he said with a surprisingly good Scottish accent. Caleb and I laughed as Parker hurried off to grab the plates.

We sat at the small dining table, and Parker told us about learning multiplication between each slurp of his saucy noodles. Caleb would throw out a random, simple equation, and Parker would use a finger technique to figure out the answer.

It wasn't often I had a home-cooked meal. Dad ordered takeout for us most nights as he didn't have the time or patience to cook. The garlic bread was crunchy, with the perfect amount of butter melted into all the nooks and crannies. The pasta was a thick spaghetti cooked al dente with a chunky red sauce that smelled like rosemary and thyme. I scarfed it all down and filled my stomach to the brim. We all did. Our plates were empty except for the smears of left-over sauce that decorated them like a first grader's finger-painting.

I popped the last corner of garlic bread into my mouth. "So, where are your parents tonight?"

"Luke's not our dad," Parker said with sauce all over his mouth.

Caleb placed a napkin in front of Parker. "He knows that. Use a napkin, please." Parker did as he was told, and Caleb looked at me. "They wanted a night away, so they're staying at a casino tonight. I'm sure they'll come home with less than they started with. That's usually the case." I could hear the frustration in Caleb's voice as he stood to collect our plates.

"Here, let me help." I picked up the dirty napkins and remaining silverware.

Parker slumped in his chair with a fake frown. "Do I have to do the dishes tonight?"

"You know the rules," Caleb shouted from the kitchen. "I cook, you clean."

Parker rolled his eyes, peeling himself off his chair.

"I'll help you," I said to Parker, who perked up with a smile.

I washed and let Parker dry, then put away the dishes. We flew through them with ease, telling each other bad knock-knock jokes. When we finished, we joined Caleb on the couch. He had already popped in a DVD.

Parker jumped into the spot beside his brother. "What're we watching?"

Caleb turned on the TV. "*The Lost World*, duh."

"Yes!"

I sat with Parker between Caleb and me. "What's that?"

Parker glared at me. "The sequel to *Jurassic Park*!"

I sunk into the couch. "Oh, right."

I liked the sequel. It was exciting, especially in one scene where two T-Rex attacked a trailer with people inside, trying to push it over a cliff. It might've been the most stressful thing I'd seen in a movie.

Parker had fallen asleep in Caleb's lap twenty minutes before it ended with his legs out over mine. The credits rolled with the famous *Jurassic Park* theme song. Caleb clicked it off and eyed me. "What'd you think?"

I shrugged, whispering, "It was good, but it can't beat the original."

Caleb smiled. "I knew I liked you." He petted Parker's sleeping head. "I'm gonna take him to bed."

I nodded. "Okay."

Caleb scooped Parker into his arms. His biceps didn't go unnoticed. Everything felt so peaceful in that trailer. I wondered how different it was when their mom and her boyfriend were around.

After a few minutes of silence, Caleb's footsteps returned from the kitchen. "You want a beer?" He asked.

"Sure," I said. I didn't like the taste of beer, but I would've accepted anything Caleb offered at that point. The bottle hissed as Caleb popped the cap off. It must've gone flying because I heard it hit the floor and topple away. Caleb swore under his breath as he chased after it. He popped a second bottle and sauntered, holding it out for me to take. Its frosty glass sent a chill up my arm when it touched my palm. I smirked at Caleb. "I thought you weren't allowed to drink."

"In public," Caleb said. "But they can't monitor what I do in the privacy of my own home." He plopped next to me and sipped from his bottle.

The beer was dark and bitter, leaving a strong, earthy taste on my tongue. "Thanks for tonight. It was sweet making dinner for me. Do you cook a lot?"

"Yeah," Caleb said as he pulled a leg up, leaning into the fluffy arm of the couch. "Parker would never eat otherwise."

"You don't think your mom would make sure he ate?"

"I don't know, she's selfish. They both are. It'd be very different for Parker if I weren't here." Caleb took another sip, and I focused on how his lips kissed the edge of the bottle. "I'm trying to save up for a place, one for me and Parker. I'd love to get him out of here, but things are slow at Lucky's. I might have to look for something else, but no one wants to hire me after a background check."

I can imagine how frustrating that is.

"I thought about going back to school, getting a degree in something to get a better job. Parker has always wanted a huge TV to make it feel like we were at the movies. He deserves that, ya know? I've avoided getting the court involved because I'm afraid they wouldn't let me be Parker's legal guardian now with my criminal record. It's tough. Sometimes, I feel like I'm raising Parker when I should be partying at some state school or something. I resent my mom because it shouldn't be my job. What twenty-one-year-old is raising a kid?" Caleb scratched his cheek and sighed. "God, that makes me sound like such a dick."

I sat up straight. "That doesn't make you a bad person. You didn't choose any of this. You're right, it shouldn't be your job. But Parker adores you, I'm sure he's grateful for you." I took a sip and forced the beer down, trying not to show my dislike for it.

"I'm sorry, I didn't mean for this to become another venting session. We can talk about something else." Caleb's eyes lit up. "Oh, hey, did you ever figure out who Michael Myers was at the party?"

I chuckled. "Yeah, it was Dan's brother, Chris."

Caleb choked on his beer. "Holy shit," he said with the liquid still in his mouth.

"But he said he was super drunk and didn't remember the party, so crisis averted, I guess."

Caleb's T-shirt hiked up as he slouched into the corner of the couch. The golden skin of his hip peeked out. I felt like Gollum, fighting the urge to grab his precious ring. I averted my eyes to the table before Caleb caught me staring. An old tin lunch box under the coffee table was the perfect distraction. I pointed to it. "What's that?"

Caleb scooted to the edge of the couch, placed his beer on the table, and reached for the metal square. He set the box in his lap. "This is where we keep pictures of our dad. Parker and I were looking through them earlier," Caleb said, opening the squeaky top. I slid closer to Caleb as he reached for the photos. He flipped through them, explaining each one. "My dad loved this motorcycle."

I focused on the picture. The colors were faded as if they'd been exposed to sunlight too long. Caleb's dad looked tall, with broad shoulders, wavy hair, and a thin goatee. In the picture, he stood beside a motorcycle with grease stains on his arms. He was handsome in a classic literature kind of way.

"He let me work on it with him a couple of times," Caleb said. "I never understood what I was doing. I just enjoyed being around him." Caleb placed the picture at the back of the stack and flipped through a few more, stopping at one of his mom and dad with their faces pushed together cheek to cheek. Caleb's mom took up most of the photo, and only half of his dad's face was present. But they both looked young, having the night of their lives. His mom's hair was teased to the sky, and she wore big hooped earrings.

The box shifted in Caleb's lap, and something rattled inside. I reached in and pulled out a long brass key with numbers carved into it. *2443*. "What's this?" I asked.

"It's the only thing my dad left behind. I found it on the floor next to his bed. I tossed it in here in case I ever figured out what it went to."

I examined the grainy key in my fingertips. "Weird." I placed it back in the box while Caleb stared at the motorcycle picture again.

"He got on that motorcycle and fled. I always think about where he could've gone. I know he has family back in Puerto Rico, so I always assume that's where he went." Caleb placed the pictures back in the lunchbox, hiding the single key underneath. "But who knows, maybe he's in Florida or Utah, or maybe he never left Texas. I wonder if I'd even recognize him if I saw him."

"I'm sure you would," I said, touching his thigh.

"When I was a kid, all I wanted to do was see him again while we were grocery shopping or walking to school. But now if I saw him, I don't even know what I'd say." Caleb reached for his beer. "I go back and forth between thinking I'd scream at him or just cry in his arms." Caleb paused, his eyes still fixed on the lunchbox. "I miss him a lot sometimes."

I knew how he felt. I would've given anything to talk to my mom one more time. I didn't feel her pain, but I felt the pain of her loss every day and craved more time with her. She would have loved Caleb. Seeing the way he took care of Parker would've been enough for her to realize he was a good guy.

I wrapped my arm around Caleb's shoulders just as he sipped his beer, accidentally whacking his arm, and spilling the frothy liquid all over his shirt.

I slid away from him. My eyes wide. "Oh my god. I'm so sorry!"

"Don't be! It's okay, it was an accident," Caleb said, waving it off. He placed the bottle on the table and pulled his shirt over his head, tossing it on the floor beside him. My gaze lingered on his chest before I pulled my eyes away, knowing I'd be trapped there until he walked away, but he didn't; he stayed put. Caleb smiled and said, "Were you trying to put your arm around me?"

My eyes hit the floor. "Maybe."

"Smooth," he said. "But I think that's against the rules."

I swallowed a lump in my throat. Something changed when Caleb was shirtless in front of me. I couldn't stop thinking about how badly I wanted to kiss him, and what I was willing to do to get it. "I broke up with Lauren yesterday." The lie flew out of my mouth like a spitball from a straw.

"Wait," Caleb said, taken aback. "When?"

"Yesterday." The word formed before I thought about the damage it could cause.

He squinted. "Why didn't you tell me?"

"I hadn't found the right time I guess? That's why I agreed to come over. I wanted to tell you all night, but it seemed weird to talk about it in front of Parker."

"Damn. Well, how did she take it?"

"She was upset, obviously didn't see it coming. But we talked for a while, and she eventually understood why we couldn't stay together."

I dug myself a grave I wasn't sure I'd be able to escape from, but lust was a powerful monster that couldn't be stopped.

"So it's officially over?" Caleb asked.

I nodded. "Officially over."

Caleb's lips pulled into a grin. "No more rules?"

My brain shouted at me to stop, but my eighteen-year-old hormones had already taken over. "No more rules."

"Come here," Caleb said as he reached for my arm, bringing me closer. He touched my chin with his thumb and gently pulled me into his lips. Caleb's hand moved to my face as my tongue found his. I placed my hand on his chest and followed the curves of his body down to his hip. I'd wondered what his skin felt like for so long I thought I might be in another dream. His skin was soft, void of a single divot or blemish. He leaned backward on the couch, pulling me down on top of him, and our kissing turned aggressive.

Caleb's warm hands explored my body; he sent his palms down my back and underneath my shirt before scaling back up. He broke our kiss, pulled my shirt over my head, and tossed it on the coffee table before our lips reconnected. My naked torso rubbed against his without an ounce of friction. His hands slid down my back again and pushed past the waistband of my underwear. My heart pounded against his chest. Caleb's hands squeezed my ass, making me nibble his bottom lip.

Caleb whispered, "Is this okay?"

His breath warmed my upper lip. I was so nervous, but I didn't want any of it to stop. I looked at him in his perfect hazel eyes and nodded. He gave me another squeeze, and it sent a ripple of pleasure up my sides. Grinding against his leg, I'd never been that hard in my life.

Caleb's hands let go of me and instead reached between us, feeling the crotch of my jeans. We continued to kiss while he attempted to unbutton my pants. He struggled to get a good grip. I could feel him smile under my kiss before I stood to take the pants off myself. Caleb did the same, still lying on the couch, revealing blue boxer briefs that hugged him, leaving little to the imagination. I'd never seen anyone so beautiful.

I stepped out of my jeans, turning them inside out. Caleb tossed his pants across the room and sat up on his knees. I kneeled against the couch and kissed him again in our upright position, allowing my hands to linger on the dimples of his lower back before pushing my way into his underwear. His peach fuzz tickled my palms. I couldn't help but return the squeeze he'd given me.

Caleb pressed his weight against me, laying me back to the fluffy cushions of the couch. He straddled me, seemingly unbothered by his excitement against my thigh. His lips explored the side of my neck, sending a lightning bolt pulsing through me. My hips writhed against his. He continued to move his kisses down my chest and across one of my nipples, sending another shot of electricity to my groin. Caleb released his tongue and pressed it against my skin, letting it trickle down my stomach, swooping over every peak and valley of my abs until he reached my hip. He slowly peeled the top of my underwear down to expose my hip bone, and he kissed it softly. I squirmed, chuckling as his lips sent goosebumps up my arms. Caleb smiled against my skin, peeling back the rest of my underwear and exposing me for the first time.

I lifted my waist to help him remove my boxers. I wanted him to see me naked; I wanted him to experience all of me the way no one else had. Caleb touched me so delicately as if I were an ancient Egyptian artifact dug up from a three-thousand-year-old tomb. Every time his lips connected against my skin, it sent another wave of pleasure over my entire existence. It wasn't until I felt his mouth around me that I gripped a chunk of his hair in my fist. I pulled a bit to make him stop before I embarrassed myself.

Caleb leaned back on his knees and removed his underwear. I couldn't stop staring. I didn't want to blink because it meant I would miss a millisecond of enjoying his perfect body. I think he knew I enjoyed the sight of him because he ran his hands over his smooth skin, with the most devilish smile I'd ever seen.

Caleb crawled over me, and straddled my crotch, grinding against me before leaning down for another kiss. My hands had a mind of their own as they locked onto his hips. I pressed against Caleb's fuzz. As soon as I gripped between his legs, a moan escaped his lips. I'd never felt someone else in my hand, but I had touched myself enough times to know what to do next.

Caleb made me a part of him that night, and I never wanted to return to anything else. Neither of us lasted long. Our lust had escaped, leaving us both gasping for air between each kiss. That kind of ecstasy was new to me. A shared state of euphoria that I craved over and over again. In our own intimate bubble, I'd never felt closer to another human. After it ended, I could still feel him on me, and I'd never felt more sure. We stared at each other, unable to look away. All I could do was smile so big that my cheeks hurt.

Caleb closed his eyes as I ran my fingers through his silky hair. "I should shower," he whispered. "Wanna join me?"

I chuckled. "Can two people even fit in there?"

Caleb stared down, still straddling me, with his hands on either side of my head, holding his weight off of me. "I don't know, but we can find out."

Caleb hopped off and collected his clothes before running into the bathroom. I thought about how Parker could wake up at any second and find us, so I grabbed my clothes just as fast and joined Caleb.

Even in the shower, we couldn't stop kissing. Letting him lather me allowed him to explore me all over again. I logged every touch, every kiss, every smile, and every inch of him into the Caleb file box in my mind. It was the best night I'd ever spent with anyone, and I didn't want to forget a single second of it.

My bike ride home wasn't as joyous. The guilt finally washed over me. I was a liar *and* a cheater. There was no way around it, I'd have to break up with Lauren the next day. I had to stop putting it off, no matter how hard it would be.

Grow some balls and do it, asshole.

THIRTY

The next morning I woke up feeling like an hourglass. My bottom half filled with guilt from the giddy high of my night with Caleb.

I entered the kitchen and scarfed down a bowl of cereal. I opened my phone before heading out the door, seeing a kissing emoji from Caleb. I couldn't stop thinking about him and his...everything.

I slid my backpack on before crossing the street, feeling a ping in my stomach as my brain switched from thinking about Caleb to Lauren. I'd officially betrayed our relationship, and it was just evil to keep her in the dark. My anxiety pushed through the roof just thinking about breaking the news to her.

The first warning bell rang as I spotted Steven at his locker in the main hall. I waved as I passed, but he reached out and pulled me into an empty bathroom.

"Spill it, bitch," Steven said, looking me up and down.

I tried not to grin. "Spill what?"

"The T-E-A, the tea! I need it!"

I stared at him with a crooked face.

Steven clapped his hands at me. "Oh my god, I'm talking about Caleb. How was Caleb's last night?!"

I shrugged.

Steven's jaw dropped. "I knew it, you guys did it, didn't you?"

"Does it matter?"

Steven punched me in the shoulder.

"Ow! What was that for?"

"For not waiting until you broke up with Lauren."

"I'm telling her today. I have to."

"Don't get me wrong," Steven said. "I'm glad you finally lost your V card, but you didn't need to drag Lauren through the mud while you were at it."

"Believe me, I feel like shit."

Steven fixed his hair in the reflection of his phone. "Then why'd you do it?"

"I've been asking myself the same thing."

"Cheating is for straight boys. It's not a good look." Steven put his phone away. "Fix it," he said, blowing a kiss before exiting the bathroom.

Thanks.

I sat at my usual desk in my homeroom and pulled out my phone to text Caleb.

ME

You at school today?

CALEB

Yep, I'll be mopping the floors during the second period.

ME

Maybe I'll have to sneak out and come find you.

CALEB

Oh, please do. ;)

. . .

My stomach sank as a text from Lauren popped up.

LAUREN

Morning babe :)

ME

Hey, are you gonna be around later? I want to talk to you about something.

LAUREN

Of course, is everything okay?

ME

Yeah, just find me during lunch, maybe?

LAUREN

Me and Dan are going to the library to do some research during second period if you want to come talk then?

ME

I don't really want to talk around Dan.

LAUREN

We can sneak away :)

ME

Sure, I'll see if I can escape for a bit.

LAUREN

Okay <3

It was hard to focus during the first period. I tried to find the right words to say to Lauren. I'd never broken up with anyone before. Hell, I'd never cheated on anyone either, and I knew it was going to make everything so much harder to say.

I glanced at Jacob Andrews, sitting beside me, scribbling notes on his spiraled pad. He and Tasha briefly dated during our junior year. The relationship lasted exactly seven days. I remember the entire break-up event outside the editing room, where we put the monthly paper together. We gathered around a computer, pretending not to watch Tasha and Jacob through the open door.

Tasha pulled a small Tupperware from her backpack and handed it to Jacob, saying, "I think we should break up, but I made you this cupcake." We had to stifle our laughter not to get caught eavesdropping. Jacob opened the container and pulled out a purple frosted cupcake that looked like she ripped it from the pages of a fairytale. Tasha walked into the editing room and closed the door, looking content, and went about her day as if nothing had happened. Poor Jacob looked depressed for the rest of the week every time I saw him until he started dating Becky Johnston. I knew that a cupcake wouldn't get close to fixing the damage. I'd need a whole Mack truck full of them.

I walked to my second-period class, still racking my brain, but nothing stuck. I hated not having anything planned to say. I was so bad at improv; I knew if I waited until I was face to face with Lauren, I would freeze up and chicken out.

I stepped into Mrs. Donahue's class with my head down as I passed her desk.

"Landon," Mrs. Donahue said, stopping me mid-stride. "Are you all right?"

I was one of the last people to arrive. The bell rang, but I'd missed it entirely.

"Yeah," I said, noticing the *Madison Monthly* on her desk, with SPECIAL EDITION stamped across the front page. "Just a lot on my mind, per usual. What's this?"

"Just came out today." Mrs. Donahue leaned her elbows on the desk. "I have to say, your piece was the best you've written."

I snatched the paper, quickly flipping through the pages. "My piece?"

"Didn't you know this was coming out today?" She asked.

I racked my brain before a flash of my hungover heart-to-heart with Tasha hit me. "I guess I forgot," I mumbled as I flipped through the pages.

"Well, really great work on this one."

"Tasha was the one that picked it. I..." My eyes caught my printed name, and I started reading. "...wait."

"What's wrong?" Mrs. Donahue asked.

My heart stopped. "I have to find Tasha. I'm sorry, I'll be right back." I turned and bolted out the door, still holding onto the paper. I power-walked through the empty halls, frantically typing out a text to Tasha.

ME

Hey, where are you right now?

I stopped and waited for Tasha to respond, lacking patience with my eyes locked on my phone screen.

TASHA

Library, why?

I picked up speed again. Pushing through the library's swinging doors, I went straight for the front desk. Mrs. Fletcher, a short woman with white hair peered at her computer screen. My sudden voice startled her. "Have you seen Tasha?"

Mrs. Fletcher squinted, surveying the large room before pointing a wrinkled finger at the computer lab.

I twisted in place and spotted her. The computer lab was a small room at the back of the library, secluded in a glass box. I weaved through the long tables of studying students and pulled the heavy glass door open. Tasha sat in front of her laptop. I hovered over her chair like a vulture flying over a dying animal. "How did you get this?"

Tasha removed her headphones and looked up at me, brows pinched. "What?"

I slapped the *Special Edition Monthly* on her keyboard. "My college application story. How did you get it?"

Tasha pushed her chair away from the desk and faced me with a raised hand. "You said I could take whichever one I wanted."

"Yes, from my desktop."

"Landon, this story was on your desktop."

My eyes widened. "Are you sure?"

"Yes, I'm positive," she said. "What's the big deal?"

I slumped into a chair and gripped my forehead. "I'm such an idiot."

Tasha stared at me.

"I was so hungover, I wasn't even thinking," I said.

Her head tilted. "I'm not following here."

"That story was never meant for anyone to read. It was for my college applications."

"But it's so good."

"Yeah, but it isn't mine."

"What?" Tasha asked. "You plagiarized it?"

"No. Not exactly," I stood and started pacing. "How many copies have gone out? Maybe we can reprint."

"All of them, during first period."

"God damn it!" I flipped a plastic chair on its side, and Tasha jumped from her seat, gasping at my sudden outburst. "This story wasn't meant for you or the paper."

"I'm sorry, Landon. If I had known..."

I pinched the bridge of my nose and clenched my eyes. "Shit, I'm sorry. This isn't your fault at all. It's mine." I picked up the chair and set it back at the table. Caleb flashed through my mind, and I wanted to scream at the top of my lungs. "I'm sorry, I'm sorry. I gotta go." I jogged back through the library, into the hallway, and pulled out my phone to text Caleb.

But his voice echoed through the empty hall, hitting me like a forceful wind. "What the fuck is this, Landon?"

I slipped the phone into my pocket as Caleb approached, holding the *Special Edition Monthly* in his hand.

"Caleb, I can explain. How did you even get one?"

"It's being passed out to everyone. And imagine my shock when I read it."

"Please don't be mad, I—" Trying to touch his chest, I stepped closer, but Caleb pushed my hand away.

"Did you think this was okay?" Caleb said. "Everything I told you about my dad... You knew how traumatized I was about the hat he gave me for Christmas, and you turned it into a story for the school newspaper?"

My hands shot up, trying to explain. "No, it wasn't meant for—"

"I don't give a fuck, Landon. This is my life! This isn't one of your little made-up stories, this is real. You exploited me!" Caleb crumpled the newspaper and tossed it into a trash bin and turned. I hurried to stop him from going, grabbing his arm, but he pulled away and faced me again, pointing a finger at me.

"Don't touch me, Landon. I knew this was a mistake."

I stood in the middle of the empty hallway while he murdered me with his words.

"God, I feel so stupid! I knew when I saw you at Lucky's—I shouldn't have started this with you," he said. "I should've trusted my gut when I said I couldn't do complicated. I trusted you, Landon! It's been really hard for me to get close to anyone since Andy. Do you realize what it took for me to have sex with you?" Caleb's eyes fixed on something behind me, and his skin went pale. "Fuck," he whispered.

Dan and Lauren stood at the library doors, frozen in place, staring at me. My stomach dropped out like a trapdoor, and my mouth went dry. Lauren and Dan had heard everything Caleb said. My entire world crashed down on me, and it was suffocating.

I ran to Lauren but Dan stepped in front of her and pushed me back.

"Dan, don't," she said.

I stared at her. My heart pounded through my chest. "Lauren."

She stepped to me and glanced at Caleb. "What is he talking about?"

My eyes welled. "Can we just go somewhere and talk?"

Lauren's questioning continued. "Is it true? Did you have sex with him?"

"Please, let's go talk alone," I begged, reaching for her hand, but she stepped back.

"I don't want to go anywhere with you. I want you to tell me the truth," Lauren said.

I glanced over my shoulder, trapped between them with nowhere to go. Caleb's head tilted.

"Landon," Lauren said, pulling my gaze back to her flushed face. "Are you gay?"

Caleb stepped closer to us, I heard his feet against the tiled floor. "You didn't actually tell her, did you?"

I spun around to face him. "Caleb, I can—"

"You lied to get me to have sex with you."

My head shook. "It's not like that. I didn't mean—"

"Stop!" Caleb yelled. "You're a manipulative asshole." He backed away, still looking at me with moist eyes. "Don't call me, don't even text me. I don't wanna hear from you ever again. Seriously, fuck you, Landon." He finally turned, disappearing around the corner.

His words impaled me at the speed of light. My jaw clenched. "Caleb!"

My hands trembled as I turned back to Lauren, holding my breath to keep the tears back. "Lauren, I swear to God I was gonna tell you. I didn't mean for it to go this—"

She slapped me across the face. The sting of her hand snapped across my jaw. I couldn't look at her after that. I honestly should've seen it coming. Lauren whimpered as she hurried back through the library doors.

Dan and I stood in the hallway alone. I expected him to punch me into the ground, but it never came.

"Should've known you were a faggot," Dan said before disappearing into the Library.

I panted, grabbing my forehead, with no idea what to do next. I paced the hall, thinking Dan would tell everyone in the library about me. A phantom pain hit my stomach like a one-two punch. My knees bent, and I leaned my hands on them, staring at the floor and breathing heavily.

Tasha appeared, pushing through the library doors. "Landon..."

I shook my head. "Don't." I could feel the anxiety reach my head, and it filled my eyes with tears. "Please, just don't." I couldn't look at Tasha. I just turned and returned to Mrs. Donahue's class, feeling deflated, empty, and alone. I wiped the tears from my eyes before entering the room. I zoned out at my desk, staring at the whiteboard lost in a daze, feeling as if I had just gone ten rounds in a boxing match where I didn't land a single punch.

I could tell word spread every time I walked through the halls. People stared at me and whispered as they passed. Like a monkey in a zoo, I was on display.

I never expected to lose Lauren and Caleb on the same day. A pile of bricks landed on my chest whenever I thought about it.

I hoped the news wouldn't reach the teachers because it might reach the principal, which meant it would get to my dad. I would've been okay going my whole life never telling him, even if it meant I had to hide someone from him. It would shatter him If I told him I was gay.

I left school that day drained, barely able to lift my feet to get home. Once I found my bed, I didn't move for the rest of the night.

THIRTY-ONE

A week passed, and every student at Madison High knew my deepest secret. Most mornings, I'd be met with a new derogatory word printed and taped to my locker. Fag. Fairy. Queer. Pansy. Steven eventually caught wind of it and started to come to school early to make sure my locker wasn't defaced before I got there. He was the only person in the entire school who could empathize. I appreciated his support, but he'd change the subject when I tried to ask about Lauren. She avoided me like I was an infectious disease. If she saw me walking toward her, she'd split down another hallway or duck into the bathroom. I wanted to apologize, but it seemed she couldn't stand to look at me.

Eventually, I caught her at her locker, putting books away. She didn't see me coming. "Hey," I said, leaning on the locker next to her. My voice made her jump.

Lauren rolled her eyes when she realized it was me.

"Look," I said. "I know you don't want to talk to me, but I just wanted to say—I'm really sorry."

"People keep asking me if I turned you gay," Lauren said as she slipped a textbook into her backpack. She slammed the locker and looked at me. "Do you know how embarrassing that is?"

"People are idiots."

"It still hurts."

"I'm so sorry, Lauren. You don't even know how bad it killed me keeping everything from you."

"You know, I keep thinking about that night in your room, and it all makes sense now. How long have you known?" she asked.

"Not long. Everything is still so new."

"Why didn't you tell me?"

"I was afraid of hurting you."

"So you thought cheating on me would be the better option? How could I ever forgive you after that?"

"I don't know if you can or even should. I fucked up, I know that. I'm saying I'm—"

"I can't do this right now I'm gonna be late." Lauren pushed by me, and I watched her disappear into the crowd.

Another week went by, and I felt more alone than ever. Tasha and Steven were the only two who spoke to me. They would switch at lunch every other day. When they weren't sitting with me, they sat with Lauren, like split custody in a divorce.

Chris was the only guy from the team that would still talk to me. Everyone else was on Dan's side. It was an unspoken pact that no one could look in my direction if Dan attended practice. They all took it out on me on the field, tackling me as hard as they could, not throwing the ball my way. Football became harder and harder to enjoy.

I walked by Mrs. Donahue's room on my way to trig when she called my name. I stepped back to peek through the open door. She sat at her desk in front of the whiteboard. It must have been her free period, as no other students were in the room.

"Come in, talk to me," Mrs. Donahue said.

I nodded and walked in, sitting at a desk in the front row.

"I just wanted to check in. You haven't been taking part in class much lately," she said.

"That's my fault, I can try talking more." I was about to get up to go, but she gave me a look that told me she wasn't done.

"Tasha told me you've been having a tough time recently."

"And you want to know if all the gossip is true?"

"It's not my business if it's true or not," she said. "But I will say that I support you either way. I hope you know you can come talk to me if you need to."

The corner of my mouth tugged weakly. "I appreciate it."

"So that story was never meant to be published, huh?"

"Tasha really likes to talk, doesn't she?"

Mrs. Donahue chuckled. "She told me you're still waiting to hear from NYU. With that story, I think you're a prime candidate."

I leaned on the desk, avoiding eye contact. "It wasn't mine to tell."

"You can't change the past, Landon. Everyone makes mistakes, I sure as hell have. A lot of them. But the beauty of making mistakes means we can learn from them and make ourselves better because of them."

"I'm learning the hard way."

"Have you thought about what you'll do if you get into NYU?"

I shifted in my seat, leaning against the chair and slouching. "I don't know. I keep going back and forth, thinking about what my life would look like at UT versus NYU."

"And?"

"I'm afraid I won't feel any different at UT than I do now. I feel like I hate football more and more every day. I want to start fresh, somewhere where no one knows me. I want to be somewhere where I can be the real me."

Mrs. Donahue stood, rounded her desk, and leaned against it. "The only person holding you back is yourself."

My eyes shot to her, and chills rushed over me. "My mom used to say that."

Mrs. Donahue smiled. "She sounds like a smart woman."

It was going on week three since Caleb broke it off with me and I left school eager to get home to shower. It had been one of the muggiest days of the year, and my sweat-stained shirt proved it. I entered the kitchen, and dropped my backpack at the closed door. Dad stood at the island. His hands leaned on the countertop, and his shoulders hunched, looking over something.

My heart dropped, and I thought, *Word finally got to him. Coach found out and told him.* I stepped to the counter. He was reading a letter.

My eyes widened. "What is that?"

Dad didn't look up, just took a deep breath and sighed. "Why didn't you tell me you'd applied to NYU?"

"What does it say?"

"Answer me," Dad growled.

"It was a late application that my guidance counselor gave me. I just wanted another option because I didn't know if I would get a scholarship. What does it say?"

Dad slid the letter toward me.

My eyes scanned the words. "Holy shit," I whispered. "I got in."

Dad looked at me and raised an eyebrow. "What the hell are you gonna do at NYU?"

"I wanna be a writer," I told him for the first time.

Dad stroked his mustache and laughed. "Don't bullshit me, Landon. You're gonna play football at UT. You're not gonna to be a writer."

"That's what *you* want me to do," I said, trying to stay calm, but my emotions from the day resurfaced. "Have you ever considered what *I* want? My entire life, you've pushed me to play football, but guess what? I'm done."

Dad crossed his arms against his chest, staring at me. "What do you mean you're done?"

"I'm done playing football," I said, staring him in the face.

Dad's cheeks went red, I could tell he wanted to raise his voice.

"Landon, don't be an idiot. You have an amazing opportunity in front of you, you have a full scholarship."

"Fuck the scholarship, Dad! I don't want it. I want to go to New York!"

"Landon, I can't afford to send you to that school!"

I grabbed my backpack from the floor and slung it over my shoulder, heading for the stairs. "I'll figure it out then."

"Landon, I—"

"You know," I said, cutting him off. "For so long I've been terrified of what other people think of me, including you. I didn't tell you about wanting to be a writer because I knew you wouldn't take me seriously. I need to think about myself and what makes *me* happy. Going to New York and getting out of this shitty town is about the only thought making me happy right now. So I'll figure it out, okay?"

Dad stood there with his arms crossed, looking appalled by my words. I waited for him to respond, but all I got was silence. He eventually shook his head and walked through the living room toward his office.

I slammed my bedroom door behind me, tossing my backpack on my bed. I sat at my desk as I read the acceptance letter over again. I'd felt so heavy for so long that I'd almost forgotten what it felt like to float. I wanted to show my mom so badly. I wanted to bust through her bedroom door and jump on her bed together, cheering and hollering.

I pulled out my phone to text Caleb the good news but recalled his voice saying the same thing I'd played repeatedly: "Don't call me, don't even text me. I never want to hear from you again."

Dad barely spoke to me for the next two days. My life force drained, leaving me emptier than I was the day before. The first thing I'd do in the morning was check my phone, hoping to see Caleb's name. My heart skipped a beat every time my pocket buzzed, only to be disappointed. After all that time of nothing, I'd assumed Caleb was entirely over me. I wondered if Parker ever asked about me. And if he did, I wondered what Caleb told him had happened between us.

For those three and a half weeks, I never once spotted Caleb mopping any floors, cleaning graffiti off the walls, or even mowing the grass. It was like he'd walked off the face of the earth. I was alone in the dark; NYU seemed to be my only light at the end of the tunnel.

Now that NYU had accepted me, I decided to leave football behind. When the school day ended, I went to the locker rooms to talk to Coach. When I knocked on his door, he was hunched over a playbook at his desk. "Hey, Coach."

"Griffin, where the hell have you been? You missed two practices. I tried calling your dad about it, but he never picked up."

"His campaign team's been keeping him pretty busy. I'm sorry I missed them, but I wanted to talk to you about that."

"Come in. Shut the door."

I did as I was told and sat across from him.

"So, what the hell's going on?"

"I wanted to let you know that I declined the UT scholarship."

Coach's eyes widened, and he closed the binder in front of him. "Why the hell would you do that?"

"Coach, my head hasn't been in the game for a while now, and I know you can tell."

"We all have our slow weeks. That's all I chalked it up to be."

I chuckled. "It's a lot more than a slow week. I've been thinking about this for a long time. I don't think football is my thing."

"You're not saying what I think you're saying, are you?"

"I'm sorry."

"Oh, come on, your dad didn't raise you to be a quitter."

"Don't you want guys on your team who are passionate on the field?

Coach's face twisted. "You can't quit. You've been playing since you were a little kid."

"Sure, I enjoyed it, and I got good at it, but I realized I wasn't doing it because it made me happy. I was doing it because it made my dad happy."

It took a second for it to really sink in for him. "Hell, I know the feelin'," Coach said. "But are you sure? Because the team needs you. At least play out the rest of the season."

I shook my head. "I'd just be wasting everyone's time."

Coach sighed, brushing a hand over his bald head. "I don't like it, but I can't force you to do something you don't want to do. I just hope you don't regret it."

"I'll come to every game, I promise."

"Bet your ass you will, Griffin. Now go clean out your locker before everyone gets here. I'll tell the guys the news."

I nodded. "Thanks, Coach."

I folded my jersey, staring at my name printed on the fabric before placing it in my backpack. I tossed my pads and helmet into a big plastic bin. The door swung open. I looked over my shoulder and saw Chris down the row. He placed his duffle bag on the bench in the middle of the aisle.

"You're here early," I said.

Chris pulled a pair of dirty shoes out of the bag and slapped them against the floor. "I know, I wanted to get some drills in before we started."

"Smart," I said with a nod.

"Team's not gonna be the same without you," Chris said as he opened his locker.

"It's that obvious, huh?"

"We knew it was comin'. I told the guys to ease up but they don't listen to me like they listened to Dan. You quitting because of them?"

"Not fully, no." I said. "Football just isn't what I'm meant to do. But you guys will be fine, you don't need me." I smiled. "I'll be cheering you on at every game." I pulled my arms through the straps of my backpack.

Chris pulled off his T-shirt, revealing a black Under Armour short sleeve. "What about the scholarship?" He reached for his shoulder pads and slipped them over his head.

"It was a tough call, but I declined it. Maybe they'll give it to Dan now."

Chris scoffed as he squeezed his big shoulder pads into his jersey. "Yeah right, he barely shows up for practice anymore."

"Has he gotten worse?"

"Most nights he doesn't come home at all."

"I'm sorry, Chris."

"It's not your fault," Chris grunted as he pulled on his knee pads. "He's choosing to do this. He doesn't even care about how worried our parents are."

I shook my head. "He's always been selfish. I should go before the other guys show up. I want to avoid all the questions." I started for the door, but Chris stopped me with his words.

"I lied before," he said.

I looked at him as he tied his tight pants.

"I wasn't drunk at the party. I remember everything.".

"Oh." My jaw clenched. "Why didn't you say anything when I came to get my bike?"

Chris sat on the bench, reaching for his shoes. "I don't know. I felt so awkward about it, and I didn't know what to say. I knew you were wasted. I didn't want to rehash it and make things more awkward."

"Just so you know, I thought you were someone else. I wasn't trying to hit on you."

"I know," Chris said, slipping on his second shoe.

"Why didn't you tell anyone?"

Chris stopped tying and leaned his elbows on his knees, staring at me with a furrowed brow. "You're my friend, Landon. I wasn't gonna out you to the entire school."

A wave of relief washed over me, and I smiled at Chris. It felt good to know he still considered me a friend. "Thank you. You have no idea how much that means to me."

Chris nodded and messed with his laces again.

"I should go, but good luck tomorrow night," I said.

"Thanks, man," Chris said without looking up.

I walked out with my head held a little higher.

The next night, I walked out of my house and could already hear the excitement of a Friday night game. The school's parking lot was packed, and the lights of the football field made it look like the middle of the day. It was the first time in years that I watched the game instead of playing. I decided to grab some popcorn to snack on before heading to the stands.

The wind picked up, and I slipped on my hoodie. Standing in line at the concession booth, I remembered Caleb and Parker tossing popcorn into each other's mouths when they watched me play. I could hear their laughter, and it made me miss them even more.

I spotted Steven's pink hair out of the corner of my eye, several feet away, talking to Lauren. Their eyes found me, and my attention shot forward. The next time I peeked over, Lauren was walking toward me. I slipped my hands into my hoodie pocket and pretended not to see her.

"Hey," Lauren whispered. It was the first time in weeks I'd heard her voice.

"Hey, hi," I said, avoiding eye contact until I noticed her smile.

"Congrats on NYU. Steven told me."

"Yeah, thanks. Congrats to you, too. Who would've thought we'd end up in the same city?" I chuckled awkwardly.

"I know, right?" Lauren smiled. "We should grab a coffee or something, like after we settle into our dorms and stuff."

I nodded. "Yeah, yeah, absolutely." I knew she was just being polite. I doubted we would ever actually get coffee after everything.

I stepped to the counter. The concession stand was a little green hut just off the parking lot. Inside was a small popcorn maker, two coffee machines, and every popular candy bar splayed out. "Uh, can I just get a bag of popcorn, please?" I looked over my shoulder at Lauren. "You want anything?"

"No thanks."

I passed a dollar bill to the small freshman boy operating the money box before he scooped some popcorn into a paper bag and handed it to me. Lauren lingered when I stepped to the side.

"I'm sorry we haven't talked much," she said, pushing her hands into the pockets of her denim jacket.

"I get it, it's okay."

"I just needed time to like, process everything, you know? I felt like I cried for weeks." She pushed a strand of hair behind her ear that the wind had blown across her face.

"I feel awful about everything," I said, eyeing my popcorn. "I didn't mean for things to play out like they did. I didn't want to hurt you, but it blew up in my face anyway, so—"

"You were gonna hurt me no matter what. But I wish I'd heard it from you."

"Me too. I tried to tell you, but as time went on, it just kept getting harder."

"I should've gotten the hint when I found Grindr on your phone."

I looked at her. "Yeah, maybe." We both chuckled, briefly avoiding eye contact. "So, did Steven force you to come talk to me?"

"Not exactly. He and Tasha have been there for me a lot. And while I can't say I fully forgive you, I do miss having you around."

I smiled. "You do?"

"Yeah. And I kinda had an idea."

"Oh god, what is Steven making you do?"

Lauren laughed. "It's something we've been talking about. Since prom is next week and my dad went through all the trouble getting our outfits, maybe we could still go together? Not as a couple, but with me and Steven."

Her offer stunned me; I thought she'd never talk to me again, never mind take me to prom. "Seriously?"

Lauren shrugged. "Yeah, we might as well use the clothes since we have them."

"Well shit, I'm down, yeah," I said with a smile. Lauren opened her arms, pulling me into a hug. I wrapped around her, still gripping my bag of overflowing popcorn. "I'm so sorry," I whispered. "For everything."

Lauren squeezed me tight.

Steven smacked into us, adding to our hug, causing the top layer of my popcorn to sprinkle the grass. "Did we kiss and make up?"

We laughed as Steven released us from his bear hug.

"Not exactly," Lauren said. "But we're good, for now."

I tossed pieces of popcorn at both of them.

"Hey, don't waste that, I'm starving!" Steven said as he reached into the bag for a handful. I threw more at him as we all jogged to the bleachers, laughing.

The three of us cheered the entire game. It was more exciting to watch than to worry about getting smashed to the ground at any second. I searched for Dan's jersey, curious if he had shown up to play, but he was nowhere to be seen. Our team lost by ten points, but everyone seemed to be in good spirits. Maybe Chris was right. Perhaps the team *did* need me. The game was a blast. It was the first time in weeks that I'd forgotten about Caleb.

Steven and I lingered at his car after Lauren had said her good-byes. The moon glistened off the hood of Steven's white sedan. A rainbow beaded necklace hung from his rearview mirror. "You still haven't heard from him?" He asked.

"Not in almost a month," I said, pulling my hood up.

"Have you tried texting him?"

I watched a black truck pull out of its parking spot. "No, I've been too afraid. I don't want to make things worse."

"Girl, we need to get you out of this funk," Steven said as he reached into his pocket, pulling out a small pack of gum.

"What funk?"

Steven unwrapped a thin rectangle piece and popped it into his mouth. "I'm not blind. I've seen you moping around school every day for weeks, you eat by yourself at lunch, and you barely talk to anyone. Tonight was the first time I've seen light in your eyes since everything happened."

"Yeah, tonight was the first time in forever I've felt like myself."

"Maybe you just need a Grindr date. That always works for me."

I laughed and crossed my arms, leaning against the hood of

Steven's car. "Every guy that messaged me seemed like a creep. I deleted it anyway, so I'll pass."

"Oh my god!" Steven did a little hop and grabbed me by the arms. "I have an idea! I can set you up with my friend!"

I shivered away from him. "I don't know, I don't think I'm ready to get involved with someone else."

"No, that is exactly what you need!" Steven pulled out his phone and typed. "You have to get back on the horse if you want to forget about Caleb." I stared with blank eyes. I didn't necessarily want to forget about Caleb, but every time I thought about him, it made me sad. I would wonder what he was doing during the day and if he was thinking about me.

Steven beamed with excitement; the brightness from his phone illuminated his smile. "My friend Blake is super cute. We used to do community theater together." He held his bright screen in front of my face. It was an Instagram picture of a guy from the shoulders up. The blurry background looked like he could've been at the beach. He had blond hair shaved on the sides but fell into his sky blue eyes from the top. "He's cute, right!?"

I looked away from the phone. "I guess. I don't know. It feels too soon."

Steven's thumbs went to work. "I'm texting him right now."

"Fine," I said, feeling exhausted. "I'm gonna go. I'll catch ya later."

"I'm gonna send him your hottest insta pic!" Steven shouted. His voice ricocheted off the light posts that lit the parking lot.

"Whatever you say!" I yelled over my shoulder, headed for the street. I thought about Blake's picture as I walked up to my house. It felt strange to imagine myself with a guy who wasn't Caleb.

Two days before prom, I finally agreed to go on a date with Blake. Steven texted me daily, bugging me about him.

STEVEN

Blake thinks you're cute.

I want to set you guys up.

I think you'd really like him!

Blake asked about you again today.

Should I tell him to follow you on Insta?

Do you have an X account?

I'm gonna keep bugging you until you say yes.

You better not be thinking about Caleb!

Bitch if you don't answer me...

Blake has such a cute dog. Caleb doesn't have a dog. Red flag!

OMG Blake said he loves gingers, go out with him! I talked to Lauren, she thinks it's a good idea too.

Kay, if I don't get back to him, he's gonna find someone else.

You're missing out, girl!

I'm just gonna tell him you're interested.

ME

Jesus! FINE! I'll go on ONE date!

Steven set the whole thing up. I hadn't even spoken to Blake, and I never texted or followed him on social media. Steven suggested it should be a blind date. Luckily, I knew what Blake looked like so I could spot him in a crowd. Steven told us to meet at Alvin's Coffee House in Madison's Downtown Square.

The square was cute at night. Small trees lined the sidewalks, lit by white string lights around their branches. The square had only been built in the last seven years. It was mostly filled with mom-and-pop shops, restaurants, and even a real estate office.

Steven suggested Blake and I meet for coffee and dessert first because it was less formal than dinner. If I didn't think things were going well, walking away from coffee would be easier than sitting through an entire meal. Steven was more experienced in dating than I was, so I did what I was told.

I approached Alvin's and surveyed the few customers inside through the large pane windows. Even with the entrance door closed, the bitter smell of coffee filled the air. I didn't see any guys with blond hair in the shop, so I waited beside the outside dining area.

I pulled out my phone. It was 8:10 p.m. Blake was late, so I scrolled through Instagram. It'd become a trend to post your college acceptance letter. I typed in Dan's name, curious to see if he had posted anything recently, but everything was from months ago.

A voice startled me. "Landon?" It came from a tall guy with familiar blond hair swooping across one eye.

"Yeah, hi," I said, pushing my phone in my pocket.

Blake smiled and reached for a handshake. "Sorry, I'm late. Got caught up in a phone call." He slicked back the falling strands of hair. He wore a gray suit, with a white button-up shirt under his blazer. He'd unbuttoned his shirt at the top, a small tuft of hair poked from it. The lenses of his wire-framed glasses made his eyes brighter than the string of lights on the trees. A brown leather satchel dangled across his torso.

"It's totally fine. Though I feel a little underdressed," I said, pulling at my tank top.

Blake waved me off. "You look great. Mind if we sit outside?" He spoke fast with a slight southern drawl on certain vowels.

"Yeah, that's fine."

"I come here all the time; it's great." Blake walked through the opening in the fence and sat at an empty table with two chairs, pulling his satchel over his head and placing it on the ground. The table was made of dark wood, and a mason jar with a tea light sat atop it. "You and Steven, y'all are close?"

"We've been friends for a while. He said you guys did theater together?"

Blake chuckled. "I did one show after my family moved here from Alabama when I thought I wanted to be an actor. It was fun, but not something I want to do again."

A woman wearing an ALVIN'S COFFEE HOUSE T-shirt approached our table. Blake didn't wait for her to greet us. Instead, he spat out his order. "I'll have a caramel macchiato and a slice of cherry pie."

The server looked at me. "I'll have the same, thanks," I said, not wanting to struggle over any coffee names.

Blake watched our server leave, then looked at me. "So, how old are you, if you don't mind me asking? Same age as Steven?"

"Yeah, eighteen. You?"

"Turn twenty next month," Blake said, leaning his arms on the table. His answer surprised me because his clothes made him look more distinguished than me. "Steven told me you play football."

"I did, yeah. I just quit the team, though."

"Oh?"

I could tell by Blake's tone that he wanted me to explain, but the server interrupted us. "Turns out that we're out of the cherry pie," she said.

"Just the drinks are fine then," Blake blurted without asking me for input. The server trotted back inside. "So, what do you do now that you quit the team?"

"I guess I can focus more on my writing now."

"Oh, you're a writer. That's cute," Blake said as the server placed our drinks on the table.

My jaw tightened. Blake's words hit me like a condescending brick. My phone vibrated, and I checked it under the table. Steven texted me.

STEVEN

How's it going?

ME

I don't think I feel a spark…

Blake and I sipped at the same time. I had no idea what to say next. I thought about the briefing Steven gave me the day before. He mentioned that I should ask about Blake if the conversation got stale because people loved talking about themselves.

My lips lingered on the cup. I could taste the sweet caramel syrup that was dripping over the edge of the mug.

My phone vibrated again, and I glanced at my lap, almost choking on my coffee. Caleb's name filled the screen. Liquid spilled over the mug's edge when I slammed it on the table. "Sorry I have to take this," I said, feeling short of breath. I shot from my seat and walked to the edge of the street.

I put the phone to my ear. "Hello?"

Caleb's voice cracked. "I need help."

THIRTY-TWO

I plugged my other ear. "What's going on?"

"Luke hit Parker," Caleb said, huffing as if he were running. My heart fell to my feet. "I'm sorry I called, but no one else was answering."

"No, don't apologize. Go to my house; I'll be there soon."

"Okay. Thank you."

I hung up, and rushed back to the table as Blake looked up from his phone. "Hey, I'm sorry to cut this short, but something just came up. I gotta go."

Blake stood. His brows tensed. "Is everything okay?"

"I'm not sure. I just have to go."

"Well, let me drive you."

"No thanks, I have my bike."

"Okay," Blake said before wrapping me in an awkward hug.

I backed away and jogged to my parked bike, not bothering to leave any money for the coffee. Blake didn't exactly look strapped for cash. I pedaled as fast as I could.

Hearing Caleb sound so worried made me panic. I hoped things hadn't gotten too out of control with him and Luke. The last thing Caleb needed was trouble with the cops again. I imagine they'd tack more time onto his probation if he got arrested. Caleb sounded so winded.

I hope he wasn't running from the cops.

I speeded down my street, spotting Caleb sitting on my front steps with Parker in his lap, leaning his head on Caleb's shoulder. I dropped my bike in the grass and hurried to them, kneeling to touch Parker's arm. "Are you okay?"

Parker nodded. His eyes were red and puffy, and a bruise formed on his jaw.

"He could use some ice," Caleb whispered.

"Let's go inside," I said, leading them to the side door. "We just have to be quiet. My dad's in his room, not sure if he's asleep yet." We entered the kitchen with Caleb carrying Parker and I clicked on the light. He plopped him down on a stool at the island.

I grabbed a washcloth and opened the freezer, pulling two ice cubes out of a small bucket. I twisted the cloth around the cubes and handed it to Caleb.

He touched the ice pack to Parker's face. "Just hold this here for a bit, okay?" Parker nodded, holding the cloth. Caleb turned to me. "I'm sorry to make you do this. I hope I didn't pull you away from anything important."

I resisted the urge to roll my eyes, thinking about Blake. "It wasn't."

"I didn't want to bother you, but I tried calling Miguel and the others, but no one answered."

"Caleb, it's fine. I don't mind at all. Let's go to my room. You guys can stay there." They followed me up the stairs, and the floors creaked with every step. I tried to tiptoe as not to alert my dad. I could hear the TV on in his room, most nights he would fall asleep to the History channel. Caleb held Parker's hand and led him into my room. I pulled some folded blankets from the hallway closet and closed my door behind me.

They sat on my bed, and Parker slumped against Caleb's arm.

I laid the blankets on the floor between my desk and my bed. "So what the hell happened?"

"I should've known the piece of shit would do it eventually," Caleb said. "I was reading in our room, and Parker was on the couch watching TV. Luke had been drinking all night, so I stayed away."

I grabbed a pillow off my bed and tossed it onto the small bed of blankets I'd created. Caleb led Parker to the pile and gestured for him to lie down before he continued. "I guess he wanted to take over the TV. He changed the channel, and Parker got mad at him. I heard Luke tell him to go to his room, but Parker refused." Caleb joined me, sitting on the bed. "The next thing I heard was Parker yelling my name. I came flying into the living room and saw Luke yank Parker off the couch and punch him to the floor."

It shocked me that a grown man could strike a kid over something so stupid. "What a fucking scumbag."

"I swear to God I wanted to kill him. I tackled him and just started punching; I didn't care where they were landing; I just lost it. And then my mom jumped on me, clawing and screaming for me to get off of him. She didn't seem to care that he'd just hit her son." Caleb looked over the bedpost at Parker, who had already fallen asleep. "When I stopped punching Luke, I grabbed Parker, and we ran."

"Jesus," I said, grabbing Caleb's hand. I was nervous he would pull away from me, but he let me touch him.

"We're not going back there," Caleb whispered. "I can't put Parker through that again."

"You shouldn't have to," I said, shuddering to think things could've been worse.

Caleb looked me in the eyes for the first time that night. "Thanks for letting us crash here."

"Of course."

"With the way we left things, I didn't think you would answer either."

"I didn't think I'd hear from you again."

"I'm sorry, I—"

"You have nothing to be sorry about. What I did was really fucked up. You didn't deserve that." Caleb glanced at our hands, still interlocked. A tinge in my stomach made me let go of him, and stand. "You can sleep in my bed. I'll take the couch."

Caleb reached out, grabbing me by the wrist before I could walk away. "Stay with me."

I sighed, unable to say no to his puppy dog eyes. I leaned to switch off the light before I got undressed.

Caleb fiddled with his clothes before we slid under the covers, and shared a pillow. We flipped on our sides, staring at each other. He pulled the blanket up to our ribs. The moonlight glistened over his bronze skin. "What made you write the story, anyway?" Caleb asked, and I could feel his warm breath against my chin.

"It was for some late college applications." I tucked my hand under the pillow, resting my arm against Caleb's bare chest. "No one was supposed to read it. I was just as surprised when I saw it in the paper."

"How'd it get there?"

"Miscommunication on my part. I told Tasha she could take a story off my desktop the morning after Dan's birthday. I was so hungover when she asked me, I totally forgot the story was there."

Caleb's hand touched my hip. "Rookie mistake." He slowly ran his fingertips up my ribs. "I didn't mean to out you like that. I swear I didn't see Lauren and Dan standing there."

"Karma caught up with me, I guess," I said. "Now everyone at school knows."

"Did people care?"

"The guys on the team started treating me differently, making fun of me. Hitting me a little harder on the field."

"Seriously?"

"Yeah, I ended up quitting the team, not because of them, but because I realized football stopped being fun a long time ago."

"I'm sorry. None of that should've happened."

"Like I said, you have nothing to apologize for."

Caleb's nose brushed mine. "And what about Lauren?"

"We didn't talk for a while. But she approached me at the game last week. I think we're okay now? I honestly didn't think we'd ever talk again."

Caleb smiled. "That's good."

He stroked my skin. It felt nice to feel his touch again.

I pushed my fingers through his thick hair. "When I didn't see you at school, I was afraid you were gone for good."

"I was really angry. I knew I wouldn't be able to be around you. I didn't wanna keep seeing you in the hallway or something. So I asked to switch to another school district to finish my community service."

"Ouch," I said.

"That doesn't mean I didn't think about you." Caleb pushed closer to me. "Just promise you won't lie to me again."

"I promise."

Caleb grazed my chin and lightly rubbed his thumb against my bottom lip.

"I missed you so much," I whispered.

He pulled me into his kiss. I gripped his hair as I let his tongue into my mouth. Caleb pressed his body against me, and my hand trickled down his spine before sliding into the back of his underwear. He kissed me harder as he shoved his hips forward. "I want to," Caleb whispered. "But Parker's right there, we shouldn't."

"You're right." I kissed him gently. I'd craved Caleb's touch for so long that it was impossible to hide my excitement pressing against him. Caleb kissed my cheek, pecked his way to my chin, then gave me a final kiss on the lips before flipping to his other side. He reached back and pulled my arm over, making him my little spoon. I laid my forehead against his back, realizing Caleb was my missing puzzle piece. I felt complete again.

My full bladder forced me awake. Caleb and I hadn't moved from our positions, still cuddled together. The sun just started to poke through my window when I slowly removed my arm from Caleb. My clock read 6:44 am. I stood, peeking at Parker before stepping to the door.

He looked so peaceful sleeping with his knees tucked close to his stomach.

I peeked into the hallway. Dad's bedroom door was still closed. I crept across the hall and into the bathroom, thinking of ways to get Parker and Caleb out of the house without Dad knowing. He didn't leave the house most days until 8:30 a.m., so I figured I could keep the boys secluded in my room until he left for the day.

I tiptoed back across the hall, wearing nothing but my underwear. Shutting the door behind me, I twisted the lock on my doorknob and stared. Seeing Caleb asleep in my bed rattled the butterflies awake again. Never in a million years did I think I'd be sharing my bed with a boy, and definitely not one as impeccable as Caleb.

I lifted the covers, sliding back into my spot as if Caleb was the mold and I was the silicone poured into it. I closed my eyes, taking in his musk.

The latch of my door unhooked, and the butterflies in my stomach turned to ash.

"Hey, I heard you were up, so I—"

I let go of Caleb, springing out of the covers, and pressed my back against the headboard.

Dad's shocked eyes moved from Parker's small sleeping body to the shirtless boy in my bed next to me.

My sudden movement woke Caleb, who rolled over and rubbed his eyes. "What's going on?" He asked.

I didn't need to look at Caleb to know he saw my dad standing in the doorway because I felt his body tense.

"Landon, get dressed and come downstairs now," Dad said. My room would've frozen over if his words controlled the temperature. Like a statue, I sat there, unable to move until my dad closed the door. I jumped out of bed and put on the clothes I wore the night before while mumbling every curse word I could think of.

Caleb sat up in bed, and hugged his knees. "You didn't lock the door?"

"I keep forgetting it's fucking broken," I said.

Caleb moved from the bed and dressed. "What should I do?"

"Just stay here," I said. "I'll go talk to him and figure it out."

I fled out the door and down the stairs. Dad sat on the edge of his recliner with his elbows on his knees and his forehead in his hand. I sat on the couch and stared at him, unsure what to say.

Dad spoke without looking at me. A visible vein pulsed at his temple. "What the hell is going on with you? Why is that boy in your bed?"

"Dad, he's not the bad guy you think he is."

His eyes hit me. "I've seen his record. I know what kind of guy he is. I don't want you getting mixed up in that."

"Dad, please—"

"Did he make you do something? Did he force himself on you?"

"What? No!"

Dad stood, towering over me. "Then why the hell is he in your bed, Landon!"

"Because I like him," I whispered.

Dad bent and looked me in the face. "I'm sorry, you what?"

"I like him," I said louder.

He stumbled back and stared at me, jaw slack. "The hell you do," he scoffed. "You aren't like that. We didn't raise you like that."

"It doesn't—"

"You're with Lauren," Dad interjected.

I shook my head slowly. "Not anymore."

"Jesus, Landon. Why are you doing this? Do you have any idea what that'll do to my campaign?"

I shot to my feet. "This isn't about you!"

Dad's jaw clenched so hard, I heard his teeth grind. "No, you're too young to know what you want. It'll pass."

"Nothing will pass. This isn't a phase or whatever you think you want to call it. I like him. That's not changing," I said. I locked my feet in place with sturdy legs. My heart pounded as I took a deep breath and squeezed my fists, imagining myself as a mountain that couldn't be shaken. "I'm gay."

Dad's face loosened and turned pale as if the word were his greatest fear. He closed his eyes, wiping a hand down his face. "I can't look at you right now," he said as he pushed by me, grabbing his keys off the kitchen counter.

I fell back onto the couch as I heard the side door slam and the car engine roar.

I stared at the empty room, wondering if I'd suffered the same fate as Caleb, never seeing my dad again.

My head slumped against the back of the couch, drained from the confrontation, yet my chest felt lighter. I had no more secrets to be afraid of.

The stairs creaked, and I perked up from the couch, almost forgetting Caleb and Parker were still there. I turned. Caleb stood at the foot of the stairs. Parker flanked him, holding his hand.

"We're gonna go," Caleb said, his eyes red.

I stood, stepping closer to them. "What? No, you don't have to—"

"I've made your life complicated enough." Caleb rounded the corner and started for the front door.

I rounded the couch, jogging after them. "Caleb."

He gripped the doorknob and pulled it open. The sunlight spilled in like a tipped-over can of paint. "It'll be better for both of us if we stay out of each other's lives."

"What're you talking about?"

"You realize I've pretty much caused every issue in your life since we met, right?"

My head shook. "That's not true."

"I don't do complicated, remember?"

"So you're running then?"

Caleb's nostrils flared as he stared at me. "I'm sorry for everything."

"Wait! Where are you gonna—"

I wanted to run for the door, but everything seemed slow. By the time I reached the threshold, Caleb had slammed the door behind them. I pushed my forehead against the door, and my whole body tightened to fight back the tears. "God damn it!"

I smacked the door with the side of my fist, vibrating pain down my arm. My face fell into my hands. I'd lost everything.

THIRTY-THREE

My head filled with static for the rest of the day. Getting Caleb back just to lose him again gave me emotional whiplash. Luckily I had Steven and Tasha to vent to during lunch.

Steven sipped his bottle of water through a straw. "So, your dad just walked out?"

I took a bite of my burger and spoke with my mouth full. "Yeah, I assume he went to work, but I haven't heard from him all day."

"I can't believe he found Caleb in your bed," Tasha said. "That must've been terrifying."

Steven rolled his eyes. "Girl, we've all been there."

I picked at my fries, drowning them in ketchup before popping them into my mouth. "Caleb's walk out was the icing on the cake," I said. "Like, do I text him?"

"Maybe let him cool off for now," Tasha said, puncturing her mac and cheese with a plastic fork.

I tisked. "The last time I did that, I didn't hear from him for a month."

Steven chuckled. "You could always text Blake."

Tasha slapped him on the arm.

"I'm sorry! I didn't realize how much of a douche he was," Steven said. "I haven't seen him since I was, like, thirteen!"

"Yeah, Blake and I didn't really click," I said, looking around the lunchroom. I wanted to see Caleb walking in to help the lunch ladies, or take out the trash. Anything that told me he was okay.

I worried about Caleb and Parker for the rest of the day. I hoped they hadn't gone back home. I pictured Parker sleeping on a cot in the kitchen at Lucky's while Caleb worked the night shift, hoping it'd never come to that.

I finished my homework for the night and sat to watch TV. Nothing kept my attention. I'd flip to a cooking show, then a 90s cartoon, and then to an action movie halfway through its runtime. I watched the screen as bullets blasted from a machine gun, shooting at an armored car speeding down the highway. I thought about something Caleb told me, "Never watch a movie on TV. They censor it and cut it to shit. No film should ever be interrupted by a commercial. That should be illegal." I could hear his raspy voice in my head. It always got higher in pitch when talking about something he was passionate about.

I switched through the channels, ending on an infomercial about a mop, when I heard a car pull into the driveway. I shot up and jogged to the side door, pushing back the thin curtain. Dad exited the car and walked down the driveway toward the street. I hurried to the window above the sink. Dad continued through the school courtyard and around the building.

What the hell is he doing?

I wondered how his day had gone. If he'd told anyone about me at his office. Or if he'd confided in Grace at all. I imagined him researching conversion therapy online or pastors I could talk to. Recalling my dream in the church made me shiver. Dad disappeared behind the school, and I snatched my hoodie off the couch and slipped it over my head.

After jogging across the street and through the courtyard, I poked my head around the edge of the building. I couldn't see anyone in the distance. I crossed the parking lot to the football field, which wasn't as bright as on game night. The track was dimly lit by a few lamp posts. Stepping onto the turf, my sneaker sank into the ground. I scanned the field and noticed a figure sitting in the middle of the bleachers.

I climbed the steps, going to Dad, who still wore his full suit and tie. I sat beside him on the bench, and the cold metal seeped through my jeans. Dad didn't look at me or say hi. He just stared out at the dark field. I could only hear his breathing in the silence, letting the wind swim between us.

"I already miss seeing you out there," Dad finally said. His voice was low and gravelly. "You were ten when I brought you to your first try-out, remember that?"

"Yeah," I whispered, focusing on the green grass and freshly painted yard lines.

"You were so excited to put on all the pads. I swear you didn't take the helmet off for a week after you made the team," Dad said with a small laugh that tapered off into the air. "I couldn't stop thinking about you today." He scratched at his stubble. "I couldn't stop thinking about this one time when you were little, your mom and I were trying to get you to eat your broccoli, or maybe it was green beans. But I remember saying, 'Don't you want to grow up to be big and strong?' And you looked up at me with your big eyes and mashed potato on your chin and said, 'I don't want to grow up, 'cause then I won't be Daddy's baby anymore.' I nearly fell off my chair. I looked up at your mom, she was practically in tears." Dad placed his feet on the bench ahead of us and leaned against his legs. "I said to you, 'You're always gonna be my baby, no matter what'," he said. "Today I kept thinking, what kind of father would I be if I lied to that little guy's face?" Dad turned to me. His eyes glistened even with the dark sky above us. "Every time I look at you, I see her face, and it reminds me she's gone. Your mom had all the answers, and I feel like I've been swimming upstream. Where I got it wrong, she always got it right, and God damn, I missed her today." A few tears slipped down his cheek, and it brought a lump to my throat. "I needed her more today than I ever have," he said. "But you know what? I kept hearing her voice in my head saying, 'you go home and you tell that boy you love him.'"

It was the first time I felt my dad truly saw me. The pressure in my throat became too hard to hold back, and I finally burst into tears. Dad pulled me in and my head fell against his shoulder as I wrapped my arms under his.

"I miss her so much," I said, trying to catch my breath.

"Me too, bud," Dad said. He wrapped his big hand around the back of my head, and his body convulsed from his sobs.

I pulled away from him, wiping my face on my sleeve. I'd turned into a complete mess.

Dad touched my shoulder. "All I want is for you to be safe," he said with a sniffle. "And I want you to be happy. If *he* makes you happy, and if writing makes you happy, then that's enough for me." He wiped his cheek dry. "I can't pretend to know what you've been going through. And I know I'm going to screw up and make mistakes, but I'm more than willing to listen and learn. You're all I have left, Landon. I can't lose you too. I just can't."

I nodded, unable to wipe my tears fast enough.

"I love you, son."

"Love you too, Dad."

Dad smiled at me. His eyes had dried. "I did a lot of research on student loans today. I think we can make this work, especially if I get elected."

"Really?"

"Really."

We sat on the bleachers for almost two hours. Dad listened to what I had to say for the first time in years. I told him about Caleb and Parker. I told him about my stories and ideas for what I wanted to write next. I told him about Steven, and how much he helped me when no one else could. I told him how excited I was about NYU and how wild living in a big city would be. Dad was a sponge, sopping up every word I said. It all felt familiar as if I were talking to my mom again. Like I'd gotten my best friend back.

I stared at myself in the mirror; I'd always felt ridiculous in nice clothes. I slipped the black dress coat over my red vest and reached for my red bow tie. I could hear Steven and Lauren chatting and laughing with my dad downstairs. Red wasn't the best color to go with my ginger hair. I often got rosy in the cheeks and was well aware I'd look like a ripe tomato during prom.

"We're gonna be late!" Lauren's voice boomed up the stairs.

"All right, I'm coming!" I did a quick check of my teeth before heading down. I gave my best dapper smile and buttoned my jacket as I entered the kitchen. I was met with over-the-top oooh's and ahhh's.

"You clean up nicely...for a jock," Steven said as he hugged me. He wore black skinny jeans, purple Converse shoes, and a matching purple blazer. He completed the look with a rainbow bow tie and glittery cheeks.

"Very handsome," Lauren said, strutting over to me.

"Look at you!" I said, gesturing to her with my mouth open in shock. She looked like a modern-day queen of hearts. Her strapless dress cinched at the waist. Her hair had an array of ribbon-like buns, and she wore black high heels. "You're stunning," I said before taking her by the hand for a twirl.

"All right, let me get a picture," Dad said from the living room. We all rushed in front of the fireplace and posed with Lauren between Steven and me. The multiple flashes made me see purple and green dots floating around the room.

"We should get going," Lauren said, reaching for her purse on the coffee table. "Tasha texted me, she's just gonna meet us there."

Dad pulled me off to the side. "Anything from Caleb?"

"Nothing," I said.

He frowned. "I have this charity dinner tonight, so I'm not gonna be home until late," Dad said as he swiped through the pictures he'd taken.

Steven and Lauren were practically out the door.

I hugged Dad and hurried to meet them.

"Have fun, guys!" Dad called out as we stepped through the side door. "And hey, no drinking and driving!"

We drove to prom in Lauren's Volkswagen Bug while most people took limos. With only three of us, we didn't see the point in our parents spending the money.

Prom, held at the Duncan Country Club and Golf Course, was a forty-minute drive from Madison. I couldn't stop thinking about Caleb as I sat in the backseat, watching the houses and trees whiz by. I wondered what it would feel like to slow dance with him in front of everyone. It was hard to fathom taking another boy to the prom. I glanced at my phone, hoping to see Caleb's name, even though I had no notifications.

He's gone for good this time.

My mind flashed back to Caleb lying in my bed. I could see him so clearly, wearing nothing but the moonlight.

We entered the lobby of the Country Club and collectively gasped. With the Winter Solstice theme, everything glistened with ice illusions and blue and white tones. A giant ice sculpture of a snowflake sat close to the ballroom's entrance. Strips of blue and white cloth decorated the walls, and large plastic snowflakes danced from the ceiling. White-clothed tables decorated with glittery snow surrounded a sizeable square dance floor in the middle of the room. Living in Texas, it was the closest to winter we could get.

We found our table and greeted Tasha with hugs. Her hair was tied up into three braided buns, mohawk style, and she wore a tight black dress. It was a corset on top that blended into a ruffled skirt.

Everyone took selfies and posted Instagram stories while we waited for food. We had to eat dinner before the dancing started. I ordered the fanciest steak I'd ever eaten and stuffed myself with mashed potatoes and asparagus. We moved on to dessert when Jordan Palicki showed up at our table, wearing a tux that looked a size too small. He passed around a flask of mysterious alcohol. I was the only one at the table that didn't take a swig. The flashbacks from Dan's birthday party still haunted me.

The lights dimmed around us, and the dance floor lit up with blue and purple hues. The DJ's voice ripped through the room: "All right, Madison High School. Are you ready to get this party started?!"

The whole senior class erupted into cheers, and music blasted. Lauren and Steven screamed in each other's faces with excitement as drums thundered through us. They sang at each other. "Ooo baby, do you know what that's worth? Ooo Heaven is a place on earth!" They jumped out of their chairs, dancing and scream-singing. I stared in amazement, laughing, not having heard the song before.

Everyone flooded the dance floor. Steven reached out, grabbed me by the sleeves of my suit jacket, and dragged me up. He and Lauren held my hands through the sea of dancing bodies. Tasha followed behind.

The colored lights flashed with the drumbeats, and spotlights circled the dance floor. We couldn't stop smiling at each other, dancing like maniacs running wild at an insane asylum. I eventually caught on to the lyrics and shouted along, realizing it was the same words on repeat.

My lower back moistened as we reached the eighth song in a row, not slowing down our crazy movement. I spotted Dan in a white tux through the crowd, dancing with his shirt unbuttoned halfway down his torso, exposing his white tank top. He brought a hand to his nose, and snorted something off his fist before throwing his head back, swaying chaotically. Dan seemed to be in his own world, not worried about getting noticed.

Another song started, but I needed a break. I trudged back to our table, took off my jacket, hung it on my chair, and rolled up my sleeves.

My feet begged for release from my tight, shiny dress shoes. I sat and checked the blank screen of my phone. Nothing new.

I glanced around the room. Everyone looked so happy.

We'll all graduate in two weeks, and tonight will just be another memory.

I'd probably never see Jordan Palicki again after graduation. I imagined him moving into a dorm at some state school and starting a successful weed business.

Jessica Walters sat on Max Gibbons' lap at the table next to mine. They'd become inseparable since she dared him to take the gum from her mouth at Dan's party. I imagined them going to the same college and promising each other they'd get married the day after graduation.

All the happy straight couples smiling, taking pictures, kissing, and grinding on each other on the dance floor made my chest go hollow.

Lauren, Tasha, and Steven popped up in front of me. Out of breath and sweaty.

"You okay?" Lauren asked.

"I think so," I said, still staring at Jessica and Max with jealousy swirling in my stomach.

Steven smiled. "Do you guys want to tell him, or should I?"

My ears perked, and my attention whipped to him. "Tell me what?"

"Well," Lauren said. "We wanted to do something special for you."

"Yeah, we were tired of seeing you sulk around everywhere, bringing the mood down," Steven said as he propped his arm on Lauren's shoulder.

I rolled my eyes. "What did you guys do?"

"Look for yourself," Lauren said, pointing behind me.

My brow furrowed, and I twisted in my seat. Caleb stood awkwardly at the ballroom entrance, wearing a fitted navy blue suit and a black skinny tie, with his hair pushed back from his forehead.

I shot out of my seat, showing all my teeth. "Oh my god! How did you get him in?"

"I pulled some strings," Lauren said with a shrug.

Steven pantomimed a hair toss.

I chuckled, flabergasted. "I have so many questions."

"It was actually Tasha's idea," Steven said. "She helped a lot."

I looked at Tasha. "Is that true?"

Tasha smirked. "I can't say I don't feel a little responsible for everything that happened after printing your story."

I stepped closer, taking her hands in mine. "How'd you find him?"

Tasha's sculpted brow raised. "If someone's on social media, I can find them." We both laughed. "It was the least I could do after everything."

"Tasha, you did nothing wrong, I promise. But thank you. You have no idea how much this means to me," I said, wrapping her tightly.

"All right, get that fine-ass man before Jessica Walters sees him!" Tasha shouted over the music, giving me a playful shove. I saluted her and started through the tables with Caleb in my sight.

"All right, let's slow things down," the DJ's voice echoed. "Let's get all the couples to the dance floor. This is Slow Dance by AJ Mitchell."

It was the first slow song of the night. The crazy flashing lights transitioned into slow pulses. The song started with charming beats and plunks of a piano. The singer's high voice bounced off the walls, easing the room.

I stopped in front of Caleb with my hands in my pockets and smiled. "Hey. What're you doing here?"

Caleb cocked his head. "I guess I just can't get enough of you." He flashed his dimples as if he knew my weakness.

"Where's Parker?" I asked.

"I finally got a hold of Miguel after we left, so we've been staying with him."

"Oh, good, good." I nodded awkwardly.

Caleb offered me his hand. Cool and relaxed. "Wanna go turn some heads?"

I took a deep breath, mentally preparing to come out to the entire room. Teachers, chaperones, and any other student that hadn't heard the gossip, but I still placed my hand in his. We both smiled as he led me to the dance floor. People caught on as we threaded through them. I imagined Caleb as a handsome prince leading me to our first dance in front of the King and Queen of the Winter Kingdom.

Caleb parked us at the center of the dance floor, and my nerves tickled my stomach. Caleb turned to me and wrapped his arms around my neck. "Is this okay?"

"Yeah, I think so," I whispered, setting my arms around his hips.

The dance floor became a wave of swaying couples. Some stared at us, but I tried to stay on Caleb's face.

"You look cute in a bow tie," Caleb said.

I hung on his every word as if he had a spell over me. "You're not too bad yourself."

"Miguel, let me borrow the suit, though I'm not sure whose it is because he's way too short to wear it."

We swayed, spinning in a slow circle. My jaw clenched as people whispered. Anxiety crawled up my throat while Caleb seemed unfazed by the stares.

"Hey," he whispered. "Just focus on me."

I breathed and asked him another question to focus on his lips. "What did Tasha say to get you here?"

"I've been sworn to secrecy," Caleb said. "But, I can say she reminded me how stupid I was for pushing you away. Life's gonna be complicated no matter what."

My anxiety eased, sliding back down my throat. "I can't believe you're here," I said before seeing Lauren and Steven dancing together, smiling at us. Steven made kissing faces, making me laugh. "I never thought this was how my prom would go."

Caleb's thumbs stroked the back of my neck. "You mean you didn't picture yourself dancing with a guy in the middle of a bunch of straight couples while they stared at us?"

"Exactly," I said with a chuckle. Caleb pulled me closer, making our bodies touch, and my stomach fluttered.

My hands rested on Caleb's tailbone. Focusing on his lips only made me want to kiss him. Instead, I said, "I just never pictured any of this. Since we lost my mom, it's felt like I've been endlessly falling with nowhere to land."

Caleb's warm hands slid to the side of my neck, his thumbs on my jaw. He looked me in the eyes. "Well, I'm here now. You can land on me."

His words smashed all the walls I'd built since the first day I saw him. Everyone's curious glances no longer mattered. I was all in with Caleb. Everyone else faded away until it was just the two of us swaying under the winter lights.

I kissed Caleb for the first time without an ounce of fear. There were no gasps from passersby, no words of discrimination thrown our way, no faces of disgust because none of it mattered anymore. I was his, and he was mine. Protected by an invisible force field that our passion for each other created.

Everything came back into focus when I pulled away from Caleb's lips. He held me close, and I rested my face against his shoulder. I looked up to a glaring Dan at the edge of the dance floor. We locked eyes. He pulled at his nose and walked off.

The slow song transitioned into an upbeat pop tune that everyone cheered for. Lauren, Steven, and Tasha hopped closer to us, singing and dancing.

I finally introduced my friends to the boy who held my heart.

Another hour and a half of nonstop dancing had passed before I put my lips to Caleb's ear. "Wanna get outta here?"

"Are you sure? What about your friends?" He asked.

"They'll be fine without us," I shouted over the music. Caleb held up an 'okay' signal and nodded. I turned to the others and shouted, "We're gonna head out!" They all frowned but quickly transitioned into one hug after the other. I held Caleb's hand, guiding him back to my table to collect my things.

We stepped outside to a drizzle, slicking the ground.

I pulled my phone out. "I'll get us an Uber."

"No need," Caleb said, casually crossing to the parked cars.

I jogged up behind him. "What do you mean?"

"Miguel let me borrow his car," Caleb said, stopping behind a Jeep.

"Caleb, you don't have a license," I reminded him.

Caleb put a finger to my lips. "Sshhh. It was a special occasion. *But* you should probably drive." He snatched the keys from his pocket and tossed them to me.

I caught them against my chest and shook my head at him.

The whole drive back to my house, I couldn't stop thinking about getting Caleb out of his suit and into my bed. I wanted to feel his hands on me again. I craved the slightly salty taste of his skin. I gripped the steering wheel to help me focus on the road, but Caleb's hand on my thigh wasn't helping.

I parked in front of my house and glanced at the school, noting how creepy it looked at night. Caleb quickly exited the car and waited at the side door, bouncing.

I strutted to him, thinking how lucky I was to be his. He leaned against the house, and I kissed his lips. His hands rested on my lower back, yanking me close. I wanted him to take me right there on the driveway.

Caleb released my kiss and stared at me, studying my face.

A smile tugged at my lips. "What?"

"Tasha told me about NYU. Why didn't you tell me that the story got you in?"

I shrugged. "I didn't want to rehash it and risk pushing you away again."

"It made me realize I don't have much time left with you now that you're gonna be a city boy. I want to spend every second with you that I can. That's what got me to come back."

"I think we can make it work," I said, pushing my fingers through his hair. The usual soft strands had gone stiff from the hairspray holding it back.

"As your muse, I think it's my responsibility to stick around. Who knows, maybe you'll write a bestseller about me."

I couldn't laugh before Caleb pulled me in for another kiss, but my smile lingered against his face.

Faint footsteps against the dampened driveway sent my heart into my throat. I turned, gasping as Dan stood there like a phantom in the shadows, still wearing his white tux. The drizzling rain stopped, and Dan's heavy breaths filled the air. I noticed his shadow before my brain registered Dan's stiff arm pointed at us. A nearby street light reflected off the bridge of the gun in his hand.

THIRTY-FOUR

My breath caught in my throat as I stared down the barrel of Dan's gun. I slowly raised my arms, still close to Caleb. "Dan," I said. "What's going on?"

"Get inside," Dan said with a flat tone. "Hey!" Dan yelled, inching toward us, aiming the gun at Caleb. "Do not reach for your phone! Turn around slowly and get inside."

"Okay, okay," Caleb said with his hands to his chest.

Dan followed us through the side door into the kitchen. My mind raced as my eyes darted around the room for anything I could use as a weapon. The knives were too far away, but a stool was an option. Caleb and I stood pressed against the kitchen island, facing the living room. Dan closed the door behind him, not once looking away or pointing the gun elsewhere.

My heart pounded through my chest. "Dan, just put the gun down. We can talk."

"I don't want to talk!" Dan shouted, moving in front of us.

"Just, tell us what you want," Caleb said with a clenched jaw. "I have some money in my wallet. You can take it and go."

Dan sniffled. His pupils took up most of his eyes. "I'm not going anywhere."

"Why are you doing this? I'm your friend," I said, my voice trembling.

"Faggots are not my fucking friends!" Dan yelled. A vein erupted from his neck. "You can't have everything."

My brow creased. "What're you talking about, Dan?"

Dan's arm rattled, pointing the gun at me, making me flinch. "You've always been the fucking golden boy! You get everything you want. The girls always wanted YOU! Fuck, even the guys want YOU! The scouts wanted YOU for the scholarship! Everything was so easy."

"Dude, you're high," Caleb said. "These are the drugs talking, not you."

Dan pointed the gun at Caleb. "FUCK YOU! You don't know me!"

"I do," I whispered. "This isn't you."

"Shut up, faggot!" Dan inched closer to me, pointing the gun at my chest. "You're so smart! You know everything, right, golden boy?"

My jaw clenched as the tip of the gun dug into my skin. My stomach swirled, trying to think of anything to make Dan drop the weapon.

"Say it again, see what happens," Dan said. "This isn't me? Say it again!"

Fear held my mouth shut.

"That's what I thought. Faggot Golden Boy doesn't have anything to say, does he?" Dan shouted, and his saliva hit my neck.

Praying Dan wouldn't squeeze the trigger, I said, "I know what you're going through."

Dan stepped back, still aiming at me.

"Steven told me what happened," I said. "And it's okay. You don't have to hide it anymore."

"Fuck you!" Dan spewed. "Whatever he told you was a fucking lie! I'm not a faggot. I don't need conversion therapy!"

"No one is saying you do," I said, keeping my voice low and calm.

Dan licked his lips. "I'm gonna kill that queer next. I'll put this gun in his mouth for spreading lies about me!"

"Dan, please," Caleb whispered.

"Shut up! Just shut up!" Dan snorted, switching his aim to Caleb.

"You and him make me sick!" Dan's head lowered, and he stared at us through his furrowed brow. "Everything would be so much fucking better if you were dead."

Dan pressed the gun to my head. I turned out of instinct, and my eyes crunched closed.

Caleb grunted, and a shot rang out next to my ear. The bullet shattered the window above the sink, spewing glass in every direction. I crouched and grabbed the side of my head as a ringing pierced my eardrum, sending a bolt of pain down my neck. My hand warmed under the slick blood trickling from my ear.

Still wrestling with Dan for control of the gun, Caleb slammed him into the side door. The weapon fired into the ceiling, spraying the boys with dust. Caleb drove a knee into his attacker's gut, and the gun slipped from Dan's grip, skidding across the floor and disappearing under a stool.

Dan roared and gained the upper hand, lifting Caleb clean off the ground before slamming him onto the cold tile. A sickening thud echoed as Caleb hit the floor. Before he could recover, Dan landed a brutal kick into his ribs. Caleb let out a sharp, pained gasp, rolling onto his back.

Dan straddled Caleb's chest, swinging a fist down hard. Still frozen, clutching my ear, I watched Caleb's blood spray the white floor with every crack of Dan's knuckles against his face. Over and over, Dan's fist flew up, coming down harder each time.

My mind screamed at me to *do something!*

I snapped out of my paralysis and lunged forward, attempting to wrap my arms around Dan's neck from behind. But Dan swung his elbow back, colliding with my nose. A crunch sent blinding pain across my face. Tears blurred my vision as I staggered back, crashing into the counter. My nose burned as blood dripped down my lip.

Through the haze of tears and dizziness, I saw Dan's arm rise again, crashing down onto Caleb's battered face. Each hit sounded like a hammer against bone, echoing in my head.

I forced myself to move, crawling on all fours. My hand brushed something cold, and my vision sharpened enough to see the gun.

Desperation surged through me as I scooped it with both hands. I stood with shakey knees and pointed the gun, gripped in both hands. “Stop!” My heart pushed against my ribs. Dan still pummeled Caleb’s face, three feet away, oblivious to me.

"DAN! STOP!" My voice trembled. "I’ll fucking shoot you!"

Dan didn’t even look up.

Tears streamed down my face. “STOP!”

I squeezed the trigger. The recoil jolted through my arms. A bullet ripped through the back of Dan’s neck. A chunk of flesh and muscle spiraled to the floor. Blood gushed from the wound like a fountain, splattering across the tiles. Dan’s fists stopped mid-swing to claw at his neck as if trying to hold the life in.

He collapsed next to Caleb with a heavy thud, blood pooling around his body as he gurgled.

My ears rang. I’d heard gunshots in movies, but they were louder than expected in real life. My elbows locked, and my arms shook. I wanted to drop the gun, but my entire body froze. The scent of hot metal emanated from the barrel of the weapon. My mouth was too dry to speak, and I could hardly swallow. I desperately wanted to reach out to make sure he was okay, but there was so much blood. It was so red and coming out so quickly. I didn’t want to shoot him, but he wouldn’t have stopped otherwise. Tears welled in my eyes. His blood was on my hands now.

I dropped the gun and crawled to Caleb, crying. Dan’s body jerked and trebled in a puddle of his blood before going still.

I pulled Caleb into my lap, out of the pooling red matter. I tried to wipe the mess from his face, but the blood was too thick. “It’s gonna be okay,” I whispered, crying over him. I pulled out my phone, barely able to click the numbers with shakey fingers. I slapped the bloody screen to my ear, listening to its ring. “I need help!” I said through gritted teeth and sobs. “Me and my boyfriend were attacked, and I can’t tell if he’s breathing. Please send someone!”

I gave my address and dropped the phone once the woman said an ambulance was coming.

I stroked Caleb's matted hair, barely seeing through the blood and tears. I leaned to his ear. "Please be okay, please be okay."

Two cops kicked through the front door and rushed their way to the kitchen with their guns drawn. I huddled over Caleb's limp body before the officers pulled me away, and two paramedics rushed to evaluate him. The officers held my arms behind my back as I watched one paramedic pump his hands against Caleb's chest, counting out loud in quick succession. The second paramedic checked Dan's limp body, searching his neck for any sign of life.

"He's gone," the second paramedic said before moving away from Dan.

My entire body trembled as I sobbed. The officers kept me from tumbling back to my knees.

Caleb coughed up a spurt of blood.

"He's got a pulse!" the first paramedic called out. "Get the stretcher."

I breathed relief and squirmed out of the officer's grip, kneeling beside Caleb. "I'm here, babe," I said, trying to wipe my tears away as they fell. Caleb slowly turned his head toward me, unable to open his swollen eyes. His hand searched for mine, and he used his finger to draw a circle on my palm. A sob escaped my throat, and I gently pressed my forehead against his. "I love you too, Caleb. I love you so much."

Red and blue lights filled the street. Dad drove up to the house as Caleb's stretcher was hoisted into the ambulance. He rushed toward me, but a pair of officers stopped him.

"That's my son!" he yelled at them. The officers eased their stance and let him through. He ran to me before I could jump in the back of the ambulance and wrapped his big arms around me as I sobbed into his shoulder.

"Landon, what happened?"

I looked at him with a wet face. "Dan attacked us. He hurt Caleb pretty badly."

"Jesus." Dad glanced at Caleb in the ambulance then back to me. "Go with him. I'll meet you at the hospital. We can talk there." He hugged me before I hopped inside, and the paramedics closed the door, leaving Dad standing alone as we drove off.

Caleb was taken into surgery as soon as we reached the hospital. The doctors told me he had a broken rib and an orbital fracture around his left eye. I voiced my concerns about his vision, but they said the break was clean, that his eye was swollen, but they could fix everything with no risk to his sight.

I was getting my ear patched up when Dad entered the room with two police officers. They made me recount the whole event from start to finish. I was so exhausted. It took hours to get all the words out.

The officers told us they'd removed Dan's body from our house and had notified his family. My stomach sank thinking about Chris and his parents. Prom had gone so perfectly. I never imagined the night would end the way it did.

"Are you in pain?" Dad asked as the officers left the room.

I sat on the hospital bed, with my legs hanging over the side. "A little. The doctors said the ringing should stop after a few hours, maybe a day at max."

Dad hugged me again before pulling back, keeping his hands on my shoulders. "Thank God you're okay. Did they tell you anything about Caleb?"

"He's in surgery now. They say he'll be all right." A wave of realization hit me. "Oh, my god. I have to tell his little brother."

"I can call his parents," Dad said.

"They've been staying with a friend. I have to call Miguel."

"Do you know his number?"

"They gave me Caleb's phone." I reached into my pocket and pulled it out. I opened the screen, but it had one of those passwords where you had to draw a pattern. I sighed. "I don't know his password." I stared at the phone, thinking of anything I could trace. I looked at Dad again. "Miguel's car is at our house, though. He let Caleb drive it to the prom."

"Okay. Stay here. I'm gonna make some calls." Dad pulled out his phone as he left the room.

I opened the screen of Caleb's phone again, and an idea popped into my head.

It can't be that easy.

I traced out the letter A on Caleb's screen, and his phone opened to see a picture of him and Parker behind the apps.

I can't believe that worked!

I clicked through his contacts, and hit the green button next to Miguel's name before touching the phone to my ear.

"Hey Miguel, it's Landon."

I was back in my kitchen, staring down the barrel of Dan's gun again, trying to tell him everything would be okay, that he didn't have to hide anymore, but I couldn't hear my own words. My mouth moved, but no sound came out.

With no warning, Dan pointed the gun at Caleb and shot him in the chest. A rope of blood hit my face. I screamed as Caleb crumbled to the ground, or it felt like I screamed, but again, my voice couldn't be heard. I glanced at Dan just in time to see the gun erupt in my face with a loud bang.

My eyes popped open, and my head lifted from Caleb's hospital bed just as Miguel and Parker entered the room. I stood, and Parker greeted me with a hug. "We have to be quiet," I whispered to Parker. "Caleb's still sleeping."

"Okay," Parker whispered back. He sat in my chair next to Caleb's bed and reached to hold his brother's hand.

I hugged Miguel before he handed me a small bag.

"I got you a coffee and a bagel," he said.

"Thanks."

"How're you holding up, sweetie?"

"I'm okay, I think." My wrist was still sore from the kickback of the gun. "Thanks again for bringing Parker."

"Of course. He's been an angel."

I glanced at the bed. Caleb was waking up. They bandaged his head, covering his left eye, but he saw Parker and smiled.

"I need to make some work calls," Miguel said. "But when I'm done, I can stay here with Parker. You should go home and get some rest. You've been here for three days already."

"Yeah, you're probably right. Thank you."

Miguel smiled and reached for my hand, giving it a little squeeze. The jingle of his bracelets reminded me of the bell that chimes when walking into Lucky's. Miguel closed the door behind him and I pulled a chair to the other side of the bed.

"When are they gonna let you come home?" Parker asked.

"In a few days, I hope," Caleb said hoarsely.

"But it's already been a week and two days," Parker said.

"The doctors just want to make sure I don't do too much before my body's ready."

"I'm gonna ask the doctor if we can go to the movies when you're out!" Parker said excitedly.

I chuckled. "I don't think they'll have a problem with that."

Caleb smiled at Parker. "How's it been staying with Miguel?"

"It's been good," Parker said. "He sprays a lot of perfume, but other than that, I like it there. He makes me a lot of sandwiches and lets me watch YouTube."

Caleb let out a small laugh followed by a grunt. "Tell Landon about your loose tooth and the sandwich."

Parker's eyes lit up, looking over the bed at me. "This one time I was eating a ham sandwich, and I had a loose tooth, but when I finished the sandwich, my tooth was gone! I swallowed it!"

Caleb turned to me. "The whole day he begged me to call the tooth fairy to make sure he still got the dollar."

"And did you?" I asked Parker.

"It was under my pillow the next morning!"

We all laughed.

Seeing Caleb smile again made my heart leap. Every day I got to hold Caleb's hand in that hospital bed, my love for him grew. I owed him my life, something I was sure I'd never be able to repay him for.

I stepped into the kitchen, yawning. The sun was up, but I could barely keep my eyes open. I haphazardly reached for a bowl and a box of cereal. I grabbed the milk from the fridge and sat at the kitchen island. My line of sight connected with the floor, where I could see Dan's lifeless body lying there in a pool of blood as if everything happened the day before. I stared, half expecting him to pick himself up and walk out the door.

"Morning, son," Dad said. His voice pulled me from the trance.

I squeezed my eyes closed for a second. "Morning."

Dad poured a cup of coffee and joined me at the kitchen island. "I just got off the phone with Principal Jamison. He said you could take your final exams online."

"Awesome, thanks."

"If you want that, of course. You can go back whenever you're ready."

"It might be good to be around my friends again," I said, pouring my cereal. Sugar wafted from the bowl.

"Jamison also told me they're having Dan's funeral today over at St. Anne's."

"Oh?" My stomach flipped. Suddenly, I didn't have an appetite.

I thought about the funeral for the rest of the day. I thought about Chris and his parents and the pain they'd surly felt. Lauren told me Chris hadn't returned to school. Part of me wanted to see him, but I was too scared to reach out.

I stepped into the living room to find Dad watching TV. "Can I use the car?"

He turned, looking over the couch at me with drooping eyes. "Sure. Going to see Caleb?"

"Maybe. Just wanna clear my head."

"Want to talk about anything?"

"No, it's okay. I'm okay."

Dad nodded. I don't think he believed me.

"Keys are hanging up," he said.

"Thanks. Let me know if you need anything while I'm out."

I didn't fully understand why I wanted to go to St. Anne's church. Maybe to see how many people showed up. It wasn't until I pulled into a parking spot that I realized it was because I hoped to see Chris.

I had a clear sightline to the church entrance as cars filled the lot. I straightened in my seat when Dan's dad walked through the main doors. Chris and his mom walked toward the church arm in arm, dressed in all black. He was so much taller than her. They stopped and greeted a few others coming in at the same time. A pit formed in my stomach when Chris turned, spotting me. He hugged his mom before she entered the church and jogged to my car. To my surprise, he didn't try to smash my windows. He knocked on the passenger window before opening the door and sitting inside.

I tried to swallow the chalky taste in my mouth and glanced at him. "Hey."

Chris stared at the glovebox. "What're you doing here?"

"I wanted to see you. See if you are okay."

"I'm all right. My mom's a mess, but I'm trying to be with her as much as I can."

"Yeah, Lauren told me you haven't come back to school."

"We thought it was best. I've been doing everything online."

"Me too," I said, nodding.

"If my parents see me talking to you, they'll flip out, so I should get back." Chris turned his pale face and pushed open the passenger door.

"Wait." I hopped out, too, and rounded the hood, meeting him at the front of the car. "I'm so sorry, Chris. I keep replaying everything in my head," I said. "Everything happened so fast. I can't sleep because I see him every time I close my eyes. I feel so fucking guilty." My eyes welled. "I just... I wanted to make sure you knew I'm sorry."

Chris pulled me into a tight hug. "It's not your fault," Chris whispered. His voice sounded weak. I shattered in his arms, and Chris held me as I sobbed into his big shoulder.

He looked at me with watery eyes. "Good luck in New York, okay?"

I nodded, wiping my wet face with my sleeve as I watched him disappear into the church. I sat in my car for another ten minutes before I finally stopped crying.

"We fucking did it!" Steven cheered.

I stood with him, Lauren, and Tasha in the school's courtyard, wearing our red and white gowns. It was Graduation day on the football field. They had set up a small stage for the speakers and white chairs on the field for the graduating class.

"Are you sure you guys don't want to go naked under the gowns? There's still time," Steven said. We all laughed.

"Hell no," Lauren said.

Tasha pulled us all into a hug. "You guys are gonna come visit me in DC, right?"

"Hey," Steven said. "We have months together before we start booking trips to see each other." Steven pulled out his phone. "My mom's on the field, I'll see you guys over there!"

We all smiled as Steven jogged off.

Lauren turned to me. "You ready?"

"I'm ready for everything to be over," I said.

Lauren smirked, "Just think, in a few months, we'll both be in New York, starting fresh."

"We all need to start fresh," Tasha said.

Lauren perked up. "Hey, there's Caleb."

I turned over my shoulder to Caleb, walking with Miguel and Parker.

Tasha nudged Lauren.

"We'll meet you on the field, okay?" Lauren said with a smile.

I hugged them both before they trotted off.

Parker ran into me face first with a hug. "Caleb said I should tell you congra—congr—tulations."

I laughed. "Thanks, bud."

"Okay, come on," Miguel said, tugging Parker's collared shirt. "Let's find a good seat." Parker let go of me and ran. "Congrats Landon,"

"Thank you!" I said to Miguel with a smile as he passed.

Caleb stopped in front of me, straightened my red cap, and playfully dusted my face with the tassel. Even with a swollen cheek and stitches through the middle of his left eyebrow, he still beamed. "This is it," Caleb said, reaching for my hands. "You're finally free of high school. How does it feel?"

"It feels like it took forever. Just wish my mom was here to see it."

"She can see it, don't you worry," Caleb said, raising my hand to his lips.

My chest warmed, thankful to have him. "How should we celebrate?"

Caleb chuckled. "Well, we have the whole summer before you jet off to New York, so we have plenty of time to figure it out."

"As long as I get to spend every day with you," I said, wrapping my arms around his neck. "I don't care what we do."

"Honestly..." Caleb held his arms around my waist and pulled me against him, planting a gentle kiss. "... That sounds perfect."

Continue reading for a Sneak Peek of *Land On Him.*

NEW YORK CITY

EIGHT MONTHS LATER.

Lauren and I picked at a chocolate croissant at The Ivory Den. The shop was overstuffed with college students taking shelter from the cold.

"I already have to write three papers by the end of the week," I said, licking the chocolate filling off my fingers.

"Not only do I have to write two papers, but I also have performances at the end of the week. So, two dance combos, two monologues, and a song from friggin' *Les Miz* to memorize."

"Jesus," I said before sipping from my cup. "Why are you even here?"

"I needed a break, believe me." Lauren ripped the end off the croissant. "These musical theater girls are bat shit."

I laughed.

"Has your roommate started to clean up after himself yet?"

I rolled my eyes, "Nope."

"Hey, I've seen your room at home. You aren't exactly Mr. Clean."

"Yeah, but this is next level," I said. "I've already used an entire bottle of Febreze since being back. And I have to wear headphones to bed because he stays up late on his computer."

"Doing what?"

"He's really into coding and hacking and stuff. He types so fast. I swear I can hear it in my dreams."

Lauren laughed, taking a sip from her cup. "How's your dad doing? He must be crazy busy since he got elected."

"Yeah, it seems pretty nuts. But you should hear what people suggest at council meetings," I said.

Lauren chewed, shaking her head. "Christmas break went by so fast. I feel like I barely got to see anyone."

"I know," I said, checking the time on my phone.

"Still nothing from Caleb?" Lauren asked before finishing her hot chocolate.

I sighed and crossed my arms. "I've texted and called him since I've been back, but he hasn't responded. He gave me a half-assed Happy Birthday when Parker called me, but that was it. I fucked everything up," I said, looking at my lap.

Lauren's voice got soft. "You both said shitty things. And you were drunk. He can't hold that against you forever."

Lauren unhooked her purse from the chair. "It's not like he hasn't gone dark before.

"It's different this time."

Lauren laid a hand over mine across the table. "He's being an asshole. Maybe I'll text him." She stood and slipped on her coat.

"I don't want to get you involved." I stared at my phone's dark screen.

"Okay, but I'll send him a text if you want me to."

"Thanks."

"I should stop procrastinating and get back to memorizing." She struggled to slip her backpack on so I stood to help her. "What're you up to for the rest of the day?" She wrapped her long scarf around her face.

"I have a writing session with Isaac, so I'm heading to his place next."

Lauren pushed the scarf under her chin and raised an eyebrow. "Who's Isaac?"

I shrugged, slipping my hands into my pockets. I could feel the chill whip in whenever someone walked out of the coffee shop. "This guy I met. He's a year ahead of me at NYU." I didn't want to spill all the beans about Isaac just yet.

"Is he cute?"

I smirked. "Yeah, I guess."

"Is he single?"

"Why? You want me to hook you up?"

"Hey, straight guys are hard to come by at my school. A girl has needs."

I laughed before pulling her into a hug. "He told me he had two boyfriends once, so I think you're out of luck."

"Two boyfriends? At the same time?" Lauren pulled back, leaving her arms around my waist.

I looked down at her. "They were a throuple, apparently?"

"Oh." I could tell the gears were turning in her head. Then she looked up at me with sincerity in her eyes. "Caleb will come around, okay?"

I nodded, forcing a smile. "I'll text you later."

Lauren flung open the shop's door, entering the human current along the sidewalk. Just as the door was about to close, I caught a glimpse of Dan standing in the middle of the sidewalk in his bloodied tuxedo, unnoticed by the people walking by, wrapped up in their winter garb. I scrunched my eyes closed and took a deep breath.

Fuck, not again.

Later that night, I sat at my desk, finishing a paper about plotting a story.

Josh popped his head out from the bathroom next to my desk. His dreadlocks swung in every direction. "Can I use your bar of soap? I'm all out."

I peered at him. "Sure," I said. He smiled and shut the door while I made a mental note to open a new bar of soap the next time I showered. Josh was cool, but co-existing with him in a small space wasn't ideal. I started typing again as I heard the squeak of the shower knob and the water hitting the porcelain.

I was on my last paragraph when a loud knock rocked my door, causing me to jump out of my skin. With a grunt, I pushed myself out of my chair, kicking a pair of Josh's boxers under his bed.

I opened the door, and my blood went cold when I saw Caleb wearing his tight jeans and leather jacket. "Caleb..." I muttered, barely able to speak.

He held a backpack that looked like it'd been through a tornado. One strap was missing, and the fabric was torn and ruffled. He entered my room and tossed the backpack on my bed.

My tongue dried up. "How... How did you get through security?"

"I snuck in," Caleb said, sounding raspier than usual as he rifled through his bag.

"That's impossible. How?"

"Doesn't matter."

I stepped closer with a huff. "What are you doing here? I've been calling you."

"Can't afford a new phone."

That's right, he smashed it on New Year's. "So you didn't hear my voicemail?"

"No."

I was relieved he hadn't heard of my mental break. "How did you get here?"

"Two buses. It was the cheapest way." Caleb finally pulled his hands from the backpack and opened them in front of me, revealing his numbered key. He looked at me, his eyes worn with bags. "He wanted me to find it," Caleb said.

"What?"

"The numbers. I figured it out."

"What about them?"

"I asked around some hardware stores, and one guy recognized it. Said someone came in asking to make a copy but said he couldn't because it was technically a federal key."

"What does that mean?" Staring Caleb in the face felt like a dream.

"He said it belonged to a safety deposit box. It took me a few days, but I finally found the bank it belonged to."

My jaw fell agape. "Holy shit."

"It gets weirder."

Caleb paced between the two beds in the room. My mind raced with questions. I hadn't been that close to Caleb in so long. I wanted to hug him and tell him I was sorry.

"The woman at the bank said I was the only person authorized to open the box. I had to show my ID," Caleb said.

"Why are you *here* then? It sounds like your dad might be in Texas."

"He isn't. There was a New York address in the box with some other stuff. I've been looking for it for almost two days, but without my phone, it's been hard to find."

"Caleb, you've been here for two days! Why didn't you come here first?" The thought of Caleb alone on the cold city streets shattered me.

"After—I thought I could do this alone, but I'm realizing I can't. I need you."

His words pierced my chest. I heard the shower turn off, and my eyes shot to the bathroom door.

"Landon," Caleb said with a whimper in his voice. My gaze went back to his hazel eyes. "I need to figure out what happened," Caleb said. "My dad is here somewhere. If I'm gonna find him, I need your help."

THANK YOU FOR READING MY BOOK!

As an author, reviews can be such a huge help in getting new eyes on the page! I'd love to see what you have to say about *Land On Me.* Please leave a review on Amazon and Goodreads!

To stay up to date with me and to get exclusives about my next book, please join my Newsletter at www.matthewrcorr.com and follow me across Social Media @matthewrcorr

ACKNOWLEDGMENTS

If you've read this far, first off, thank you! If you are someone who doesn't know me in real life or if you are someone who I didn't personally ask to read this book, I am forever grateful to you, a stranger, for giving a new author a chance. I hope I entertained you and I hope you took something away from this experience. This whole thing started as a short story I wrote on Tumblr years and years ago, so the fact that it's now in your hands as a full-fledged novel, it's almost hard to fathom. Just know that I am so appreciative that you spent your hard-earned money on a little gay indie book. Thank you, thank you, thank you!

There are a ton of people to thank that helped make this dream come true. My parents should be the first, you know, since I wouldn't be here without them. Mom, Dad, you've been nothing but supportive of me my entire life. You supported me when I came out, when I said I wanted to be a performer, when I moved to New York City to go to college, when I made it to the professional stages and the TV screens, and then when I said I wanted to write a book. But even when I made mistakes, and trust me there were plenty, you were both behind me 100% and I feel very lucky to have you. It sounds cliche, but I couldn't have asked for better parents. And of course, the rest of my family followed suit. To both my grandmas, Danny Martinez, Cheryl VanLuven, Kenny Dias, you all had a little something to do with this book. Whether it be throwing me a few dollars for an editor or promoting the book on social media, it all mattered to me. Thank you!

To my boyfriends, Ryan LaForest, and Kyle DePriest. Wow, where would I be without you? You've both been so patient with me throughout this entire process. I know I sacrificed a lot of time with you guys so that I could get this done, but you never faulted me for that. You both encouraged me to keep going, no matter what. I think I was even writing on Thanksgiving! Ryan, thank you for reading every version of this story and for celebrating me, and popping a bottle of champagne just for finishing my first draft. That feels like forever ago now. Kyle, without you I wouldn't have a title! Thank you for brainstorming with me and giving me your brilliant, mostly sarcastic ideas. This title means more to me than you know. Thank you for giving it to me.

To my amazing friends, you have been my life-force throughout all of this. To Katie Pickett, who was my original editor-in-chief, the only one who would read this thing...You gave me so much. I'm sorry it took years to finish, but I hope you're happy with the final product! To Will Wolz, who, besides Katie, was the first friend who actually read it when I asked, and it was only like ten chapters back then, thank you for your kind words! To Sarah McIntyre, who has read the first four chapters about five times and nothing else until I released the book, you actually had an enormous impact and even helped shape Landon's dad into who he is. Thank you. To Grayson Kilgo, who was my point man for strategy, you're so smart and intuitive. I value our friendship so much. And to Betsy Rinaldi, my ride or die, thank you for being my personal cheerleader since day one. Who knows where I'd be now without you? Thank you for always having my back through every life choice I've made over the past "90 years" of our lives. Now please move to New York City so we can be together forever!

I've been so lucky to have an amazing professional team of women by my side. To Quill Hawk Publishing and Amy M. Le, what started as a simple Facebook conversation turned into an amazing friendship. Without you, I would've gone into this business blind. Thank you for giving me the tools to grow as a writer and for helping me navigate this crazy landscape. To Dessiree Perez, my fantastic cover artist, I'm sorry I worked you to the bone, but damn did you deliver! Our collaboration and your talent means so much to me. Thank you for bringing my vision to life through every detail. To Alicia Dean, my editor who cleaned up this mess of a manuscript. You truly are a saint. Thank you for all of your positive light.

This story would be nothing without my team of Beta Readers. You all single-handedly shaped this story and made it a hell of a lot better. I had long conversations with all of you about these characters and their struggles. For that, I am indebted to you. Thank you Savvy Jones, Alyssa Venora, Christian Krenek, Justine Melvin, Jeremy Haig, Jesse Kramer, Dana Semmel, Brandy (Eva) Lovell, Emerald Ketope, Amanda Cusack, Chris Arceo, Karen Mann, and Jessica Osborne.

To my fellow queer authors who I've made friends with throughout my journey, you've all taken me under your wings and made me feel like I could truly achieve this. Thank you for constantly dealing with my annoying questions, especially Jeff Adams, Alex Blades, Jordon Greene, Jason June, and Robbie Couch. (Please go support these amazing authors!)

If I didn't mention you by name that doesn't mean you weren't an important part of bringing this book to life. If you read it, wrote a review, shared it, told a friend about it, bookstagrammed it, made a TikTok about it, tweeted it...you mean the world to me! Thank you for being part of *my* story!

ABOUT THE AUTHOR

Matthew Corr was born and raised in beautiful New England. Coming out as gay in high school in his small town fueled his big city dreams. Matthew moved to New York City, where he gained a degree in musical theatre. After countless performances on stages across the country, his passion for writing finally stepped into the spotlight. Matthew is a huge nerd for film and everything Marvel related. He currently lives in Brooklyn, NY. To learn more about Matthew, and the release of his next book, please visit www.matthewrcorr.com or @matthewrcorr

www.ingramcontent.com/pod-product-compliance
Lightning Source LLC
Chambersburg PA
CBHW030549310726
48979CB00010B/2087/J

* 9 7 8 1 7 3 5 1 1 9 4 7 2 *